THE WHITE GHOST

Billy Boyle
The First Wave
Blood Alone
Evil for Evil
Rag and Bone
A Mortal Terror
Death's Door
A Blind Goddess
The Rest Is Silence

THE WHITE GHOST

A Billy Boyle World War II Mystery

James R. Benn

Published by Soho Press, Inc.
853 Broadway
New York, NY 10003

Library of Congress Cataloging-in-Publication Data

Benn, James R.
The white ghost / James R. Benn.
(A Billy Boyle WWII mystery)

ISBN 978-1-61695-511-3
eISBN 978-1-61695-512-0

1. Boyle, Billy (Fictitious character)—Fiction. 2. World War,
1939-1945—Fiction. 3. Murder—Investigation—Fiction. 4. Kennedy, John F.
(John Fitzgerald), 1917-1963—Fiction. I. Title.
PS3602.E6644W48 2015
813'.6—dc23   2015014945

Map courtesy of the United States Government

Printed in the United States of America

10 9 8 7 6 5 4 3 2 1

Dedicated to the memory of my mother,
Trude Ross Benn
Born in the Old World, lived and loved in the New World.

The convoys of dead sailors come;
At night they sway and wander in the waters far under,
But morning rolls them in the foam.

—From "Beach Burial" by Kenneth Slessor (1944),
Australian poet and war correspondent.

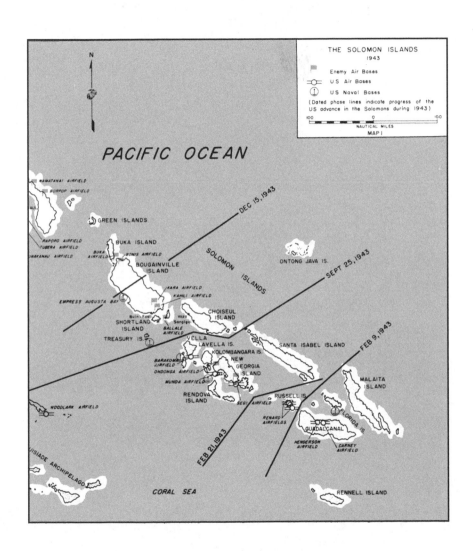

THE SOLOMON ISLANDS
1943

▪ Enemy Air Bases
⊐o US Air Bases
ⓘ US Naval Bases

(Dated phase lines indicate progress of the
US advance in the Solomons during 1943)

100   0   100
NAUTICAL MILES
MAP 1

PACIFIC OCEAN

NAMATANAI AIRFIELD
BORPOP AIRFIELD

GREEN ISLANDS

RAPOPO AIRFIELD
TUBERA AIRFIELD
INAKANAU AIRFIELD

DEC 15, 1943

BUKA ISLAND
BUKA AIRFIELD
BONIS AIRFIELD
BOUGAINVILLE
ISLAND

SOLOMON ISLANDS

ONTONG JAVA IS.

SEPT 25, 1943

KARA AIRFIELD
KAHILI AIRFIELD

EMPRESS AUGUSTA BAY

Buin-Fosi
SHORTLAND
ISLAND
Vozo
Sangigo
BALLALE
AIRFIELD
TREASURY IS.

CHOISEUL
ISLAND

SANTA ISABEL ISLAND

FEB 9, 1943

VELLA
LAVELLA IS.
KOLOMBANGARA IS.
NEW
GEORGIA
ISLAND
MUNDA AIRFIELD

BARAKOMA
AIRFIELD
ONDONGA AIRFIELD

MALAITA
ISLAND

RENDOVA
ISLAND

WOODLARK AIRFIELD

SEGI AIRFIELD

RUSSELL IS.

RENARD
AIRFIELDS

FLORIDA IS.

GUADALCANAL

FEB 21, 1943

HENDERSON
AIRFIELD

CARNEY
AIRFIELD

LOUISIADE ARCHIPELAGO

CORAL SEA

RENNELL ISLAND

PREFACE

SEVENTY YEARS AFTER the Solomon Islands Campaign—that hard-fought duel between the Allies and Japanese forces on the doorstep of Australia—top secret documents are still being declassified after decades of mandated confidentiality.

Under the requirements of the Espionage Act (Title 50 of the US Code) certain US Navy and State Department reports and communications relating to the Solomon Islands Campaign have been sealed these many years. Through Executive Order 13536 (Sections 1.4 and 3.7) some of those documents were recently declassified and made available through government archives.

Now, the story of how Billy Boyle came to journey to the South Pacific in 1943 can finally be told.

Astute readers may have noted Billy's absence between the invasion of Sicily (*Blood Alone*), which occurred in July 1943, and his appearance in Jerusalem in November 1943, before being sent on assignment to Northern Ireland, as recounted in *Evil for Evil*.

He was not idle during those months.

With the governmental veil of secrecy lifted, the events of 1943 immediately following Billy's Sicilian assignment are chronicled here for the first time.

CHAPTER ONE

I TURNED AWAY from the hot wind gusting against my face, gave up watching for incoming aircraft, and went inside. Again. I glanced at the clerk pecking away at his typewriter, avoiding my eyes. I'd asked him the same question so often he'd begun to ignore me, in the polite fashion of a busy corporal who didn't want to be pestered by a dime-a-dozen second lieutenant who'd drifted in from another outfit.

When is the flight expected in?

Dunno, sir.

Who am I supposed to meet?

Dunno, sir.

Where is your commanding officer?

Dunno, sir.

He was very good at not knowing anything. I paced the room, back and forth along the tall windows that fronted the airfield, watching the sky for a glimpse of B-24 bombers. It was cool inside, the white-washed stonework keeping out the midday Moroccan heat.

"Relax, Billy," Kaz said. He tilted back in his chair, crossing his legs, but not before shaking out the crease in his trousers. Kaz dressed only in tailored uniforms, even when it was desert khaki. Lieutenant Piotr Augustus Kazimierz—Kaz to his friends—was with the Polish Army in Exile, attached to General Eisenhower's headquarters. Kaz was a real baron as well, which he usually only brought up when trying to get a decent table at a restaurant. In French Morocco or Algeria, a

baron easily outranked a colonel, at least as far as any decent maître d'
was concerned.

"Relax? I *was* relaxed, back at the Hotel Saint George in Algiers,"
I said, knowing I sounded half-crazed. Yesterday I'd been ready for
some well-needed leave with my girl in the swankiest joint in Algiers,
and now here I was waiting for who-knows-what at an army airfield
six hundred miles away. "How can I relax when even General Eisenhower didn't know about these orders?"

"If worrying and pacing would help, I would join you," Kaz said,
tossing aside the week-old newspaper he'd been reading. It was the
Miami Herald, dog-eared and yellowed after its long journey. Anfa
Airfield was on the Air Transport Command run from the States.
Miami to Puerto Rico, then down to Brazil, over the Atlantic to Dakar
and up to Casablanca. The flight office was a good place to pick up
discarded newspapers from home and see what the civilian world was
up to. I glanced at the front page and saw that coal miners were out
on strike, even though the United Mine Workers had made a no-strike
pledge when the war began. FDR was threatening to end deferments
for any miners who stayed out on strike, but only a few had returned
to work. Steel mills had been shut down for two weeks without coal to
fuel their furnaces. No coal meant no steel. No steel meant no tanks,
bayonets, or destroyers. I should have gone straight to the funnies.

"They came direct from the War Department," I said, dropping
into the chair next to Kaz, struggling to keep my voice low. "Signed
by General Marshall himself, Army Chief of Staff. He's *Ike's* boss."

"I am well aware of who General Marshall is," Kaz said. "If I had
not been, the twenty or so times you have told me since we left Algiers
would've sufficed to inform me."

"Don't you find it strange that our boss's boss is sending us orders
direct from Washington D.C.? And that General Eisenhower doesn't
have a clue what it's all about? Never mind the fact that we're stuck
here waiting for a courier and no one seems to know anything?" I failed
utterly at keeping my voice low. The corporal ceased his typing and
looked up at me, shaking his head wearily.

"It is strange," Kaz said. "But then, life is strange, is it not? I never thought I would serve in the British Army, much less work for our general, and with you to keep me company. So what is one more small surprise? Patience, Billy."

"I don't have time for patience," I said, and rose to get back to my pacing. I thought I heard Kaz stifle a laugh, or maybe it was the corporal. I didn't care. I'd left Diana Seaton back in Algiers, which was where I wanted to be right now. Diana is an agent with the Special Operations Executive. She's a lady, an authentic British aristocrat. I'm Boston Irish, and hardly a fancy-pants kind of guy. We make one damned odd couple. Diana's last assignment had been a rough one, and we had both been looking forward to a week of time to ourselves. Maybe this summons would amount to nothing and I'd be back at the Hotel Saint George in time for dinner. Hell, if worrying doesn't help, as Kaz said, why not be an optimist? I tried, but he was much more practiced at nonchalance than I'd ever be.

Kaz hasn't had an easy time in this war either, but that's a long story. The scar he got last year has healed as well as expected, but it's still the first thing you notice when you see him. A jagged line from eye to cheekbone, it's a constant reminder of all he's lost. Both of the people I'm closest to over here have lost what's most dear in their lives, so I tend to be protective of them. Quite a job in wartime.

Two P-38 Lightning fighters swept in over the airstrip, distracting me from thoughts of personal losses. They banked low and disappeared beyond the rolling green hills facing the sea. I strained my eyes and thought I saw tiny dots in the distance. The B-24s? Perhaps the fighters had been their escorts.

"Lieutenant Boyle?" A door slammed and a major in rumpled khakis strode into the flight office, a cigarette dangling from his lips. He glanced at the corporal who indicated me.

"Yes sir," I said. "Can you tell me anything? We've been waiting for hours."

"All I know is I'm supposed to give the two of you use of my office, to meet with a US Navy officer on this incoming flight from Dakar. He'll be brought straight here." He drew on his cigarette and spit out a bit of tobacco. "And don't ask me any goddamn questions because I don't have any goddamn answers. Make it snappy and clear out of my goddamn office pronto, I've got an airbase to run. Understood?"

"Yes sir," I said. We followed him down the hall to an office facing the runway, floor-to-ceiling windows giving a clear view of incoming aircraft. The sign on the door said Major Kilpatrick, Executive Officer. Whoever was behind all this had enough clout to make a major nervous. For all his bluster, I could tell Kilpatrick was putting the best face on a bad situation. Hell, it made me nervous, too.

"Do not sit at my desk, Lieutenant," Kilpatrick said. I nodded my agreement as he crushed out his cigarette in the overflowing ashtray, leaving it smoldering as he departed, curses issuing from between clenched teeth. Kaz flopped into one of the chairs facing the tall windows overlooking the runway.

"As usual, we have not made a friend," Kaz said, his smile tight, almost a grimace, where it touched the scar. "Mere lieutenants with orders from powerful men are viewed with such suspicion. It shows how insecure most officers really are."

"For some guys, the rank is all they have. Junior officers with clout upset their view of the world," I said. "I knew a few cops like that back in Boston. But you can't blame Major Kilpatrick. No one likes being tossed out of their digs, even for an hour."

"Perhaps," Kaz said. "Although he could have been more courteous. I am tempted to sit at his precious desk in retribution." Kaz's eyes sparkled behind his steel-rimmed spectacles, and I was glad to see his impish humor hadn't entirely disappeared. Kaz was thin-framed, his motions languid, as if he could barely be troubled to endure the follies of the world. In the right light he reminded me of Leslie Howard, the English actor who'd been killed while flying over the Bay of Biscay a couple of months ago. More so now that Howard was dead, I think. Death became Kaz. It haunted him and he haunted it right back. I was worried that one day he'd follow the grim reaper wherever he led him, but until then I kept my eye on my friend, trying to keep him amused. And alive.

"There," I said, as an array of dots coalesced into a formation of B-24s approaching the airfield. PB4Ys, as the navy called them. I could make out the camouflage colors, white on the bottom and a dull grey on top. These guys were probably headed for antisubmarine duty, hunting U-boats in the Mediterranean or off the Atlantic coast of France. What that had to do with me, I had not a clue.

The big four-engine bombers lumbered in for a landing, jeeps and trucks racing out to direct them as they taxied off the runway. We watched as engines switched off and crews exited the aircraft, stretching after hours in cramped, cold quarters. No one seemed in a hurry. Crewmen began climbing aboard trucks which rolled off toward buildings on the other side of the runway. Mess hall, perhaps. If they'd flown in from Dakar, they'd probably been making the South Atlantic run from the States. I'd be hungry myself, but if I carried orders from General Marshall I might put that aside.

"Perhaps this is not the flight we are waiting for," Kaz said.

I was almost ready to agree when a jeep with an officer at the wheel raced across the runway, straight for us. It was a navy officer, still wearing his fleece-lined leather jacket in the North African heat. That had to be our man.

The jeep braked hard a few yards short of the window, spraying a cloud of dust that swirled around the driver. He got out and removed his flying cap and leather jacket, tossing them nonchalantly on the seat as he looked around, waiting for someone.

Then I recognized him. Square jaw, thick black hair, gleaming eyes. It was Joe Goddamn Kennedy.

CHAPTER TWO

"WHAT THE HELL are you doing here?" I said, advancing on Kennedy as he stood by his jeep, casually stowing his aviator's sunglasses.

"Inside, Boyle, and don't think I like this any better than you do," Kennedy said, brushing past me and ignoring Kaz as if he were invisible. He stood at the door, expecting to be escorted inside, like a rich snob waiting to be taken to the best table in a restaurant. I led the way, and shut the door to Kilpatrick's office once we were all inside.

"What gives, Kennedy?" I said. I saw Kaz trying to catch my eye, but I was in no mood for introductions. Or caution, if that was what he was trying to signal.

"Simmer down, Boyle," he said, moving to sit at Kilpatrick's desk, commandeering the seat of authority. Typical. "I've been flying since Miami. Any chance of getting a cup of coffee around here?" His glance lighted on Kaz, as if he were a servant with nothing better to do.

"We just got here ourselves. So if you want coffee, go look for it yourself," I said, my curiosity doing battle with my astonishment and resentment. The former won out and I decided to make introductions. "This is Lieutenant Piotr Kazimierz, of the Polish Army in Exile. Kaz, this is Joe Kennedy Junior." I stressed the word junior.

"Lieutenant," Kennedy nodded, his lack of interest palpable.

"It's Baron Kazimierz, actually." As soon as I said that, Kennedy's eyes registered interest, and he looked at Kaz as if he was a real person, not simply staff to do his bidding.

"We met several years ago, Lieutenant Kennedy," Kaz said. "At Cliveden, when we both were guests of Lady Astor."

"Oh yeah," Kennedy said, recognition dawning. "It was one of those English weekend things at her country place. You left early, didn't you? We didn't have a chance to talk."

"Indeed. Lady Astor's pro-Nazi statements were too much to bear, not to mention her anti-Catholic comments. I'd been invited by her son, Jakie, but I think he, too, was embarrassed."

"Jakie?" Kennedy said, furrowing his brow. "You mean Jacob? How is he?"

"Fine, the last I heard," Kaz said. "He's serving with the Special Air Service. Perhaps to maintain the family honor after being associated with the Cliveden Set." That was the name given to the pro-Nazi appeasers associated with Lady Astor. Joe Kennedy would fit right in. SAS was a British commando outfit, and old Jakie must have felt the family needed some serious rehabilitation. Not that I cared about aristocratic Brits, or Bostonians, for that matter. But I did care about what brought Joe Junior here.

"Okay, that's enough of old home week," I said, taking a seat and leaning back, hands clasped behind my head in what I hoped was a show of disdain for Kennedy. "What do you want?"

"I don't want a damn thing from you, Boyle," Kennedy said, gazing out the window. "But Father does."

"What does Ambassador Kennedy want with us?" Kaz asked.

"Former ambassador," I said.

"You retain the title after your service," Kennedy said. "So it's Ambassador Kennedy." Joseph Kennedy Senior, in return for his substantial support for President Roosevelt, had been made ambassador to Great Britain in 1938. He lasted less than three years. Joe Junior sounded exasperated having to make the point about the title. The Kennedy family liked titles.

"Okay," I said. "Tell us what your old man wants and why you're here."

"I'm merely the messenger, Boyle. I'm on my way to England, to fly antisubmarine patrol over the Bay of Biscay. Father thought it best that I deliver the orders in person, so there would be no confusion."

"And of course the War Department had no problem arranging that," I said.

"Of course not," Kennedy said, not picking up on the sarcasm. And of course they wouldn't. "Here's the deal. It hasn't hit the papers yet, but it will, very soon. My kid brother, Jack, managed to get his PT boat sunk the hard way. He was run over by a Jap destroyer."

"I didn't know Jack was in the Pacific," I said. "I'm surprised they took him." Joe's younger brother wasn't the healthiest specimen of a man.

"Yeah, well, you know how that goes," Joe said, meaning influence, political pressure, and all the other tools of the Kennedy family trade. "Jack was supposed to have a desk job in intelligence, but then he got in trouble with some dame in D.C. and they transferred him out. Somehow he wrangled himself a combat assignment zipping around in those plywood boats."

"Was he hurt?" I asked, still wondering what this had to do with me.

"Mainly his pride," Kennedy said with a snorting laugh. The Kennedy brothers were highly competitive, and if Joe was just getting his first combat assignment, it must have been tough on him to have his kid brother already in the fight. It was common knowledge that old man Kennedy had high hopes for his namesake. To live up to his father's plans, Joe Junior needed to come out of this war a hero and not second best to his rail-thin sickly brother.

"His crew?" Kaz asked.

"Two dead, one badly burned," Kennedy said. "They spent a week on some island eating coconuts before they were rescued. Jack got his feet pretty cut up on coral and got sent to a navy hospital on Tulagi. That's in the Solomon Islands."

"Yeah, I read *Stars and Stripes*," I said. "And you need an ex-Boston cop for exactly what?"

"Jack has been involved in the death of a native scout. Apparently losing his boat wasn't bad enough; now he's got himself mixed up in a murder," Joe said. "Father wants you to help him out."

"In the South Pacific?" I said, not quite believing what I was hearing.

"Sure," Kennedy said, reaching into his flight jacket for a thick manila envelope. "Here are your orders, signed by General George C. Marshall himself. Also there's a file on what we know about the incident. The native was part of the Coastwatchers operation. You know, those Australians who stayed behind on Jap-occupied islands?"

"Wait a minute," I said, not giving a hoot about Aussie Coastwatchers. "Why send me? The Boyles and the Kennedys aren't exactly a mutual admiration society."

"You're right, Boyle, we aren't. That's why Father chose you."

"For what exactly? I'm not navy. Don't you have the shore patrol or something like that?"

"Let me lay out some facts for you," Kennedy said. "First, the shore patrol is only whoever the master-at-arms can lay his hands on. They get a baton and are sent ashore when swabbies get their leave to make sure they don't burn down the town. They're a joke, unless you're a drunken sailor wising off to one of them. The Office of Naval Intelligence investigates crimes against US Navy personnel. But as I said, the victim here was a native. Jurisdiction is murky. The Solomons are a British protectorate, administered by the British and Australians in peacetime. Now it's mostly Japs and Americans up and down the islands."

"And the Melanesians," Kaz said.

"Yeah, the natives," Kennedy said. "So there's no one really in charge when it's a crime against one of them. The Melanesians."

"Is Jack actually a suspect?" I asked. I wouldn't admit it to Joe, but my curiosity was getting the better of me.

"At least one of the local brass contacted ONI asking for direction," Kennedy said. "The navy doesn't want to turn one of their own over to the Australians without sufficient evidence. And since we're the only thing standing between Australia and a Japanese invasion, the Aussies are being careful not to ruffle any feathers. Father wants the record set straight now so there are no future repercussions."

"You don't mean he wants the truth?" I said.

"Jack's not a killer," Joe said. "Your job is to find out exactly what happened and put this behind him. We don't know yet if the navy is going to court-martial Jack for losing his boat or make him their latest hero. Either way, he doesn't need a murder charge hanging over his head. It would embarrass the family."

"You still haven't said why you want Billy on the case," Kaz said. "I assume you are primarily interested in him."

"Two reasons," Kennedy said. "And you're right. Boyle is the man we want on the case, with your assistance, of course, Baron." He gave a polite smile, flashing pearly white teeth like a shark before he takes off your leg. "Father thinks that if you clear Jack of any potential charges, no one will question your judgment."

"Because of our mutual past," I said.

"Exactly," Kennedy said, nodding as if to encourage a slow pupil. "You'd be more apt to convict him, based on family history."

"Maybe," I said. "Although as an investigator I do have an interest in what the evidence tells me."

"Sure, sure," Kennedy said with a wave of his hand. "Look for all the evidence you want."

"I take it the other reason is the reverse of the one you stated," Kaz said, drumming his fingers on his knee, his eyes narrowing as he took the measure of the man seated across from us.

"How do you mean?" Kennedy said.

"That if Billy finds evidence which implicates your brother, it can be written off as a grudge."

"Baron, how can you say that? I might take that as an insult," Kennedy said, his smile still stretched across his gums as his eyes darkened. "Besides, that isn't the other reason."

"What is it?" I asked.

"You owe us," Kennedy said in a whisper, leaning over the desk, pushing aside Kilpatrick's paperwork with his elbows.

"For what?" I said, anger rising inside me. "I don't owe your family a damn thing."

"Your father never told you, did he?" Kennedy leaned back, glee rising in his voice. "How do you think it all happened? Your sudden appointment to the War Plans Department right out of Officer's Candidate School? While the other second louies went off to get shot to pieces as platoon leaders, you got a soft posting with Eisenhower. Someone had to make that happen Boyle. Someone with clout."

"The Ambassador," Kaz said. He knew my story. How my dad and uncle hated the idea of me dying in another war to save the British Empire, as their eldest brother Frank had in the last war. How they cooked up a scheme to get me appointed to the staff of a distant relative—on my mother's side—who worked in an obscure office in Washington D.C. And how shocked we all were when Uncle Ike got sent off to Europe as head of all US Army forces, and took me with him.

"Yeah," Kennedy said, his eyes locked onto mine. "Father was the one who pulled the strings. Even after he came home from London in 1940, he still had his contacts in government, still had favors owed. Your father and that lunatic uncle of yours approached him to get you appointed to General Eisenhower's staff. You're here because the Kennedys put you here, Boyle. It's time for payback." He clasped his hands behind his head, the same pose as I'd so confidently presented a few minutes ago. I didn't feel quite so sure of myself anymore.

"I can see that," I said, marshaling my thoughts as I tried not to show my dismay at being in thrall to the Kennedy clan. "Your old man could pull a few strings back home. But how did he pull this off? Getting General Marshall to order me halfway around the world for your kid brother?"

"It doesn't hurt that the director of the Office of Naval Intelligence used to be Father's naval attaché in London," Joe said with a smirk. He liked to brag about family connections, even when it would be best to keep his mouth shut. I decided to push further.

"Come on, Joe," I said. "Even ONI couldn't make all this happen so fast. Somebody other than your old man must be calling the shots."

"Wake up and smell the coffee, Boyle. There's an election coming up in '44. FDR wants a fourth term, and there are plenty of people who think he never should have had a third. His health isn't so good, either, although he does a good job of hiding it."

"Is your old man going to challenge him?" I asked. There had been rumors of Joe Senior wanting a shot at the presidency.

"No, that's not in the cards," Kennedy said. "The country's not ready for a Catholic president. Not yet. But millions of Catholics vote. Father can deliver a lot of that vote, especially the Irish Catholics."

"Or not," I said. "If he sits on his hands next year."

"Jack always said you were a dumb bastard, Boyle. I think my little brother got that wrong."

CHAPTER THREE

"AN UNPLEASANT MAN," Kaz said as Joe Junior went off in search of chow and a bunk.

"Not all Boston Irish are the happy-go-lucky types," I said as I leafed through the orders he'd left with us. Joe Kennedy was a loudmouth lout, as far as I was concerned. But his big mouth told me a few things that were interesting. ONI was not to be trusted in this investigation, and Joe Senior was ready to do anything to clear Jack's name, guilty or not.

I didn't much care for the news that the former ambassador was behind my appointment to General Eisenhower's staff. I'd always known the Boyle tribe traded political favors, and a few markers had been called in to get me my posting. What worried me was what the Kennedys wanted in return. I stopped reading the orders and gazed out the window, wondering what it had cost Dad or Uncle Dan to approach Joe Senior. Not in terms of the quid pro quo, but rather in their own self-respect.

"What is the nature of your past acquaintance?" Kaz said, breaking the silence. "It sounds like it must be an interesting story."

"Yeah, and a long one. Two stories, actually, but I'll have to fill you in later. These orders say we need to depart immediately. It's going to be a long trip, Kaz."

"Made twelve hundred miles longer by the summons to Morocco," Kaz said as we left the room. "All to listen to insufferable Kennedy demands."

"You must have been prepared, having met him in London," I said, quickstepping it to the flight office.

"I had a low opinion of his father, having heard his comments favoring the appeasement of Hitler. Lady Astor and her friends were in the same camp, but I must admit I paid little attention to the son of the American ambassador. My only recollection is that he seemed obsequious around the titled British and brusque with everyone else."

"That must have been a fun weekend," I said.

"The high point was hearing Lady Astor lament that Hitler looked too much like Charlie Chaplin to be taken seriously," Kaz said. "Jakie and I then retired to play billiards and drink a bottle of Blandy's Bual Madeira to recover our equilibrium."

We showed General Marshall's orders to our corporal pal who gasped and called in Major Kilpatrick, who cursed and hustled us down the runway where he pulled a war correspondent and a colonel off a packed C-47 transport about to take off. Once again, a couple of lieutenants trumped the bigwigs, making no friends in the process. Not that it mattered. So far I hadn't run into many of the senior brass who cared a fig about second lieutenants, so I made sure to return the favor.

The C-47 held twenty-eight passengers. Mainly officers above the rank of captain with one remaining war correspondent and a congressman on a fact-finding junket. Those last two were seated directly across from us. They told us that the reporter we'd replaced was from the congressman's hometown and the colonel was with Army Public Relations and carried the liquor supply in his pack. The congressman asked who the hell we were to rate special treatment, in a southern drawl that told me I couldn't sell either Kaz or myself as coming from his district. So I told him it was top secret, which wasn't far from the truth. Close enough for a politician, and it shut him right up.

"What does the report tell us?" Kaz said as soon as the C-47 had gained altitude and the ride smoothed out. I took out the paperwork from the envelope and leafed through it. No letterhead, nothing to indicate who had written it up or to whom it was sent. Meaning

Ambassador Kennedy had his sources. The file also held a thick sheaf of official navy documents, including a service record.

"The deceased is Daniel Tamana," I said. "From Guadalcanal. He was originally a native scout with a detachment of the British Solomon Islands Protectorate Defense Force. Apparently those are natives who work with the Australian Coastwatchers and as scouts for the marines. He'd recently become a full-fledged Coastwatcher."

"How was he killed?" Kaz asked, leaning closer and adjusting his glasses as he read along.

"Head bashed in," I said. "He was found on a beach at Tulagi, near the naval hospital."

"Found by whom?"

"Kennedy," I whispered. It wasn't an uncommon name, but I didn't want to arouse the curiosity of the reporter or politician seated across from us.

"Didn't Joe say his feet were badly cut up from the coral?" Kaz said. "That might make it difficult to get around, not to mention kill a man."

"That's something to check out," I said. "All it says here is that he was being treated for fatigue, abrasions, and lacerations. No way to know how incapacitated he was."

"Who was it that reported the incident to ONI?" Kaz asked. I flipped through the carbon copies, wondering who had possession of the original.

"It's not entirely clear. Maybe Lieutenant Commander Thomas Garfield, commanding PT Boat Squadron Two," I said, finally finding the name. "Or someone above him. Squadron Two is Jack Kennedy's squadron. He's the skipper of PT-109. Or was. Says here a Japanese destroyer rammed his boat and cut it clean in two."

"One wonders how young Jack got into that predicament," Kaz said. "His brother mentioned the navy might court-martial him."

"It's possible, I guess. But that would be bad publicity. If the navy operates anything like the army, some admiral will pin a medal on Jack and send him on a war bond tour. Did you ever run into him in England? I know he spent some time in London when the old man was there."

"No," Kaz said. "I heard about him chasing women and being seen at the best nightclubs every evening, but we didn't travel in the same circles. I was rather surprised when he wrote a book and it became a bestseller. I didn't peg him as the intellectual type."

"He's a Harvard boy," I said. "He had to write a thesis. And when you've got his family connections, it'd be a snap to get it published. Did you read it?"

"I skimmed parts," Kaz said. "Intriguing title. *Why England Slept.* He argued that appeasement was the logical course to follow, since Great Britain was not well prepared for war. I had to admit there was some logic to that. At least he did not support appeasement for its own sake, as did his father."

"The rumor was dear old dad bought thousands of copies and stored them in the basement of their place on Cape Cod."

"The path to success is always easier for the rich," Kaz said.

Not always, I wanted to say, but bit my tongue. Kaz was rich, but had little success to show for it. He'd been a student at Oxford when the war broke out and Germany invaded Poland. His entire family had been murdered by the Nazis, not long after the Germans and the Russians carved up Poland between them. Kaz's father had seen bad times coming, and was readying his family to leave the country. He'd transferred his bank accounts to Switzerland before hostilities, but was too late in getting himself and his family out. That left Kaz alone in the world, stranded in England with a small fortune to remind him of all he'd lost.

"We have to be careful," I said, leaning closer to Kaz and keeping my voice low. "If Jack is involved, his old man will come down hard on us. On me, to be precise."

"Do you think he still has the influence?" Kaz said.

"He's got deep pockets and connections everywhere," I said. "What Joe said about the next election is true enough. It may be the old man's last card, but he'll play it for all it's worth."

"Then I hope we find that the younger Kennedy is guilty of nothing more than bad seamanship," Kaz said.

"He's been sailing small craft off Cape Cod since he was a kid. If he got into a jam out on the water, I'll bet it wasn't due to faulty seamanship," I said. "If he's innocent, our problem is going to be how to find out who killed Daniel Tamana. The Solomon Islands are not exactly my home turf."

"You have managed to work things out in England and Algeria," Kaz said. "Therefore you must use the same techniques in the Solomon Islands."

"Think the luck of the Irish will hold on the other side of the world?"

"Jack Kennedy's Irish luck held," Kaz said. "He's a living example."

"If you call luck getting your PT boat sawed in half and losing two crewmen," I said. "My dad had a saying about luck like that. If he'd been really lucky, it wouldn't have happened in the first place."

We were interrupted by turbulence, a gentle bumping as the C-47 flew into a cloud bank, grey mist enveloping the wings. The congressman across from me turned white and then went a pale shade of green, as I prayed for the ride to smooth out or for someone to bring him a bucket. The bumps turned to crashes as heavy winds slammed into the aircraft. Every loose item on board took on a life of its own, hitting the ceiling and sides of the fuselage as we tossed about. I felt the plane gain altitude and the turbulence calm as patches of blue sky showed outside the windows.

Nervous laughter broke out among the passengers, and the congressman began to assume his regular shade of blustery pink. I leaned forward to pick up papers that had slipped from the thick file I'd been holding. It was Jack Kennedy's service record, complete with a photograph of him in his dress blues, a newly minted naval lieutenant.

"Hey, isn't that Joe Kennedy's son?" bellowed the congressman, squinting his eyes to study the photograph. "The younger kid, not the good-looking one."

"Joe who?" I said, raising my voice to be heard over the roar of the engines as I gathered up papers and stowed them in the heavy manila envelope.

"Joseph P. Kennedy," he said. "His kid wrote a book, and that's him, I'd swear to it."

"I don't read much," I said, looking to Kaz to come to the rescue.

He shrugged, seeming to enjoy my predicament. I tended to provide Kaz with a good deal of amusement.

"Don't tell me you never heard of Ambassador Kennedy," the congressman said, poking the reporter in the ribs to get his attention. "He almost ran for president last time around. What are you doing with a picture of his kid? John, I think his name is."

"Did you read the book?" I asked.

"Of course I did," he said, in an indignant tone of voice that suggested he hadn't cracked the spine yet. "The ambassador himself sent me a copy." I wasn't surprised. He probably sent every congressman in Washington a copy. Nothing like greasing the skids for the next generation. "What business do you have with the Kennedys?"

"Listen," I said, leaning forward and stifling a desire to smack this guy. "It's—"

"It is all part of a joint public relations effort," Kaz said, his hand on my shoulder gently pulling me back into my seat. "We are developing a series of stories on where the children of famous politicians are serving. Of course Ambassador Kennedy's sons are on the list. How about you sir? Do you have any sons in the service?"

That unleashed a torrent of parental pride. He had a daughter about to complete nursing school who'd already volunteered for the Army Nurse Corps. His son was in the navy, serving on the *USS Little*, a destroyer transport in the South Pacific. Kaz cautioned the congressman and the reporter that the whole thing was not yet for release, and dutifully wrote down the names of the politician's two kids, Kennedy offspring long forgotten.

"Thanks," I whispered, after the ride had smoothed out and the congressman was cutting ZZZs. "Good story."

"I thought it preferable to you punching the gentleman," Kaz said. "Now tell me, what is it with the Boyles and the Kennedys? What sort of feud do you have going?"

The congressman yawned and his eyes opened. I wondered if he'd heard the magic word.

"Later," I said. "It's a long story." I closed my eyes and tried to forget I'd ever heard the Kennedy name.

CHAPTER FOUR

WE PARTED WAYS with the congressman in Cairo where we were rushed aboard a Stirling transport aircraft, its four engines warming up as we boarded, holding onto our hats against the prop wash. The door shut tight behind us as the pilot began taxiing down the runway even before we could grab the last two seats, nowhere near each other. Conversation wasn't in the cards, so I focused on ignoring the glares from a couple of British generals and a gold-braided admiral. Or he might have been the doorman from the Copley Square Hotel, it was hard to say. Cairo became Karachi, where we dined on Spam sandwiches and tea as the Stirling was refueled for the southerly hop along the coast of India to China Bay in Ceylon. Kaz chatted with a general whose son had attended the same college at Oxford as he had. Of course, Kaz knew the kid and that loosened the general up. A hip flask made an appearance, but before it could make it in my direction, we were off again. I slept the length of the Indian subcontinent.

The rains hit as soon as we landed in Ceylon. The China Bay airstrip was next to the harbor, and we were scheduled to take a Sunderland flying boat as soon as the weather cleared. We ran from the Stirling to the nearest Quonset hut, musette bags held over our heads against the downpour. It didn't help.

"It is monsoon season," Kaz said, shaking off the wet as we made for the tea kettle and tray of cheese sandwiches. We were the only passengers on the next leg of the journey. The Sunderland was flying reconnaissance, on the lookout for Japanese naval forces from Java or Sumatra making a run to the Indian Ocean. "We may as well settle in. I doubt they can take off in this weather."

"It's a flying boat, Kaz," I said, dumping sugar into my tea and grabbing a couple of sandwiches. "A little rain shouldn't bother a Sunderland." It was actually a lot of rain, as if the earth had turned upside down and the oceans were being emptied on our heads. Kaz wasn't fond of rough seas. "I'm sure we'll have to wait for a while, if only so we won't get swamped being ferried out to the Sunderland."

"Let us talk about something else, Billy," Kaz said as he sipped his tea. "Tell me about the Kennedys, now that we are away from prying ears. How did this enmity begin?"

"Okay," I said, glancing at a couple Royal Air Force officers in the mess hall and the few stewards cleaning up. No one was paying us any mind. Plus the drumming rain kept a beat on the Quonset hut roof that made it impossible to hear a conversation two yards away. Perfect conditions for talk of Kennedys, Boyles, and bootlegging.

"It was 1929," I began. "My dad had finally made detective. He'd been on the force for ten years and it was a big deal to make the grade to plainclothes detective. He said he'd never dreamed of a big Irish lug like himself dressing up in a suit and tie every day. I told you how he got into the department, didn't I?"

"Yes, the great Boston Police Strike of 1919," Kaz said.

"Yep. Over a thousand rank and file walked off the job," I said. "A new recruit was still making only two bucks a day, the same wage as sixty years before."

"It seems the strike was justified," Kaz said. "Although it must have been illegal."

"It was," I said. "And the sad truth is they all lost their jobs when Governor Coolidge broke the strike with the National Guard. The police commissioner fired those who had gone off the job and hired fifteen hundred new cops."

"Your father and uncle among them," Kaz said. I guess I'd told him the story before. Maybe a few times, now that I think about it.

"Yeah. Them and hundreds of other veterans who'd just returned home from France. Most of them Irish, since it was hard to find work when you spoke with a brogue and had a moniker from the auld sod. Dad would have been glad to get work in a factory or digging ditches, anything to put food on the table. Instead, he and Uncle Frank wound up bluecoats, and worked hard at it. Frank had made detective the year before, working vice out of the downtown headquarters."

"What was your father's assignment?" Kaz asked. This was territory I hadn't covered before.

"He was warming a chair in the commissioner's office," I said. "Awaiting a transfer, learning administration and procedures, that sort of thing." Dad had alluded to a payoff in order to land a plumb assignment like homicide, but I could never get any details out of him. I never even knew if he'd been assigned to the commissioner because he'd paid up or had refused to.

"It is hard to imagine your father as a police bureaucrat," Kaz said, "after all you have told me about him."

"It didn't last long, not after the prohis showed up."

"Pro-hee? What is that?"

"No, Pro-heez. Short for Prohibition agents, from the US Treasury Department," I explained.

Kaz smiled as he sipped his tea. "You Americans do not like your words overly long, do you?"

"We're too busy for big words, Lieutenant Kazimierz," I said, drawing out his last name for as long as I could manage. "But since we're grounded here, I'll take my time. You've heard of Eliot Ness?"

"Yes, of course," Kaz said. "The Untouchables. Chicago, Al Capone." Kaz loved American gangster movies and especially slang associated with mobsters. Otherwise he was pretty much of an egghead. An armed and deadly egghead, that is.

"Same bunch. The Bureau of Prohibition sent a squad to Boston with orders to cooperate with visiting agents from the Canadian Royal Commission on Customs and Excise. Taxmen, just like the US Treasury boys. Since they were on our turf, someone had to be assigned to them."

"Your father," Kaz said. "Because he was the least senior detective. No one else wanted to be associated with the prohis." I could tell Kaz liked the new slang.

"Yep. Local cops used the Prohibition laws when it suited them. If it would help to nab a mobster, fine. But no one wanted to bust open barrels of beer and keep honest folks from a little relaxation. But the Treasury men from the Bureau of Prohibition, they had a calling, all right."

"They were simply upholding the law, Billy," Kaz said.

"A ridiculous law that made gangsters rich and politicians more crooked than ever. But you're right, the law is the law, and Dad was told to help the Canadians and the prohis any way he could. Since it was his first assignment, he figured he had to do a decent job if he wanted to make a name for himself."

"Without overdoing things," Kaz said. We both turned to look outside as the rain drumming on the metal roof lessened. It was still coming down heavily, but a sliver of light gleamed at the horizon.

"Now you get the picture," I said. "He had to walk a tightrope. Especially when the Canadians explained what brought them to Boston."

"Let me guess," Kaz said, lowering his voice. "Joseph Kennedy."

"On the money," I said. "They were after him for unpaid liquor export taxes. They had his name on a few shipping documents, but had no conclusive evidence. The prohis had their eye on him as well, but had even less evidence."

"But there was no Prohibition in Canada," Kaz said. "Surely an American could be in the liquor business there."

"Yeah, and he was. Kennedy owned a liquor distributor called the Silk Hat Cocktail Company out in Vancouver, British Columbia. They exported liquor overseas and paid the export tax. The excise agents said they suspected some of the ships never left port. Instead of steaming off to Mexico or Japan, the skipper would simply dock at another berth and unload directly onto trucks."

"Which would then smuggle the alcohol across the border," Kaz said, staying one step ahead.

"Right. Nice and clean. That way the books balanced. Then Kennedy got greedy, according to the Canadians. Their theory was that he'd set up operations on the East Coast, bringing in booze on small boats, skipping the fiction about legal exports."

"What evidence did they have?" Kaz said.

"Not much at first. Kennedy did supply all the booze for his Harvard class's tenth year reunion in 1922. Cases of the stuff. That brought him to the attention of the Treasury boys, but even they couldn't go up against that kind of influence. Half the guys at that reunion had enough cash and clout to shut down any investigation. But when the Canadians came calling with a lead a few years later, it was a different story."

"How so?"

"It was an open secret that toughs from Southie—the Gustin Gang—were bringing in booze from ships out in international waters."

"Rumrunners, yes?" Kaz asked.

"That's what they were called," I said. "Small, fast boats that could be beached and unloaded easily. The Gustin Gang—named after the street where they hung out—distributed to speakeasies all over Boston. Then they decided there was an easier way to do business."

"What?" Kaz asked.

I smiled, challenging him to figure it out.

"Easier than unloading from ships at sea," he said, thinking out loud. "While still ending up with the liquor. Of course! Steal it from other gangs, yes?"

"I'll make a cop of you yet, Kaz. Or a criminal. Hard to say which we are, in this business. Yeah, the Gustin boys started knocking off rival shipments. Worked great for a while, but then the other gangs began to fight back, and soon no one was getting their booze."

"There must have been angry customers," Kaz said.

"As well as angry mob bosses. The big guys, not street thugs like the Gustins."

"Let me guess," Kaz said. "Someone was eliminated."

"Well, yeah, but how? The gangs had already been fighting, but no one had scored a knockout blow."

"Hmmm," Kaz said, drumming his fingers on the table. "I have it! A sit-down, yes? Is that not what a meeting among gangsters is called?"

"Yep. An Italian gang offered to arrange it. Frank Wallace and Dodo Walsh were offered safe passage to discuss a truce. They were gunned down as they walked in. That's a Mafia truce. Hard to argue with it."

"This is a fascinating story, Billy, but what does it have to do with the senior Boyle and Kennedy?"

I was about to get to that when an RAF officer came for us. The rain was pelting down, but the sky to the east was clearing, and that was where we were going. I was groggy from too much time in the air and not enough sleep, but I was aware enough to understand what that meant. The wide Pacific Ocean and a new enemy, one even more alien than the Germans. All of Europe could be swallowed up and vanish in the broad stretches of sea and sky conquered by the Japanese.

"To be continued," I said.

CHAPTER FIVE

THE SUNDERLAND WAS like a flying house. It came equipped with bunk beds, a galley, and indoor plumbing. Even with all the creature comforts, Kaz was not feeling his best as the plane wallowed in the swells waiting for takeoff. When the four powerful engines finally started up, the hull slamming against waves as we built up speed, he crawled into the sack and groaned for the next hour when he wasn't swearing in Polish. I don't speak Polish, but I know a curse when I hear it.

The flight itself wouldn't have been too bad if the pilot had climbed above the clouds. But we'd hitched a ride on a reconnaissance mission, which meant the Sunderland had to fly low enough to scan the ocean waters for Japanese ships or a submarine cruising on the surface. Winds buffeted the fuselage, rattling and shaking the aircraft, vibrating the metal hull until I thought the rivets might pop out. I followed Kaz's lead and crawled into a bunk, keeping my curses to myself. Some were aimed at the weather, but mostly I cursed the fates that had brought the Kennedys back into my life.

I'd had enough of Jack back in Boston, and would've been happy if our paths had never crossed again. But now he needed me, so here I was, flying around most of the world to smooth things out for the skinny little bastard. Again. I'd begun the story of how the Boyles and the Kennedys first came into contact, and as soon as Kaz was back on solid ground, I'd finish it. But I wasn't sure about my story. Jack's story,

I should say, since he always preferred to be center stage. Unless there was trouble, that is.

Truth was, I was embarrassed. I didn't want to admit to playing the sap for a spoiled rich kid.

I awoke to a smooth ride and blue skies, the ocean dazzlingly bright beneath us. We landed in a lagoon at Keeling Island, a flyspeck in the Indian Ocean halfway between Ceylon and Australia. A barge motored out and refueled the Sunderland. As we took off, RAF crewmen watched us from the white sandy beach, palm trees swaying lazily in the breeze. What was it like to spend a war in a tropical paradise? Did they count themselves lucky, or dream of distant battles and pester their commanding officer for transfers?

"It must be teatime somewhere," Kaz said through a yawn, startling me as I gazed out the window. He looked disheveled and even paler than usual. "I don't think I even know what day it is."

"Tuesday," I said, with more certainty than I felt. We made our way to the galley and got the tea going. There are worse ways to travel.

"Finish your story," Kaz said as he stirred milk into his tea. I dumped sugar into mine. "About your father and Joseph Kennedy. Entertain me. We still have hours to go until we land. Or whatever they call it when one of these things comes down in the water."

"Okay," I said, leaning back in my seat and thinking about the stories Dad and Uncle Dan had told around the dinner table. I'd been in school back then, getting my knuckles rapped by the nuns and struggling with geometry. "Dad tags along with the prohis and the Canadian excise men, getting the lay of the land. They have some decent inside dope about gangs active in hijacking trucks with both legal and illegal cargoes. So Dad figures he'll show them where the gangs operate and maybe pick up a few leads to use after they're gone."

"I take it he was more interested in the hijacking of trucks belonging to legitimate businessmen?" Kaz said.

"Yes and no," I said. As usual, explaining how things worked wasn't as straightforward as you might expect, especially with Prohibition thrown into the mix. "A lot of the guys involved in rum-running were ordinary businessmen. Tavern owners, distributors, greengrocers. Their business had been hurt by Prohibition and they were only looking to keep their heads above water."

"What about the rest?"

"That's different," I said. "The bosses at the top were the real crooks. Some were career criminals, others were rich bastards who didn't think the rules applied to them. Rich men who didn't think they were rich enough. They made the real money, while everyone else ran big risks for small rewards."

"Joseph Kennedy the elder being one of those?" Kaz raised his eyebrow as he asked the question, a smile playing on his lips. I had to remind myself that Kaz himself was rich and might have heard people disparage his own family's wealth, jealous of their comforts and prestige, back when it was possible for any Pole to be comfortable.

"Dad said the Canadian evidence was interesting, but not enough to build a case on," I said. "So they went to work on picking up the rest of the Gustin Gang. They were in hiding after the Mafia hit on Frank and Dodo. Frank's brother, Stephen Wallace, was running the gang, such as it was. They were back to rum-running, bringing in bootleg booze from offshore."

"But they had learned their lesson about stealing liquor from other gangs," Kaz said.

"Yeah, and there were rumors the hit had been ordered from high up," I said, lowering my voice to a whisper.

"Higher than the Mafia?" Kaz asked.

I nodded.

"Kennedy?"

I shrugged. "It was a theory," I said. "The Gustins had upset the natural order of things, drawing too much attention to what was going on. Nobody in that business likes attention."

"Did your father ever find evidence?" Kaz said.

"He got close," I said. "They picked up Wallace and brought him in. The prohis threatened to let him go very publicly and leak word that he'd cooperated with them. An old trick."

"But a smart one," Kaz said. "It must have frightened Mr. Wallace, following the Mafia hit on his brother."

"Yes, but too smart, as it turned out. Wallace talked, and claimed he could implicate Joe Kennedy. Dad wasn't too sure; he thought Wallace might have been trying to impress the Feds, and if Kennedy were actually involved, he wouldn't be in contact with lowlifes like the Wallace brothers."

"What happened then?"

"Governor Allen sent one of his men to intervene. It seems Dad and his pals were getting too close, either to Kennedy or someone else with political connections. Wallace was sprung and the whole thing was forgotten. By most people, that is."

"Your father had threatened a powerful man," Kaz said.

"Yep. And he paid the price. He got sent back down to the uniform division. A signal to the rest of the department: it doesn't pay to cooperate with federal agents, not when they have their sights set on Joe Kennedy and his like."

"But you don't know if it was Kennedy," Kaz said, his tea gone cold.

"No," I said, shaking my head. "Funny thing is, that guy from the governor's office—Joseph Timilty—got himself appointed police commissioner back in 1936. He's known to be in the back pocket of Joe Kennedy, and he's as corrupt as they come. A few months ago he was indicted on charges of corruption. He didn't even lose his job. The indictment was quashed by a friendly judge, and Timilty is still running the Boston police."

"By friendly you mean a friend of Ambassador Kennedy's," Kaz said.

I nodded. He caught on fast.

"Your father became a detective, though."

"He did. Not long after we got a new governor and one of his pet projects was a police academy. Dad helped him with that, and pretty soon he was back in plainclothes, working homicide."

"Did Commissioner Timilty make things difficult for him later?"

"No need," I said. "The point had been made. Everyone knew the story. Remember, these people don't like attention if there's even a whiff of impropriety. It was easier to move on and leave Dad alone to do his job. There's an invisible world out there, run by money and power. The rules are unwritten, even unspoken, but anyone who comes into contact with it comes to understand them damn quick. Secrecy and order are what it's about. Everything needs to run as normal to complete the illusion that all is right and proper with the world. Dad threatened all that when he drew attention to a possible link between Kennedy and the smugglers. He got away easy with a slap on the wrist."

"Attention," Kaz said. "That is why we have this assignment, is it not? To make sure the younger son does not receive unwarranted attention."

Kaz was a quick study. I nodded, turning away in hopes the conversation was over.

"That tells me why the Boyles would not think much of Joseph Kennedy Senior," Kaz said. "But it does not explain your antipathy towards Joe Junior and Jack."

"No, it doesn't," I said, folding my arms across my chest and gazing out over the blue rippling ocean.

CHAPTER SIX

THE BIG SUNDERLAND took us to Australia in style. First a stop at Darwin, then on to Port Moresby in New Guinea. The flying boat landed on calm waters and motored up to a dock where we got off and stretched our legs. The sun was bright, the water blue, and Kaz wasn't the least bit seasick. A good day so far.

We walked along the dock as men secured the Sunderland and a fuel barge motored alongside. A flurry of activity surrounded the small boats tied up along the waterfront, sailors and GIs hauling supplies and rolling drums of fuel over the splintered, sun-bleached wood. Farther out in the bay, a couple of destroyers stood at anchor.

"Lieutenant Boyle?" A figure emerged from the crowd, a lanky guy with naval aviator's wings on his rumpled khaki shirt and a crush cap pushed back on his head. "Lieutenant White. I'll be flying you to Guadalcanal." Freckles dotted the skin beneath his teardrop sunglasses, and I resisted the urge to ask if his daddy had given him the keys to the plane. Instead I introduced Kaz as White led us to a jeep waiting on a hardpack road that fronted the harbor.

"We're fueled and ready to go," White said as he gunned the jeep up a winding hill, passing an array of European-style buildings with broad verandahs next to native thatched-roof houses and army pyramidal tents. The ascent became steeper as the road curved around an antiaircraft emplacement.

"We are not going by flying boat?" Kaz asked.

"Yeah, but we're a PBY unit. We have retractable landing gear and can land on water or dry land. Not as comfortable as that flying hotel you came in on, but we'll get you there. The airbase is just over this next hill." He took another switchback and had to use first gear to inch up the steep incline. We had a clear view of the town and harbor, the rich greens and vivid shades of blue strange after the North African climate we'd grown used to. White braked and I thought he was about to play tour guide for us tourists from the European Theater of Operations.

"There," White said. He grabbed a pair of binoculars and scanned the western sky. First I heard it, that familiar insect-like distant drone. Then I saw the spots in the distance coalesce into a formation.

"Ours?" Kaz asked.

"Japs," White said, "headed our way. Betties." He floored the jeep and we held on as he sped along the hill. We saw antiaircraft crew swiveling their gun in the direction of the incoming aircraft.

"Are they going for the airfield?" I asked, holding onto my hat as White shifted into high gear.

"No," he said. "They're coming in over the water, so they're after the ships and docks. But if they have fighter escorts, the Zeroes don't mind a strafing run on the airstrip to slow down pursuit."

We crested the hill and saw that the bombers were closer. Antiaircraft fire rose up from the destroyers and emplacements along the harbor. One of the bombers blossomed into flame, its wings trailing fire and belching smoke as it fell, twisting and turning as if trying to shake off the grip of the red blaze. White barely slowed as we took a turn that nearly spilled us from our seats. The chatter of machine guns and the rhythmic *thuds* of larger antiaircraft shells filled the air with noise and explosions. Another Betty blew up, descending in a fireball to the sea.

Then they dropped their bombloads. I could see the bombs descend as the aircraft turned away, climbing from the barrage clawing at them from every point in Port Moresby. The bombs exploded in neat rows, ripping into the docks and small ships moored in the harbor. I saw the Sunderland lifted from the water, its back broken by a direct hit.

We were spared the sight of any further destruction as White took the jeep down the hill toward the airfield, where a flight of P-40 Warhawk fighters roared down the runway and took to the air in pursuit of the bombers. We raced past hangars until he slammed on the brakes near a Consolidated PBY, its two engines already warming up. It was painted a flat black, even the US Navy insignia done in a dull grey. There was no time for questions as we scrambled aboard, the crew and copilot already at their stations.

We began to taxi, then had to wait for another half dozen Warhawks to get in the air. When it was our turn, White lost no time leaving the ground behind. The waist gunners manned their thirty-caliber machine guns in the distinctive blisters that afforded a wide view of sky and sea. But no Japanese Zeroes challenged us, and as White gained altitude and headed south, the only thing we saw was smoke blackening the sky above Port Moresby.

"Keep your eyes peeled, boys," White said over the intercom. "I'm headed for that cloud bank at nine o'clock." He tossed the headset aside, told his copilot to take over, and leaned in our direction as we stood in the lower passageway leading to the cockpit. "We've got you guys to thank for saving us from those Betties."

"How so?" I asked.

"We normally berth in the harbor," White said. "But we needed some quick maintenance to make this run to Guadalcanal. So we flew up to the airstrip this morning. We would have been right under those bombs. We owe you."

"I will take a smooth flight as thanks," Kaz said. "Why do you call them Betty?"

"That's our designation for the Mitsubishi G4M bomber," he said. "They give Jap planes code names to make it easier to remember. I hear the Nips call them the Flying Cigar."

"Why?" I asked.

"Because they light up so easy," White said with a grin. "The Japs don't have self-sealing gas tanks on 'em, so even small-arms fire will turn a Betty to toast. You saw those two go up over the harbor, right?"

"Hard to miss," I said. "You expect to run into any other enemy aircraft today?"

"You never know, but don't worry. We'll get you to Guadalcanal in one piece."

"Will it be a water landing?" Kaz asked, eager as always to avoid choppy seas.

"No, we'll put you right down at Henderson Field. What's the Polish Army doing in the South Pacific anyway, if you don't mind my asking?"

"I do not mind at all," Kaz said. "But neither can I say."

"That's okay," White said. "I've seen all sorts out here. French, Dutch, not to mention the Brits, Aussies, Kiwis, and the Fuzzy Wuzzies, of course."

"I know Kiwis are New Zealanders," Kaz said. "But who are Fuzzy Wuzzies?"

"The natives," White said. "They have those big haloes of curly hair, you know? So Fuzzy Wuzzy."

"What do the natives think of that?" Kaz asked.

"Well, I don't know. Back in New Guinea I guess they're actually Papuans, but I don't know what they're called out in the Solomons. What I do know is that every Aussie soldier I talked to who fought on the Kokoda Trail said that they couldn't have stopped the Japs without them. They fight, carry heavy loads through the jungle, and help evacuate the wounded. And they really hate the Japs."

"Where's the Kokoda Trail?" I asked.

"It's the trail over the Owen Stanley Mountains that leads from the Jap-occupied east coast of New Guinea to Port Moresby on the west. If the Aussies and the Fuzzy Wuzzies hadn't stopped the Japs there and pushed them back, we might be having this conversation in the Australian Outback while the Japs hunt us down."

"Never heard of it," I said. "All I read about in the *Stars and Stripes* is how MacArthur is winning the war out here."

"Well, if he is, he's doing it from Lennon's Hotel in Brisbane," White said. "Why don't you two give the waist gunners a hand and stand lookout in the blisters? We'll be in the clouds soon, but extra eyes are always welcome."

We headed back. The gunners watched the sky while we scanned the ocean below. The clear acrylic blisters bowed out from the fuselage, giving a spectacular view in all directions. I looked at Kaz and grinned, the bombing and destruction almost forgotten in the thrill of the ride. The waist gunners craned their necks, checking every quadrant. The PBY had a decent defensive armament, but getting jumped by a Zero would definitely be bad news.

The sea and sky were empty as we headed into the cloud bank. Mist enveloped the aircraft, muffling the noise of the twin engines as it created an eerie sense of vulnerability. We were hidden, yet it was impossible to know what awaited us beyond the thin veil of fog. I thought I'd relax, but I grew tenser by the moment, straining to see anything in the greyness. It sort of summed up the whole war. An occasional false sense of security between bouts of boredom and sudden death.

"Gets to you, huh?" the waist gunner said. I nodded and felt a little better knowing he sensed it, too. But not much.

I tried to stay alert, but the monotony of the droning engines and the zero visibility made it a challenge. After ten minutes or so, I thought I heard a variation in the engine sound, but then it faded.

Then it returned.

"Something wrong with the engines?" I asked the waist gunner. He cocked his head to listen and shrugged. The sound was gone again.

I peered out of the blister, pressing my face against the cool acrylic, trying to pick up any change in vibration or sound. I swore I heard it again, the engines going louder and suddenly softer. The waist gunner cupped his ear, finally picking it up himself.

"Holy Christ," I said in a whisper, backing away instinctively from the waist blister. "It's another PBY!" The sound I'd heard was their engines as the aircraft drifted closer and then away, both of us unaware of how close we were.

"Where?" The waist gunner leaned in next to me. It had vanished again.

"Right there," I said. "Slightly above us. I saw a waist blister and the high wings. Look!" It had drifted close again, a large fuselage that looked about to drop on top of us. Then I saw it. That big red ball that made it clear it was not one of our floatplanes.

"Kawanishi!" Yelled the waist gunner. "Port side."

He opened up with his machine gun as the PBY banked to starboard. The narrow interior was filled with screaming voices, thunderous bursts of fire, and the metallic clatter of ejected shells bouncing on the deck. Terrified, I grabbed the edge of the blister and caught a brief glimpse of a face staring openmouthed from the waist position in the Jap plane, like some macabre mirror image. His machine gun spat fire, but his shots were as wild as ours—an instinctual reaction on both sides to put hot lead and distance between the planes and the possibility of collision.

But was the Jap plane heading for home? Were that gunner and his pals as scared as I was? Or were they circling around, hunting us in the clouds? I kept watch for a while, nothing but mist and murk as far as the eye could see, which was no farther than the acrylic bubble.

"That was close," White said when I went forward. "The Kawanishi is larger than us, a four-engine job. He might have survived a collision, but he would have crushed us." He put the PBY into a slight dive until he found the bottom of the clouds and evened out, staying right below the unending fluff, not a yard from cover if needed.

"Kawanishi? No code name?" I asked. "Patty or Maxene maybe?"

"Mavis," he said. "But everyone in the Solomons knows the Kawanishi. It's the Jap version of the PBY. Long range, and not bad at night either. I guarantee that won't be the last one you see."

"I just hope the next one isn't that close," I said.

"I hope it is in flames, like the Flying Cigar," Kaz said.

"You got the right attitude for the Solomons, Lieutenant," White said to Kaz. "Welcome to our South Pacific paradise."

CHAPTER SEVEN

THE PBY PUT us down on Henderson Field on the north side of Guadalcanal. It had been less than six months since ground combat had ended on the island with the last of the Japanese troops vanquished. The airstrip was alive with fighters, transports, and bombers, all in various stages of readiness as crews swarmed over them, fueling, rearming, and unloading supplies. Seabees smoothed out the runway with bulldozers shoving crushed coral into bomb craters.

"I guess the girls paid a visit," I said. "Betty and her friends."

"Let us hope they've grown tired of this island. I already am. What do we do now?" Kaz asked, eyeing the repair work as we stood in the hot sun. Lieutenant White had already taxied down the runway for his return leg. We walked to the nearest hangar, haversacks slung over our shoulders. The heat was thick and humid, nothing like the breezy warmth of Port Moresby. The place had a smell about it: oil and gasoline mixed with stale sweat and fetid decay.

"Boyle and Kazimierz?" A navy lieutenant in bleached-out khakis called out to us as he emerged from a Quonset hut. His shirt was soaked with perspiration and rivulets of sweat ran from his black wavy hair.

"That's us," I said, mopping my forehead. "You got a heat wave going on here?"

"Funny," he said. "This is actually the nicest day we've had in a week. Welcome to Henderson Field. I'm Dick Nixon, Air Transport Officer."

"Billy Boyle, and this is Kaz," I said as we shook hands.

"Commander Cluster is waiting for you," Nixon said, leading us to an open pavilion with a palm-frond roof. A crudely painted sign read: NICK'S HAMBURGER STAND.

"That you?" I asked as we followed Nixon.

"Yeah, we organized that for pilots coming through. We grill burgers and try to put out whatever food we can scrounge. A lot of the guys bring stuff from Australia when they can. Even cold beer once in a while."

"All the comforts of home," I said.

"That's the idea. There's Commander Cluster," Nixon said, waving to an officer drinking coffee at the end of a long wooden table that had been cobbled together from packing crates. "I'll have some chow sent over for you fellows. We don't see too many Poles out here, Lieutenant Kazimierz. Is the Polish Army in Exile sending troops to fight the Japs?"

"We Poles have enough war in Europe," Kaz said. "Between the Germans and the Russians, we have our fill of enemies. The Polish government did declare war on Japan following Pearl Harbor; however, the Japanese rejected the declaration." We walked into the shade of the open-air hamburger joint, thankful for the slight coolness and the familiar aroma from the grill.

"Rejected a declaration of war?" Nixon said. "That's a new one. Why'd they do it?"

"Prime Minister Tojo said Poland had been pressured into it by Great Britain, since we were dependent upon their support. Tojo probably rejected it purely for propaganda purposes, since we obviously pose no threat to them in the Pacific."

"Well, don't try telling that to the first Jap you see," Nixon said. "The finer points of diplomacy are lost on them. So what exactly are you two doing here?"

"Long story," I said. "We're looking into a possible murder. One of the natives who works with the Coastwatchers got himself killed over on Tulagi."

"You're lucky," Nixon said. "Tulagi is a tropical paradise compared to Guadalcanal. That's why the British made it their district head-quarters for the Solomons. Is one of our guys involved?"

"That's what we're here to find out," I said. "Say, you wouldn't happen to know a pal of mine from Boston, would you? PT skipper named Jack Kennedy? He had his boat sunk recently." I made it sound casual, to see if any scuttlebutt had reached across the bay about Jack being involved with the killing.

"Kennedy?" Nixon said, tapping his finger against the dark stubble on his cheek. "No, never heard of him. PT boats get sunk all the time. Wouldn't exactly be big news. Sorry. Good luck, fellas." Nixon waved to Cluster and we headed over to him. We did the salutes and intro-ductions. Cluster was good-looking, tanned and blond. A walking advertisement for PT boats.

"Have a seat," he said. "I understand you boys have come a long way."

"How'd you hear that, Commander?" I said in my most polite voice. As far as I knew, a commander in the navy was close to a colonel in the army, so until we knew how things worked out here, it paid to observe the niceties of military rank. He also wore an Annapolis ring, so I figured he'd be a stickler for that stuff.

"Between the pilots coming through here and the navy base on Tulagi, you can pick up a lot of gossip. I heard about two hotshots sent out here all the way from Europe to investigate us," Cluster said, eye-ing me as he sipped coffee from a chipped mug. "Figured I'd better check you out myself."

"Must be two other guys," I said. "We came from North Africa. To look into the murder of a native, not to investigate the navy."

"Sounds like you might be ready to make an arrest," Cluster said. "I heard you mention one of my men to Nix."

"Jack Kennedy is one of yours?"

"I have two Motor Torpedo Squadrons up at Rendova. Jack is one of my best skippers, and he's been through a lot."

"We heard about his boat being sunk," I said. "And I know Jack from Boston. That's why I was asking about him."

"You're a friend of his?" Cluster asked.

"We're acquainted," I said. "It's been a while. But we have no plans to arrest anyone. We've simply been sent here to look into things." Cluster looked at Kaz, then back to me. He set his cup on the table and leaned back, taking our measure.

"You know Jack, but you avoid calling him a friend," he said. "You're both from Boston, but your accent doesn't sound as Harvard as his."

"South Boston," I said. "I was a cop before the war."

Cluster nodded, his face grim. "So either Jack's father sent you, or someone who is an enemy of the old man," he said. "Or this is the biggest coincidence of the war."

"No coincidence," I said. "We were picked for the job, you're right. But it won't be a whitewash. Or a witch hunt. You have my word."

"Okay," Cluster said. "And if that's true, I don't envy you the assignment."

"Tell me about it, Commander. I could use some of that coffee. Is it any good?"

"Best in the Solomons," he said, signaling for two more to a sailor at the grill. "Nix takes care of his pilots. Like I take care of my PT crews."

With that subtle warning in mind, we ate hamburgers and drank coffee. The chow wasn't bad, and the hot joe was welcome even in the sticky, humid air. An occasional breeze blew the heat around, but it wasn't long before our khakis were drenched with sweat. Many of the guys were shirtless or wearing grimy T-shirts.

"Proper uniforms do not seem to be the order of the day here," Kaz said.

"Not on Guadalcanal," Cluster said. "The rot is in the air. You can smell the decay. Those leather shoes of yours would be mildewed by morning and falling off your feet by nightfall. The humidity eats at everything. If there wasn't flat ground for an airstrip, no one would want this place." He shook his head as if in disgust at the very notion of the island.

"Nixon said Tulagi was better," I said.

"A lot better," Cluster said. "Which is why the hospital and naval headquarters are there. I'll bring you over on my boat."

"Boat?" Kaz asked. "Is it a long journey?"

"Less than thirty miles," Cluster said. "An easy run. Unless the Japs make a daylight raid, but the action has mostly moved to the northwest, up to Rendova and New Georgia. They're more likely to come at night. We still have a few hours before dusk, but we might as well get started."

"Why at night?" Kaz asked as we left the thatched-roof grill and blinked our eyes against the blinding sun.

"A raid in force could come at any time. But after dark our propellers churn up the phosphorescence in the water when we're under way. So the Kawanishis like to fly low and slow looking for phosphorescent wakes. They patrol the Slot—the main channel running through the Solomons—nearly every night. The wake is like a big arrow pointing right at us. We can't see the Jap planes but they can see us. Not a good combination."

"We already had a run-in with a Kawanishi," I said. "Our PBY almost collided with one in a cloud bank."

"Don't worry," Cluster said. "It won't be your last."

We walked along the runway, heading for a line of vehicles. A burned-out bulldozer and a wrecked aircraft—Japanese and American, respectively—sat rusting in the sun. Weeds and vines grew through gaps in the shredded steel and aluminum, testament to the jungle pressing in on us.

"Even metal doesn't last long on Guadalcanal," Cluster said, waving his hand over the pile of battle debris. "Rust, rot, and the jungle will swallow all this up. I wonder if people will remember this place when it's all over. Seven thousand soldiers, sailors, and marines dead. The brass guess about thirty thousand Japs dead, all told. Out there in the channel, there's so many sunken ships they call it Ironbottom Sound. Except for the occasional bombing, it's basically a backwater, a stopover on the way to the real war."

"How long have you been out here, Commander?" Kaz asked.

Cluster stopped, staring at the wreckage. He didn't answer. Which was an answer. Too long.

"Come on," he finally said. "Let's get you two outfitted for the Solomons."

"Whatever you say, Commander," I said. We got in his jeep, tossing in our haversacks. I got the sense that we'd passed some sort of test. He'd warmed up, or maybe simply figured out that I was a pawn in someone else's game. No threat to his men, at least not compared to the Japanese.

CHAPTER EIGHT

THE ARMY SERGEANT waved away our orders as I began to unfold them.

"No need," he said. "If you're with the commander, you're okay by me." We were in a large tent with the sides rolled up, surrounded by K rations, Spam, artillery shells, grenades, medical supplies, and all the other tools of assault and sustenance.

"Ditch them shoes," the sergeant said. "They won't last unless you're going to sit at a desk over on Tulagi. And then not for long anyways."

"You have those new jungle boots?" Cluster asked. The sergeant nodded and eyed our feet, then reached into a crate to grab a couple pairs.

"Try these on," he said. "They don't last long either, but they're rubber soled and made of canvas. Water drains right out, and you can count on getting soaked plenty around here."

"So what good are they?" I asked as I slipped one on.

"Leather combat boots mildew and rot," he said. "Plus they keep water in when you get wet, so you end up with all sorts of fungi. The canvas boots don't hold up over the long haul, but they're a damn sight better than the old clodhoppers."

"Comfortable," I said, lacing up the boots. It was like wearing tennis shoes. "Anything else we should have?"

"You might want to get rid of that wool cap, Lieutenant," the sergeant said to Kaz, who wore his British Army service cap.

"I shall keep the hat," Kaz said. "Otherwise I may be mistaken for an American."

"I wouldn't worry about that," I said, to which Kaz raised a languid eyebrow.

I swapped my garrison cap for a billed cap, or M41 HBT Field Utility Cap, Sage Green Herringbone Twill, as the army insisted on describing it. Shading my eyes from the glare of the sun would be important out here. I took a canvas holster to replace my leather one, figuring it would be hard enough to keep my .45 automatic clean without worrying about the holster decomposing around it. Kaz already had a tan canvas holster for his Webley revolver, which he had chosen because it matched the color of his web belt. Always the clotheshorse. Once the sergeant gave us an extra set of cotton khaki shirts and trousers, we were all set to win the battle against mildew and jungle rot.

I hoped that was as much fighting as we'd need to do.

Cluster drove to the docks at Lunga Point where his PT boat was docked. As he braked the jeep to a halt, a low wail rose in the air, a familiar sound from London and North Africa. Air-raid sirens. Seconds later came the snarling engines of Navy Wildcat fighters, the sound growing louder as the planes rose in the sky and flew overhead, due north.

"Let's move!" Cluster yelled as he leapt from the jeep and made for the docks. We scrambled after him, haversacks in hand. The PT boat engines were rumbling; sailors held lines, ready to cast off. We raced up the gangplank as Cluster barked orders to the crew. Other PT boats were already underway, opening up their supercharged Packard engines as soon as they cleared the docks. Within seconds we joined them, sailors manning the two twin fifty-caliber machine guns swiveling their weapons skyward, searching for the enemy.

"What's happening?" I asked above the sound of the engines. Kaz and I hung onto the rail behind the bridge as the boat thumped against the waves in the open water.

"Jap air raid," Cluster shouted over his shoulder. "When we scramble fighters in a rush it means one of the Coastwatchers radioed in a warning."

"I thought you said the Japs hardly ever came over in daylight," Kaz said, wincing as the boat plowed through a swell that nearly knocked us off our feet.

"They must have known you were coming," Cluster said with a grin as he spun the wheel to starboard, putting distance between our boat and the others scattering into Ironbottom Sound. After that all eyes were on the sky, searching for enemy aircraft.

But our first sighting was a formation of four Wildcats. They climbed away from us, probably worried about itchy trigger fingers. It wouldn't have been the first time.

Then we saw what the Wildcats were after. A large formation, twin-engine bombers. Betties, they looked like, heading for Henderson Field. From above the Betties, Japanese fighter planes dove into the Wildcats, trying to intercept them before they had a chance to turn a Betty into a fireball. Cluster shouted an order to the engine room and the PT boat picked up speed, headed away from the dogfight and the oncoming bombers. The wind whipped against us, salt spray coating our faces. I glanced at Kaz, who had a landlubber's pale look to his face. Me, I'd grown up going out into Massachusetts Bay with my dad's fisherman buddies, so I enjoyed a ride across the wave tops. It was the men in aircraft trying to kill us I could do without.

I saw one plane go down in flames, but it was hard to tell what it was. The sky was a confusion of contrails, smoke, flame, and the distant chatter of machine guns. A few minutes later, Cluster eased up on the engines.

"What gives?" I asked.

"We're getting close to Tulagi," he said as an island came into view. "We don't run the engines at full bore for long. Wears them out. We've put enough water between us and the Jap planes. They're probably going to hit Guadalcanal in any case."

That was a reasonable guess, but in short order we were watching two fighters circle, dive, and climb in a fight for advantage. As they dueled for position, they drew closer to us and farther from the other aircraft to our rear.

"Looks like a Wildcat," I said. "What's the Jap fighter? A Zero?"

"Nah, we don't see many Zekes down this way," the gunner next to me said. "They're carrier-based. These are Jap Army planes from their bases on Bougainville, probably."

"It's a Tony," the other gunner yelled. "He's headed for us!"

The Wildcat dove to the deck, trailing smoke and heading for home. The Tony—I guessed fighters were boys and bombers girls—swung around to come at us from the port side. Kaz and I ducked behind the low bulwark behind the bridge and peeked out to watch the Tony's approach. Cluster zigged and zagged, making for Tulagi and the protection of the antiaircraft batteries there.

The Jap fighter was too fast for us. We were still a mile or so out when he opened up, his machine guns sending up spouts of water in our wake. Our machine guns and the twenty-millimeter cannon on the aft deck returned fire, sending the fighter into a climb to escape the tracers seeking him out. He made a giant arc across the sky and came at our starboard side. I saw a thin wisp of white smoke coming from his engine. Had we scored a hit?

Then the Tony did. Rounds chewed into the bow of the PT boat, narrowly missing the bridge. Our guns followed the fighter as he roared overhead, staying with him this time. The trailing smoke grew as black and orange flames spread across the fuselage. A cheer went up from the crew, just in time to see the pilot bail out. The plane went into a spin and crashed into the ocean as his parachute opened, stark white against the blue sky.

"Let's go get ourselves a prisoner, boys," Cluster announced as he steered the boat toward the downed flyer.

As we neared the pilot, I leaned over the bulwark and watched him release his parachute and fumble with his life jacket. A crewman with a gaff stood at the bow, ready to pull him in. Jap prisoners were rare; I'd read about their last-ditch banzai charges and how they'd commit suicide with grenades rather than be captured. But this guy waved his arms as if he couldn't wait to be hoisted aboard.

Cluster shouted an order to the engine room and the PT boat slowed as we came within reach. The sailor extended the gaff to the pilot who took hold of it, jerking on it suddenly and pulling the crewman into the water. He reached into his life jacket and came up with a pistol. He fired two shots at the bridge as he screamed, his face now contorted with hate and fury. Paddling with his free hand for a better angle, he squeezed off two more rounds, aiming at Cluster and his executive officer. He was so close, the machine gunners couldn't depress their guns to fire a burst at him. More shots rang out as the crew ducked for cover and the sailor in the drink swam for it.

Kaz and I drew our weapons. Kaz crouched behind the bulwark and fired over the top, hoping to distract him. Our first shots went wide, and I saw the pilot load a new clip into his automatic, all the while yelling what may have been curses at us or prayers to the emperor. I heard Cluster order the engine to be reversed as we popped up again and fired, only to duck as rounds whizzed by our heads.

"Stay down," a voice said from behind, followed by the welcome sound of a Thompson submachine gun wielded by a gunner's mate. He fired two quick bursts, hot ejected shell casings showering our shoulders. "Now you can get up, lieutenants. Welcome to the Solomons."

We stood. The top of the pilot's head was gone, the sea around him stained red.

"Nice shooting, Chappy," Cluster said, tossing a life ring overboard for the crewman still in the water.

"Everyone okay?" I asked.

"Yeah, he put some holes in my boat but no one got hit," Cluster said. "And for the record, that bulwark isn't metal, it's plywood. If he shot at you through that, you'd get wood shards as well as a bullet." Kaz rapped on the low wall and got the hollow sound of three-quarter-inch wood.

"Is there anywhere safe on this boat?" I asked.

"Hell no," Chappy, the gunner's mate, said. "We're a plywood boat sitting on three thousand gallons of high-octane aviation fuel. That's why we like to go real fast."

Recovering the gaff and the overboard sailor, Cluster had the pilot's body pulled in to search for documents. There were a couple of maps in his flight suit and a picture of a young girl in a kimono in his shirt pocket. Cluster kept the maps. The body was tossed overboard, the photo flipped into the sea as an afterthought. The engines roared into life as the PT boat made for Tulagi and a safe harbor. Kaz and I stood on the bridge, the cool breeze and calm coastal waters a relief after the blood and terror of crossing Ironbottom Sound.

"I should have seen that coming," Cluster said as the island loomed closer. "It's never over with the Japs. The warrior code of Bushido and all that. They consider surrender a dishonorable disgrace to the soldier and his family."

"It's hardly surrender when you're shot down during aerial combat," I said.

"Death in battle, especially if many enemies are killed in the process, is the most honorable fate for a Japanese soldier," Kaz said. "To that poor fellow, there was no difference between the machine guns in his fighter and the pistol in his hand. It is what he was taught."

"I have a hard time thinking of him as a poor fellow," Cluster said. "A classmate of mine, a marine officer, was on Guadalcanal in the early days. After a failed banzai charge at the Tenaru River, marines went out to help the Japanese wounded. The Japs set off grenades. Blew themselves and the marines who were helping them all to hell. That was the last time he let any of his men go to help Jap wounded."

"It's a different war out here," I said.

"The Germans can often be barbarians," Kaz said. "Very occasionally, honorable. You never can tell. At least out here you know what to expect. No quarter, no surrender."

"That's what our boys learned real quick," Cluster said. "If you give up to the Japs, they'll probably torture or kill you, so you might as well go on fighting. Shoulda seen it coming." He shook his head the way people do when they can't believe how gullible they've been. I shook my own head, trying to rid it of the vision of the pretty girl in a kimono.

Cluster skirted westward of Tulagi, coming into the harbor at the PT boat base at Sesapi. Across from the larger Florida Island, the Sesapi anchorage provided secluded and calm waters for the small craft and seaplanes tied up at the docks. Cluster eased his boat into his mooring and we clambered off, Kaz especially glad to be on dry land.

"The base commander radioed that he arranged a jeep for you," Cluster said. "You should report in. The driver will take you." A vehicle was parked along the wharf, a sailor waiting at the wheel.

"What about you?" I asked.

"We're based here, but I'm headed up to Rendova to check on one of my squadrons. Ask around if you need me, it's a small town." Cluster grinned as he stretched his arm out to encompass the shacks, Quonset huts, machine shops, and thatched-roof huts which lined the wharf. It had the air of a fishing village on hard times with a surplus of oil, men, and not much in the way of women, soap, or fresh laundry.

"Charming," Kaz said. "Are we to stay here in Sesapi?"

"No," Cluster said. "I hear Captain Ritchie set you up in the old assistant district commissioner's house at the east end of the island. That's near the hospital."

"Who's in the district commissioner's house?" I asked.

"Captain Ritchie, of course," Cluster said. "Good luck."

Without telling us if he meant with Ritchie, the investigation, or the Japanese, Cluster set about assessing the damage to his boat as his men secured the vessel. We walked up to the jeep and a smart-looking swabbie jumped out, snapping a salute. He was dressed in clean dungarees, blue shirt, gleaming white cap, and shined shoes. Amidst the greasy tumult of Sesapi harbor, he looked like he'd stepped out of a recruiting poster.

"Yeoman Howe, at your service," he said, taking our bags. "I'm to take you to Captain Ritchie and show you to your quarters, sir. And sir." The second sir was for Kaz. Seaman Howe was well trained.

"Take us to the base hospital first," I said.

"Sorry sir, Captain's orders. He wants to see you right away. And it's nearly time for supper. The captain gets upset if he's late for supper."

"Then by all means, let's not keep the good captain waiting."

"Excellent idea, sir." Well trained. I doubt Yeoman Howe ever ran into an officer with a bad idea.

We drove along a ridgeline, cresting it after about a mile. On our left, a jumble of huts and small buildings crowded the beach. "That's the Chinese village," Howe told us. "There's a lot of them on the island—merchants and that sort of thing. Tulagi's only about three miles long, so you get to know it pretty well."

As we descended along the rocky spine of the island, we were rewarded with a view across the sound with Guadalcanal in the distance. The sun was nearing the horizon, golden rays gleaming on the placid water. It was so peaceful you could easily forget about all the bones and steel lying on the seafloor.

"There's the captain's quarters," Howe said. "And yours next to it." A row of European-style houses lined the road, built high off the ground with large wraparound verandahs.

"Were these all for the British colonial administrators?" I asked.

"Not all, sir. The Lever Brothers managers lived there, too. You know, the soap company?"

"Soap? How'd they make soap out here?"

"Something to do with coconuts, sir, I really don't know. There's a group of Australian Coastwatchers staying in the Lever houses. Some sort of big confab going on."

"The Lever guys haven't come back?" I asked.

"No," Howe said. "They need a lot of native labor for whatever they do. The Japs control most of the Solomon Islands, and in the rest the coconut plantations haven't recovered from the fighting yet."

"There must be a demand for native labor," Kaz said.

"Yeah," Howe said. "One of the Coastwatchers told me the Japs use them as slave labor, so a lot of them hide in the jungle or make their way down here. They get paid and treated pretty fair, from what I can tell. It's gonna be hard to keep 'em down on the farm after a few US Navy paydays."

"You hear anything about the native who was killed recently?" I asked.

"Sure," Howe said. "But I'll let the captain tell you about that." He slowed for a switchback and downshifted as we made the hairpin turn. "Base headquarters is ahead at the east end of the island, right by the hospital. The land thins out here, and there's always a nice breeze off the water from one side or the other."

"Just the right place for headquarters," I said.

"I meant for the patients, sir. But the captain doesn't mind either."

"How about you?"

"I like what my commanding officer likes," Howe said. "Do they run things differently out in North Africa? Sir?"

"Please excuse Lieutenant Boyle," Kaz said, placing his hand on Howe's shoulder from the backseat. "He has the police detective's habit of asking questions even when there is no need."

"No problem, sir, glad to help." Without actually having helped, Howe parked the jeep near a Quonset hut and a couple of weathered clapboard buildings that once perhaps reminded a European of home, but were now ready to decay into the ground. They all had wide verandahs, which I figured was standard because of the heat. It had to be stifling indoors at midday, even with the breeze wafting in from twenty different directions.

Howe offered to wait and drive us to our quarters. I figured he was going to report our every move to Ritchie, so I told him to knock off for the day. On an island as small as Tulagi, we couldn't get lost for long. He looked dejected as we turned away and took the rickety steps up to the base commander's office. A sailor on duty showed us into Ritchie's office, where we found the captain reading from a file. There were two chairs in front of his desk, on which we were not invited to sit. As a matter of fact, Ritchie didn't react at all. He kept reading, turning each page over carefully as if his superior officer might give him points for neatness.

Howe had been right. The open windows on each wall let in a cool seaside breeze. The view wasn't bad either, with Guadalcanal in the distance and the lush green of Florida Island on either side. A ceiling fan revolved slowly overhead. A sheet of paper moved about a half inch as the air wafted in. Ritchie put it back, aligning it with the others. I caught a few upside-down words, *Boyle* and *Kazimierz* among them. *Uncooperative* was there, too. No US Navy letterhead either, only flimsy paper that looked like it came out of a teletype.

Salutes weren't done indoors except when reporting to a superior officer, and I wondered if Ritchie was waiting for his due. We weren't under his command, but perhaps he liked that sort of stuff.

I glanced at Kaz, who had his British service cap tucked under his arm. I stiffened my posture into a semblance of attention and he caught on quick, snapping his heels and doing one of those Brit palm-out salutes, his arm practically vibrating above his eyebrow. I did the best I could, but I didn't have the panache for it.

"Lieutenants Boyle and Kazimierz reporting, sir!" I intoned.

"Glad to see the army taught you basic military discipline," Captain Ritchie said. He had about ten years and twenty pounds on us. His wavy brown hair was in retreat and his voice was a combination of sarcasm and weariness with a thin layer of disdain as a chaser. I could see we were going to be great pals.

"Our orders, sir," I said, holding out the crumpled sheets I'd been carrying halfway around the world.

"I know all about your orders, Lieutenant Boyle," Ritchie said, looking me in the eye and ignoring the proffered papers. "I'm the one who contacted ONI and asked for an investigator to be sent in."

"Yes sir," I said.

"Are you clear on what you are here to do?" Ritchie asked. I had about half a dozen theories on the subject, but figured I'd better stick to the official version.

"Yes sir. To find out who killed Daniel Tamana and bring him to justice."

"The native, yes, of course," Ritchie said. "It is vital that we treat his killing seriously."

"But?" I said, urging him along in the hopes he'd offer us a seat.

"It must be done in a manner that reflects well upon the United States Navy," Ritchie said, his chin jutting out as if it were the bow of a battleship cutting through the water.

I thought about that. And about the teletype sheets, and how the Office of Naval Intelligence had its fingerprints all over this investigation.

"You worked in ONI, didn't you, Captain Ritchie?" I said.

"My previous assignment has nothing to do with this situation," he said, the disdain a little heavier in his tone.

"I don't believe that, sir," I said. Then I sat down. Kaz followed suit. The hell with this guy and his pompous airs. "I didn't understand how ONI got on top of this so fast. But once I saw you had a report with our names in it, I knew you had a connection."

"I didn't invite you to sit, Lieutenant," Captain Ritchie said as he closed the file in front of him, nervously patting it down as if it might spring open and scatter pages for all to see.

"And I don't think your commanding officer would take kindly to you doing political favors in a war zone, Captain. I bet you and Alan Kirk were at ONI at the same time, right?" Kirk was Joe Kennedy's naval attaché in London, who had gone on to head ONI. He didn't last long, and was heading up a bunch of destroyers in the Mediterranean last I heard.

"What of it?" Ritchie said, worry lines appearing in his forehead.

"Kirk is connected to Joe Kennedy Senior," I said. "You're connected to Kirk. Jack Kennedy gets himself involved in the murder of a local native, and the first thing you do? You don't investigate, you don't bring in the British or Australian police, instead you contact your buddies at ONI, who can get to Joe Senior. Then things begin to happen and favors accrue. I bet old Joe would pay a bundle to have his son's name cleared."

"I don't have the time or inclination to listen to your preposterous theories," Ritchie said, standing and sucking in his gut. That was our cue to leave. "Find out what happened to Tamana and try not to disgrace the uniform while you do it. Report to me if you find out anything useful." I felt his glare on my back as we left.

"That was interesting," Kaz said as we stood on the verandah, surveying the bustle of soldiers, sailors, and natives around the headquarters area. "When were you sure about Ritchie and ONI?"

"When he didn't throw me in the brig for sitting in his damn chair," I said, watching a crew of natives loading a truck from a supply tent. "And the few words I caught in that report didn't sound like a military memo. It was the lowdown on us. On me, probably direct from old Joe himself."

"Do you think Ritchie is really being paid off?" Kaz asked.

"Not with money or anything that can be traced," I said. "But I bet he'll get a promotion and a plum assignment next."

"Unless we do not proceed in a manner that reflects well on the United States Navy," Kaz said, in a rough attempt at imitating Ritchie's growl.

"I'm tempted to disgrace the navy just to see him transferred to Greenland," I said. "Come on, let's find Jack and see what the hell he has to say about all this."

We maneuvered the jeep through the heavy traffic around headquarters and the nearby docks. Seaplanes floated near their moorings offshore and a steady stream of small craft motored men and materials back and forth. Tulagi had become a backwater island when the fighting moved on up the Slot, but it was still a busy backwater.

The hospital was a long whitewashed cement block building with a red cross against a white background prominently painted on the roof. It sat high on a slope facing the sound, with breezes off the water drifting through the wide-open windows. I asked a clerk at a desk in the main corridor which room Jack Kennedy was in.

"He's up the hill, Lieutenant," the clerk said. "Go out the back door, third hut on the right."

"In a hut?" I asked, expecting to find Jack bandaged and bruised, stretched out on white sheets.

"Yeah, the VIP lounge we call it," he said. "It's for officers with minor wounds. Not much different from in here except we don't have to check on them that often."

"No nurses here?" I asked, noticing the all-male character of the staff walking the hallways.

"Not of the female persuasion, not yet anyway," he said. "Captain Ritchie says it ain't good for morale to have a few women around with so many guys who ain't seen a dame in months."

"The captain must not be the most popular officer around," I said.

"Let's say if he were laid up here, he wouldn't have many visitors,"

the clerk said. "Not like Lieutenant Kennedy. He's got people coming
to see him around the clock. Nice guy."

"Yeah, he's swell." We stepped out the back, taking a well-trodden
path to a shaded palm grove with island huts arranged on either side.
They were built up on stilts, the walls made of woven palm fronds.
The roofs were thatched and makeshift windows were propped up to
let the air circulate. We went into the third hut, where four hospital
beds were arranged around a central table. A card game was in progress.
Bridge, by the look of things. No one was in bed nursing their wounds.
VIP lounge, indeed.

"Hey guys," I said, waving my hand in greeting. By the bottles on
the table and the wrinkled clothing, it didn't seem any of them were
sticklers for rank. "I'm looking for Jack Kennedy. Is he around here
somewhere?"

"Crash? He's on a date," one of the players said as he tossed back
a shot of bourbon.

"A date?" I said. "The kind with a woman?"

"I guess you don't know our Jack," another guy said.

"Oh, I know him all right," I said. Then I began to laugh. The table
joined in, probably to be polite, because I couldn't stop. I come halfway
around the world to save Kennedy from a murder charge, and on this
small island with no women, he's out on a date.

Jack, you sonuvabitch.

CHAPTER NINE

"NEM BLONG MI Jacob Vouza," a booming voice said in my dreams. "Hu nao nem blong yu?"

I opened one eye, struggling to remember where I was. Tulagi. The assistant district administrator's house. Asleep, under mosquito netting.

"Wanem nao yu duim?"

All I could make out was a hazy silhouette in the door, sunlight filtering into the room at his back. I scrambled out from under the netting in my skivvies, still half asleep, to find an imposing figure standing square in the doorway, his arms crossed, shooting a glare at Kao, the houseboy who came with the joint. Kao was a skinny little kid. Our visitor looked like he could snap him in two.

"Your name is Jacob Vouza?" Kaz asked, sitting up on the edge of his bed. I could see he was working out what the native was saying.

"Ya, Sergeant Jacob Vouza. Blong Solomon Islands Protectorate Armed Constabulary. Twenty-five year. Retired. Now marine." He pronounced the English words precisely, with some island dialect mixed in.

"Blong," Kaz said, standing to face Vouza. "Belong? The name which belongs to you?"

"Ya," Vouza said, speaking slowly as if to a pair of slow children, pointing to each of us with an exaggerated gesture. "Nem blong yu?"

"Nem blong mi Kaz. Nem blong him Billy," Kaz said, keeping

things simple. I pulled on my trousers and watched as Vouza and Kaz exchanged a few more words. Kaz was the one with the language skills, so I left the lingo to him as I took in the man before us.

He was dressed in a *lap-lap*, which looked like a sarong to me, but Kao had corrected me on that point last night. Vouza was tall, broad, bare-chested, and wearing a web belt with a mean-looking machete and a .45 automatic slung off it. His hair was thick and frizzy, his skin a dark, rich brown. He had a broad, flat nose and sharp eyes which kept a watch on Kaz and me as I cinched my own web belt and pistol.

The scars were something to behold. His chest, throat, and ribs were decorated with thick, knotted scar tissue. Not the puckered scar of a gunshot wound, or the scattered rips and tears from shrapnel. Knife or bayonet, I guessed. Kao squatted on the floor, gazing at Vouza with awe. Maybe fear.

"Sergeant Vouza is a retired constable," Kaz said, turning to me. "From the neighboring island of Malaita. He says he works with the marines and the Coastwatchers organization."

"You got all that from what he said?" I asked.

"He's speaking Pijin, an island dialect. It is very closely related to English," Kaz said.

Vouza threw a glance at Kao and said, "Kopi." Whatever that meant, Kao ran out of the room, nodding his head and smiling.

"You mean pidgin?" I asked.

"Not exactly," Kaz said. "Solomon Island Pijin is related to other Pacific dialects. Pidgin is a less precise term. Pijin is a trade language, originating with the first whalers who visited these islands in the last century. It allowed the natives and the seamen to speak a common language. A quite interesting evolution, actually."

"I'm sure," I said, cutting Kaz off before he composed a monograph on the subject. "But why is he here?"

"I gather he wants to know why *we* are here," Kaz said.

"Does he know Daniel Tamana?" I asked, looking to Vouza for a reaction. His eyes widened for a split second at the mention of the victim's name.

"Mi wantok blong Daniel," Vouza said. "Angkol."

"Angkol?" Kaz repeated. "Uncle? You are Daniel's uncle?" Vouza nodded solemnly.

"Wanem nao yu duim?" It was the same thing he said when he first came into the room. I was beginning to get the hang of this. Most of the words were English, pronounced with a unique accent, and perhaps a slight speech impediment.

"What are we doing?" I guessed.

"Now," Kaz added. "What are we going to do now?"

Vouza nodded, folding his arms across his massive chest and waiting.

"We are here to find out who killed Daniel, and why," I said. Another nod. Then I smelled coffee brewing, and I learned another Pijin word. Kopi. I needed some.

We sat on the verandah, the three of us sipping steaming kopi while Kao worked his magic with powdered eggs and Spam. Vouza was silent, content with the view and his sugared brew.

"Do you think he plans to stick with us?" I asked Kaz.

"I sense he may be impatient, and with good reason," Kaz said. "If Captain Ritchie has done nothing so far, the trail has certainly gone cold."

"We need to talk to Jack and check out the scene of the crime," I said. "Then find out who may have had a beef with Daniel. The sergeant should be able to help with that, at least among the natives."

"Yes, and the Coastwatchers as well," Kaz said. "We need to find someone among the navy personnel who isn't worried about offending Captain Ritchie. We should talk to Commander Cluster before he leaves."

"Yeah, he doesn't seem the type to worry about a pencil pusher like Ritchie," I said.

"Have you spoken with Captain Ritchie?" Kaz asked Vouza, who had made a sour look at the mention of the name.

"Nomata yu talem hem, baebae hem i no lisen. Hem i nating savvy," Vouza said as Kao came out with the breakfast plates.

"No matter what you tell him," Kaz said slowly, replaying the Pijin words in his mind, "he will not listen. But I do not understand 'nating savvy.'"

"He understands nothing," Vouza said, in British-accented English, tucking into his Spam, which disappeared as quickly as his Pijin. I heard Kao chuckling as he brought out more coffee.

"I DID NOT know your purpose," Vouza said as we drove to the hospital. He was going to a nearby villa where his Coastwatcher boss was headquartered. "I wanted to hear you speak when you thought I would not understand." He spoke slowly, his voice not quite right, the words slurred and thick. I wondered if the scar on his neck had anything to do with that.

"You speak English very well," I said.

"They taught me well at the Evangelical Mission on Guadalcanal," he said. "But Pijin comes easier. You learn kwiktaem, Kaz." I guess I'd be the slow-time one.

"You're worried we're here to cover things up?" I said.

"No mi wari," Vouza said. "Hem kill Daniel wari." That was easy enough to figure out.

"Do you know Lieutenant Jack Kennedy?" I asked, wondering if Vouza had him on his list of suspects.

"Sure. Hem loosim boat. Two fella dead. Hem wari all day. Hem hate Japan man. Kennedy barava." Brave. It wasn't the first word that sprang to mind about Jack, but it had been a while.

"Did he know Daniel?" I asked.

"Ya. Daniel friend with Biuku and Eroni. They brought message to navy to send boat. Save sailors. They all visit Kennedy. Next day, Daniel dead. You think Kennedy kill Daniel?"

"I don't know," I said.

"I think no," Vouza said. "Hem good man. Also weak from loosim PT boat, no helti. Daniel strong. Hem faetem Kennedy easy."

"That fits what we know about his condition after the rescue. We need to talk to Jack," I said. "You know his father is a very important man?"

"I do not know his father. Big man?"

"Yes," I said, figuring Vouza deserved the truth. "Very big in America. He had us sent here. But he doesn't own us."

Vouza looked at me from the passenger seat, then turned his gaze to Kaz. He pursed his lips, nodding to himself.

"No wari," Vouza said. "You tell me Kennedy no kill Daniel, I believe you. You tell me Kennedy kill Daniel, then I kill Kennedy. Kwiktaem."

There wasn't much to say after that.

CHAPTER TEN

I SAW JACK before he spotted me. He had always been skinny, but I wasn't prepared for how frail and bone-thin he looked. But the smile was there, the same one I remembered. The kind of grin that took you in and swallowed you whole. There was no denying a smiling Jack.

"Billy Boyle!" Jack exclaimed from his hospital bed, where he'd been reclining while a striking brown-haired female nurse changed bandages on his feet. He swung his legs off the bed, trailing a swath of gauze and nearly knocking the girl off her chair. "Sorry I can't get up; we're in the middle of something. How are you, Billy?"

His Cambridge accent was as strong as ever. They tell me folks from Southie have a bit of an accent, but we all sound normal to my ears. Jack's accent was pure Harvard, with that British upper-class drawl and those leisurely *rrr*'s. I took his proffered hand and shook. His skin was deeply tanned, but that was the only part of him that looked healthy. Or helti, as Jacob said. He had dark bags under his eyes and a weariness that his jovial greeting couldn't hide.

"I'm good, Jack," I said. "How are you?"

"Fine," he said. "Deanna is taking great care of me. Deanna Pendleton, this is an old pal of mine from Boston, Billy Boyle. A swell guy." Jack looked up at me while Deanna smiled politely and maneuvered his legs back onto the bed. She smeared ointment on the bottom of his feet. They'd been badly cut up from what I could see. Healing, but it didn't look like Jack would be running the hundred-yard dash anytime soon. I looked away, feeling Jack's gaze grow steely. He didn't like his weaknesses on display.

"Jack, this is Kaz."

"Lieutenant Piotr Kazimierz," Kaz said. "A pleasure to meet you, Lieutenant. I met your brother several years ago in England, at a house party given by Lady Astor." Kaz carefully left out the recent meeting in Morocco.

"My condolences, Lieutenant," Jack said. "Sounds dreary. Joe can be a bore at times. Always so serious."

"I assure you, Lady Astor was so offensive I took little note of anyone else."

"Very diplomatic," he said. "At least regarding my family. Are you with the Polish Government in Exile?"

"Detached," Kaz said, avoiding the fact that he now worked for General Eisenhower.

"Kaz is a baron," I said, steering the conversation in a direction a Boston Brahmin might appreciate, even an upstart Irish Brahmin.

"What clan?" Jack asked. It was the first time I ever heard anyone ask that question. Everyone else was surprised that Poles had barons.

"The Augustus clan," Kaz answered, pride evident in his voice. "But please call me Kaz. Most Americans do."

"Then so shall I," Jack said. "I had no idea there were Polish forces in the South Pacific. Are you two stationed around here?" He sounded genuinely clueless about why we were here. But the Kennedys didn't get on top by telegraphing their moves, so I thought I'd play along and see what was what.

"For the time being," I said, which was true enough. "We met Sergeant Vouza this morning, and he came along." Vouza stepped closer, his hand raised in greeting.

"Hao Nao, Jacob!" Jack said.

"Mi olraet nomoa!" Vouza said. "Jack savvy gud Pijin. Hao Nao, Deanna." He grinned and gave Deanna a salute, which she returned with a gracious nod, her hands busy wrapping a roll of gauze around Jack's foot.

"Jacob taught me some," Jack explained as Deanna tied off the bandage, ignoring her and whatever pain she inflicted on his foot. "It's not hard to pick up if you pay attention."

"I go now," Vouza announced. "Captain Sexton and other Coast-watchers wait for me. Jack, soon we kill many Jap fella. All inna ground. Lukim iu!" With a wave of a hand, he was gone.

"He's an excellent fellow," Jack said. "The Coastwatchers organiza-tion is having a major confab in a villa down the road. Jacob is a big wheel with them." I wondered if he'd be as admiring if he knew Vouza was ready to use that machete on him if necessary.

"Lukim iu?" Kaz asked.

"Goodbye," Jack explained. "See you, to be precise."

He winced as he moved to a chair and motioned for Kaz to join him. He walked gingerly on the heels of his feet, which obviously were not fully healed. He shifted a few times in his seat, getting his back as straight as he could. His back was always giving him fits, and being run over by a Jap destroyer couldn't have helped much.

After a deep breath, Jack began asking Kaz questions about Poland and the Polish Government in Exile. What was their position regarding the Soviets? Post-war borders and the British government? It was like watching a sponge absorb water. Jack had a way of taking all the intelligence you had to offer and giving little in return except his undivided attention. It was charming and callous at the same time.

"So, Miss Pendleton, I didn't think there were any Australian nurses on staff here," I said, making conversation while Kaz and Jack talked about the consequences of the Treaty of Brest-Litovsk.

"There aren't, and I'm from New Zealand," she said, her accent soft and melodic. She wore army coveralls which were way too large for her. The belt was cinched twice around her tiny waist. "Call me Deanna, please. I am a nurse, but I was with the Methodist mission on Vella Lavella. We stayed behind after the other civilians were evacuated, hoping the Japanese would respect a religious community providing medical care for the Melanesians."

"I'm guessing they didn't," I said.

"No," Deanna said, shaking her head as she absently twisted the white bandages around her hand. "We heard rumors of Catholic nuns on Bougainville being bayoneted. As word of Japanese atrocities against the natives filtered out, I decided to get out. A Coastwatcher on Segi sent a canoe, and I ended up working as his radio operator until they brought me here."

"That's the short version, Billy," Jack said. "Deanna helped rescue two B-17 crews and came back here with fourteen Jap prisoners." He turned back to Kaz and talked of Stalin's plans for Poland without missing a beat.

"That's impressive," I said, meaning it.

"It isn't," she said. "I wasn't alone, and the Japanese were fairly meek. They have no concept of surrender, so when they are taken prisoner—which isn't often—they have no behavior to fall back upon. They feel cut off from Japan and believe they can never go home, having shamed themselves. Pathetic wretches, really."

"Why did you stay on with the Coastwatchers? Couldn't they have gotten you out?"

"My sister was a nurse with the army. Stationed at Singapore," she said, her voice low and halting. "They brought the nurses out on the last ship before the garrison surrendered, but it was torpedoed off Sumatra. They all made it ashore in a lifeboat, where unfortunately the Japanese were waiting. They shot the wounded men and then forced all twenty nurses to walk into the water."

"Back into the ocean?"

"Yes. Then they machine-gunned them. One of the women was only grazed by a bullet and simply floated until the Japanese left the beach. Natives gave her shelter and she worked her way to Australia. That's when I found out my kid sister was dead."

"You wanted to avenge your sister," I said.

"I never thought of it that way," she said. "I simply didn't want anyone else to suffer like that because they'd been captured. And I wanted those prisoners we had to know what their people did."

"You told them?"

"Yes, one of the officers spoke English. He told the others and they wept. What a strange people they are. Chopping off heads, shooting and bayoneting women, and then squatting in their loincloths and crying a river of tears for my dead sister."

"Perhaps they were ashamed," I said.

"I think they were, Lieutenant," Deanna said. "But that may have had more to do with the carbine I had pointed at them. Not only did they fail to die for their emperor, they were prisoners of a mere woman." She laughed, softly, to show it was a bit of a joke. But the laughter ended on a sharp note, and I knew there was a measure of vengeance in it.

"Enough of me, Billy," she said, brushing the dark hair away from her face. "What brings you to Tulagi?"

"Looking up an old friend," I said. "We heard about Jack's boat and decided to see how he was doing. We missed him last night."

"We were at a party. Hugh Sexton is in charge of the Coastwatchers in the Solomons. He's got a bunch of his chaps in for a confab and we got together for drinks. They don't see each other too often, so it was an occasion for celebration."

"What was it like being a Coastwatcher? Lonely?"

"Hardly," Deanna laughed. "You're much too busy to get lonely. Lugging a heavy radio set, working with the natives, always looking for a better observation post, and evading Japanese patrols tends to focus your attention."

"Are the natives on our side?"

"Oh yes," Deanna said. "Even the ones who didn't appreciate the British administration long for those days. The Japanese abuse them terribly. The Japanese might have done better if they'd befriended them, but word spread quickly about their brutalities."

"The Japs did us a favor," Jack said, his interrogation of Kaz complete. "Otherwise the natives might not have been so helpful." Cynical, but true.

"I'll let you fellows get on with your visit," Deanna said, gathering up her medical supplies. "Jack, I'll be back after lunch and we'll take a walk, alright?"

Jack nodded as Deanna gave him an affectionate peck on the cheek and patted his shoulder on her way out. Even in army coveralls, she cut a great figure, which Jack viewed with proprietary interest.

"Are you up to walking, Jack?" I said, bringing us back to the present.

"Yeah, I get around okay," he said. "I have deck shoes I wear loose, and a pal of mine gave me this cane." He hoisted a long wooden cane with a heavy knobbed head and intricate carvings. "He said he got it from a native chief, but who knows? Sometimes friends keep the truth to themselves."

Silence filled the hut as the three of us stared at each other.

"Are we friends, Jack?" I tried for an offhanded tone, but the bitterness hung in the air.

"I think we're about to find out," Jack said. "Now that we're alone, why don't you come clean and tell me why General Eisenhower's personal cop comes all the way from North Africa to this dump. Are you going to arrest me for the murder of Daniel Tamana?"

"We don't know who killed him, Jack," Kaz said. "We only know that you found the body. But his death is why we are here. Or specifically, why Billy is here."

"Let me guess," he said. "Father pulled some strings." He shook his head as if in disbelief that his father's control extended so far.

"Not only did he pull them," I said, "he thinks I'm still attached at the other end. As far as I can figure, if I come up with any evidence of your involvement, he'll claim I'm biased against you." Which had a ring of truth to it.

"You won't," Jack said. "I didn't kill Daniel. I wish I knew who did."

"That would save us all a lot of trouble," I said. "Has anyone asked you any questions?"

"Not really," Jack said. "Captain Ritchie came around and said he'd have it investigated. Some of Sexton's Coastwatchers were district commissioners before the war. They would have been the local authority, but it's the US Navy in charge around here now."

"Meaning Ritchie," I said. I outlined the captain's connection to ONI and Ambassador Kennedy.

"Ritchie's an idiot," Jack said. "Headquarters down here is FUBAR."

"Fucked Up Beyond All Recognition," I explained to Kaz, not certain if he'd picked up that bit of Yank slang.

"Do you have any ideas who went after Daniel? Did he have enemies?"

"I didn't know him well enough to say. I'd met him only the day before, when he came to visit with his native pals, Biuku and Eroni. They were the natives who found us on that island. Daniel was a Coastwatcher. Seemed like a smart kid. Spoke English like he went to Oxford with Kaz. I went over to Sexton's that same day, and Daniel was there for a while, but left soon after I arrived."

"Deanna and Jacob both mentioned a big Coastwatchers meeting," I said.

"Yeah," Jack said, leaning back in his chair, the trace of a wince crossing his face. "We've moved up the island chain recently. We took Rendova, which freed up a number of Coastwatcher teams. Sexton brought in some of the others for resupply and to make plans for the next offensive. There's about a dozen of them, which is probably the largest gathering of the war so far."

"Is Deanna going out again?" I asked.

"No," Jack said. "Sexton wouldn't go for it. She did her part, but she's a civilian. All the Coastwatchers, even the ones who were plantation owners before the war, have been made officers in the British Navy. It's supposed to give them protection under the Geneva Convention, but the Japs don't care. If a Coastwatcher is caught, it's the bayonet for him. Or her. And the closest villagers are killed as well, since the Japs figure they helped them."

"Did any of them hold a grudge against Daniel? Maybe he slipped up and got some villagers killed?"

"Not that I've heard," Jack said. "He comes from Malaita Island. Not too many connections to the tribes in this area. You're thinking a blood feud?"

"Too soon to tell," I said. "Can you show us where you found the body?"

"Sure. I'll take you there. Toss me those shoes, Kaz." We waited while Jack pulled on the white canvas deck shoes over his gauze-encased feet, the laces tied loosely. I grabbed his cane and handed it to him. It was a handsome dark wood, with artistic carvings at the top.

"What do the carvings mean?" I asked as he limped out of the hut, leading us downhill toward the water.

"Nothing," he said. "You'll find all sorts of stuff for sale down by the harbor. Grass skirts, canes, and all sorts of carvings. But it's meaningless. Literally."

"What do you mean?" Kaz asked, offering a hand to steady Jack as he took uneven steps on the path. Jack shook it off, an irritated look on his face. A Kennedy didn't need help. His gait improved as we walked. Maybe he was shaking off the stiffness, or maybe ignoring the pain. Hard to tell with that guy.

"GIs and sailors saw grass skirts in Hawaii when they shipped in," he said. "So they expected to see them everywhere. When they came through these islands, they wanted souvenirs like they found in Hawaii. The natives were too polite to tell them they never heard of a skirt made out of grass. But they were smart enough to see an opportunity. These canes are another good example. Every sailor around here will tell you they got theirs from a village chief. There aren't that many villages in the Solomons."

"The islanders must enjoy the newfound wealth," Kaz said.

"Yes," Jack answered, leading us through the bushes on a narrow track. "But remember, the white settlers and plantation people here call themselves islanders. The Melanesians are natives. The English and Australians are touchy about the distinction. Besides, the islanders don't like all the money the natives are making, whether from souvenirs or working for the navy. They say it'll be hard to get them back to work on the coconut plantations after the war. Here we are." We stepped out onto a small stretch of beach, soft sand about twenty feet wide. Crescent-shaped, the beach fronted a small lagoon. Waves lapped against coral-encrusted rocks. Peaceful and quiet. The perfect secluded spot for a bit of mayhem.

"He was over there," Jack said. "Close to where the trail empties out onto the beach."

"Show me exactly," I said. "Where was his head?"

"He was on his stomach," Jack said. He drew an outline in the sand with his cane. Legs pointing toward the water. "His head was bloody, but it was dried. I don't know about these things, but it seemed he'd been dead a while."

"What time did you find him?" Kaz asked.

"A little after seven o'clock," Jack said. "I'd taken a walk to get some strength back in my legs."

"With those cuts?" I said. "They must have been pretty bad last week. They're still healing."

"A few scratches from the coral," he said with a shrug. "No big deal."

"Still, it must have been hard," I said. "You did okay today, but you weren't exactly limber."

"You're right. It wasn't as easy last week," Jack said bitterly. He wouldn't have liked being incapacitated then, much less admitting to it now.

"But you had your cane, right? Or did your friend just give it to you?"

"No. He brought it over the first day I was here," Jack said. "What's your point?"

"I don't know," I said, studying the cane as Kennedy put weight on it. "I guess I wonder why you chose this spot."

"I like the view," Jack said impatiently. "Listen, Billy, anyone could have followed Daniel down here and surprised him."

"Sure," I said, taking the cane from his hand. "But how many of them came prepared with a blunt object?" I slammed the round end of the cane into the palm of my hand.

It packed a wallop.

CHAPTER ELEVEN

JACK GRABBED THE cane out of my hand, told me to go to hell, and stalked off, waving the cane like a saber at a clump of tall grass, beheading it neatly. I'd half expected him to swing at me, but he was too smart to incriminate himself, so the vegetation suffered in my place.

"Interesting fellow, your friend Jack," Kaz said as we watched him disappear into the bushes.

"I never claimed he was my pal," I said, walking along the water's edge, trying to imagine what had brought Daniel Tamana to this spot. I walked to where Jack had drawn the outline of Daniel's feet. "It would help to know which side of his head he was hit on."

"Why?" Kaz asked.

"It might tell us if he was trying to get away, or was taken by surprise," I said. "He was close to the path, and it seems like he was facing away from the water. Had he started to leave? Run? Or did someone take him by surprise?"

"I see," Kaz said. "If he were hit from behind, he wasn't taken by surprise since his assailant would have been in the open, close to the water."

"Yeah," I said, kneeling and studying the surface of the beach as if it might yield a clue after all this time. "Not that it matters much; it won't tell us if he knew his killer. Too bad there wasn't a real police report or a morgue with the body on ice."

"We're a long way from anything so organized," Kaz said. "I wonder what did happen to the body."

"Let's ask Jacob Vouza," I said. He'd told us he was headed to Hugh Sexton's place, where the Coastwatchers had gathered. I figured it wouldn't be hard to find.

"Good idea," Kaz said. "While we walk, you can tell me about your history with Jack Kennedy. What happened back in Boston?"

"What did you think of Jack's reaction to seeing me this morning?" I asked as we took the trail to the main road by the hospital.

"Pleased to see you, I'd say. Fairly normal for running into an old friend. Or acquaintance," Kaz said.

"Right. It was like nothing had happened, nothing of importance," I said, feeling the anger rise in my throat. "Except that the last time I had anything to do with him, he nearly cost me my job."

"Why?" Kaz asked.

"Because it was convenient for him, and I was handy," I said. "Which is all that matters to Jack. But that's enough ancient history for today." Being with Jack reminded me of what a chump I'd been, how I'd assumed a friendship that was never real, never on an equal footing. We got into the jeep and drove in silence down the winding narrow lane, following the directions we'd been given to Sexton's place. Palm trees arched overhead, shielding us from the midday sun. It was already hot, and our khaki shirts were damp with sweat. North Africa had been hot, but this was a different kind of heat: thick, humid, cloying. And this was Tulagi, the paradise of the Solomon Islands.

I wanted to find Daniel Tamana's killer and get the hell out of here, away from the sweltering heat and Jack Kennedy. We drove away from the hospital, navigating around a couple of trucks from a signals company stringing communications wire through the palm trees. Tulagi probably never had a single telephone before the war. Now it had all the trappings of civilization: bombs, Spam, and telephone calls.

"There," Kaz said as we approached a large house with a wide verandah where Jacob Vouza stood talking with a man wearing an Australian slouch hat. The building sat on a cleared hillside alongside a smaller house on the right. Across the road on the water side, a weather-beaten dock jutted out into the clear water, where an even more weathered boat bobbed gently on the waves. It had one blackened funnel, a broken window in the pilot house, and peeling white paint down to the waterline. Two dugout canoes were beached nearby.

I pulled the jeep off the road and we walked up the steps—coconut logs set in the hill—to the house.

"Hao Nao, Jacob!" Kaz said. Jacob smiled and waved us onto the verandah.

"This is Captain Sexton," Jacob said, introducing us to the wiry, tall fellow at his elbow.

"Pleased to meet you," Sexton said, shaking hands. His blond hair was bleached nearly white by the sun, or perhaps worry. Coastwatching was not for the faint of heart. His face was deeply tanned and crow's feet radiated from the corners of his eyes. "You've come to find out who killed Daniel, I hear." Sexton spoke with an upper-class English accent and wore an easy grin. The dark bags under his eyes hinted at something far deeper.

"We'll do our best," I said.

"Daniel deserves no less," he said. "If there's anything I can do to help, let me know."

"We'd like to hear more about Daniel," Kaz said. "From both of you. What he was like, his work, his friends."

"Let's go inside," Sexton said. "I'll show you."

The main room held a large table strewn with maps and charts. Sexton cleared off the top layer, revealing a dog-eared map with Guadalcanal at one end and Bougainville at the other.

"This is my area of operations," Sexton began. "As you can see, Guadalcanal and Malaita anchor the Solomons to the southeast. The island chain runs to the northwest, where Bougainville, the largest landmass, ends it. Beyond is New Georgia and New Ireland, both firmly in Jap hands."

"This is the Slot," Jacob said, tapping his finger on the channel between the central Solomon Islands. "Jap ships come at night, planes by day."

"It's our job to maintain posts on the Japanese-held islands and radio in reports of ships and aircraft," Sexton said. "When the battle for Guadalcanal was being fought, it was about the only advantage we had."

"Shoot down many fella Japan Kawanishi," Jacob said.

"Do they still come down this far?" I asked.

"Not usually," Sexton said. "But as you saw, we'll get the occasional raid. The whole show has moved up the Slot. We've recently taken Rendova, so the action is around New Georgia now." He tapped his finger on a clump of islands at the center of the Solomons. "That's why we're here. Reorganizing and moving new teams up. We still have observation posts on nearly every island, but the main focus is the advance up the Slot."

"Where was Daniel stationed?" Kaz asked.

"Choiseul. Big island," Jacob said.

"Mount Vasau," Sexton said. "Excellent observation point. Unfortunately an obvious one, so Daniel and Dickie Miller were constantly on the run."

"Miller?" I asked.

"He worked for Burns Philp before the war," Sexton said. "One of their plantation managers. He escaped Bougainville and joined our group when the Japs invaded."

"He knew Daniel well?" Kaz said.

"They in bush together one year," Jacob said. "But he gone Austrelia. Got pekpek blut bad."

"Pekpek?" Kaz asked.

"Dysentery," Sexton explained. "We evacuated them both when we heard how sick Dickie was. It's fairly common, but Dickie was very ill, nearly died. We sent in a fresh team when we got the two of them out."

"How did Daniel come to join the Coastwatchers?" I asked.

"He work on plantesen on Pavau," Jacob said, tracing a line on the map to an island north of Choiseul. "Japan man come, Pavau man kill one fella Japan. Japan kill many fella Pavau. Daniel escape, takim boat to Choiseul. He help nuns escape too, bringim to Tulagi."

"That's when he volunteered," Sexton said. "He spoke English very well and was adept with the radio. He was very good."

"Did he and Dickie Miller get along?" I asked.

"Like barata," Jacob said. "Faetem lot, but strong together."

"Like brothers," I said.

"Yes," Sexton added. "When two people spend that much time together in the bush, there's bound to be arguments. But Daniel didn't leave Dickie's side until he got on a transport at Henderson Field."

"When was that exactly?" I asked.

"The day before he was killed," Sexton said. "He came over here, but didn't stay long. He said he had to see a relative from Malaita. He was due a few days' rest, so that wasn't a problem."

"Do either of you have any idea why he would have gone down to that beach?" Kaz asked.

"No," Jacob said. "I come over later in the day, weitim here. No Daniel."

"We were surprised," Sexton said. "We'd told Daniel that Jacob would be here to meet him. They hadn't seen each other in two years."

"Did anyone see him after he returned from his visit?" I asked. The two men shook their heads.

"The only man to see Daniel after that was Jack Kennedy," Sexton said. "Not counting the fellow who killed him, of course." At the mention of Jack's name, Jacob's eyes narrowed as he looked away, gazing out over the water.

"Where is everyone, anyway?" I asked. "I thought you were having a pow-wow."

"Each team is being briefed on the new teleradio sets over at the naval base, courtesy of your signals section," Sexton said. "They'll be back this evening. Every Coastwatcher has to be thoroughly versed in radio repair and maintenance. It is a matter of life or death."

"Is that the new radio?" Kaz asked. A large transmitter and receiver were set up on a table.

"Yes, the Teleradio 3BZ," Sexton said. "Has a range of four hundred miles."

"Plenty heavy," Jacob said. "Fourteen fella to carry."

"Fourteen?" I said. "Why so many?"

"You've got the transmitter and receiver," Sexton said. "Plus the microphone, headset, and spare parts. Then a gasoline generator to run the thing, not to mention the fuel itself. Batteries for when the fuel runs out. Fourteen fella, just like Jacob said."

"It must be very difficult," Kaz said with typical English understatement. "Is four hundred miles a sufficient range?"

"No, especially if we sight aircraft coming in from Rabaul. So we relay messages from one post to another, until they're received by the signals unit on Guadalcanal. That's why it's vital we have teams on every island, and that the teleradios remain operational. It's not easy when the men are constantly on the move and staying off the trails to avoid Japanese patrols," Sexton said. "And of course, the best observation point is always on the highest ground."

"I had no idea," I said.

"Good," Sexton said. "We can't brag about our work. The less the Japanese know about us, the better."

"They always lukluk," Jacob said. "Come to every island. Ask where radio? Kill the people if they no tell."

"Do they tell?" Kaz asked.

Jacob shrugged.

"Only once in a great while," Sexton said. "It's usually someone from another island who has no ties to the local families. The Japs might have had better luck when they first came if they didn't destroy gardens and shoot people indiscriminately. Now they're thoroughly hated. If they send a small patrol to an island, they're often never heard from again."

"Daniel was from Malaita," I said. "But he'd been on Pavau and then Choiseul. Could he have gotten involved in a dispute with the local natives?"

"Who then followed him to Tulagi?" Sexton said. "Not likely. If there was a dispute on Choiseul, it would have been settled there."

"Sorry," I said. "I'm trying to get a sense of where to begin. We usually get a chance to study the crime scene and view the body. We don't even know where Daniel was struck."

"On head. You want lukim?" Jacob said.

"I thought the body would have been buried by now," I said. "Especially in this climate."

"Yes," Jacob said. "Body buried. But you can lukim Daniel's head. I take you."

"Take us to Daniel's head?" Kaz said.

"Yes," Jacob said, as if explaining the obvious to a slow learner. "Head about ready now."

CHAPTER TWELVE

"I DO NOT like boats in general," Kaz said, "and I do not like this boat in particular." He used Jack's cane as we boarded, the small craft rolling gently as waves slapped the hull. I didn't mind boats in general, but I did wonder about this one.

We'd gone back to the hospital and commandeered the cane from a none-too-happy Kennedy while Sexton organized a crew for us. Once I told Jack it could eliminate him as a suspect, he calmed down a bit. Eliminating the cane as the murder weapon was closer to the truth, but I saw no reason to go into detail with him. Or to explain that Jacob was apparently taking us to Daniel's head, *sans* body, on Malaita. That was the kind of thing Jack might see as a marvelous adventure and insist on coming along for the ride, the fact that he was a suspect notwithstanding.

"Don't worry, Piotr," Deanna said, patting his arm. "It's only sixteen miles."

"Round-trip?" Kaz said hopefully. Deanna laughed at what she thought was a joke. She'd returned to Sexton's place as we were leaving, and asked to come along to provide what medical care she could to the natives. She'd arrived on board with a knapsack and musette bag full of medical supplies, a machete, and an M1 carbine.

"It's been a while since they've seen a lik-lik doctor on Malaita," she said. "That means little bit, by the way. It's what they call nurses and the medical orderlies the government used to send out. Little bit doctor, that's me."

"Lik-lik GI," I said. "Where'd you get the carbine?"

"A gift from a marine lieutenant," Deanna said with a smile. "You haven't heard the story?"

"No," Kaz said. "Do tell and take my mind off this impending journey."

"When Hugh first had me brought out from Vella Lavella, someone started a rumor that Amelia Earhart had been found. When we docked at Tulagi, there were about a hundred cheering men there to meet us. I had to disappoint them all. But one lieutenant was very gallant and gave me the carbine in case I ever found myself back on a Japanese-held island."

"Jack and that marine probably weren't too disappointed," I said.

"A damsel in distress in the Solomon Islands will have no shortage of admirers," Kaz said, as suavely as he could manage while holding on to the cane and the quarterdeck for dear life. "Even if she is not Amelia Earhart."

"That's sweet, Piotr," Deanna cooed. "Ah, here's Jacob with our brave crew."

"Silas Porter's the name," the first man to board said in a thick Australian accent. "Glad ta meet'cha." He wore a slouch hat and wrinkled khakis of undetermined nationality. He was tall, six feet at least, wiry with a fringe of long brown hair showing from under his headgear. Heavy boots, a big knife, a holstered revolver, and a Lee-Enfield rifle slung over a shoulder completed the picture. "We made it back from the briefing first, so Hugh told us to take you out. Nice day for a cruise, ain't it?"

Next on board was a native, wearing a calico *lap-lap* with a web belt, bare-chested but otherwise similarly armed.

"Nem blong mi Billy," I said slowly, showing off my linguistic skills before Kaz could beat me to the punch. I spoke slowly, so the native would be sure to understand.

"Pleased to meet you, Billy. I'm John Kari," he said, speaking English that would pass muster in Parliament. I pretended not to hear Deanna giggle as Kaz introduced himself. In plain English, of course.

"John Kari speak English pretty damn good, eh?" Jacob Vouza said, grinning as he came aboard, well-armed himself. This got another round of laughter.

"Now don't you two worry about the looks of this ship," Porter said as Kari went below to start the engine. "It's a bonzer vessel, and that's the dinkum oil."

"Silas not speak English so good, eh?" Vouza said, laughing and slapping the Aussie on the back as they crowded into the small bridge. Engine noises rumbled up from below deck as Kari popped up from the engine room hatch.

"It's a fine ship, and that's the straight truth," Kari translated. "Silas lays on the Australian pretty thick when he first meets an American. All in good fun. He's really a bastard." He disappeared with a smirk on his face as Deanna cast off the lines and we headed out.

"Does anyone here speak plain old American English?" I asked.

"Sorry, mate, we're having a bit of fun with ya," Silas said as he leaned back. "We call a good friend a bastard. Meaning he's a good egg."

"But not the Englishmen," Jacob said as the boat picked up speed.

"No, never," Silas grinned. "Then he's a Pommie bastard, and that's a real bastard!" They both laughed, and I wondered at the wisdom of an ocean-going voyage with these madmen.

We left Tulagi and circled around Florida Island, getting our first view of Malaita in the distance. Smoke belched from the stack as the engine chugged and wheezed, but the boat moved at a decent clip. Bonzer enough for this short crossing.

"I understand Jacob is taking you to see Daniel," Deanna said, the wind nearly whipping her words away.

"Perhaps not all of him," I said. "Do you know what he's talking about? Are there headhunters on Malaita?"

"No," Deanna said. "They're in New Guinea. It's better that you see for yourself. Keep in mind this has much religious significance for Jacob and his people. While many Malaitians have taken to Christianity, they still revere their ancestors. And Daniel is with the ancestors now."

"Well, I've been to a few Irish wakes, so I'm familiar with strange burial customs. Tell me, are you expecting trouble over there? You're all loaded for bear."

"Bear?" Kari said, poking his head above deck.

"Ready for anything," Kaz explained. I was glad we had some jargon of our own to throw back at him.

"Ah, yes," Kari said. "You must always be ready in the Solomons. Even though there has not been much fighting on Malatia, the Japanese have landed there a number of times. They had an observation post at the north end of the island, working much as we do to warn of attacks."

"What happened to it?" Kaz asked.

"Marines raided it," Kari said. "There were about thirty Japs. Most were killed or captured. A few escaped into the bush but the Malaita-men caught up with them." He drew a finger across his throat.

"They still land troops and patrol the island looking for Coast-watchers and radioing back intelligence," Deanna said. "But they don't stay long. They get no help from the natives and soon they're out of food and ready to leave Malaita behind."

"Do we know if there are any Japs there now?" I asked.

"You never know, mate," Porter said from the bridge. "Always assume the enemy is right around the bend."

The wind and waves picked up, and Kaz went below to the small cabin to be miserable. I stayed topside, staring at the horizon the way my dad had taught me, to minimize the pitching sensation. Soon we drew close to Malaita, the shore now visible and the water calmer. I clambered up to the bridge to get a better view.

"Is that where we're headed?" I asked, as a cluster of huts at the water's edge came into view.

"Wouldn't go in there," Porter said. "That's Laulasi. Back when you Yanks landed at Guadalcanal, seven of your planes bombed Laulasi, thinking it was the Jap observation post up at Afufu. Killed twenty-eight people, mostly kids. So we don't go to Laulasi much, and never with a Yank in tow."

I watched the village as we motored by, wondering what it must have been like for people who lived such a primitive life to watch bombs dropped on their children. Not that dropping bombs was all that civilized to begin with.

Fifteen minutes later, Porter eased the boat toward a small bay, steering between coral reefs and letting the waves usher the boat into calm waters. Ahead, a river emptied into the bay, and Porter guided the craft to the cover of sheltering palms.

"That's that," he said. "Japs shouldn't spot us from the air, at least."

We debarked, Kaz wasting no time getting onto dry land. Vouza led the way into the bush, with Porter at the rear. We stayed on a trail along the riverbank for about a half mile, then went into the bush. The hot air was thick with humidity and the sunlight faded as we pressed on under the dense canopy and through the thick undergrowth. All around us vines wound around tree trunks and hung from branches, snaking up from black muck like parasites, choking the trees. There was nothing of the pleasant sea breeze that wafted over Tulagi here. The cloying odor of rotting leaves and wood rising from the mud assaulted our nostrils, and I was already soaked in sweat.

"Welcome to Malaita," Vouza said, glancing back at us. He was barefoot, wearing only a *lap-lap*, and he looked totally at ease.

"Can you tell us where we are going, Jacob?" Kaz said, leaning on the cane as I gasped for breath.

"Kwaiafa," Vouza said. "Up the mountain."

"There isn't a road?" I asked.

"Yes, there is road," Vouza said. "But long way around. We take shortcut. You need rest?"

"I don't," Deanna said, taking a swig from her canteen.

"Not me," I chimed in, wishing Deanna had wanted to take ten. We soldiered on.

"Where are you stationed?" I asked John Kari as we crossed a small river at the base of a thirty-foot waterfall. We stopped to scoop up the clear water and rinse our faces. The open air was refreshing after the jungle gloom, and even Jacob paused to stare off into the clouds. Or maybe he was on watch for Jap aircraft.

"San Jorge Island," Kari said. "Off the coast of Santa Isabel, next island up the chain. Perfect for coastwatching; a nice mountain peak with a view of the Slot and plenty of bush to hide in."

"Friendly natives," Porter chimed in. "To us at least. Not like Malaita, not one bit."

"Because of the bombing, you mean?" Kaz asked, soaking his cap in the cool water.

"No," Vouza said, his eyes still on the sky. "Some Malaitamen still cannibal. High up on mountain." With that, he climbed the riverbank and vanished into the lush green.

"Isn't that where we're going?" I asked as the group hurried to follow him. No one answered, and I ran to catch up.

"The villages along the coast have all become Christian," Deanna explained as we came out of the thick jungle and assembled on a narrow footpath. "But the farther up the mountain, the more they cling to the old ways. Ancestor worship and occasional cannibalism, from what I understand."

"It's not occasional if you're the one in the pot," I said.

Vouza signaled for us to wait, and went ahead to scout.

"They'll probably only roast your liver," Kari said. "So don't worry about being boiled alive."

"Very funny," I said.

"No, it's true," Kari said. "The liver, I mean. Malaita cannibalism is ceremonial, to show disdain for a defeated enemy. The point is not the actual eating of flesh, but taking an extreme form of vengeance. At least that's what I have read on the subject."

"Let us hope we can continue to rely on secondary sources," Kaz said.

Vouza reappeared and motioned for us to get a move on. I thought I caught a glance of movement in the thick greenery, but then it was gone. I picked up my pace, forgetting about the rivers of sweat running down my back.

Fifteen minutes later, we came to a small gorge with a sluggish stream at the bottom. Three logs had been felled to form a crude bridge. On the other side, a half dozen or so native buildings stood in a half circle facing the stream. They were on stilts and thatched with palm fronds. Women and children gathered to watch our arrival.

Vouza led the way across the bridge. As I glanced back to make sure we were all there, six native men quietly stepped out of the bush. Not a single leaf or branch moved as they took to the trail and followed across the bridge, rifles slung on their shoulders.

The villagers gathered around Vouza and the six men flanked us, holding their rifles at the ready. Four British Lee-Enfields and two Japanese Arisaka models.

"What's going on, Jacob?" I said, not certain if this was our escort or our guards.

"Japs," he said evenly. "But far away. No wari."

Deanna was the center of attention, the children swarming her and chattering in Pijin. Kari and Porter stayed with her as she set up shop on the porch of the largest house, where the armed men stood watch.

An older woman approached Vouza with leaves and flowers held in a thick, large leaf, rolled and tied tight. The fragrance rose up from her hands as Vouza took the greenery and spoke to her. It gave off a sweet, pleasant odor, like walking through a garden in bloom. They spoke in low voices while the woman patted Vouza's hand, tears in her eyes. She walked away, ignoring us.

"Daniel's mada," he said, then held the bouquet to his nose and inhaled. "She wrap puchupuchu in taro leaf. Now, I take you to Daniel." It wasn't far, a few hundred yards from the village, but there was no trail or sign that others had come this way.

The smell hit us before we saw it.

Flies swarmed and buzzed as we approached a cairn of rocks. I swatted at the darting insects as I tried to make out what was protruding from the rock pile, breathing in quick, shallow gasps.

It was a head. Daniel's head.

His eyes and lips were gone, all the soft flesh eaten or rotted away in the fetid jungle heat. The outline of his skull was clearly visible, hidden only by patches of dried skin. Kaz and I had seen death before, but this was something new. The autopsies I'd attended in Boston were nothing compared to what came next.

Vouza grabbed the head and twisted. A cracking sound marked the severing of the neck from the spinal column. Kaz turned away. I wanted to, but the scene was so unreal I couldn't take my eyes off it.

"This is ravuravauni," Vouza said, standing over the cairn which presumably enclosed Daniel's body. He waved his package of leaves at the flies zooming around the head.

"The grave?" I asked.

"No, no grave. Only hed is important. Only hed matters," he said, tapping his own skull. He unrolled the leaves and flowers and began to stuff them into the mouth, eye sockets, and nasal passages. "Good puchupuchu," he added, rubbing the remaining leaves into his hands. "Now Daniel ready."

"For what?" Kaz asked, steadying himself on Jack's cane as he stepped closer.

"Clean," Vouza said. "We go down to the beach. Then you lukim Daniel's hed. He sit in the sun for few days, then go rest with ancestors." He carefully wrapped the head in the giant taro leaves and tied it off with vine. Holding it under one arm, he took his rifle in the other and started off. We trotted along after him, glad the puchupuchu had done its job.

"There," Vouza said as we neared the village. Farther up the hill were a group of small wooden structures. They were steep-roofed and decorated with necklaces and other garlands. Inside, protected from the elements, were stacks of skulls. "Ancestors."

"Fascinating," Kaz said as we hurried to keep pace with Vouza. "This reminds me of Hallstatt, an Alpine village in Austria."

"Austria is probably the last place this island reminds me of," I said.

"They share a similarity," Kaz said. "Lack of proper ground for burials. Hallstatt is perched between a steep mountain and a deep lake. People can be buried in the church graveyard for only a year. Then they are disinterred and their bones deposited in the church crypt. The skulls are prominently displayed. I happened upon a disinterment procession when I was touring the country. Quite festive, actually."

"You're right," I said. "We haven't seen much cleared land. Those giant roots and vines would make hard going for a gravedigger."

"Yes," Kaz said, warming to his theory. "And the climate is perfect for rapid decomposition. The combination of salt water and sand makes for a viable cleaning agent. We should be able to make out Daniel's wound quite clearly."

The path to the beach took us down the other side of the mountain, to the eastern shore of the narrow island. Waves broke over a coral reef, sending sprays of saltwater into the air. Before us stood open ocean, the great South Pacific. The view was marred by nothing more than a few white, fluffy clouds and the horizon looked a million miles away. The wind off the water was refreshingly cool after the trek from the village, and Kaz and I plunked ourselves down as Vouza unwrapped the head of Daniel Tamana.

The odor of death wafted up on the breeze as he peeled away the taro leaves. He wordlessly removed the puchupuchu and carried the head into the water, giving it a thorough soaking. Then he rubbed the fine white sand all over it, seemingly oblivious to the decayed skin and flesh sloughing off. More water, more sand, more rubbing, followed by careful, delicate scraping with his knife. I wondered what had happened to the brain matter, but we remained silent, aware that this was a funeral ritual as sacred as any church service.

"Daniel is ready," Vouza said, setting the skull on a taro leaf and placing it before us. The surface of the bone was clean, the smell of decay nearly gone. Vouza turned and walked into the water, bathing himself, rubbing gobs of wet sand over his hands.

"Here," Kaz said in a whisper that seemed appropriate to the moment. He placed a finger in a depression on the rear of Daniel's skull, behind the ear. "His parietal bone was evidently struck."

I took Jack's cane and held the round knob at the top against the indentation. It was a perfect fit. A killing blow.

"Cane blong Jack?" Vouza said, standing over us with his rifle in hand.

"Cane blong Jack," Kaz said. "But it might not be the cane that killed Daniel, or someone other than Jack could have used it. It might have been given to Jack to frame him for the murder."

"Maybe," Vouza said. "Maybe not." He lifted Daniel's skull from the ground and placed it in the cleft of a rock overlooking the beach. "Morning sun work on Daniel. Three, four days, he be ready to join ancestors. Nice and clean, white like teeth. Come, we leave him alone now."

WHAT TOOK A half hour going down took three times as long going up. Finally we came to the village, where Jacob Vouza received another warm welcome. He seemed much loved by his people, or perhaps it was because of the ceremony he'd conducted. Or both. Deanna was finishing up with her last patient, a child with a laceration on his leg. Deanna sprinkled sulfa powder on the wound, singing to the child as she wrapped a bandage around the thin limb.

Porter and one of the natives were engaged in a rapid-fire Pijin conversation. He was pretty good at it. The native indicated the general direction of our boat, and I was able to make out "Japan fella" but nothing else.

"A Jap pilot was shot down over the Slot," Porter told us. "He parachuted and landed close to shore near our boat."

"What about the Jap patrol?" Vouza asked.

"They've been spotted on the coast road from Malu'u," Porter answered. "They must have seen it, too."

"Good," Vouza said. "We get pilot and kill many fella Jap, too."

"We should get a move on," Porter said. "It'll be dark in a few hours."

Vouza nodded, accepting a drink of water from a gourd given him by the old woman we'd seen earlier. Four of the native men trotted off across the bridge and melted into the bush.

"Are you sure we can handle that?" I asked. "We're not exactly a combat patrol."

"Most assuredly," Kari said with a grin, the excitement causing his voice to rise. "There is a ten-thousand-dollar bounty for every live pilot we bring in."

"Even split three ways, it's damn good money," Porter said. "Sorry, mate, only goes for Coastwatchers."

"Don't let me stand in the way of cash money," I said, with more bravado than conviction.

Vouza said his goodbyes to the villagers and made for the bridge. We followed to the cries and laughter of children saying goodbye to Deanna, trailing us as we crossed the ravine.

"You're popular everywhere you go," I said.

"Who doesn't like Amelia Earhart?" she answered.

Our exchange drew a muted hush from Vouza. Deanna unslung her carbine, and suddenly the jungle seemed even more threatening than ever.

We stayed on the path this time, wending our way down switchbacks until mountain steepness gave way to rolling hills. I saw one of the natives come out from the bush ahead and talk with Vouza before vanishing again. We had an escort. Which meant there was something close we needed protection from.

I unsnapped my holster.

Twenty minutes later we came to the river, probably the same one we'd crossed farther upstream when we went cross-country. Vouza motioned for us to wait, and we moved into the underbrush along the riverbank. I drew my automatic, feeling the sweat in the palm of my hands. I looked at Vouza, who put a finger to his lips. He didn't need to tell me twice.

I caught a glimpse of movement across the river. I raised my pistol. Vouza shook his head no, lowering the barrel with his hand. I finally made out the figure more clearly. One of the men from the village, followed by the three others. The villager silently pointed downstream, to where a series of large, flat stones made for an easy crossing. Vouza nodded, and led us to the spot. But we didn't cross.

The natives moved along the riverbank, jumping from stone to stone, not making a sound. Before coming opposite to our position, they climbed the riverbank in swift, fluid movements, their brown skin streaked with shadows as they filtered into the dark green jungle, gone before I could blink the sweat from my eyes. Then I understood.

The Japanese were coming. And we were going to ambush them as they crossed.

The only sounds came from the flowing water and the thumping of my heart. I tried to catch Vouza's eye to get some sense of what was going on. How many Japs were there? Did he know? Did he care? He stayed focused on the riverbank, which at this point was the smart move, so I did the same after checking to be sure Kaz was in a good position. He and Deanna were behind a moss-encrusted rock. Kari was closer to the water, prone behind a fallen log. I couldn't spot Porter.

We waited.

Then I heard sounds. The kind of sounds infantrymen make even when they work at being quiet. The subtle creak of leather, the slap of a canteen on a hip, the wood-on-metal clatter of slung rifles. Faint, but unmistakable.

A minute later a figure emerged from the bush, near the stepping stones. His uniform was a pale khaki brown, his shirt as sweat-stained as ours. He wore a cloth cap with a neck flap, and clutched an Arisaka bolt-action rifle that was almost as tall as he was. Stepping cautiously into the river, he looked upstream and down, crouching as if ready to run at the first sign of trouble.

Vouza held steady, and without a word spoken, we all knew he was calling the shots. No one was going to fire until he did. He let the lone soldier cross, coming within five yards of us. As soon as he gained the bank, he stood on the bare earth and scanned the thick underbrush, nervously poking at the greenery with his bayonet. When he was satisfied, he turned and waved to the rest of the patrol. Three other Japs came down the bank, followed by an officer wearing a sword, and then about ten soldiers clustered around the pilot, wearing a white silk scarf, khaki flight suit, and leather boots. His shoulder was bloody and he cradled the injured arm with his good one. The scout climbed the bank, turned and sat on a rock to watch the others cross, unaware of the hidden threat on both sides of the water.

A flash of shadow and spray of blood. John Kari with his hand on the Jap's jaw and a knife drawn across his neck. Then the scout was gone, no sounds other than the faint rustle of Kari dragging him into the bush and a gush of blood on leaves as the soldier's heart beat its last.

One of the Japs in the river looked up and called out. He spoke to the others and they laughed. Probably a joke about the scout taking time for a piss. A few more steps and the first of them were almost on top of us, the rest strung out, jumping from rock to rock.

Vouza fired.

We opened up on the soldiers to our front. Three, then four dropped quickly, the others shooting wildly, not certain where we were. The rapid semiautomatic fire from Deanna's carbine behind me and the louder, slower Lee-Enfield single shots rang in my ear. I steadied my automatic with both hands and aimed two shots at the closest Jap and saw him crumple, blood staining the smooth rock beneath him.

More shots came in our direction as the remaining soldiers spotted us and fired, but they were in a panic, their shots high, zipping through the foliage like angry bees. The noise was deafening as everyone seemed to fire at the same moment. Porter came charging out of the undergrowth, firing and leaping behind a boulder, giving him a better angle on the enemy rear.

An explosion behind me left my ears ringing as I fell forward, tensing against the expected flow of blood or feel of red-hot grenade shrapnel. I was unhurt, as was Deanna, who winked as she raised her carbine.

Vouza dropped a soldier at the edge of the group protecting the pilot. Then the officer pointed with his sword to the opposite bank, obviously telling his men to retreat. Kari got another one and that hurried them on.

Right into the trap.

The natives opened fire from the bank and more Japs went down, the rest huddled in confusion, firing at the new threat and looking to their officer for orders. A bullet took him in the throat and he fell, his hand clutching his neck as spurts of blood escaped through his fingers. His other hand clutched the sword, now swung in our direction. He tried to get up but fell as his men got the message and charged our position. There were five of them left, plus the pilot, who staggered after them. He must have felt invincible with all the lead leaving him unscathed. Or did he know his bounty price?

Vouza stepped forward, firing at the men on either side of the pilot. I followed, but Kaz was even faster, jumping into the water and firing his Webley revolver, taking out the Jap right in front of the pilot. The last two men charged with their bayonets, their faces a snarl of anger, fear, and resignation. Shots from the far side of the river sent them sprawling, the water washing their blood from the rocks.

The pilot stood alone and forlorn, bodies all around. He gaped as Kaz and Porter checked him for weapons.

"Good shooting for such a little guy," Porter said, slapping Kaz on the back. "Didn't even nick this fella once!" He turned the pilot roughly and pushed him back across the river with his rifle barrel.

Vouza went to the officer, who was still holding his throat, blood bubbling out across his hands. He picked up the sword from the side of the dying man and leaned on it as he studied him.

"You seeim these scars?" Vouza said, touching each of the knotted scars on his chest and throat. "Japan man give me these. But I no dae. You dae." With that, he swung the sword, separating the body from the head, severed hand still grasping the wound as the head rolled into the water to be taken away by the current.

CHAPTER THIRTEEN

FORTUNATELY THE JAPANESE patrol hadn't discovered our boat. We boarded with our reluctant passenger, who was at turns surly and morose. Getting shot down, wounded, then rescued is one thing. But to watch your rescuers massacred before your eyes must have been a real shocker. Then to see the motley force responsible, well, that would be enough to drive any sane man over the edge. We tied him up and thankfully left Malaita, heading into the setting sun.

"You all did well," Vouza said. "No one even scratched and a pilot to bring back." He sat on a crate and lifted his face to the cooling sea breeze.

"What happened?" I asked Vouza as we lounged on the deck. "The scars, I mean."

"Last year, on Guadalcanal," he said. "Mi lukim Jap positions. I go as native wanting work. They grab me and search me. I had hidden a small American flag marines gave me, folded in lap-lap. They found it and beat me. Tied me to tree, ask where marines are. I tell them nothing. They hit me with rifle butts, and still I say nothing. The officer tells his men to use bayonet, not to waste bullets."

"You received those wounds all at once?" Kaz asked.

"Yes," Vouza said, caressing each of the rough scars. "Here, here, and here. Jap officer stab my throat with his sword, cut off part of my tongue. Thought he killed me."

"How did you get away?" I asked.

"They leave me for dead. I see many Japs headed for the marines. Two, three hundred. A big attack. So I chew through the ropes to get loose and crawl back to marines. I tell them attack coming. They had time to get ready. Kill many Japs."

"That's the Battle of the Tenaru he's talking about," Kari said. "The big attack on Henderson Field. Almost the whole Jap force was wiped out, seven hundred at least."

"All because Jap officer didn't want to waste one bullet on me," Vouza said, and gave out a throaty laugh that got us all going. Except for the pilot, who hung his head and studied the deck.

WE DOCKED AT Tulagi and turned the Japanese pilot over to navy intelligence. As soon as news of our encounter got around, Hugh Sexton organized a party to celebrate. There was beer and booze, mangoes, sweet potatoes, rice, and fish cooked on an outdoor grill. And more booze. I decided Coastwatchers survived months in the jungle by thoroughly pickling themselves.

Deanna had freshened up and looked like she'd been at a hair salon all day instead of providing medical aid and covering fire. A couple of striking Chinese women made up the rest of the female contingent. Clad in bright silk, they added color and cheer to the khaki and brown assembly. Kaz and I cleaned up as best we could, threw on clean shirts, and went out looking forward to the evening and the company.

Until Jack showed up. I should have known his radar for the fair sex would have picked up on a party with three beautiful women, especially on the male-dominated island of Tulagi.

"Well, do you have my cane?" Jack asked, his nonchalance masking any real worries he may have had about our investigation.

"We do," I answered. "But we need to hang on to it a while longer. It fits the hole in Daniel Tamana's skull far too well."

"Really?" Jack said. "You found his body?"

"On Malaita," Kaz said. "They have the most interesting burial customs there. Let me tell you." Kaz steered Jack into a corner of Sexton's spacious verandah. I watched as they talked, the genuine interest evident in Jack's posture and gestures. He was an expert at soaking up information in which he was interested, and at discounting anything he didn't want to think about. Or need to think about. He had the rich kid's belief that any problem life threw at him could be fixed.

Not that I still hold a grudge after all these years. Six and a half, to be precise.

"Billy, come meet Fred Archer," Deanna said, sliding her hand through my arm.

"Don't you want to spend time with Jack?" I said. They hadn't spoken but a few words since he arrived.

"He gave me the cold shoulder. He was polite enough, but a girl can tell. He's zeroed in on one of those Chinese women."

"Jack can be moody," I said. But I knew what the deal was. Jack was all about the pursuit, and my guess was that he had already landed in the sack with Deanna and was now bored with her company. But that wasn't anything I'd say to a nice kid like her.

She introduced me to Fred Archer, a tall, rangy planter who was in from his Coastwatching station on Ranongga. His accent was English, but he had the same weathered look as his fellow islanders.

"I came out with a small group of sailors from the *Helena*," he said. "One of your light cruisers that went down in Kula Gulf. Most of the men were picked up by destroyers, but these eleven made it to Ranongga on a life raft."

"Nice piece of work, that," Porter said, joining us with a large whiskey in one hand and a cigar in the other. "Henry Josselyn on Vella Lavella had a hundred and sixty blokes wash up on his beach. That was a handful, to be sure."

"Were they all rescued?" I asked.

"My lot was," Archer said. "The natives hid them from the Japs and we organized a PBY to come get them as soon as the weather permitted. We—my partner, Gordon Brockman, and I—hitched a ride with them for this radio course. The plane took us to Rendova and then we came by boat to Tulagi. Josselyn had a damn hard time of it. One hundred and sixty sailors, many of them wounded, weren't easy to care for. He and the Reverend Silvester hid them for more than a week, until destroyer transports could take them off the beach. Ah, here's Gordie now." Archer waved his pal over, and made introductions. Gordie was short and stocky, going bald, and halfway in the bag.

"Archer filling you with tales of our island exploits?" Gordie said, his Aussie-accented words slurring. "Don't believe half of it, at least not the half that involves me!" He thought that was hilarious and laughed as much as everyone else put together.

"I was telling them about the sailors from the *Helena*, Gordie," Archer said, an indulgent smile on his lips.

"Oh yes, a close-run thing," Gordie said. "We're lucky our small island didn't get as many as Josselyn did. Wouldn't have known where to put 'em."

"Who is the reverend you mentioned?" I asked.

"Reverend Silvester is the Methodist minister I worked with. He stayed behind to tend to his flock. And his radio," Deanna said.

"He's a Coastwatcher?" I asked.

"Not officially," she said. "But he already had a radio to keep in touch with the outside world, so it was the natural thing to do."

"Seems to me the natural thing to do would be to get out," I said. "Hiding alone in the jungle for months, on the run from the Japanese—now that sounds unnatural."

"That's us," Archer said. "Crackers, as the Australians say."

"I'll drink to that," Porter said. "Tell me, Archer, who are the Chinese ladies? I haven't seen them around before."

"Sisters to one of the Chinese merchants that came out with the *Helena* crew," Archer answered.

"What were Chinese doing there?" I asked.

"Hiding from the Japs," Archer said. "Most of the small merchants in these islands are Chinese. Since Japan is at war with China, they generally don't fare well under occupation. When the Japs landed in force on Vella Lavella, a small group of Chinese headed into the interior. They were fairly safe, but when the *Helena* crew had to be evacuated, it made sense to bring them along."

"Since they couldn't thank Henry Josselyn in person, the sisters came tonight to give their thanks to Hugh for helping to rescue their brother," Deanna said.

"Sam Chang," Archer explained. "Fairly well known in the local waters. You must have run into him, Silas. Pavau isn't that far from Vella Lavella."

"Yeah, I heard of Chang. We tried to do business with him, but we were too far off his route. Decent fellow, had a good reputation from what I knew," Porter said.

"He visited the mission often," Deanna said. "Had a thriving business before the war, buying and selling, importing Western food, that sort of thing. There's a call for the comforts of home among the islanders. Marmalade and gin are favorites."

"Why isn't Chang here himself?" Porter asked, looking around.

"I heard he fell and reinjured his leg," Archer said. "He broke it on Vella Lavella when he was in the mountains. He's in the hospital here on Tulagi. His sisters live in the local Chinatown. They own their own stores and have done very well for themselves. Important in the community, from what I hear."

"War is usually good for business, until it's on your doorstep," I said.

"Damn right, Boyle," Gordie put in. "When the Japs poured into the Solomons, it ruined a lot of us. Archer here had a thriving plantation on Bougainville, and I was set up on New Georgia, both of us doing well selling copra to Lever Brothers."

"Copra?" I asked.

"The dried meat of the coconut," Archer explained. "They have to be opened, shelled, and dried, usually in kilns. Hot work, I'll tell you."

"And it'll be hotter work paying off debts to Sam Chang, eh?" Gordie said, a bitter laugh punctuating his statement. "First the Japs take our plantations, run off the workers or enslave them, then old Sam takes to the hills, account ledgers and all. He says we still owe him, the bugger!"

"Are we talking serious money?" I asked.

"Well, before the war, when business was booming, no," Archer said. "Everyone close to Vella Lavella did business with Sam. Even when the Japs attacked back in December '41, we still had our plantations to run. We were stockpiling copra and waiting for the regular Lever transports to make the island runs. But by April '42, the Japs were on our doorstep."

"Still had workers to pay and expenses, you know," Gordie said. "A lot of us owed Sam a fair bit when the Rising Sun was hoisted over the Solomons. We lost everything, and to be fair, so did Sam. The Japs seized his goods and would have finished him off if he hadn't taken to the bush. Can't blame the fellow. He's alive and he wants his money. Wish I had it to give."

"What was your business, before the war, Lieutenant Boyle?" Archer asked, draining his whiskey and looking like he wanted to put an end to talk of debt and loss.

"I was a cop," I said. "Detective in Boston."

"Billy's here to look into Daniel Tamana's death," Porter said. "Haven't you heard?"

"Right, right," Archer said. "How is that going? Daniel was a good man. I wouldn't mind getting hold of the bastard who did him in."

"We're still gathering information," I said, giving the standard police response. "Do you know of anyone who had a problem with Daniel?"

"No, I don't think so," Archer said, rubbing his chin. "But I always wonder about chaps like him. And John Kari. Well-educated natives—between two worlds, aren't they?"

"What would that have to do with murder?" I asked.

"I don't know," Archer said. "But there's bound to be problems somewhere along the line. Daniel was a Melanesian who spoke the King's English, like Kari does. Smart, too. Easy enough to run into a white man who doesn't appreciate a Fuzz Wuzzy who speaks better than he does, if you know what I mean."

"Or a native who doesn't like one of their own acting like a white man," Porter said. "I've seen that often enough. So I know what you mean about him being between two worlds."

"It is true enough," John Kari said, joining the conversation.

"No offense meant, John. I was simply making a point," Archer said.

"I quite understand," Kari said, with exaggerated politeness. "And it is a valid one. The only question is, does it apply to Daniel's death?"

"Well, there aren't any members of Daniel's tribe here on Tulagi," Deanna said. "None I know of, except for Jacob."

"True," Kari agreed. "But remember what expert paddlers we have in the Solomons. Biuku and Eroni took their canoe thirty-five miles through Japanese waters to deliver Kennedy's message to Rendova. A journey from Malaita is much less than that."

"Who are Biuku and Eroni?" I asked, recalling that Jack had mentioned their names but not much else.

"They're scouts for Reg Evans on Kolombangara Island," Archer explained. "Excellent chaps."

"So it wouldn't be out of the question for someone from Malaita to take their dugout canoe to Tulagi," I said.

"Not at all," Kari said. "Hardly any open sea to worry about, for a Melanesian, anyway."

"But we don't know of any Melanesian who had it in for Daniel," I said, steering the conversation back from possible to probable.

"No," Porter said. "And believe me, if Jacob Vouza knew one of his people killed Daniel, he'd have taken care of it himself. Kwiktaem." There were nods and general murmurs of agreement.

"So it must have been a white man," I said. "Or at least someone not from Daniel's clan on Malaita."

"Thanks for not leaving me out," Kari said, and everyone laughed. But I had deliberately amended my statement to include him, or any other potential Melanesian suspect.

"I don't know anyone who had a fight or a problem with Daniel," Deanna said.

"It could have been something he saw or heard," I said. I didn't reveal that the wound on Daniel's skull suggested he knew his attacker, at least well enough to turn his back on him. "He might not even have comprehended the reason."

"That makes it tough to figure who did it, right?" Porter said.

"Yep, it does. We need to talk to Dickie Miller, Daniel's Coast-watcher partner," I said. "They were together constantly; maybe he could shed some light on this."

"You'll have to go to Brisbane. They took him there to the Royal Navy base hospital," Deanna said.

"Uh-oh, here comes trouble," Archer said. I followed his eyes to a group of American naval officers. They were tanned and dressed in wrinkled, bleached-out khakis. They had the look of privileged pirates. PT boat skippers, most of them Ivy League, I'd bet.

"What trouble?" I asked.

"Lieutenant Phil Cotter and his pals," Deanna said. "Jack's not happy with Cotter. His boat was on patrol in Blackett Strait with Jack when PT-109 was rammed."

"Word is," Porter said, leaning in to whisper, "Cotter reported back that he'd searched the area after seeing Jack's boat run down by the destroyer. But he didn't, at least not so any of the 109's crew saw him."

"Now that's a motive for murder," I said. I watched as Kaz made his way over to us. Jack was deep in conversation with one of the Chinese ladies, and hadn't yet noticed Cotter. I edged closer, interested in how Jack would react when he did.

"Phil Cotter," Jack said, finally catching a glimpse of Cotter at the drinks table. "I'm surprised you found the place."

The room went silent. Apparently everyone knew about Cotter's claim to have searched for survivors. There was a sudden ripple of nervous laughter at Jack's barb, then the room filled with silence again. Cotter faced Jack, a drink in his hand.

"Don't be an ass, Jack," Cotter said.

"I mean, after all," Jack said, ignoring the comment, "you searched for PT-109 and couldn't find it, even with flames shooting a hundred feet in the air. So how'd you make it here in the pitch black?"

"Go to hell," Cotter said, turning his back on Jack.

"Ah, there's the side of you I know better," Jack said with a grin. With that, he extended his arm to the woman he'd been talking to, and they left the room, heads touching, lost in a whispered intimacy.

Cotter's face was red, but he kept mum. A good idea with Jack, who excelled at sarcasm and managed it in a way that left you defense-less and usually looking the fool.

Deanna rolled her eyes as Jack walked past her without a word. Good for her. She'd gotten his number quickly enough. Our little group broke up as people wandered off for fresh drinks or food.

"Interesting," Kaz said, watching the couple depart. "It seems your friend Jack harbors a grudge."

"He's not my friend," I said. "I'm not sure he knows the meaning of the word. I'm bushed, Kaz, how about you?"

"I think I will stay and talk with Jai-li a while longer," Kaz said, looking faintly embarrassed. "Since Rui left with Jack, she is unac-companied. I will offer to drive her home, if you can find your own way back to the house?"

"First-name basis, huh? You've been busy."

"She is quite fascinating. You never know what dope I might pick up," Kaz said, the American jargon he loved so much sounding odd with his Continental accent.

"Go ahead, I'll hitch a ride or walk back," I said. "We'll figure out our next steps in the morning."

I wished Kaz luck and walked outside, breathing in the cool night air, so welcome after a day of heat and sweat.

"I see our friend Jack has dropped Deanna," Fred Archer said as he appeared by my side with two bottles of beer, handing me one. "Maybe I'll take another run at her. Charming lass."

"You tried before?" I asked.

"I did, but she was besotted with the Kennedy boy. She's a nurse, and he's a rich, good-looking lad who needed tending. It came natu-rally to her, I guess, even though he's a bit of an ass."

"Is that jealousy talking, Fred?"

"Well, he's likable enough at a party, I'll give him that. Not a stu-pid chap by a long run, but as a PT skipper he leaves a lot to be desired. First one I ever heard of who got his boat run over by a destroyer. And have you heard his nickname? Crash."

"I did hear him called that," I said. "What's the story?"

"He was racing another PT boat into base after a mission," Fred said, relating the tale with obvious relish. "You see, they have to refuel as soon as they get in, and it has to be done one boat at a time. So every skipper wants to be first, which gives his crew more time to rest up before the next patrol. Well, Kennedy pulls ahead, but as he gets close, something goes wrong with the engines, and he can't stop or even slow down. He crashes into the refueling dock and destroys it. Hence the nickname."

"I'll bet he doesn't like that much," I said.

"I don't think he minds," Archer said. "He's not that sort. Kind of a glamorous name, and as time goes by, fewer people will remember the real story behind it. Like I said, he's not stupid."

I had to agree with Fred's assessment. We clinked bottles and he went back to the verandah to speak with Deanna. I watched the conversation and it went well for a while, the two of them chatting amicably. But then Deanna shook her head back and forth, and put her hand on Fred's arm. The way you do when you give someone bad news. Kind of pitying. He didn't take it well and spun around, heading directly for the drinks table, probably looking for something stronger than Victoria Bitter.

Too bad for Fred, but when there's one girl per thousand guys on the island—not counting the natives living in grass huts straight out of *National Geographic*—he had to understand Deanna was well practiced at saying no.

I was ready to leave, so I sought out Hugh Sexton, pulling him out of a conversation about rugby that was as heated as it was incomprehensible.

"Will you be here in the morning, Hugh?" I said. "I want to talk to you more about Daniel."

"At your service, Billy," he said. "Good work today on Malaita, by the way. Was the trip useful?"

"Yeah, we learned a lot," I said, although doubtful that I'd ever need to know how to stuff a skull again. "Say, do you know anything about this feud between Kennedy and Cotter?"

"The whole island knows about it," he said. "Cotter came back from that patrol claiming he'd searched for survivors after Kennedy's boat was hit. Kennedy said he didn't."

"Who do you believe?"

"Kennedy. We had a report from Reg Evans on Kolombangara that he saw the flames from the explosion. He didn't know what it was at the time, but in the morning he sighted the overturned hull of PT-109 drifting on the current. If he saw the flames, then Cotter should have had an easy time searching if he stayed in Blackett Strait."

"But he didn't," I said.

"Pretty sure not," Sexton said. "He fired off his torpedoes at the destroyers coming through the strait, but then headed home. He reported all hands lost on the 109. The base even held a memorial service for them. The story went that Kennedy was incensed when he heard about it."

"Why do you think Cotter came here tonight?" I asked.

"Booze," Sexton said. "That's why they all came. I only invited my Coastwatchers, but fish on the grill and liquor on the table draws a lot of uninvited guests."

Not Jack, I thought, as I made my way out. He never was a big drinker. A few beers here and there, but he never touched the hard stuff. He came seeking a new conquest, and Rui Chang was what he found.

As for Kaz, I was glad he showed any interest in a woman. It had been more than a year since he lost the love of his life. Daphne Seaton was the sister of Diana, my own true love. Daphne had been killed during our first investigation. A bomb had ended her life and scarred Kaz's face, leaving him with an aching loss, alone and adrift without family or the woman he cherished by his side. The war had taken everything and given nothing but a jagged scar in return.

Death comes in many ways, I thought. Quick and violent, lengthy and lingering. Kaz was dying the long death of loneliness and sorrow, and if an exotic, beautiful woman on this South Pacific island could give him a moment of forgetfulness, then hurrah for the human spirit.

Me, I missed Diana. I worried about her. But stuck on this side of the world, there wasn't a damn thing I could do about it. What I could do was find out who killed Daniel Tamana. But first, I had to answer that nagging unanswered question: *Why* had someone murdered him? And what, if anything, did Jack have to do with it?

CHAPTER FOURTEEN

"KOPI, BOSS?" KAO asked, squatting outside the mosquito netting, holding a steaming mug of joe.

"Sure," I said, blinking the sleep from my eyes as I parted the netting to escape the bed. "Where's Kaz?"

"Verandah, boss," Kao said, heading back to the kitchen. I shuffled out of the bedroom in my skivvies and T-shirt, grasping the java and taking that first blessed sip. I sat next to Kaz on the wide verandah. His khaki pants were clean and pressed, the crease crisp and sharp. His shirt had been starched as well.

"When did you get in?" I asked, noting he had already shaved.

"An hour ago," he said, sipping his coffee and avoiding my eyes.

"You had a busy night," I said. "Getting your pants pressed and all."

"Jai-li has a number of servants," Kaz said. "When it became apparent I would be spending the night, they took my uniform and cleaned it. To good effect, I might add." I swore he blushed as he said it. I'd known Kaz for a while and couldn't remember ever seeing him that shade of red.

"Nothing like getting your uniform cleaned," I said.

"A gentleman does not discuss such matters," Kaz said, setting down his cup and saucer with a clatter. Then we both laughed. A short burst of laughter, followed by a smile. But it was enough.

"Did you see Jack?" I asked.

"No, Jai-li and Rui live in separate houses on the same lane. But one of the servants said Lieutenant Kennedy was with Rui for about an hour and then departed."

"He never was one for long, drawn-out relationships," I said.

"I did hear something interesting," Kaz said. "Daniel Tamana had come looking for Sam Chang the day he was killed."

"Really? Any idea why?"

"No," he said. "It must have been after he left Dickie Miller at Henderson Field. He came to Chinatown and asked several people if Sam Chang was there."

"This was after the rescue of the *Helena* crew from Vella Lavella, right?"

"Yes," Kaz said. "I assume he heard about that after being withdrawn from Choiseul."

"He and Miller were in radio contact with the other Coastwatchers," I said, thinking it through. "He must have known about the rescue in general, but probably not the details, such as the Chinese in the group."

"That makes sense," Kaz said, standing and leaning on the railing. "So somewhere between Henderson Field and Tulagi, he hears Sam Chang was in the party rescued from Vella Lavella. He looks for him on Tulagi, and then is found dead the next morning."

"Discovered by Jack Kennedy," I said. "Who went home last night with Sam Chang's sister."

"If accompanying one of the Chang sisters makes one a suspect, that would include me," Kaz said. "Kennedy's presence last night was likely a coincidence, but Daniel's interest in Chang does bear scrutiny."

"I need to retrace his steps," I said. "We may learn something from who told him about Chang, and when."

"It seems Sam Chang must be considered a suspect," Kaz said.

"Could be," I said. "It fits in that Daniel was from the general area in which Chang operated. He may have had a beef with him. I'll visit Chang in the hospital before he gets out. At least we know where to find him. But you need to get started; you've got a long trip ahead of you."

"Where am I going?" Kaz asked.

"Brisbane. To talk to Dickie Miller."

"Good. I shall sleep the entire way," Kaz said, stifling a yawn. And a smile.

I CLEANED UP enough to be seen in public with Kaz, and after breakfast we drove to base headquarters to ask Captain Ritchie to arrange air transport to Brisbane for Kaz. Yeoman Howe jumped up as if he'd been expecting us.

"Go right on in, sir, Captain Ritchie is expecting you," he said. I opened the door with an inquisitive glance to Kaz, who simply shrugged.

"Captain Ritchie," I said, coming to a semblance of attention. Remembering our last encounter, I thought it best to forego the vinegar and try the honey this time. "Thanks for seeing us, sir. I'd like to request immediate air transport for Lieutenant Kazimierz to Brisbane, to follow up on a development."

"Very well, Lieutenant Boyle," Ritchie said. "Tell me what you've discovered."

"We know from examining the skull of the deceased that he was struck from behind. Since he was found on the beach in a manner which suggests he was about to take the trail back, I'd say he knew his attacker. And the weapon used was similar to the wooden canes the natives sell." I thought that was a nice touch, not mentioning that Jack had one of those canes. There was no need to worry Ritchie and have him bulldog our every move.

"What's the reason for the trip to Brisbane?" asked Ritchie.

"To interview Tamana's Coastwatcher partner, Dickie Miller, sir. He may have known Tamana better than anyone else around here. I have a lead to follow up here while Lieutenant Kazimierz is away."

"Sounds like you've got a lot of nothing so far," Ritchie said, tossing down a pencil. "But talking to Miller sounds sensible. Have you looked into the incident at the hospital?"

"No sir," I said, wondering if something had happened to Jack. "What is it?"

"My God, lieutenant, some detective you are!" Ritchie exclaimed. "That Chinaman Sam Chang was found strangled early this morning in my naval hospital. Half his family has already been in here demanding an explanation. I told them you would look into it, since you're the closest thing we have to a real investigator. One of the head women, May Lee or something like that, said that was satisfactory. It calmed them down and got them the hell out of my office."

"Jai-li," Kaz corrected. "Sir."

"I don't care what her name is, I want peace and quiet on this base so we can get on with the war. These Chinese run most of the businesses around here, so we need to keep things on an even keel. They're our goddamn allies, after all."

"Captain, this is the first we've heard of his murder. I'll get over to the hospital right away. But we still need that air transport."

"Very well," Ritchie said. "You may be late on this Chang affair, but your timing is good on getting to Brisbane. There's a PBY in the harbor that makes a daily run, leaves in thirty minutes. Yeoman Howe will give you the details. Now get out."

"When did all this happen?" I asked Howe once the door to Ritchie's office closed behind us. "He sounded like we should have known about Chang getting killed."

"News does travel fast around here, Lieutenant," Howe said. "As far as I know, he was found dead around dawn. His family was informed and in short order they'd marched in here demanding justice. I guess they thought the captain needed a push in that direction."

"Why would they think that?" I said.

"Because Captain Ritchie puts the navy first," Howe said, lowering his voice.

"And justice comes second," I said. "For Melanesians or Chinese?"

"Your words, Lieutenant, not mine," Howe said. "Is there anything else?"

"Yeah, Lieutenant Kazimierz needs to get on that PBY headed to Brisbane, pronto. Ritchie gave his okay."

"No problem," Howe said. "You need anything else like that, come see me. No need to bother the captain." I liked the sound of that. But it was the only thing I liked the sound of this morning.

"This must have happened after I left this morning," Kaz said. "There was no hint of anything unusual in the household."

"Hurry back," I said as we descended the steps outside the office. "I may need you to help run interference with Jai-li. The last thing we need is a second case and a bunch of angry Chinese on our tail. Ritchie seems more worried about them than about Tamana."

"Perhaps he has lost interest in serving the Kennedy interests, since you demonstrated how obvious his links are to the ambassador. The Chinese can certainly close ranks and make his administration of Tulagi irksome. They are here, and the Kennedy family is far away," Kaz said.

"Yeah, maybe. The good news is we might stumble upon a link between Daniel and Chang if we can find out why Daniel sought him out," I said as I started the jeep.

"I'd say there is bad news and good news," Kaz said. "The bad news is that if there was a link, with both men dead, we may never know what it was."

"And the good news?"

"The good news is I will not have to suffer another boat ride to Guadalcanal."

I drove Kaz to the harbor where he did have to endure a brief journey in a launch out to the waiting PBY. It was seven or eight hours to Brisbane, so depending on when he got to the hospital and saw Dickie Miller, he'd be gone two or three days. I hoped it would be worth the trip.

I proceeded to the hospital, wondering what the death of Sam Chang meant. A blood feud between gangs? There were a number of triad organizations active among the Chinese communities in the South Pacific. Like Mafia families, they often fought with each other. But from the little I'd heard about Sam Chang, he was a straightforward business-man, not a criminal. Maybe he borrowed money and couldn't pay it back. The triad wouldn't like that. Or maybe he loaned money and the bor-rower paid him back with a tight grip around the neck.

Or, perhaps somebody didn't want us making the connection between Daniel Tamana and Sam Chang. Well, I had one now: both of them murdered on Tulagi.

"Lieutenant Boyle?" asked a sailor as I took the steps up to the hospital entrance. He was dressed in blue dungarees and a white Dixie cup hat and sported an SP armband. Shore patrol.

"If you know my name you know why I'm here," I said. "Lead the way."

"The doctors are in a snit waiting for you, sir. They keep saying they have to move the body. The other patients don't like a corpse on their ward, if you know what I mean."

"Can't blame 'em, sailor," I said. "But no one's touched the body, right?"

"Yes, sir. My buddy is standing guard."

He took me to a small ward off the main corridor. A small room, really. No nurses station, just six beds, three along each wall. All the patients were Chinese. In unison they began chattering at me, jabbing fingers at Chang's body, obviously not happy. Neither was Sam Chang, with his broken leg in traction, the bed sheets thrown off, and his open eyes fixed on the ceiling.

"Does anyone speak English?" I asked.

"Already tried that, Lieutenant," the second SP said. "No one even understands the question."

"You finally made it." The voice belonged to a harried doctor with disheveled hair, a heavy beard, and a rumpled white coat over his navy khakis. "Captain Ritchie ordered us not to move the body until you looked at it. So look."

"I'm Lieutenant Boyle. And you are?"

"Captain Schwartz, and I've been on duty for twenty-four hours, so hurry it up, please."

"Okay, Captain, but first tell me, are these patients civilians? What are they doing here?"

"We expanded the English colonial hospital when we first took the island. Medical facilities had been overwhelmed with natives and other refugees fleeing the Japanese. So we have a few rooms set aside for them. We put the Chinese patients together so they could communicate with each other."

"That's great, but I'd like to know what they're saying now," I said over the din of the continuing complaints.

"They wish my brother's body to be treated with respect," a soft, melodious voice said from behind Captain Schwartz. "And not left in such an undignified position."

"Miss Rui Chang," I said, recognizing the woman Jack had left with last night. She wore a white silk dress, buttoned high to the neck. I knew white was the Chinese color for mourning. "We mean no disrespect."

"Even so, Lieutenant, our beliefs dictate that when a person dies, their body must be treated gently and with kindness. The spirit remains for a time near the body. Unless the spirit can move on in a state of happiness, it may not be reborn for a very long time. And any spirit would be distressed upon seeing my poor brother's body."

"Of course," I said, taking in the traction device that held Chang's broken leg up, not to mention the bruised neck and the open, sightless eyes. "I need only a few minutes, and the body can be released."

She nodded and retreated to the corridor.

"When was he found?" I asked Schwartz as I leaned over the corpse.

"Around five o'clock. Orderlies check the rooms at night every hour. Everything was fine at four. He was found like this at five."

"Death by manual strangulation, obviously," I said, turning his head to see the bruises on either side of his neck. Schwartz nodded his agreement. "Was he being treated for anything other than a broken leg?"

"No," Schwartz said. "Re-broken, to be precise. He sustained a fracture on that island he was evacuated from, and then fell and reinjured it getting off ship in the harbor. We reset it, and he would have been fine."

"Did he have a lot of visitors?"

"Lieutenant Boyle, the Chinese have large families," Schwartz said. "They're in and out of here all day long."

"White men? Melanesians? Anyone other than family?" I asked.

"No," Schwartz said. "Not that I know of, but we don't really keep track of visitors, especially when we don't speak the same language."

"Didn't Sam Chang speak English? It seems he did business with lots of islanders; he must have known the lingo," I said.

"He did. But still, this is a naval hospital. We treat civilians as needed and then get them out. Chang was here mainly because his injury was sustained while disembarking a naval vessel."

"So no one else besides his family came to visit him?"

"No, not exactly," Schwartz said, rubbing his chin absentmindedly.

"What?" I asked.

"Lieutenant Kennedy—you know that guy who got his PT boat rammed?—I saw him in the hallway last night, late. He stopped and looked in the Chinese ward. But then he left."

"What time?" I asked.

"It was a little after two o'clock. I was headed to the mess for some coffee when I saw him. I asked if he needed any help, and he said he was looking in on a friend, then heading for his hut."

"You watched him leave?"

"Sure," Schwartz said. "I didn't follow him, if that's what you mean. But he went in that direction, down the main corridor." He hitched his thumb in the general direction of the long hallway leading to the rear of the hospital and the grass and bamboo huts for the walking wounded of the officer class.

"Hang on a sec, Doc," I said, brushing past Schwartz.

"That's Captain," he said, without much enthusiasm.

"Miss Chang," I said, noticing for the first time that she was accompanied by two large guys standing on each side of her. Their eyes focused on me as I drew closer, and one stepped in front of Rui while the other intercepted me. Classic bodyguard moves. She spoke sharply, and they eased back into position.

"Are you done, Lieutenant Boyle?" she asked.

"Almost, Miss Chang. Could you or one of your associates ask the other patients if they saw anyone enter the ward during the night?"

"Such an obvious question, Lieutenant. We asked hours ago. No, none of them saw anything. Two patients, including the man opposite my brother, had been given sedatives. My brother as well was given a sleeping pill. The assailant could have easily entered in silence and done his work."

"Forgive me saying so, but the men with you appear to be body-guards. Is that because of the murder of your brother, or is it how you usually travel?"

"My sister and I always go out with one escort," she said. "Due to the perilous times in which we live. The second man is because of my brother." She spoke very precise English, each syllable clipped and exact. Her posture was equally as exact. She stood erect, completely still, not a wasted movement, even in her hands, which were demurely clasped in front of her. Her eyes were dark, her lips red, and her cheek-bones finely sculpted. Jack always did go for the finer things in life.

"I see. Is it possible he was killed as the result of business dealings? In these perilous times?"

"No, Lieutenant Boyle, it is not," she said with the ghost of a smile. "My brother had been trapped on Vella Lavella for months. He had no opportunity to engage in a dispute that would have resulted in such an attack. In any case, very few people knew he got out and was on Tulagi, and most of those were American navy or Coastwatchers. I am afraid you must look to your own people for the killer."

"I understand Lieutenant Kennedy visited you last night," I said, watching for a reaction.

"You saw us leave the party together, so you know that," she said.

"I don't mean to pry, but did you mention your brother's presence here to Jack? Ask him to stop and visit?"

"Yes, I did," Rui said. "I gave him a bamboo plant and asked him to leave it on Shan's bed table. Or Sam, as you call him. I saw it there when I looked in earlier. It is a symbol of good luck, and I thought it would cheer Shan up when he awoke." Her eyes brimmed with tears, but she kept them in check.

"Did your brother know a Melanesian named Daniel Tamana? He's also a Coastwatcher."

"Not that I know of," Rui said. "Is that not the man who was recently murdered?"

"Yes. I understand Daniel was looking for your brother the day before he was killed."

"As you know, Lieutenant," she said, "if he found him, it would have been in this room. Shan was hardly in a position to attack and kill him, if that is what you are alluding to."

"No, not at all. I simply thought it might shed some light on Daniel's activities the day of his death."

"If I hear of anything, I will inform you," Rui said. "Shan may have known him on Vella Lavella, but I would have no knowledge of that."

"One last question, I promise. What time did Jack leave you?"

"Perhaps one thirty, a little later."

"Thank you, Miss Chang. I am very sorry about your brother's death. I will do everything I can to find the killer."

"Do so, Lieutenant Boyle," she said, and left. A woman used to getting her way. I watched the bodyguards flanking her, and thought that even from a hospital bed, a Chang family member would have no trouble getting their dirty work done for them.

"Okay, Captain Schwartz," I said, returning to the room and noting the glass vase with sprouted bamboo. "How long would it take to strangle him?"

"Hard to say. He could have struggled, fought back," Schwartz said.

"Don't worry, Doc, I won't ask for a second opinion," I said. "And remember, he'd been given a sleeping pill."

"Right," Schwartz said, consulting the chart still hanging at the end of the bed. "Supposing his assailant could get into position without waking him, it would take about ten seconds of firm, steady pressure to render him unconscious. Then another minute and it's all over. The sedative would have made the job easier."

I hefted the glass vase with the bamboo plant set in among smooth, rounded pebbles. It would have made a decent cosh, but there had been no need. I checked the drawer on the nightstand, but it was empty. Not surprising since Chang probably came in with nothing but the clothes on his back. Or if there had been anything valuable, his sisters would have taken it for safekeeping. I rolled his body, looking for anything hidden in the bed. Nothing.

"I don't see any other marks or bruises, do you?"

"No," Schwartz said, unbuttoning Chang's pajama top and getting a good look at the marks left by the killer's hands. "Strong hands, I'd say."

"Why?"

"Even with the sedative, he would have woken up," Schwartz said. "The natural response is to thrash about, and if he moved that leg at all, it would have been painful. A sharp, sudden pain that would make anyone gasp or scream, sedated or not."

"But he was being choked," I said.

"Right, but some sort of sound would have come out, unless the grip was very tight, which also would have rendered him unconscious more quickly. My conjecture is that his assailant was very strong and determined, otherwise Chang would have made more than enough noise to wake someone in this room."

"Strong, determined, and with big hands," I said, placing my own around Chang's throat. "Bigger than mine."

"Right," Schwartz said. "The killer might be right-handed, as well. See how the right thumbprint shows? People usually grasp things first with their dominant hand."

"You know your way around dead bodies, Doc."

"You do your residency at County General in Chicago, you see a lot of violent injuries in the ER," Schwartz said. "Couldn't help learning a few things from the questions cops asked."

"Thanks, Captain, you've been a big help. Okay to move him out." I arranged Chang's hands on his chest, closed his eyes, and drew the sheet up over his face as Schwartz loosened the wires holding Chang's leg in traction. I left, wishing Sam Chang a quick trip to the next life and hopes that it'd be a peaceful one.

As for Jack, my mind wasn't made up. I knew he had a temper, and it wasn't impossible to think of him taking a whack at a guy in a rage; I could see him killing Daniel in an unguarded moment. But could he throttle a man to death? It wouldn't have been his style in Boston, but in the South Pacific, surrounded by blood, decay, and death, who knew?

I didn't.

CHAPTER FIFTEEN

"JACK?" I SAID, announcing myself as I entered his hut. The place was empty, his bed unmade and clothes heaped in piles on the floor. Neatness was never a big consideration for Jack, as far as I remembered. I sat at the table, strewn with yellowed newspapers, a couple of old *Life* magazines, and some correspondence in progress. I sat to wait and flipped through *Life*, reading about the army training women pilots in Texas to ferry aircraft overseas from the States. Not a bad idea. Another article was about General Charles de Gaulle, which wasn't even a close second in the not-a-bad-idea department. I tossed the magazine aside and let my gaze wander over to Jack's letters.

One envelope had a return address from Charlotte McDonnell. The letter next to it was in Jack's handwriting, with a note from Charlotte scrawled across the top in large letters: *Can't keep all the girls straight?* Jack's letter to *Dearest Darlyne* had gone in the wrong envelope and was obviously not appreciated. Especially the part about looking forward to a return engagement, not of the matrimonial kind.

No, Charlotte, I thought, Jack can't keep all the girls straight.

I craned my neck to spy on the letter Jack was obviously in the midst of writing. *Dear Lem*, it began. Lem Billings, Jack's best friend from his private school days. I'd met Lem—it was hard to know Jack and not meet Lem—and liked him. A decent guy. We'd stayed in touch off and on, mostly through Christmas cards and the occasional postcard from distant lands. He had bad eyes and couldn't get into the service, but had volunteered for the American Ambulance Field Service, and probably saw more action in North Africa than a lot of guys in the army.

Jack's letter started off by informing Lem he was about to be discharged from the hospital, and was well enough *to have sampled the delights of the Orient, if you know what I mean. Last night was my first excursion into the Far East, and I did my nation proud.* And so on. Now I'm no prude, but something in Jack's bragging about his conquests didn't sit well with me. It seemed like he needed to announce his every escapade, and I wondered if the telling was more important for Jack than the act itself. I'd heard plenty of rumors about his old man stepping out with the ladies, so maybe he was trying to live up to his father's reputation.

I walked outside, putting some distance between me and evidence of my snooping. Just in time, too. Jack approached, wearing shorts and tennis shoes, a towel slung around his neck.

"Billy, what's new? Did you have a good time last night?"

"It was okay," I said as I followed him into the hut. "How about you?"

"Terrific. Rui took me home to Chinatown," Jack said, grinning as he flopped into a chair and tossed the towel on the floor. "Did you meet her?"

"Yeah, a little while ago," I said. Jack sounded like he hadn't heard about Sam. "As I was checking her brother's body for evidence."

"What?" Jack said, his eyes wide with surprise, or a reasonable imitation.

"Sam Chang was murdered early this morning," I said. "A few hours after you were seen in his room."

"Oh Jesus, that's all I need," Jack said.

"Yeah, I imagine he felt the same way when he was being strangled," I said, pulling up a chair next to Jack and leaning in close. "Tell me why you were there."

"Rui asked me to drop off a bamboo plant," he said. "It's for luck."

"Yeah, all of it bad. What time was that?"

"I'm not sure, around two o'clock, I think," Jack said. "I went in and put the plant on the table; Rui told me which bed Sam was in. He was asleep, and so was everyone else in the room."

"Did you see anyone else?"

"A few people in the corridor, maybe a doctor and a few orderlies," he said. "I really wasn't paying attention, I just wanted to hit the sack. Strangled, huh? Poor bastard."

"Did Rui talk about her brother? Did she mention anyone who had a beef with him?"

"Other than her? No," Jack said, and began shuffling through the letters on the table. He looked at the returned letter from Charlotte and laughed as he ran it under his nose. "I can smell her perfume, but I don't think I'll ever get close to it again."

"Wait," I interrupted, amazed by the nonchalance with which Jack dropped that tidbit of news. "Rui Chang and her brother Sam had problems? What was that all about?"

"Money," Jack shrugged, indifferent to a commodity he found so readily available. "The Chang family runs a lot of business ventures, but the two sisters are based here on Tulagi and Sam up on Vella Lavella. Or at least he was. Rui said he borrowed from them to expand his stores and his shipping right before the war broke out. Bad timing."

"So he owed his sisters money?"

"Apparently," Jack said. "I got the impression the bamboo plant was a bit of a joke. Like saying he'd need good luck to get out of the mess he found himself in. It actually reminded me of my own brother. Joe would pull a prank like that."

"Would your family commit murder over money?" I asked, knowing that some of Joe Senior's more questionable associates might.

"You don't think Rui had him killed?" Jack asked. "It's her brother for Chrissake. And how would she ever collect what he owed?"

"Inheritance?"

"Her timing would be off for that," Jack said. "She mentioned a lot of planters had been running a tab with Sam when the war began. He'd have to collect on that first. Like I said, his timing was terrible. Anyway, I don't believe she had anything to do with it. I got the impression it's a hard-nosed family when it comes to business, but murder is a different story."

"Probably so," I said. "Now tell me why you said 'that's all I need' when I told you about Sam's death."

"Listen, Billy, I need you to keep quiet about Sam and my late-night visit. Al Cluster is coming by later today. He's my commanding officer and he's the one who can send me home or give me another boat. I don't want him to start thinking I'm a problem child he'd be better off without."

"How are your injuries?" I asked. "Bad enough for a ticket home?"

"No, my feet are healing up fine," he said. "There's a navy tradition that says a captain who's had his boat sunk gets sent stateside. If Al wants me gone, he can use that. If he doesn't, he'll ignore it. So do me a favor, Billy, and forget about this Chang thing."

"How's your back?" I asked, without commenting on the favor. There'd been a few too many favors done between the Kennedys and the Boyles, and I didn't want to start another round. "You must've gotten banged up pretty bad when that destroyer hit you."

"It's the same," he said. Which meant not so great. "Here's the deal, Billy. I can't go home now. I haven't really done anything worthwhile out here. The truth is, these PT boats are next to worthless. Our torpedoes are a joke. Half the boats don't have radar, and the brass thinks we're a bunch of Ivy League pansy yachtsmen who don't give a damn about the real navy."

"That last part sounds true," I said.

"Yeah," Jack laughed. "Guilty as charged. Al Cluster is one of the few Annapolis men who went into PT boats. He's a good officer and I don't want to disappoint him. Or myself for that matter. I got two men killed, Billy. Harold Marney and Andrew Kirksey. I need to do right by them."

"You saved the rest," I said. "Ten men survived, that should count for something."

"All I did was get my boat sunk," Jack said, scratching his damp hair. "I swam around for a while looking for help, hoping the rest of the squadron would return to search for us. All that did was get my feet cut up on the coral. It was a Coastwatcher who sent the two natives out to look for us. If it weren't for them, we would have died out on the little island. Or been captured by the Japs, which amounts to the same thing."

"It was a pretty long swim from what I heard," I said. "Didn't you tow a guy who was badly burned?"

"Yeah, Pappy. He was in the engine room. I guess he was lucky to get out alive. The doctors said he'll be okay. Even though his hands were burned, he kept flexing them all the time. They said that saved them, kept scar tissue from forming and tightening his hands into claws." He closed his eyes, turning his head away. Finally, something had gotten to Jack Kennedy.

"Jack, it could have been a whole lot worse," I said, sensing the depth of his emotion. It was the first time I'd ever seen him even close to feeling guilty over something he'd done.

"It could have been avoided," he said, slamming his hand down on the table. "It's criminal that none of the radar boats told us they were leaving the strait. It's criminal that no one came looking for us. They gave us up for dead. I can't forget that, not ever."

"What do you mean about the radar boats, Jack?"

"I told you, half the boats don't have radar, including the 109. The boats that had radar saw the Jap destroyers barreling down Blackett Strait. They fired their torpedoes and got the hell out of there. They didn't score one hit or bother to radio that they were leaving, much less that we had company headed our way. When that destroyer sliced the 109 in two and our fuel exploded, the other boats hightailed it for home."

"Sounds like a FUBAR nightmare," I said.

"The sea is dark and huge, Billy. More so when you're abandoned and left to die. Cotter lied. He claimed he searched the area, but we never saw anyone. With all the burning fuel on the water, it would have been a cinch to find us. He ought to be court-martialed. Or worse."

"Jack, threats aren't going to help you get another boat," I said. "Calm down, okay? You and your men got a raw deal, but you're mixed up in two murders already."

"Jesus, Billy, I'd never laid eyes on Sam Chang until last night. I had no reason on earth to murder him or Daniel Tamana. Give me a break, alright?" That was more like the old Jack, asking for a favor, special treatment, for me to be a pal. I'd been down that one-way street before.

"You told me that you'd met Daniel the day before he was killed, at Hugh Sexton's place," I said. "Who else was there?"

"Besides Hugh and Daniel, there was Fred Archer and Gordon Brockman," Jack said. "Along with John Kari. Deanna Pendleton, too."

"Why were you there?"

"I wanted to ask about Reg Evans, the Coastwatcher who sent the natives out to find us. Hugh told me he was still out on Kolombangara, so I asked him to pass on my thanks. And besides, I'd heard about Deanna and hoped she'd be there as well. I got lucky."

"What can you tell me about Daniel?" I asked, more interested in the murder victim than Jack's luck with the ladies. "Did he seem upset about anything? Get in an argument with anyone?"

"No," Jack said slowly, tilting his head back and closing his eyes. "Not that I can remember. There was a lot of talk about the new radios and getting back out on station before the next big offensive."

"Any mention of Sam Chang?"

"Never came up," Jack said. "It was business as usual; they talked radio frequencies, supply drops, that sort of thing. Silas Porter showed up too, but that was after Daniel had left."

"What was Daniel like?" I asked. I knew I was grasping at straws, but Jack was a shrewd judge of character and a keen observer.

"Smart. That was the first thing you noticed about him," Jack said. "Well, after the dark skin and fuzzy hair. He was sharp, didn't waste a lot of words. And when he asked a question, it was straight to the point. Observant and intelligent."

"What are relations like between the white islanders and the Melanesians?"

"It varies, from what I've seen," Jack said. "It's not like Negroes and whites back home. The natives here are so different; it's like some of them are still living in the Stone Age. To no great disadvantage, either, for many. Daniel was raised near a mission and learned English from an early age. It seemed that Sexton and the other Coastwatchers accepted him as one of their own. I don't get the sense that whites here have a problem with a native adopting Western ways."

"So no resentment about an uppity native taking on airs, that sort of thing?"

"No, not that I saw," Jack said. "In general I think the English treat the natives as nothing more than a convenient labor pool for their plantations. On an individual basis, there are some genuine friendships. Whatever the relations, it's going to be hard after the war to get the natives to go back to the old ways. They've been fighting the Japs alongside us and earning good money unloading ships for the navy. They're not going to fancy returning to plantation work for cheap wages."

"That's fascinating, Jack, but it still doesn't tell me why Daniel got his head bashed in." As usual, Jack looked at the big picture. I needed a cop's take on things, not a politician's.

"Money or sex, isn't it always one or the other? That's what you told me back in Boston."

"Yeah," I said, sighing at how little I had to go on. "Daniel didn't mention Sam Chang, did he?"

"No, I wasn't aware they knew each other."

"I'm not sure they did. Thanks, Jack. Good luck with Cluster. I'll drop by to see how you made out."

"I can fill you in on how I make out with Deanna as well," Jack said with a smirk. "I'm taking her to lunch in Chinatown. There's a joint on the docks that does great things with fresh fish."

"Making up for ignoring her at Sexton's party, Jack?"

"Deanna's a good kid, don't get me wrong," he said. "But you can't blame a guy for enjoying the few other available women in this dump. I don't mind that she was sore at me; can't blame her for that either."

"Well, enjoy," I said. Jack may have been a cad, but he was such an easy-going one, it was hard to stay mad at him.

"Hey, Billy," Jack said as I rose from the table. "What are you going to do about Sam?"

"You mean about you being seen in his room?"

"Yes, that," Jack said, his easy grin fading as he turned serious. "I really need to get another command, Billy. Give it some thought, okay?"

"Sure, Jack. See you around."

He must have seen it in my eyes. I wasn't going to give him a free pass. Like I said, Jack could really read people. That's why he changed tack and asked me to give it some thought. Hard to say no to that.

CHAPTER SIXTEEN

I WAS LOOKING for food, Hugh Sexton, and Jacob Vouza. I struck gold on the verandah of Sexton's place, where the two of them were eating off tin plates. Rice, fish, and breadfruit, which is kind of like a potato. White and starchy, anyway. Hugh went inside to fix me a plate and returned with three cans of beer, kept moderately cool in his ancient refrigerator.

"What have you found out about Daniel?" Jacob asked around a mouthful of food.

"I'm afraid not much," I said. "Did he know Sam Chang?"

"Poor chap's dead, we heard," Sexton said. I gave them what details I had.

"I don't know if he knew him," Jacob said. "Maybe did. Daniel went to Rendova after he finish school. No work there except in the plantation kilns, drying coconut. Not right for educated young man. Then he got a job on a Pavau plantation, keeping the books and overseeing the loading of copra when the Lever ship come. It's not far from Vella Lavella. He would have heard of Sam Chang for sure."

"Right," Sexton said. "Chang was a prominent merchant, most everyone up in those islands knew his name. Hard not to. Why, is it important?"

"It seems Daniel went looking for Sam right after he came back from Henderson Field. Did he ask either of you?" Sexton shook his head no.

"I was with marines on New Georgia when Daniel came to Tulagi," Jacob said. "Plenty fighting there. Never saw Daniel here. I sent a message, but he was not around when I came by."

"Any idea why he'd be looking for Chang?" I asked.

"No," Sexton said. "We'd been in radio contact about the pickup for him and Dickie the day before. He didn't say anything then or here on Tulagi."

"But we know he did look for him. Would he have heard Chang's name in any of the radio transmissions?" I asked.

"He could have," Sexton said. "We used Chang's name several times when arranging the pickup for him and his people."

"But Daniel didn't react to that at the time," I said. "It seems that it only happened when he came to Tulagi. Odd that he never brought up the connection while you were all together."

"Daniel a smart boy," Vouza said. "If something was not right, he would not speak of it until he knew who his friends were."

"Wasn't he among friends?" I asked.

"Comrades, to be sure," Sexton said. "But some of the chaps had never met the others. Remember, these are mostly volunteers who stayed in place after the Japanese occupied the islands. I've been in touch with them all, as has the Coastwatchers HQ on Guadalcanal. But other than hearing clipped reports on the radio, lots of the fellows have no idea who's who. We use call signs for each team, so as not to tip off the Japs. If they learned the names of islanders, they might deduce their location."

"Right," Vouza said. "I don't think Daniel knew Silas Porter or John Kari, even though he work on Pavau. Or Fred Archer. We both met Gordie on New Georgia before the war, but Daniel did not know he was a Coastwatcher."

"We've another group coming in tomorrow," Sexton said. "Same thing, most will be strangers except for their teleradio call signs."

"Jacob, what did you mean when you said Daniel worked on Pavau, but didn't know Porter and Kari?"

"Silas is from Pavau," Vouza said. "He owns plantation on north end of island. He escape when the Japs landed. His assistant manager was not so lucky, or the workers. Japs kill them all when they caught them."

"I think you told us someone from Pavau killed a Jap and they retaliated," I said.

"Yeah, they kill plenty," Vouza said. "Daniel work on the south side. Big mountain in between, no roads. But he heard the Japs were landing and got out kwiktaem. Him and a few fellows in canoe. John Kari work on a different plantation, got out on last boat before Japs come. I'm certain Daniel and John did not know each other."

"You told me Daniel kept the accounts and managed shipments of copra. Maybe someone he worked with there could help shed light on his murder," I said.

"Pavau full of Japs now," Vouza said. "Two plantations on south side of island where Daniel worked. Both owned by Lever Brothers. Their managers ran off before Japs got close. Left workers behind."

"Most native workers are brought in from the bigger islands," Sexton said. "They contract for a certain number of months and then go home."

"What about Rendova then?" I asked. "That's under our control, isn't it?"

"It's pretty well cleared out," Sexton said. "But there's intense fighting on New Georgia, a few miles across Blanche Channel. We've taken the airfield at Munda Point, but there are still strong Jap forces on the island."

"You go to Rendova easy enough," Vouza said. "PT boat base there. Ask for the Coburn plantation. Old Scottish fella run it, grow coffee beans. That's where Daniel worked."

"He moved on, though. Why?" I asked.

"Hard work in the fields," Vouza said. "Daniel was a smart boy, knew he didn't want to be a common laborer. He wanted to use his head, not his hands." That fit with everything I'd learned about Daniel.

"Josh Coburn returned not long ago, after Rendova was retaken, much to our surprise," Sexton said. "We thought he was dead. The Japs almost caught him on Bougainville, but somehow he got away to

Choiseul. From there he went straightaway to French New Caledonia. Word is he's now looking for his old crew of workers, most of them from Malaita. You might find someone there who knew Daniel."

"So Coburn didn't abandon his people?"

"No. There's a big difference between a man who manages for Lever and a man who owns his own place," Sexton said.

"Coburn is tough one," Vouza said, nodding his agreement. "Story was Japs got him on Bougainville, where he had another coffee plantation. We only find out a few weeks ago that he took a canoe and paddled himself all the way to Choiseul. Pretty good for a seventy-year-old fella."

I agreed that few in their right mind would fight for a big business like Lever, and that Josh Coburn sounded like an extraordinary character. But that didn't have much to do with Daniel, so I decided to dig a little deeper into his last day alive.

"I've been trying to figure out why Daniel went looking for Sam Chang when he did," I said. "Can either of you tell me more about Daniel's movements the day he came to Tulagi? In detail, I mean."

"Well, he arrived about mid-morning," Sexton said.

"Go back further," I said. "What route did he take to Guadalcanal?"

"We sent a PT boat to pick them up at Kuku, a small coastal village on Choiseul," Sexton said. "It was a dangerous spot, but Dickie was so ill we didn't think he could travel far."

"Why dangerous?" I asked.

"It is an obvious landing area," Vouza said. "Small cove, no rocks. Easy. Means Japs watch it."

"But we had good luck that night," Sexton said. "They made it back to the PT base on Rendova and then via PBY to Guadalcanal. As I said, Daniel stayed with Dickie at Henderson Field until he got on a C-47 transport bound for Australia."

"Who was with him?" I asked.

"None of us," Sexton said. "I'm not sure exactly how Daniel got here from Guadalcanal, but there's always vessels going back and forth; easy enough to hitch a ride."

"Turns out it was the same boat that brought us to Tulagi," Archer said, joining our group. "Me, Porter, Kari, and Brockman. Left Rendova, stopped at Guadalcanal, then docked here. Daniel and I figured it out later when we were chatting. Didn't know it at the time."

"How come you all didn't fly in with Daniel and Dickie?" I asked.

"The others came out sooner," Sexton explained. "The tender had already left Rendova before we got poor Dickie there. He was sick enough to get priority air transport. Nearly all Coastwatchers come out of the jungle with some sort of illness, but the rest of the bunch only had minor complaints. They were treated onboard the tender. It's a pretty big ship, with a crew of a hundred or more."

"So Daniel joined the group when he boarded the tender and sailed for Tulagi?" I asked.

"Sounds like it," Sexton said, shrugging. "It's a short trip on a large, crowded vessel. Daniel wouldn't have known who was on board. They could have run into each other or missed meeting completely."

"Okay," I said. "The PT tender docks at Sesapi, here on Tulagi. That's the harbor out past Chinatown where we landed. So how does he get to your place?"

"Good question. We had a truck waiting to pick up the other four men, since we knew when to expect them," Sexton said. "I recall Daniel showed up about an hour after they did. It didn't seem important to ask how he'd gotten here; we were just glad to see him. Besides, there's always military vehicles traveling to and from Sesapi. He could have hitched a ride easily enough."

"Jack Kennedy told me he dropped by that day," I said.

"Right," Sexton replied. "He was looking for Reg Evans, the Coastwatcher who sent the two native scouts to find him. Reg is still on station, I'm afraid. Tough spot out on Kolombangara."

"If I recall, Jack said Archer and Gordie were here, Daniel, Deanna, and John Kari. What about Silas Porter?"

"Silas was late, now that I think about it. John said he'd met a mate of his on the tender, another planter who'd been out to Rendova to check on his holdings. They went off for a drink, then Silas showed up here sometime in the afternoon," Sexton said.

"After Daniel left?" I asked.

"Yes, about a half hour or so, I think. Daniel had asked permission to leave, said that he'd heard an aunt of his was sick," Sexton said. "I told him to be back in the morning, and that was that."

"No aunt sick from Malaita," Vouza said. "Daniel made up story so he could look for Sam Chang without raising suspicion."

"But suspicion of what?" I asked. "Why keep that a secret?"

"Because Daniel and Sam Chang both knew something," Vouza said. "You find out what, you find out who killed them."

"Is Kennedy really a suspect?" Sexton asked.

I glanced at Vouza, whose steady gaze betrayed nothing.

"No one is ruled out," I said. "It could have been anyone who knew Daniel, who could get him to meet on a deserted stretch of beach. What was his frame of mind? Did he seem distracted?"

"Not that I noticed," Sexton said. "Although we had a lot of information to go over. Daniel was very professional. His briefing about the situation on Choiseul was concise but in depth. He did seem in a hurry to leave when he finished, but I attributed that to a desire to see his aunt before the situation worsened."

"But in reality, he wanted to find Sam Chang," I said. "I need to find out who he talked to in Chinatown, assuming that's where he went to look for Chang. He may have said something important."

"Everything a man says on the day he goes to the ancestors is important," Vouza said. Hard to disagree with that. "What will you do after Chinatown?"

"Looks like I'm going to Rendova," I said. "I'll talk to this Coburn fellow and see what he remembers about Daniel. Then snoop around the PT base and see if anyone remembers Daniel and Dickie coming through."

"If you want, hitch a ride with Porter and Kari," Sexton said. "They're leaving later this afternoon for Rendova. The two of them are getting their teleradio gear and supplies sorted right now."

"On that crate we took to Malaita?" I asked.

"No, your navy is sending them up on a PT boat from Sesapi harbor," Sexton said with a chuckle. "You'll make better time. It's about a hundred and fifty miles, which should take four or five hours, the last few after dark. Or you could go with Archer and Gordie tomorrow, same route."

"Watch out for the Kawanishi," Vouza said. "They see you in the daytime and they see your wake at night. Watch when light, listen when dark."

"If you're looking up and the stars suddenly disappear, say your prayers," Sexton said.

"And get ready to greet your ancestors," Vouza said, and drained his beer.

"I might as well go today," I said. "That way I can be back when Kaz returns from Australia."

"You think Dickie will be of any help?" Sexton asked.

"To tell you the truth, I have no idea who can help. I can't find any sort of motive, except the possibility that Daniel and perhaps Sam Chang knew some secret that endangered the killer."

"Enough to murder twice?" Vouza said. "That is plenty danger."

"Yeah, the stakes would have to be significant," I said. "If the killings are connected, then someone has a great deal to lose. Otherwise, why risk it? But I wonder what would be so valuable out here, with half the Solomons occupied by the Japanese? What's worth killing your own people for when the Japs are ready to oblige?"

"It was a Melanesian and a Chinese who were murdered," Vouza said. "Maybe neither was the killer's people."

He was right. Jack had mentioned sex and money as potential motives. Hatred ran a close third. Was this a white man's crime, committed by someone who saw himself above the law? I didn't like the direction that line of thought was taking.

"Anything else unusual either of you can remember about that day?" I asked.

"No, I don't think so," Sexton said, closing his eyes as if to see the scene in his memory. "Wait, Daniel spoke to Deanna before he left. A quick, whispered conversation on the verandah. No idea what they talked about."

"Did anyone overhear them?" I asked.

"I doubt it," Sexton said. "Daniel was close to her, his voice too low to hear. I could see them from inside, we all could, through the open windows and doorway."

"Did it look like an argument?" I asked.

"No, I don't think so," Sexton said. "I really didn't pay much attention."

"Deanna was from Vella Lavella," I said, "just like Sam Chang."

"Where is the girl now?" Vouza asked.

"With Jack Kennedy," I answered, and ran to my jeep.

CHAPTER SEVENTEEN

I BLASTED THE horn as I sped along the rutted lanes that passed for roads on Tulagi, sending natives, sailors, and the occasional goat scurrying into the bush or stumbling into the drainage ditch lining the roadway. Deanna was from Vella Lavella, and had been sought out by Daniel Tamana, as had Sam Chang, who lived on the same island. I didn't know the reason why, but in my gut I knew she was in danger. If I was wrong, then she and I could share a laugh over it.

Jack had said they were going to Chinatown to eat somewhere along the docks. I drove over the crest of the hill behind the hospital, negotiating a couple of switchbacks way too fast, braking and skidding my way onto the coast road before reaching the outskirts of Chinatown. I scanned the vehicles parked by the water, watching for Jack and Deanna.

Nothing.

I parked along the waterfront and jumped from the jeep, following a clutch of navy officers who hopefully were headed for the best restaurant in town. A wharf jutted out from the dock area, bearing a jumble of weathered wooden buildings on stilts, the waves crashing onto the shore beneath. Fishing craft bobbed on the incoming tide. Sea birds flocked overhead, scouting the leavings from the boats and the rickety stalls shaded with palm fronds, selling the catch of the day. The aroma of fish, saltwater, and spices filled the air, reminding me of another Chinatown half a world away. Some Boston streets I knew smelled a lot like this, especially in the stifling August heat.

I wiped the sweat off my forehead with my sleeve and walked the dock, getting the lay of the land and keeping my eyes peeled for Deanna. I walked by a few open-air markets and a fried fish stand where the cook offered his dishes served on a taro leaf. Across the street, stores sold rice, vegetables, and a few scrawny chicken carcasses. None of them the sort of place Jack described.

As I neared the water, I spotted Jack leaning against a railing on the wharf, next to rows of tables and chairs set out under a thatched canopy. Spicy aromas drifted out from the kitchen, along with the clatter of pans and the chatter of the cooks. A normal day, doing a land-office business with officers searching out a change from mess hall rations.

But it wasn't a normal day. I could tell by the look on Jack's face, before he spotted me. He was irritated. A glance at his watch. A frown.

Deanna hadn't shown.

"Jack," I said, as I worked my way through along the crowded wharf, packed with khaki, calico *lap-laps*, navy blue dungarees, color-ful silk dresses, and pale linens. He saw the worry in my eyes.

"What's wrong, Billy?"

"Have you seen Deanna?" I glanced around, hoping to see her at any moment, trying not to think of the worst.

"No," he said. "We were supposed to meet here a half hour ago. Are you looking for her?"

"You said you were *taking* her to lunch, Jack, not *meeting* her," I said. "Where is she?"

"I don't know," Jack said, backing up a step in the face of my barely contained anger. "She said she had to do something first, and we arranged to meet here."

"Do what first?"

"I told her it was crazy," Jack said. "But she insisted on talking to one of the Chang sisters."

"What do you mean, crazy?"

"She said either Rui or Jai-li would do, but I figured she was going to have it out with Rui. I told her to relax, that it was no big deal."

"Jesus, Jack," I said as I slammed my fist on the railing. "This wasn't about you catting around. Is that why you didn't bring her yourself? So you could avoid what you thought would be an uncomfortable scene?"

"Well, yeah, Billy. Who would want to get in the middle of that? We had a few words about it and then decided to meet up separately. It's not the end of the world, you know."

"Jack, get it through your thick skull. It wasn't about you, you self-centered bastard!"

"I don't have to listen to this, Billy," he said, stepping around me.

"Yes you do," I said, and pushed him back against the railing. He stumbled and barely righted himself, avoiding falling flat on his ass by grabbing the rail and pulling himself up. It had been like pushing against a bag of bones. I grabbed his arm to help him up and was struck by how little muscle there was. Jack was positively gaunt, the extent of his weight loss hidden by baggy khakis. He shook off my hand, his eyes filled with smoldering resentment. "Sorry," I said. I knew his back was a constant worry, and he didn't need to injure it again in a shoving contest with me.

"Forget it," he said, leaning on the railing and looking out across the harbor, and not at me. "So what the hell is this about?"

"I just heard that Daniel Tamana spoke to Deanna on the day he was killed. It was at Sexton's place, and they were seen whispering about something out on the verandah."

"Do you think Daniel told her why he was looking for Sam Chang?" Jack asked.

"No way to know for sure, but there has to be a connection. She came from Vella Lavella, like Sam. Sam gets killed, and maybe Deanna put two and two together. That's why she said either of the Chang sisters would do for her purposes. My guess is she wanted to talk to them about what Daniel said. It probably didn't register as important until she heard Sam Chang had been murdered."

"Why not tell me, or you, for that matter?"

"She might have told you, Jack, if you hadn't jumped to conclusions. I don't know why she didn't come to me first; maybe she planned to if she found anything out. She's not exactly a wallflower."

"That's for sure," Jack said. "Most women get jewelry from their admirers. Deanna got a carbine. Let's look for her, okay?"

"Yeah," I said, clapping him on the shoulder. He nodded, and with that, our dockside tiff was forgotten. It was easy for Jack. Most things rolled off his shoulders. Easy for me, too, when it was penny-ante stuff. "Do you know how she got here?"

"She said Archer and Gordie were going over to Sesapi, and she'd hitch a ride with them," Jack said as we strode along the wharf.

"They were both there when she and Daniel spoke," I said. "Along with Sexton and John Kari. I don't think Porter was around at that point."

"Any of them could have mentioned it to half a dozen people, as Sexton did to you," Jack said. "You really think she's in danger, don't you?"

"Let's hope she's having tea and lost track of time," I said. "Where's Rui's house? We can start there."

Jack led the way onto the main thoroughfare. Shops and bars ran along the water side, with an array of houses higher up on the hill, overlooking the harbor. Narrow lanes branched off the main road, packed with neat little abodes shaded by palm trees. A pleasant-looking town, at least now that it wasn't under Japanese occupation. We walked past shops and a couple of bars. Most of the signs were in Chinese, but one read BEER, which said it all to the sailors who drifted in and out. The next bar sported half a dozen Chinese girls in low-cut dresses, which of course attracted even more noisy sailors.

A few ancient trucks puttered down the road, their bodies showing more rust than paint. One was filled with small, squealing pigs, another with a load of coconut logs that threatened to finish off what struts were left. A sailor driving a truck behind them, probably bound for Sesapi, was in no hurry, but a jeep zipped out of line, gunned the engine, and passed them all.

It was John Kari. No reason why he shouldn't be in a hurry, but it still made me nervous.

"Up there," Jack said. Ahead was a well-kept house with the standard wide verandah, the clapboards painted in a pale blue pastel that almost made you feel a cool breeze. We hurried down the street but stopped short to check on the raised voices not far behind us.

A knot of people had gathered in front of a bar, its corrugated iron walls streaked with rust. There was a lot of excited yelling and a panicked waving of arms. It took a second to realize it was directed at us. Jack and I turned and trotted over, a Chinese guy detaching himself from the group and waving us on.

"A woman dead," he said. "White lady." He looked to the alleyway between the bar and the next building, a dilapidated storehouse with crates of fruit and vegetables spilling out onto the sidewalk. Music from an ancient gramophone set up near the open windows echoed a scratchy tune from inside the bar. Sweat chilled my spine and I could feel the fear in my face: hot skin, short breaths, and an empty feeling behind my eyes. The classic symptoms of a cop steeling himself to see what he doesn't want to, but knows he must.

"Wait here, Jack," I said, my hand on his shoulder. The music stopped as someone lifted the needle off the record, the dance tune silenced with a harsh scratch.

"It's okay, Billy, I can take it. She could be alive, right?"

"I know you could, Jack," I said. As for the chances that this was another white woman or that Deanna was still among the living, I didn't say. "But you need to stay here."

He shook off the hand resting on his bony shoulder. He got it. No reason to allow a suspect near the murder victim. He didn't like it much. I didn't care.

I pushed through the crowd, telling people who likely didn't understand English to leave the scene. The alleyway was narrow and dark, only about three feet wide. The first thing I saw was her feet. The rest of her was buried under a pile of rotten sweet potatoes. Flimsy crates lay broken on the ground, and it made sense to me that the killer forced her into the alley and knocked the crates over, covering most of her corpse. A rush job.

I wasn't in a hurry.

I picked up the sweet potatoes, most of them covered in a dusting of mold that left my fingers covered in a grey, musty mess. I uncovered a blue polka-dot skirt, then a white blouse stained red just below her left breast.

I gently removed the last of the remaining debris from her neck and face. Her throat was bruised. Not heavy bruising like Sam Chang's, but the imprint of a single hand could be seen. Thumb mark on the right side, finger marks on the left. The killer used the knife in his right hand. It was easy to imagine the scene. The two of them walking along, the gentleman on the street side. He sees his chance amidst the frantic hustle and bustle and shoves her into the alley, his hand on her throat, keeping her from screaming. Then a knife thrust, between the fourth and fifth ribs from the look of it. Not a lot of blood. What bleeding she did was probably internal, until the violated heart stopped beating. It would have taken seconds.

The collar of her blouse was stained. I leaned closer and saw that some of what I'd thought was bruising was really a brown, greasy stain. I rubbed my finger along her collar and the odor of petroleum rose up from it. Cosmoline, I guessed. The greasy stuff they pack guns in to prevent rust.

I wiped my hands on my trousers and sighed. What had Deanna done to deserve this? Her eyes were open, gazing at the sky, seeing nothing. I closed them. I found her wide-brimmed straw hat and placed it over her face. The flies had begun to descend, and I didn't like the idea of them crawling over her. Didn't like the idea of seeing that in my dreams.

It had gone silent in the alley, but it was only my thoughts that crowded out the sounds from the street, the eager onlookers, the debaters, the drunks, and maybe a killer watching the aftermath of his handiwork. I rose, and a wave of noise—combined with a foul stink of alcohol, heat, garbage, and sweat—hit me. I pushed people back and spotted two sailors and a GI in front of the bar, bottles of Ballantine's Beer clutched in their hands. Jack was nowhere to be seen.

"Hey, you guys," I said, shouting at them from the entrance to the alley, not wanting to leave Deanna's body unattended. "Is there a telephone around here?"

"Yes sir," the GI said, indicating the comm wire strung along the street. "There's a harbormaster's office on the dock. They're connected to the base switchboard."

"Get down there on the double. Call the hospital and tell them we have a body to transport. You two, lose the bottles," I said to the sailors, beckoning them over to where I stood. "You're on guard duty. No one gets in the alley."

"Is it true it's a dame, Lieutenant?" asked the freckle-faced sailor who looked like he should be in high school instead of on Tulagi with the two stripes of a petty officer second class gracing his denim shirt.

"Yeah," I said. "Deanna Pendleton. She was a nurse who came down from Vella Levalla."

"She was the one everybody thought was Amelia Earhart, right? I heard about her," he said, his voice a quiet drawl. "What happened?"

"She was murdered, knifed by the looks of it. Did either of you see anybody with her?" I asked. I watched their reactions. A dead body was one thing. It could have been an accident, a fall, heatstroke, any of a number of calamities. But when murder is mentioned, it's always a shocker.

"Jeez," the young sailor said. "No, we woulda noticed her. Nothing but Chinese girls around here."

"I think I saw that skirt," his pal said, leaning in to take a look. "From behind. I didn't see her face 'cause she had that big sun hat on. But I remember the polka dots."

"Was she alone?" I asked.

"No, I don't think so," he said slowly. "I'm pretty sure there was a guy walking next to her. But to tell you the truth, Lieutenant, I wasn't studying the guy much at all."

"Could it have been the navy officer who was with me?" I asked.

"That skinny guy? I dunno. Maybe. I can't even be sure the fellow was actually with her. They coulda just been walking in the same direction. Hard to tell with all the khaki hereabouts."

"Where'd you see her?" I asked, changing tack.

"Down that way," he said. It was in the direction of Rui Chang's house, where Jack and I had been headed. "We walked down the street to check things out, you know? There was nothing down that way, so we turned around and headed for this bar. I spotted them a little before we got here. Hey, you don't think—?"

"Yeah," I said. "Maybe. That could have been right before he killed her. How long ago?"

"We ain't been keepin' track of time, Lieutenant. We got twelve hours of liberty, you know? But maybe an hour ago, a little longer. Can't say for sure."

"Okay, fellas, stay put until I get back, okay?" They nodded and I went into the dive with the record player. The bar girls spoke some English, but the bartender was a better bet. He was positioned to see out the wide-open windows, and probably kept an eye on the foot traffic. He spoke decent English.

"No, no white lady come in here," he said, shaking his head more than he needed to. "We have no trouble here. Honest establishment." He was still shaking his head emphatically as he drew out each syllable of the last word.

"Hey, I'm not the shore patrol, okay? I only want to know if you spotted the woman in the white blouse and blue polka-dot skirt."

"European lady?" he asked.

"American," I said. "Was she with anyone?"

"European ladies do not come here," he said, starting up the head shake after a brief rest. "Plenty sailors, nice Chinese girls, but no white ladies."

"Were the Japanese good customers when they were here?" I asked, trying another tack.

"It was very bad," he said, and his head settled down as he sighed. "Bad for business. Worse for girls. Japs take what they want, you understand?"

"Yeah," I said. "This white lady, she was a Coastwatcher, from Vella Lavella. A brave woman."

"Really?" he asked. I nodded, and he leaned on the bar, glanced around to see if anyone was listening, then spoke in a low whisper. "She come in here, ask where Rui Chang lives. I say I don't know. Not good for business if Changs hear I tell anyone about them."

"Was she alone?" He nodded, a quick affirmative. "How long ago?"

"Hour and a half, maybe more," he said. "I didn't see her again."

"Even though she must have walked right by?" With the shutters wide open, the street scene was in plain view.

"Mister, people walk by all day, every day. Big blur to me. I am sorry. If she was a Coastwatcher, she was brave lady indeed. If I could help, I would."

"Then tell me where Rui Chang lives," I said, leaning in to whisper myself. He told me, the same house Jack had been leading me to. I figured he was on the level if he dared to share that dangerous dope with me. Not that it helped much.

I worked the street as best I could, asking shopkeepers and anyone who didn't turn away at my approach about Deanna. Most didn't understand, or played at it. I got the idea pretty fast that this was a company town and that the Changs were top dog. Again, not that it helped one bit.

I returned to the alley to find the GI who'd gone to the harbormaster's office waiting with his sailor buddies.

"I made the call, Lieutenant," he said. "They're sending an ambulance."

"Good," I said. I wanted a doctor to examine her for anything I'd missed, and to take a close look at the stab wound. It appeared damn professional to me. "How'd you know they were patched in to the base hospital?"

"Signals company, Lieutenant," he said. "We strung all this comm wire you see around here. Call ourselves the Tulagi Telephone Company."

"The PT base at Sesapi, too?"

"Sure. Hospital, Base HQ, the Government Wharf, the district commissioner's house, this place, and a bunch of smaller units."

"The Coastwatchers, too?" I asked.

"Oh yeah. Captain Sexton has a field telephone like everyone else. There's a switchboard at headquarters and all calls are connected through that."

I spotted the ambulance seconds later, the Red Cross bright against its olive drab paint job. I told the sailors to get back to their drinking and asked the GI where the signals company was stationed.

"In the old police station, Lieutenant, on the south shore. Corporal Wilbur Warren. Ask for me if you need anything."

I told him I might. Something was buzzing through my mind about telephone lines and lies. I needed to puzzle out how the killer intercepted Deanna right when she'd be alone. There really hadn't been a lot of time; if she'd found Rui Chang's residence, she would have been safe there, as far as I knew. And after that, she would have been with Jack. Safe? Yeah, safe. Jack was a lot of things, but I didn't see him sticking a knife into a woman. My back, well, yeah.

The hospital sent a driver and a medic, just in case. But all the medic had to do was help get Deanna's body on a stretcher and drape a sheet over it. I told them to get her into the morgue, if they had one, ask Dr. Schwartz to take a look, and tell him I'd be by later. Then I went to find Jack.

He was where I first spotted him, leaning against the railing outside the restaurant. I filled him in on the details, telling him it had at least been quick.

"What's going on, Billy?" He seemed at a loss, his eyes searching for an answer. It was an unusual look for Jack. "Why Deanna?"

"I don't know the big picture yet," I said, leaning my elbows on the paint-chipped rail. "I think Daniel Tamana saw or heard something between Henderson Field and arriving on Tulagi. He spoke to Deanna and went in search of Sam Chang. Whoever killed the three of them knew what Daniel was up to."

"But why wouldn't Daniel speak up right away?" Jack said. "Why endanger Deanna?"

"The odd thing is, she didn't seem in danger right away. Remember, Daniel was killed his first day on Tulagi. But both Sam Chang and Deanna were killed some time after that."

"So he was an immediate threat," Jack said. "The other two a potential threat. What changed to make the killer silence them both?"

"Chang would have been released from the hospital at some point, so if he knew something—"

"No, Billy," Jack said. "If he knew something, he knew it, hospital or not. That doesn't add up. What would he *do* once he got out, that's the question."

"Come here, to stay with one of his sisters, I'd guess."

"Which is where Deanna was headed as well," Jack said.

"To see one of the Chang sisters," I said. "And you."

"Look, Billy, let's get this out in the open. Do you think I killed her?"

"I don't have evidence to say you did. But you were there, and you're connected to her." I wasn't sure Jack was the type to drive a blade into a woman's heart. Break it, certainly. I noted there was no trace of blood on his right shirtsleeve. The knife thrust up into the heart wouldn't have sent blood spraying everywhere, but some trace would likely be on the murderer's hand and clothing.

"What about Tamana?" he asked.

"I could see you in a fight with Tamana," I answered truthfully. "Especially if he made some crack about getting run over by a Jap destroyer. I get the sense it would be easy to get under your skin about that. You didn't like losing your boat, and two men dead to boot. You don't want to be sent home, a failure, to face your old man while Joe Junior, the golden boy, gets his share of the glory in Europe."

"Don't call me a failure, goddamn it, and leave Joe out of this!" Jack turned to me and grabbed my arm. "And my father, too, if you know what's good for you."

"Like I said, Jack, I could see you getting into a fight no problem." I shook his hand off of my arm. "You've got a short fuse."

"Okay," he said, avoiding my eyes. "Point taken. What do we do now?"

"The bartender told me Deanna had asked him where Rui Chang lived. He didn't tell her, but we should check and see if Deanna found her. Or I should. You need to get back and talk with Cluster, right?"

"I have a little time," he said. "Want me to take you to Rui?"

"Nah, you go ahead and get back. No reason for you to get any more involved than you already are. One question, Jack. Do you own a knife?"

"Yes, I do," Jack said, his mouth set in a grim line. "I still have the sheath knife I wore that night in Blackett Strait. Right now it's in my footlocker back at the hospital. I thought I wasn't a suspect, Billy."

"Doesn't mean I don't have to ask questions, Jack. You're still someone with a connection to three murder victims. Don't get all huffy about it. And don't touch the knife."

"Billy, if I were going to kill anyone with a knife, I wouldn't be stupid enough to use my own. In case you hadn't noticed, there are weapons everywhere around here."

"Okay, okay," I said, my hands up in mock surrender. "You're right, but I have to have an answer in case anyone asks. Otherwise they'll accuse me of playing favorites, and you'll come under suspicion all over again. I'm only doing my job here, Jack."

"I guess I can't blame you for that," Jack said, sounding like he'd still like to. He removed his service cap and ran his fingers through the bushy hair hanging over his forehead. "First Kirksey and Marney, then Deanna. I got them killed on the 109, and if I hadn't asked Deanna out today, she'd still be alive. Someone has to answer for this, Billy."

"They will. That's why I'm here, Jack."

"You make sure you find out who killed Deanna and the other two, Billy," Jack said, tapping his finger on my chest. "And don't get in my way while you do it. I'm getting another boat and the Japs are going to pay for what they did. Bet on it."

With that, he was gone, leaving me on the wharf to wonder if Jack Kennedy had to put half a world between himself and his family to start acting like a man. Back home, he'd been shielded from any need to be responsible for others. Out here, it was different. No lawyers or police commissioners to call on when the going got tough. Jack knew how to take care of himself well enough. He'd been in and out of hospitals for his bad back and stomach problems plenty of times, and had done it alone, God help him. But I doubt he'd ever done much for anyone outside his family. People did things for the Kennedys, not the other way around.

This wasn't a mess he was walking away from, and I felt a bit of Boston Irish pride in his newfound grit.

CHAPTER EIGHTEEN

THE FIRST THING I needed to do was tell Hugh Sexton. He deserved to hear the news firsthand. Then Captain Ritchie.

Driving to Sexton's place, I began to notice all the communications wire. It was strung up along the road, on palm trees and hastily erected poles, occasionally branching off to a nearby building. Every military facility on Tulagi was connected via the headquarters switchboard. The wire was so much a part of the background I hadn't really noticed it.

Did Deanna make a call and unwittingly ask the killer to meet her in Chinatown? Or had someone overheard her plans with Gordie and Archer and arranged a rendezvous? However the killer found out about her visit there, it was seeking out the Chang sisters that triggered the killing, I was sure of it. There was no other reason for the killer to have waited so long to go after Deanna. He'd thought he was safe until she made that move. Jack didn't need to feel guilty about meeting her in Chinatown; he'd been secondary to her real reason for going.

I climbed the hill to Sexton's headquarters and was glad to find him alone. I had no desire to handle any more shock, grief, and anger than I had to. He smiled when I entered the room, but the grin didn't last as he took in the look on my face. I gave him the basic facts, quickly. Always best to get everything out right away, my dad always said. It's hard getting the news of a friend's or loved one's death, and sometimes people want to deny it, say it must be a mistake. But the more details you give them, without being unnecessarily gruesome, the quicker they accept the truth of what you've come to tell them. I found he was right about that, and that it was easier on me, too, whenever I handled things this way. Which may have been his point.

"Bloody hell," Sexton said, slumping in his chair next to the map table. "When is this going to end? It's awful enough losing people to the Japs, but to be murdered on a Chinatown street in Tulagi, that's appalling."

"Listen, Hugh," I said, wishing I had a precise answer. "I saw John Kari driving through Chinatown just before we found Deanna. He was in a hell of a rush."

"Do you think he—?"

"I don't know, but I have to talk to him. He may have seen something important and not even be aware of it," I said. Or, he may have killed her. I almost hoped so, since that would mean I had a real suspect.

"Quite right," Sexton said. "I think under the circumstances I should delay their departure for twenty-four hours. Do you still wish to go with them to Rendova?"

"Yes, unless something further develops here. That should give me enough time. You sure there's no problem?"

"No, not if it's only for one day. Weather's supposed to improve tomorrow, so I'll tell them that's the reason for the postponement. Let me know if you need anything else."

"Tell me more about Fred Archer," I said, recalling my conversation with him here the other night. He hadn't taken Deanna's rejection very politely. "Is he the type to fly off the handle?"

"Fred?" Sexton said, with a raised eyebrow. "You don't think he's involved in this?"

"You didn't answer my question," I said.

"Billy, it takes a certain kind of man to survive as a Coastwatcher. Fred had a reputation from before the war. He wasn't known to treat his workers with kindness. He paid them what he owed, no question about that. But he'd use his fists if he thought they were slacking off. I heard he once challenged any man who didn't like how he ran his plantation to take him on in a bare-knuckle fight. No one stepped forward."

"He sounds like the type to settle an argument with violence of one sort or another," I said.

"It's hard to judge islanders by our more civilized standards," Hugh said. "Often it's one plantation owner or manager and a larger crew of natives. And they can be quite cut off, like Silas Porter's place on Pavau. The only way in there is by boat, or footpath over the mountain. No way to summon help if you're hurt. Silas had a reputation as a hermit. Kept to himself, and quite happy about it, until the war came along. It's not a life every man takes to. Plenty come out to the islands to make their fortune and end up slinking back to Australia or England, dead broke."

"I get it," I said. "But I'll still have to check Fred's whereabouts. Jack said Deanna was getting a lift from Archer and Gordie to Chinatown. I'll need to see if that story checks out."

"Understood," Hugh said. "He and Gordie left for Sesapi to liaison with the PT boat skipper scheduled to take them to Ranongga. They're due at the communications center later to get their teleradio equipment packed up. Then they'll return to Sesapi and remain there organizing supplies this evening. I'll get in touch and let them know you'll be coming."

"You can call from here?" I asked.

"On that," Sexton said, gesturing to the field telephone in its canvas case on a table against the wall. "We call the main switchboard at the main navy base and they patch us through."

"They don't ask who it is at the switchboard?"

"Other than Coastwatcher Station, no. Feel free to use it if you want."

"No thanks, not unless I can make a collect call to Boston." I left, and it seemed clear that any number of people could have used this telephone, or others like it all across Tulagi, without being detected. But who was on the other end?

Sexton had said he'd contact the PT skipper to confirm the delay and inform him I might be along for the ride tomorrow. I'd stressed that the weather delay had to be believable. Otherwise, Kari could bolt and disappear into the bush on any one of several of the Solomon

Islands. Sexton understood, but I could see he was nearly as concerned at the prospect of losing a good Coastwatcher as he was about Deanna's death.

I decided to stop in Chinatown on my way to Sesapi. I needed to talk to Kaz's girl, and it was probably best to do it while he was away. I didn't want him to be offended by my questions and get gallant about it. In a murder investigation, pushy questions are sometimes all you have. In this investigation, that was true in spades. Besides, it was important to talk to her and Rui Chang in case they'd heard anything about Deanna's death. I was sure they didn't miss much of what happened in their domain.

I pulled over close to where Rui Chang's house was and surveyed the street. There were a half a dozen or so places where Jai-li could've lived, but I didn't feel like knocking on that many doors. I chose an establishment that sold vegetables and asked the storekeeper if he knew where Jai-li Chang lived. That got a lot of negative headshaking as he showed me strings of red peppers hanging from the low beams, apparently offering me a good price. I declined, backing out under a barrage of Chinese that could have been curses or the special of the day.

I got out into the street in time to see what I'd hoped to spot. A kid racing out the back of the store, cutting through the rear of two buildings, and showing up close to a house painted a gleaming white with azure blue awnings shading the windows from the hot sun. I walked closer and waited, hands clasped behind my back, away from the automatic in my holster.

It didn't take long. A single guy descended from the house, dressed in a loose white shirt that obviously covered a pistol in his waistband. He was big for a Chinese guy, broad shouldered, with big hands. I caught his glance off to my side and knew there was another guy behind me, but that was okay. I didn't come for trouble. I hoped the same was true of them.

"I'd like to speak with Jai-li Chang, please," I said.

"She is grieving the loss of her brother," the big guy said. "She sees no one."

"Tell her I've come to pay my respects," I said. "I'm a friend of the baron's, and I'm investigating the murder of Shan Chang." I figured this would have been one of the few occasions when Kaz had thrown his title around.

"Follow me," he said, after a moment's consideration. I'd guessed right.

We took the steps up to the house and stood under the shade of a palm tree. The bodyguard tapped my holster and I nodded. He took my pistol and handed it off to his silent partner, then patted me down. I had a jackknife in my pocket, which he also handed off.

"Apologies, but no weapons in the house," he said. He knocked on the door, which opened a few seconds later, the metallic sound of bolts and latches being released evident even through the heavy wood door.

"Is this the usual level of security?" I asked.

"A member of the family has been killed, and another murder committed nearby," he said. "I am Zhou. It is my duty to allow no harm to come to Jai-li Chang."

"Has anyone tried to harm Jai-li recently?" I asked.

"Piotr said you were quite direct, Lieutenant Boyle," a voice spoke from the shadows. Jai-li moved into the hallway, the light sparkling off her white silk dress, the design of a ferocious dragon embroidered in golden thread across her breast.

"Miss Chang," I said, giving a little bow in her direction. I don't even know why I did it; maybe she seemed a bit like oriental royalty. "Please accept my condolences. May I ask you a few questions?"

"Certainly, Lieutenant Boyle," she said, and led me into a sitting room. The rattan chairs were set at a far end of the room, away from the open windows. Zhou glanced outside and then retreated to the doorway. This was a very careful household. "I will assist in any way I can."

"Thank you. First, can you tell me if you knew Daniel Tamana?"

"The Melanesian boy who was killed? No, I did not."

"Were you aware he'd been asking for your brother the day he was killed?" I asked.

"We did hear reports that someone was asking for a member of the family," she admitted. "As you can see, we are very careful about such things." I gave her points for honesty. Rui Chang hadn't disclosed any such knowledge.

"Do you have any idea why Daniel would have been asking for him?"

"None," Jai-li said. "Do you?"

"Not yet. But I believe there is a connection between the two deaths. I think it is possible that Daniel knew your brother from Vella Lavella. He worked on a coffee plantation on Rendova and then for a coconut planter on Pavau."

"It is possible," Jai-li said, her hands folded gracefully in her lap. She had a soft, rounded face, and full lips adorned with red lipstick. Rui might have had a few years on her, plus sharper cheekbones and heavier makeup. Wisps of black hair fell across Jai-li's face, giving her an innocent and youthful look. I knew she was young, but I wasn't certain of her innocence. "Shan did much business on Rendova, less so on Pavau, I think. It was somewhat distant and isolated."

"Are your brother's business interests the same as yours?" I asked, trying for the most delicate phrase.

"Piotr said you were a police detective before the war," Jai-li said with a gentle laugh. "And I see you still are."

"All I do is ask questions," I said, spreading my hands in an open gesture. "Which often makes people uncomfortable. In normal conversation, people avoid a question they don't want to discuss. The person who inquired feels bad and drops it, maybe even apologizes for intruding. But the police don't mind making people uncomfortable. It often helps to reveal the truth, even if it may be unpleasant."

"Yes," she said. "We do not discuss family business quite so readily here."

"A Chinese custom?" I asked.

"Perhaps," she said, with a small shrug of the shoulders. "It may have more to do with our status as outsiders. The English tolerate us because we run many small businesses and keep the goods and supplies they rely on flowing to them. The Melanesians like the things we sell them, since they have no means to produce much on their own. But there is always a resentment of outsiders lurking beneath the civilized veneer of this colonial outpost, don't you think? Especially successful ones."

"Oh, I think the civilized veneer is stretched pretty thin everywhere these days," I said. "Now, I must ask again about your brother's business interests and your own."

"Let me say this, Lieutenant Boyle," Jai-li began, folding her hands demurely in her lap. "If either Rui or myself were found to have been killed, there would be questions. Are you familiar with the triads?" The last word came out as a whisper.

"Yes," I said. "Chinese gangs, like the Italian Mafia."

"Societies," she said, with a slight shrug, as if to show it was all in how you looked at things. "We are not members, but we are associated with the Wo Shing Wo triad. We provide assistance from time to time. Assistance of a nature I decline to discuss."

"You're a Blue Lantern, then," I said.

"Lieutenant Boyle, you surprise me," Jai-li said, gracing me with a smile. "Yes, that is the correct term. We are not initiates, but rather associates. I only tell you this much to draw a distinction between my brother and Rui and I. He wanted no part of such business. Even though he was the oldest, he never sought to continue in our father's footsteps. He wanted his own life, free of any obligations to the society."

"But he needed money, I understand."

"Yes. When the Japanese came, he lost all his goods and had to flee into the jungle. Since he was a kind man, many of the planters owed him money. Who knows when they would have paid? After the war? Or might they simply walk away from their losses? Shan was not in a good position, financially."

"The bamboo plant your sister gave Jack Kennedy to deliver—that was not simply a gift, was it?"

"No, I am afraid not," Jai-li said. "Rui is a better businesswoman than I. Ruthless, some say. She wanted to remind Shan of his obligation to us, and his foolishness in striking out on his own. I hope you do not need to speak further of this. It does not reflect well upon our family."

"I will have to speak to Rui," I said.

"That will not be possible for a few days," she said. "My sister has sailed for New Caledonia. A business trip to meet with our French colleagues there. Necessary, even with Shan's death."

"Thank you for being honest with me, Miss Chang," I said. "It helps us narrow the investigation."

"Please, call me Jai-li, Billy." she said. "The baron spoke so much about you, I feel we are already friends." I was surprised but pleased that she allowed this informality, so I decided to press my luck.

"Then let me take a little more of your time, Jai-li. I assume you've heard of the killing today. Deanna Pendleton was stabbed not far from here."

"Yes, of course. I was very sad to hear of it. We met at Captain Sexton's and I was impressed by her bravery."

"Do your people have any idea who could have done it?" I asked.

"Only that it would not have been anyone from Chinatown. We frown on violence here. We do not wish to be declared off limits by your shore patrol. It is important that the servicemen who come here feel safe. Safe enough to freely spend and contribute to the community."

"When you say you frown upon violence, what do you mean exactly?" I understood the part about contributions. Every merchant in town paid a percentage to the Changs, so it was in everyone's interest to keep crime down. The gritty street type of crime at least.

"That it would make Zhou extremely unhappy, which would not be good for the parties involved. Or their families. Is that clear enough?"

"I expect that approach works quite well," I said. "So no reports of suspicious strangers or a sighting of someone with Deanna?"

"Billy, to most of the people here, all *gwai lo* look alike."

"White ghost," I said. "Or is it white devil?" I'd heard the term plenty back in Boston's Chinatown, never uttered in a kindly tone.

"It does mean white ghost, from the color of your skin," she said. "Is there a connection between Shan's death and the others?"

"I think so," I said, suspecting I could trust Jai-li, at least as long as I didn't borrow money from her. "I believe Daniel Tamana, your brother, and Deanna all knew something that got them killed. Shan may not have been aware of what he knew, or the implications of it. Daniel knew for sure, and Deanna must have figured it out for herself."

"And all three are dead, with no trace of the killer," Jai-li said. "It is indeed a white ghost you are seeking."

CHAPTER NINETEEN

As I WAS leaving, Jai-li told me to please ask for any assistance I might need to find her brother's killer. She told me to ask for Zhou. Jai-li said goodbye and left me with Zhou in the hallway, waiting for my automatic to be returned. In a few minutes a servant delivered the .45 and my jackknife on a platter. Classy.

"They've been cleaned," I said, feeling a slight oily sheen on the knife.

"In this climate, rust is the enemy of any metal," Zhou said. "I hope you don't mind that we took the liberty."

"Not at all," I said, holstering the pistol, wondering if a pressed uniform and well-oiled pistol were specialties of the house. "I'll be in touch."

"Ask anyone in Chinatown for Zhou," he said. "They will bring you right to me."

"What if I ask for Jai-li?"

"They will bring you to me even faster." I think he almost smiled.

It DIDN'T TAKE long to drive to the PT base at Sesapi, where Kaz and I had first stepped foot on Tulagi. By now, if luck were on his side, he would have seen Dickie Miller. Considering his choice of Chang sisters, luck was definitely running Kaz's way. Or had Jai-li chosen Kaz? Still, it was good luck any way it shook out.

I hoped for some of that luck to rub off when I talked to John Kari. I had him at the scene of the crime, but that was it. I needed something else, any kind of clue to support his involvement. I remembered that the signals unit was housed in an old police station, and hoped I'd have need of a cell there before long, at least for one of the murders.

I parked the jeep near the wharf, where a line of ten PTs were moored. Sesapi was hardly the garden spot of Tulagi. On the steep bank opposite the wharf, tents and jury-rigged lean-tos held everything from crew's quarters to machine shops. Palm fronds and coconut logs were the mainstay of these structures, which gave shade and looked like they might keep out the rain if it held to light showers. This was a working PT base, miles from the kind of navy Captain Ritchie was so fond of.

Well-trodden paths led in every direction, some of them to winding steps set into the embankment. I took them through a beehive of activity as sailors rolled steel drums of aviation gas to be stacked up under crudely painted signs.

FLAMMABLE. NO SMOKING.

Yeah, no kidding. I reminded myself to take a different route back, not that it would matter much if one of these fifty-five gallon cans went up. I was after PT-157, Lieutenant Liebenow commanding. Sexton had told me I could hitch a ride to Rendova with them, since they were taking Porter and Kari in that direction. I found it by spotting Silas Porter sitting on a crate dockside, a pile of radio gear beside him. Next to him was John Kari, cleaning an M1 carbine. They wore identical sheath knives.

"Hello, Billy," Kari said, looking up from his work.

"Hear you're coming along for the ride to Rendova," Porter said.

"I am. I got held up in Chinatown, but then I heard you wouldn't be leaving until tomorrow." I watched their faces. Both gave weary nods, the sad acceptance of death in wartime.

"Poor Deanna," Porter said. "Hard to believe after all she endured."

"Any idea who did it?" Kari asked, wiping his hands and wrapping the carbine in heavy waxed paper before taking a Thompson submachine gun and rubbing a greasy brown substance all over it.

"No, but I have a couple of clues," I said, taking a seat on one of the wooden crates. "What is that stuff?" I asked innocently as I ran my fingers along the stock of the Thompson, and the Cosmoline came away brown, the color of the stain on Deanna's collar.

"Cosmoline," Kari answered. "It's to preserve the weapons. We're going to stash a couple of crates in the jungle, for use by the Zeleboes on Choiseul."

"They're a tribe who are quite anti-Japanese," Porter explained. "They lost a lot of men when the Japs invaded. Plantation workers, that sort of thing. When we retake Choiseul, these will come in handy. We'll hit the Japs from behind while your lot take the beaches."

"But until then, the metal would rust and the wood rot without lots of Cosmoline," Kari said. "It's easy to put on but the devil's own work to clean off." He started to disassemble the Thompson and work the greasy mixture into the weapon.

"Looks like you've been at it all day," I said, trying to sound impressed with his work ethic.

"Silas is the one with the hard job," Kari said, nodding in the direction of the radio parts. "When he tested everything this morning, he found a bad output coil in our transmitter."

"We had a spare, but it wouldn't do to start off using it right away," Porter said. "John fetched one from the communications section back at the base. So we were glad enough of the delay. Can't nip off for spare parts once you're out in the bush."

"Right," I said. "John, I think I saw you on the road when I was in Chinatown. Driving pretty fast, if I recall."

"Yes, on my way back here. I saw the ambulance but had no idea it was for Deanna. It's so hard to believe, even now." He shook his head sadly, and I thought Porter shot a glance in my direction. Protective, or did he have his own suspicions? John Kari was a hard read; with his dark skin, bushy hair, shell necklace, and precise English accent, he was a walking contradiction. Not like anyone I'd ever met before. I was having a tough time deciding if he was a practiced liar or expressing genuine grief and surprise.

"John always drives fast," Porter explained. "He'd never driven a vehicle before he was nineteen. Not many in the islands. Not many roads, for that matter."

"I do like speed, I must admit," Kari said with a gentle laugh. I watched him work, his small, delicate hands caressing the weaponry as he spread the Cosmoline everywhere. Were those the hands of a killer? I looked at their knives again. He and Porter wore identical sheaths, the narrow grip of a dagger visible.

"What kind of knives are those?" I asked. "They don't look like regular army issue."

"They're not," Porter said, drawing his out and handing it to me. "They're Marine Raider stilettos. A Raider battalion came through here a few weeks ago and we traded for them."

"They feel deadly," I said, hefting the cold cross-hatched grip in my palm, the weight of it heavy, making it well suited for a sudden thrust.

"That's all they're made for," Kari said. "Killing."

"The Marine Raiders were getting a new knife issued," Porter explained. "It's called the Ka-Bar, and it's a combination fighting-and-utility knife. This stiletto is too thin and pointy to be of any practical use, like opening a can of rations or prying open a crate. But for a quick kill, it's perfect. It's designed to be lethal and good for little else."

"It sounds like you've used it," I said.

"Not this Marine model, no," Porter said. "I had an Australian commando stiletto, and used it on a number of occasions. But it was lost on the way here, so when I saw the Raiders were trading theirs, I snapped them up. Gave them to Hugh, Fred, Gordie, John, and a few others."

"See how the pommel has a small, hard knob?" Kari said. "Good for bashing heads if the blade doesn't do the job." There was an edge of steel at the end of the grip, and my first thought was of Daniel Tamana being hit from behind. But the knob was too small. It would definitely crack bone if the strike were forceful enough, but it wouldn't make the kind of depression fracture we saw on Daniel's skull.

"If you had to use it, I guess it would mean you were in a tight spot," I said, handing it back to Porter.

"True enough," Porter said. "I had to take out a Jap sentry once. A small patrol had gone by on a path we were about to cross. We had ten natives with us, carrying the radio to a new location. The patrol halted and left one man to guard a bend in the trail as they took a break about twenty yards away by a stream. We could've waited them out, but the bugger wandered into the bush to relieve himself. Stepped right on one of the native's hands. The lad was well hidden and didn't let out a sound, but I could tell the Jap knew something was wrong. He was still pissing when I grabbed his jaw from behind and stabbed him in the heart. Bastard was dead before he hit the ground. I hope these Yank blades are as good as that Australian one. Pity I lost it."

"I hear Archer and Gordie are going out soon," I said. "They taking theirs along?"

"I saw them not half an hour ago," Kari said. "They had them on, alright. Impresses the PT crew, makes them think we're dangerous."

"What about you, John? Have you used a knife up close?" I watched his eyes, alert for any telltale nervousness.

"Not the knife, no," he said. "Rifle and machete, yes. Of course, I wouldn't have had a chance to use *this* knife, since Silas gave it to me only a fortnight ago." He smiled, forgiving me my error.

"Of course," I said. "Where are Gordie and Archer, by the way? I need to talk to them about Deanna. I understand they were the ones who dropped her off in Chinatown this morning."

"End of the dock," Porter said. "PT-169. That's Phil Cotter's boat. The fellow who left Kennedy and his crew adrift in Blackett Strait."

"I hadn't heard it was Fred and Gordie who brought Deanna to Chinatown," Kari said. "Do you think—?" He let the question hang in the air. Porter gave me a studied glance again, then looked away.

"Listen, John," Porter said before I could answer, "Fred was sweet on Deanna, but he wouldn't hurt her, would he?"

"The man has a temper, there's no denying it," Kari said.

"I heard he was pretty tough on his workers, but that's not the same thing as murdering a defenseless woman," I said, watching again for a reaction. "Who would do that?"

"That's what you're supposed to be finding out, isn't it?" Porter said, his tone harsh and demanding.

"Is that true, what I've heard?"

"Yes, it is," Kari said, wiping his hands on a greasy rag. "He's the type of man who enjoys a fight and doesn't mind a few split knuckles along the way. I wouldn't want to work for him, but I wouldn't mind having him on my side in a fight either."

"That's helpful," I said. "Thanks. See you later."

I ambled off to find PT-169. I was sure that Deanna had been killed with a dagger or stiletto. Her wound was small and the external blood loss was minimal. The fact that half a dozen or so Coastwatchers, and whoever else the Marine Raiders traded with, had the right kind of knife for the job didn't help matters. In any case, I'd wait for Doc Schwartz to confirm my theory when I saw him at the hospital.

Lieutenant Cotter was at the back of my mind as well. Jack had practically called him a coward for leaving the crew of PT-109 in Blackett Strait that night. And a liar for claiming he had searched for them. If the Coastwatcher's report of seeing a burning hulk from Kolombangara was accurate, I couldn't see how Cotter missed it in the dark Pacific night. Unless he was headed in the opposite direction.

Did that make him a suspect? It was hard to see how, except for the possibility that he'd tried to frame Jack to get back at him and discredit his accusations. One killing was worth considering. With each additional death, it made less and less sense. He could have followed Jack into the hospital, watched him deliver the plant to Sam Chang, and then strangled him, hoping that frame would fit.

But Deanna? Could he kill a woman in cold blood? No, not even my fevered imagination could work that one out.

The 169 had a lived-in look. A canvas tarp was hung across the deck to provide partial shade for the crew busy cleaning the twin fifty-caliber machine guns and the twenty-millimeter cannon mounted aft. Skivvies and sun-bleached khakis were draped over lines, drying in the sun. Fred and Gordie were on the dock, under a canvas lean-to doing the same Cosmoline job that John Kari had been working on.

"What ho, Billy!" Gordie said in greeting, holding up a brown, grease-covered hand. "What brings you here?" Fred gave me a curt nod, then returned to slathering Cosmoline over a carbine.

"I'm going up to Rendova with Silas and John," I said by way of an answer. I pulled a crate into the shade of the lean-to and joined them. "You've heard about Deanna, I suppose."

"God-awful," Gordie spat. Sweat dripped from his bald head and he wiped it away with a shirtsleeve.

"Is it related to the other deaths?" Archer asked, his mouth set in a grim line.

"Why do you say that?" I asked, glancing at their web belts. Each wore a knife identical to the one Porter showed me.

"Well, seems odd, doesn't it? I mean, we've seen plenty of death in this war, but I always thought murder might take a holiday, you know? Now all of a sudden, we've got three bodies."

"Yeah, it's strange," I said, as if the thought hadn't yet occurred to me. "I understand you fellows gave Deanna a ride into Chinatown. Is that right?"

"That we did," Gordie offered. "She seemed awfully keen on getting there in advance of her luncheon with the Kennedy boy. We left Hugh's place, made a stop at the signals section, picked up these weapons and a case of Cosmoline from the quartermaster, then made the stop in Chinatown."

"Did she seem upset or worried?" I asked.

"Not that I saw," Gordie said. "Fred?"

"She was her usual self," Fred said. "Friendly and warm. Who'd want to hurt her, that's what I'd like to know." His voice caught on those last words, and his emotion seemed sincere. When people lie about an emotion, it's easier to tell. Most times they oversell it. But Fred was working at keeping it bottled up, and that's harder to fake.

"Did you see anyone approach Deanna after you dropped her off?"

"No," Gordie said, giving it a bit of thought. "Not at all. She asked us if we knew where either of the Chang sisters lived, but we hadn't a clue. Did you see anything, Fred?"

"I watched her for a minute," Fred said, "to make sure she was alright, you know. But she disappeared into the crowd on the sidewalk. No sign of her after that."

"I went into a couple of stores," Gordie said. "Never laid eyes on her again."

"Were you with him, Fred?"

"No," Archer said. "Gordie likes those hot dried peppers the Chinese grocers sell. He went off in search of a supply of those. I stayed with the jeep."

"They don't agree with Fred's stomach," Gordie said. "But I like a bit of spice out in the bush. Helps when you have nothing but taro or rice to eat."

"I bet," I said, wondering how long Fred had while Gordie was gone. "I might get some myself. Which shop?"

"Fei Long's place, near the south end of the wharf. I wanted one of those long strings, not loose peppers. Took a while to find."

"I'll check it out," I said. "Good luck with the Cosmoline. Nasty stuff."

"But worth it," Fred said. "When we have to retrieve these carbines, they'll be as good as new. And the quartermaster chaps did us a favor. They greased a half dozen. Saves a bit of time." He gestured in the direction of two crates, stenciled with US CARBINE, CAL. .30, M1. There were smears of dried Cosmoline on the side of each one.

"Messy," I said absently, running my finger across the nearest case, feeling the waxy goo.

"That's what Deanna said, poor thing," Gordie said.

It was a mess. I left them to their work, wondering what the hell to do next. I had four Coastwatchers, all armed with the kind of knife that could have killed Deanna. Three of them were near the scene of her murder. They'd had plenty of contact with Cosmoline during the time in question. So had Silas Porter, but there was no evidence he'd been in Chinatown. I hadn't known many hermits in my time, but I'd bet not many got mixed up with enough people to want to murder three of them. At least not after hiding themselves away from the world for so long; no one made enemies that fast. Still, all four had commando knives, and all four had handled Cosmoline. Even so, Deanna could have picked up a smudge on her own at the quartermaster's.

It looked like I wouldn't need that jail cell anytime soon, unless I were willing to toss them all in.

CHAPTER TWENTY

I DROVE BACK to the hospital, trying to put together what I knew about Deanna's death.

She'd been at Hugh Sexton's in the morning. Then Fred and Gordie headed out with her in their jeep, making stops at the signals section and the quartermaster's, both on the naval base. They took on cases of carbines, two of which were smeared with Cosmoline, which Deanna could have picked up, smudging her collar. Meanwhile, over at the Sesapi PT base, Silas Porter calls the signals people to tell them John Kari is on his way for a new transmitter doohickey. Kari leaves, his hands probably still greasy with Cosmoline. Fred and Gordie stop in Chinatown. Wait—had they and Kari crossed paths? Maybe not. There were a couple of routes to take once past Chinatown, so they may well not have spotted each other.

So Fred and Gordie drop off Deanna. Fred stays in the jeep, watching her walk into the crowded street. Gordie goes off to buy hot peppers. Either one of them could have followed Deanna, pulled her aside, and taken her into that alleyway. A secret to be shared, no one must overhear. She'd trust them, wouldn't she? Or would she be nervous about Fred pulling her off the street, after his behavior at the party? She'd be more likely to trust Gordie. Cheerful, portly Gordie.

Or, did John Kari stop on his way back from the base? Then jump into his jeep and flee the scene at top speed? But why would he attack Deanna? I had no answer for that. Even Fred Archer's temper and desire for Deanna didn't add up to murder, at least not this kind of murder. His kind of guy might go too far late at night, half drunk and in a jealous rage. But in the light of day, while preparing for a mission? I couldn't see it.

I couldn't see much at all. Means and opportunity were everywhere. Motive was missing in action. If I caught a glimpse of the motive that drove these murders, all might be revealed. I parked the jeep in front of the hospital, hoping Kaz would be back soon to help me muddle through all this.

I went off to find Schwartz. He wasn't happy when I did.

"Boyle, I'm not the local coroner, dammit," Schwartz said as he led me into the damp basement morgue.

"If the Brits had one here, he skedaddled to Australia long ago," I said. "Sorry, but I wanted to be sure a medical expert examined her for evidence."

"In here," he said, opening a thick wooden door, leading into a chamber dug out of the side of the hill the hospital stood on. It was cool, about as chilled as anywhere on Tulagi could be. He pulled a cord and a harsh light illuminated a shroud-covered body. Deanna Pendleton.

"You probably saw the marks," Schwartz said, pulling the sheet and uncovering her head and shoulders. Her eyes were milky and skin pale, but her face was still beautiful. "A strong left hand, I'd say. In strangulation cases, you often see oval finger marks, with the thumb doing the most damage, like on Sam Chang's neck. You can see here that the other fingers left fainter marks." He traced a finger along the left side of her neck.

"Was she strangled?" I asked, working at not looking into those dead eyes.

"No, I don't think so," Schwartz said. "It was a very forceful grip, but I didn't see any other swelling or evident damage to the larynx. I could open up the neck and check if you want."

"No," I said, my voice a clipped whisper. I wanted to say *her* neck, but I held back. He was just being clinical.

"It doesn't really matter," he said, covering her face before folding the sheet up on her right side, treating her with more modesty than a real coroner would have. "Not with this knife wound. Right between the fourth and fifth ribs into the heart." The blood had been washed away, and all that was left was a narrow slit, a tear in the pearly white skin to the side of her left breast.

"That would have killed her, right?"

"Yes, and quickly, too," Schwartz said. "Look at the incision left by the blade. See how it's tapered at both ends? That means the blade was sharp on both sides. Fairly thin, too, based on the width of the opening."

"Like a Marine Raider stiletto," I said.

"I wouldn't know," Schwartz said. "I've never seen one of those. But on nearly any Saturday night in the County General ER, you'd see a wound like this. Usually made by an Italian switchblade, sharpened on both sides." He covered her back up and sighed, shaking his head.

"Thanks, Doc," I said. "What'll happen now? With her body, I mean."

"I contacted Graves Registration, but since she's a civilian, they're not sure what to do. You have any idea how to contact next of kin?"

"All I know is she worked with a Methodist missionary still hiding out on Vella Lavella."

"Damn," Schwartz muttered as he turned off the light and shut the heavy door behind us. "Any idea who did it?"

"*Gwai lo,*" I said. "The white ghost."

I made my way back to my quarters, the air still thick with heat even as the sun set over the Slot. Kao was waiting on the verandah with a message from Captain Ritchie, who wanted to see me, in his quarters this time. He had the old district commissioner's place, a short walk up the dusty lane. I took my time, trying to figure out a way to report on what I'd found that made any sense at all.

I came up empty.

"Lieutenant Boyle," Ritchie greeted me from a chair on his verandah, beckoning in a casual manner.

"You asked to see me, Captain?" I said, snapping a salute and standing at attention, sweat dripping from my brow.

"At ease, Boyle," Ritchie said. "Take a load off." He gestured with his thumb toward the worn wicker chair next to him, clinking the remains of ice cubes in his glass. "Join me?"

"Wouldn't mind it a bit," I said. "You have ice?"

"Yep. Got an icebox inside and a refrigeration unit on base. They deliver a block of ice every day. Keeps the food cold and the bourbon the way I like it. Sali, more ice," he hollered in the general direction of the house. In two shakes his houseboy, dressed in a *lap-lap* much like Kao's, raced out with a glass and a bowl of chipped ice. Sali retreated inside and Ritchie poured the bourbon, leaving the ice to me. I took enough to chill the amber liquid, but not enough to look greedy. Out here, ice probably commanded a high price on the black market.

"Cheers," I said, raising my glass. We touched glasses and drank. Ritchie took a long gulp, and I wondered how long cocktail hour had been going on.

"Sad business about Miss Pendleton," he said, a sigh escaping his lips as he worked a piece of ice around in his mouth.

"Yes sir," I said. "I think there's a good chance all three killings are related. Tamana, Chang, and Deanna."

"Sounds like you're making progress," Ritchie said, in an encouraging voice. I liked him a lot better with bourbon on the verandah than during office hours.

"Some," I said. "I know Daniel Tamana went looking for Sam Chang in Chinatown. He'd heard Chang was on Tulagi, but didn't know he was in the hospital. And Tamana and Deanna were observed having a hushed conversation the day Daniel was killed. I think whoever murdered Daniel is cleaning up loose ends."

"Surely you don't suspect Lieutenant Kennedy of killing all three people? Especially since he was involved with the Pendleton girl." Ritchie took another drink and topped off our glasses.

"I don't think he killed Deanna," I said. "But a guy is always a suspect when his girlfriend is found dead, until he's ruled out."

"But in this case there's no evidence against him?" Ritchie said.

"No, sir."

"If the killings are related, and you don't think Kennedy killed the girl, then you probably don't suspect him in the other two deaths, right?" It was an undeniable piece of logic; I could see the bourbon wasn't getting in the way of clear thinking for Ritchie.

"I can't be certain about Daniel yet," I said. "There's something about Jack's state of mind that makes him volatile. He can take offense easily, and I don't know what may have passed between Daniel and him if they met on that beach."

"What about the Chinaman? Chang. Do you suspect Kennedy of his death?"

"No, Captain, I don't. Jack might have a sudden fit of temper, but he wouldn't strangle a man in a hospital bed."

"It sounds to me, Lieutenant," Ritchie said, taking another sip and smacking his lips, "that you're hanging onto the slightest pretext to suspect Kennedy of being involved in Tamana's death. Should I suspect you're prejudiced against him?"

"I know him pretty well, Captain," I said. "Which means I know his faults as well as his strengths."

"Fair enough," Ritchie said. "I want you to think all this through very thoroughly. Then tomorrow, unless you come up with any evidence to the contrary, I want an official report by the end of the day, exonerating Kennedy of any suspicion in regard to these killings." With that, he crunched ice between his teeth.

"Regardless of the facts, Captain?" Now it was my turn to drain the glass.

"You don't have facts, Boyle. You have suspicion and maybe jealousy, I don't know. And I don't care. What I do know is that back in the States you wouldn't have enough evidence to arrest Kennedy, would you?"

"No. But he'd still be a suspect in any decent investigation," I said.

"That's in a perfect world, Boyle. Perhaps you haven't noticed, but we're in the Solomon Islands and at war. Hardly perfect. Now listen and listen good," Ritchie said, leaning forward, his elbows resting on his knees. "The navy has decided Jack Kennedy is a hero. Not too long ago, there was talk of a court-martial, but that's changed. You can guess why."

"He doesn't consider himself a hero, Captain."

"Do you imagine what that little runt thinks matters a whit? The navy needs a hero, so now that's his job. He's getting a new command and everyone is going to look sharp about it. No lingering suspicions. Understood?"

"Yeah, I get it, Captain. Joe Senior pulled the strings in Boston and I end up with iced bourbon on Tulagi for my troubles." To my surprise, Ritchie laughed and poured me another. I'd half expected to be arrested for insubordination.

"You might not be far off the mark, Boyle," he said. "I've learned not to question the origin of orders like these. It was a strong recommendation, actually. Nothing in writing, of course. Merely a comment that it would be in the best interests of the service."

Maybe it was the bourbon, or the ice, but I did feel for Ritchie. He was in a tight spot.

"Sali!" he yelled. "Play the piano, willya?"

"Yes, boss," Sali answered, and soon we were serenaded by a tune that sounded familiar, on a piano that was almost in tune.

"You do have all the comforts of home," I said. "Is that 'I'll String Along With You' he's playing?"

"A reasonable facsimile," Ritchie said. "Sali actually knows classical stuff, too. He learned at the mission school. Let me tell you a story about that piano. You know this was the Japanese commander's place after the Brits bugged out in early '42?"

"Best house on the island," I said.

"Of course. Well, when I arrived, not long after the marines secured the island, the place was all shot up. There'd been fighting along this road, and the Japs didn't give up easily. For some reason, that piano had been moved outside. Maybe the Jap commander thought it would be safer, I don't know. Anyway, I come walking up the path, scouting out the housing, and I find a marine playing that piano. One leg was splintered and the whole thing was at an angle, but he was playing the same song. Better than Sali is. There were dead Japs all around, shell craters and weapons lying everywhere. But that marine was lost in the song."

"Something about not being an angel, right?" I said.

"Yeah. Because angels are so few. I'm a lot like that piano, Boyle. Left out to rot on Tulagi. But I can still play a tune. String along with me, Boyle. You're no angel, but you'll do."

I sat back and drank the bourbon, savoring the ice as it sloshed into my mouth. I didn't like being told what to do. By anyone, much less a navy captain who was following orders originating from half a world away in Hyannisport. But I had to admit, the facts didn't amount to much of a case against Jack. I knew I was close to digging in my heels on this one simply because Ritchie was Ritchie and Jack was a Kennedy.

"If I write this report, Captain, what happens then?"

"As far as I'm concerned, Boyle, you can go back to where you came from."

"How about I stick around? Find out who really killed those three?"

"I get my report? Full exoneration for Kennedy?"

"First thing in the morning," I said.

"Sali! More ice!"

CHAPTER TWENTY-ONE

THE NEXT MORNING, Yeoman Howe kept my coffee cup filled as I pecked away at a typewriter outside Captain Ritchie's office. Which was fortunate, since the bourbon and ice had gone down smoothly last night. I needed the java to counteract a headache and to withstand Ritchie's prompting to get on with it and type faster. He was definitely the type of officer best experienced through a haze of alcohol.

I worked it like a police report. Short sentences and to the point. I kept the statement focused on Jack and Daniel Tamana, no mention of the other murders. Jack had recently met the deceased. He found the body of the deceased on his morning walk from the hospital grounds. No evidence of any connection between the two other than a brief conversation the day before. Lieutenant Kennedy had been cooperative in all respects. Well, that was laying it on a bit thick, but thick was what Ritchie wanted.

I dated and signed it, and handed it over to Yeoman Howe, who brought it into Ritchie's office. I helped myself to more coffee with a heaping teaspoon of sugar. One thing about the navy; they had all these ships, and besides fighting, they carried tons of supplies all over the world. Cold beer, ice, sugar, the kinds of things in short supply in North Africa and Sicily—on army bases, at least.

"Very good, Lieutenant Boyle," Ritchie said, waving the report in my direction as Howe returned to his desk. "See Yeoman Howe if you need anything, and keep me posted." He shut his door and I could hear him whistling a tune. "I'll String Along With You," of course.

"I'm at your service, Lieutenant," Howe said. "The captain's a happy man this morning."

"I live to make captains happy," I said. "Can you find out if Lieutenant Kazimierz is coming back from Brisbane today?"

"I'll send a radio message. They'll have a manifest for the PBY flight and I can find out if he's on it."

"Okay. I'm heading over to Sesapi. I'll call or swing back here later this morning."

I drove the now familiar route to the PT base at Sesapi, wondering what the payoff would be for Ritchie. A promotion? A job after the war with the Kennedy business empire? Maybe politics? Well, good luck to him, whatever it was. He'd find out soon enough there was always a price to be paid, even when you thought you were square with the Kennedy clan.

I parked the jeep and walked around the fuel dump this time, the odor of gas heavy in the humid air. The tepid harbor water did little to cool the oppressive air. Men were already stripped to the waist, glistening with sweat as they carried supplies aboard PT boats, cleaned machine guns, or worked on engines in what shade they could find. Speed was their best defense, and lives depended on those engines being in top shape. Jack had been idling on only one engine when he'd been hit, and I'd heard him harshly criticized, since it had given him no time to get out of the way of the destroyer. But what else could he have done? If all the engines had been running at more than idle, the phosphorescence from the churning water would have highlighted his position to any Kawanishi in the night sky. Jack had played the odds, but sometimes fate has a way of dealing a losing hand even when you're holding aces.

A clanking rumble jolted me out of my musings as cries of warning echoed from above. I looked in time to see two steel drums careening down the hill, straight at me, each full of high-octane aviation gas. I dropped and rolled toward the embankment, hoping to evade the avalanche. One drum hit a rock and bounced over it with a metallic *clang*, crashing into the dock a few feet from my head. The other rolled straight down and into the water, missing me by inches.

A gaggle of sailors ran to me, yammering a bunch of excuses and apologies. No one knew how it could have happened; all the drums were supposed to be secured on pallets; thank God I wasn't hurt; was I okay?

"Don't worry, boys, accidents happen," I told them as I picked myself up. But I doubted this was an accident. I scanned the gathering crowd and the wharf for a familiar face. A suspect. I didn't see any of the cast of characters running through my mind. But who would hang around? The place was a warren of paths and rickety wooden stairs. The stairs through the fuel dump had a couple of switchbacks; it would have been a simple matter to shoulder a couple of steel drums from their resting place while no one was looking.

I moved on, eager to see whoever I might run into. I spotted Silas Porter and John Kari, disembarking from PT-157. An officer in bleached khakis was following them to the shade provided by camouflage netting draped from the bow of the boat to poles set along the dock.

"Billy," Kari said, waving me over. "Come meet Lieutenant Liebenow. He's in command of the 157." He was all innocent smiles. Porter looked nonchalant, even bored.

"Call me Bud," Leibenow said. "I hear you're coming along for the ride to Rendova." None of them made any mention of the accident, not that it would have rated headlines. Sesapi was a busy place, thick with weapons and machinery, accidents waiting to happen.

"I might wait for my partner to get back from Brisbane," I said, studying their eyes. No telltale flickers of guilt. "If he makes it in later today, we'll hitch a ride with Gordie and Archer tomorrow, if that's okay."

"Your choice," Bud said. "If you're not here at sixteen hundred hours, I'm sure Phil Cotter won't mind one more on the 169."

"I'm a friend of Jack Kennedy, from back in Boston," I said, stretching the truth a bit to see Bud's reaction. "Think Cotter will mind me tagging along? There seems to be bad blood between them."

"Hey, I'm a pal of Jack's, and this is the boat that picked him and his crew up on that island," Bud said, indicating the 157 with his thumb. "Know what he said when he first saw me? 'Where the hell have you been?' He wasn't kidding around, either. Jack can be pretty hard on his friends, but we've gotten used to it."

"Has Cotter?"

"Well, that's a special case. Jack thinks Cotter abandoned him," Bud said.

"What's your opinion?" I asked.

"Hard to know," he said, puffing out his cheeks in exasperation. "We fired all our torpedoes at what we thought were landing barges, but they turned out to be destroyers. Then we returned to base, which is standard operating procedure. We were long gone when Jack lost his boat. I don't have the facts to call Cotter a liar, but it is hard to believe he didn't see the flames."

"Cotter seemed pretty sore at Jack, who basically did call him a liar," I said.

"At the Coastwatchers party?" Bud asked. Porter and Kari nodded. "I heard about that. I hope neither of them has to depend on the other again. It won't be pretty. I have a few last-minute details to check on, so I'll see you later. Or on Rendova."

"Bud's a good sort," Porter said, taking a seat on a crate of Spam under the dappled shade. "So Billy, what is your Polish pal doing off in Brisbane?"

"Talking to Dickie Miller," I said. "Daniel Tamana's partner."

"You think he may know something of what got Daniel killed?" Kari asked.

"It's possible," I said. "It was right after Daniel saw him off on Henderson Field that he began acting strangely; lying about having to visit a sick relative, and looking for Sam Chang. Perhaps he told Dickie about whatever was bothering him." I moved a wooden crate of K rations into the shade and sat next to Porter.

"Right, you mentioned that at the party, didn't you? I hope Dickie came through all right," Porter said. "I heard it was a serious case of dysentery."

"Do you know him? Either of you?"

"Not personally, no," Kari said.

"Same here," Porter said. "All we knew was the call sign for the Choiseul coastwatching station. But I never met the guy."

"You never were much for socializing," Kari said to Porter with an easy laugh. "On Pavau they called him Silas the hermit, Billy. Never stepped foot off his plantation."

"Well, there was nowhere to go, was there?" Porter said. "But I admit, that's why I bought the place. Far from civilization, that's what I thought, until the Japs showed up. Goes to show, you can't escape from the world."

"What happened exactly?" I asked.

"We saw their boats in the distance," Porter said, casting his gaze out to the horizon. "When two destroyers headed straight for us, I told my assistant manager, bloke by the name of Peter Fraser, to round up the workers. They were all from Choiseul or Malaita. We'd known it was likely the Japs would come, but I did harbor a hope that the war would pass us by. It's a small island of no military value—hardly a decent harbor to be had, and no airstrip."

"You weren't a Coastwatcher then, were you?" I asked.

"No, I didn't have a radio, and didn't really care to be part of the government. I'd come out here to be on my own, but that's another story. Anyway, as Fraser was gathering the workers, I went down to the dock and moved my boat. It was a forty-foot launch with twin diesel engines. An old tub but seaworthy. She could make eleven knots, which would serve to get us to Choiseul and then to Vella Lavella if need be."

"Why did you move it?" I asked, as I wiped the sweat from my forehead.

"I figured the first thing the Japs would do is shell the dock or send an aircraft to shoot up any shipping. I took her to a protected cove and hid her as best I could. Fraser was to have brought everyone there, but when they didn't show, I went looking, heard a shot in the distance. I ran along the track until I got within view of the plantation. I could see the Jap soldiers shooting, and then the house began to burn.

There was nothing I could do. They killed everyone, or most everyone, far as I can tell. There was rumor that someone had fired on the Japs as they marched towards the plantation. Maybe it was Fraser, maybe one of the workers. Or the Japs were simply out for blood."

"So you were alone," I said.

"Alone, yes. Ironic, isn't it? I bought that place on Pavau to enjoy being on my own. But when I finally came to be truly alone, it was the most horrible moment of my life. It'll never be the hermit's existence for me again, I tell you." Porter laughed, the gruff growl of a man who had learned a hard lesson too late.

"Did you join the Coastwatchers to get your revenge?" I asked.

"It seemed the only thing to do," Porter said, rubbing his face with his hands as if washing away a memory. "I know I'm not the type for the army, to go marching around and saluting. I figured this suited me best. I wouldn't mind a bit of revenge though, I don't mind saying." He rested his hand on the hilt of the stiletto at his belt, his fingers flexing around it. I didn't doubt he had his own personal reasons for the war he fought.

"What about you, John?" I asked. "You worked on Pavau, right? How did you get away?"

"I worked for Lever Brothers," Kari said. "At the small harbor on the south side of the island. It was where the other plantations brought their copra. Lever ships first went to Silas's place, then to the main docks for the rest of the shipment. I kept track of copra deliveries and worked the sale of supplies the ships brought in. Lever did a good business selling supplies to the planters. Whiskey especially."

"Did you escape on one of their ships?" I asked.

"No, Lever canceled the last run when the Japanese took Rabaul in the Bismarcks. It was every man for himself when we heard the Japs had landed on the north side. I got on a small boat and worked my way south to Tulagi. That's where I met Silas and Hugh Sexton and joined the Coastwatchers."

"Why?" I asked.

"These are my islands, Billy," Kari said. "I'm from Bougainville. I wanted to do my fighting here."

"I can understand that," I said. "Daniel Tamana must have felt the same way. Did either of you know him on Pavau?"

"He didn't work for me," Porter said. "I never heard of Daniel except when his name was mentioned around headquarters. John, did you ever cross paths with him?"

"No, but I'd only been on Pavau for three months. I was glad to get a job that didn't involve drying copra in those kilns or harvesting it in the fields. Really hot work. But so is this," Kari said, giving Porter a meaningful look.

Porter rose and hoisted a rope from the water, tied to a burlap bag, from which he extricated three bottles of Ballantine's Beer. It wasn't exactly cold, but it hit the spot.

"That's what I heard about Daniel," I said, returning to the subject after a long gulp. "It must be hard for a well-educated native to find a decent position."

"It's not so hard," Kari said, passing the bottle opener back to Porter. "The trick is to get them to pay you a decent wage. Lever didn't mind saving a bit of money on salary, knowing people like me were looking for a step up." He drank, shrugged, and stared at the horizon, trying to disguise his bitterness with nonchalance.

"I'm surprised you and Daniel didn't meet up on Pavau," I said. "Since his job involved keeping books and recording outgoing ship-ments of copra."

"We probably would have at some point," Kari said. "But the days the boats came in were incredibly busy, and I was focused on every detail of the supply shipments and billing the planters. I didn't want to make a mistake and give Lever a reason to dismiss me. For all I know, we did exchange paperwork at the docks, but I wasn't paying much attention."

"Was Sam Chang in competition with Lever?" I asked.

"No, he was trying to supplement what they offered," Kari said. "He saw an opportunity, and it would have been a good one, too, if not for the war."

"Lever brought in the basics," Porter said. "Liquor, tinned meats, that sort of thing. They didn't do much with anything that might spoil, since they only came around once a month." He finished his beer with a long swallow, and tossed the empty bottle into the drink.

"With the planters doing well before the Japs came along, they were ready for more frequent resupplies, and more luxuries," Kari said. "Chang delivered what they wanted."

"If you don't mind me asking," I said to Porter, "did you end up owing Sam Chang money?"

"He never came my way," Porter said. "Too far for only one customer, on the north side of the island. We face the open ocean, and the waters can be heavy."

"But he did go to Pavau," I said.

"Indeed," Kari said. "A good businessman. He let me know he had no intention of replacing Lever's business, and asked me to pass that information on, which I did."

"So he did supply the other planters?" I asked.

"Right," Kari said. "Except for Silas's place, the plantations on Pavau are all on the south side of the island, on New Georgia Sound, where the waters are calmer. Chang made regular stops every week, except for when the Lever boats came in. He was smart. He didn't want to antagonize them, so he worked around their schedule."

"Did you guys meet on Pavau?" I asked, wondering if Porter and Kari had anything in common other than their Coastwatchers service.

"No," Kari said, laughing. "Silas the hermit didn't have a reputation for putting out the welcome mat. Besides, there was only a jungle track over the mountain. His end of the island was quite inaccessible except by boat."

"And being a dedicated hermit," Porter said, "I never ventured off the plantation, by land or sea."

"I'm surprised you took on an assistant," I said. "Didn't cramp your style?"

"The price of success, I'm afraid," Porter said. "We were doing rather well, and I couldn't be everywhere at once. It takes a deft hand to work with a native crew. You have to be firm and let them know who's boss, but not be so harsh that they'll retaliate."

"Retaliate how?" I asked.

"Oh, there's been a few who were set upon by their workers. There's dozens of them and only one of you, so you have to take care. Archer is one who uses fear and his fists to deal with them," Porter said. "I favored firmness and a decent wage."

"How did Peter Fraser take to the isolation?"

"He didn't seem to mind a bit," Porter said. "But it had only been six months. Perhaps it would have worn on him, had he lived."

"So what about after the war, for both of you?"

"You mean after a hot bath and a soft bed?" Porter said with a grin. His plans didn't go beyond rebuilding the plantation and getting off the island now and then. No more of the hermit's life for him. John Kari hoped to attend university in Australia, if it was allowed.

"I have a feeling things will change after the war. There's talk of independence for the Solomon Islands," he said.

"Good luck with that," I said. "The English don't let go of their colonies easily, believe me."

"I don't think Lever Brothers and the other companies who profit from cheap native labor will be happy either," Kari said. "But we've seen and done things because of this war that will change the Solomons forever." There was no bitterness when Kari talked of the future, only hope. He finished his beer and carefully set the bottle on the wharf.

"It's true," Porter said, with a shake of his head. "For better or worse, the world has descended upon these islands. The simple times are gone."

"Well, we've still got a war to win first," I said, standing and stretching my legs. "I've got to see Lieutenant Cotter. Thanks for the beer."

"Bye-o," Porter said, lighting a cigarette as he leaned back against a stack of crates, all labeled FRAGMENTATION HAND GRENADE, MK2. Out here, you took your comfort where you found it.

John Kari waved and smiled, perhaps practicing for his future career as a politician. He had a good start. He'd been lying through his teeth when he claimed he hadn't met Daniel Tamana on Pavau.

CHAPTER TWENTY-TWO

WE ALL LIE from time to time. But John Kari's lie was about Daniel Tamana, a guy who'd brought me to these tropical isles and ruined my leave in Algiers with Diana by getting himself killed. There were plenty of reasons to hide the truth, and Kari may have had a good one, but I needed to find out if it had anything to do with Daniel's death.

I turned it over in my mind as I walked the length of the dock, heading to where Cotter's PT-169 was moored, the blistering sun grilling my exposed skin. Daniel Tamana's job on the Pavau plantation was to keep the books and oversee outgoing shipments of copra. John Kari's job was to record those shipments for Lever at the docks. How could they not have met? How many well-educated Melanesians were there on one island, speaking the King's English to perfection?

Kari was also in charge of billing planters for the Lever supplies. Daniel would have handled those bills. Another intersection of events that certainly would have brought them into contact. But why lie? Even if they'd only met briefly and had cursory business contacts, why hide the fact?

Porter had not been there when Daniel first came to Hugh Sexton's place, which explained why he had asked Kari if he'd ever met Daniel before. Would Porter have known either man on Pavau? No, not isolated as he was on the north end of the island. But I had my doubts about Kari not knowing Daniel.

I scanned the dock for any sign of Gordie or Archer, but couldn't pick them out from the press of sailors moving in every direction. Another section of dock jutted out from the shore just ahead, with only a single larger vessel moored alongside. It was about the size of an LST, but with cranes and pulleys, the kind you see on merchant ships for loading cargo. Two PT boats were anchored alongside; I figured this was a PT boat tender, the kind of vessel Daniel and the others took from Guadalcanal. It was bigger than I'd expected, and I decided it'd be interesting to see what the view was for your average passenger.

I approached the 169 as Cotter was descending the gangplank. I introduced myself and told him I might need to hitch a ride for Kaz and myself tomorrow. I offered to show him my orders, but he waved me off.

"Not a problem, Lieutenant, even for a pal of Kennedy's," Cotter said, his hands on his hips, his chin jutting forward. His words were friendly enough, but his stance was a fighter's. "Be here before fifteen hundred hours tomorrow, and keep your gear light. We've got plenty on board already, courtesy of our Coastwatcher passengers."

"Got it. And Jack Kennedy and I are acquaintances, not pals," I said. "How about you? Were you and he pals?"

"We were friendly enough, before that patrol in Blackett Strait. A skipper dumb enough to get his boat sliced in two while dead in the water shouldn't criticize his squadron mates for not finding him."

"You searched?" I asked, figuring a direct question was the best way to get the measure of this man.

"We not only searched, we sent a radio warning before the 109 was hit. We saw the phosphorescent wake of what I thought was a destroyer and radioed to all boats in the vicinity. No acknowledgement from Kennedy." He turned and spat into the oily water.

"Why wouldn't he acknowledge?" I asked.

"Good question," Cotter said. "I asked his radioman, Maguire, why he hadn't answered. He said he was up on deck, chatting with Kennedy. Chatting, can you believe it? That's the kind of skipper he was. Sloppy. If I was in a night action and my radioman left his post, I'd kick his ass and put him on report. Anything else you want to waste my time over?" Cotter took a step closer, his arms akimbo. If I backed up, I'd end up in the drink with his spit, which seemed to be his plan.

"Why is it a waste of time?" I said. "I told you he's no friend of mine."

"Because he's a rich man's spoiled kid, that's why. What the hell do you think the navy's going to do with him, send him home in disgrace?"

"It's doubtful," I agreed. Cotter let his hands drop and took half a step back, his anger vented for the moment. "Did you happen to know the fellow who was killed near the hospital? Daniel Tamana?"

"The Coastwatcher? No, but I heard Kennedy was the one who found him. You the guy they got investigating that?"

"Yep, that's me. You hear anything I should know about?"

"Yeah," Cotter said, brushing me aside. "I hear Papa Kennedy got a Boston Irish cop to come out here and clear his son. Have I got that right?" He didn't wait for an answer as he hustled off the dock. I felt half a dozen eyes on me as his crewmen stood on the deck of the PT boat, watching.

"Basically, he does," I shouted at them. They scattered.

Gordie and Archer were nowhere to be found. Maybe one of them left after rolling a couple of steel drums in my direction. Or both? Anyway, I figured there'd be time tomorrow to talk more with them. I didn't ask if any of the PT-169 crew knew where they were, figuring they might send me to the wrong end of the island just for my Southie accent, if they agreed with Cotter.

I made my way to the base HQ, such as it was. A stifling hot Quonset hut, the commanding officer nowhere to be found, manned by a single sailor in shorts and a denim shirt with the sleeves torn off. Not exactly recruiting poster stuff, but I couldn't blame him once I set foot inside. I felt the sweat evaporate off my skin in a heartbeat, and instantly understood why the CO had found business elsewhere. The sailor made a call for me to Yeoman Howe, who had learned Kaz would be on today's flight from Brisbane. Good news.

He followed me outside and collapsed into a chair set under a canvas tarp strung from the side of the metal hut, gulping water from a canteen.

"Is that big ship at the end of the dock a PT boat tender?" I asked.

"Yes sir," he said. "That's an AGP-21, a converted LST."

"Are there others in the Solomons?"

"No, that's our one and only. She runs between here and Rendova pretty regular. Guadalcanal, too. That covers all the PT bases in the Solomons."

"Who's the XO?" I knew better than to bother the ship's captain, but his executive officer would want to know what I was doing aboard, so better to start off by being polite and observing the naval courtesies.

"Lieutenant Kelly, sir. He left here about a half hour ago. They're getting ready to pull out tonight, so he's probably on board."

"Thanks. Don't get heatstroke in there."

"Don't worry, Lieutenant. I only go in when I hear the telephone or see an officer coming. If I'd known you were army, I would have stayed out here."

"Smart," I said. "They should promote you."

"The navy don't work like that, sir."

I told him the army wasn't much better and headed for the tender. Moored hard against it was a PT boat swarming with sailors brandishing wrenches and muscle as they worked to remove the heavy torpedo tubes. I saw that the depth charges were already gone and wondered what was in store for the stripped-down vessel.

I clambered up the tender's steep gangplank, remembering to stop near the top and salute the colors. The navy liked its traditions and formality, and since I'd basically be wasting the XO's valuable time prior to departure, I thought it best to play by their rules.

"Permission to come aboard," I said, saluting the officer of the deck even though he was just an ensign. I asked for the XO and he sent a swabbie to find him, leaving me to gaze out over Sesapi harbor from the deck of the PT tender. I spotted Archer and Gordie stopping to talk with Porter and Kari. I wondered what the conversation was about. Their upcoming assignments? Deanna Pendleton? Or other secrets I wasn't even aware of? I made a mental note to ask Archer and Gordie what they knew of John Kari's business on Pavau, to try and get a hint of why he'd lied to me.

"What can I do for you, Lieutenant?" The XO popped out of a hatch, his uniform sweat-soaked, sleeves rolled up, wiping greasy hands on an oil-stained rag. He looked about thirty or so, tall and dark-haired. He reminded me of commercial fishermen I'd known back home. The kind of guy who appeared at ease on a boat of any size.

"Billy Boyle," I said, extending my hand, thinking Kelly would wave me off, given the condition his were in. He didn't. But he did toss me the rag with a grin.

"We don't see the army much," he said. "You must be that second louie who's snooping around. Why do we rate a visit?"

"Because people have been murdered," I said. "Three so far." I wasn't surprised he'd heard about the investigation. It was a small island packed with guys who had little else to do other than their duties. A murder inquiry was a prime piece of gossip.

"Okay," Kelly said, his voice tempered by the mention of three deaths. "Let's get out of the sun." He led the way up a ladder to an open, flat area amid ships, flanked by cranes. It was covered with a large tarp hung over a cable, creating a tent under which men worked on several engines and other disassembled equipment—another ingenious method of countering the blazing sun. Kelly leaned against a crate and lit a cigarette, sighing as he exhaled.

"You might not see the army much, but I'm not used to seeing officers with grease under their fingernails," I said.

"This isn't exactly an admiral's flagship," Kelly said. "We're a repair and supply vessel, and the PT crews we service are even less spit-and-polish than we are. See those cranes? We can hoist two PT boats up onto this deck for repairs. And half the time we're close enough to the Japs to keep all the antiaircraft guns manned. As long as our weapons are clean and the engines working, I don't give a damn about dirty fingernails. But you didn't come here for a speech about the glamorous life aboard a PT tender, so shoot. What do you need?"

"Do you recall making the trip from Rendova to Guadalcanal, then here, about ten days ago, ferrying some Coastwatchers?"

"Sure," Kelly said, taking a drag off his Lucky. "Two teams, I think. Four in all, one of them a native. Spoke English like a professor. Don't remember their names, but I can check the manifest if you want."

"No need," I said. "What about another native Coastwatcher, picked up on Guadalcanal?"

"For the trip across to Tulagi?" Kelly asked. "I don't recall, but it's a short hop and we'd take anyone over who asked, really. Ironbottom Sound is a rear area now, and things are pretty casual between the two islands."

"Where would your passengers be?" I asked. "Would they have the run of the ship?"

"Not the bridge or the engine room, but otherwise they could take a look around. We brought a few walking wounded out from Rendova, and they stayed in sick bay. But the others were mostly above decks. On the fantail, mainly. The stern is out of the wind and a good place to enjoy the ride. I had coffee and sandwiches brought out, I remember that much."

"Anyone else other than the wounded and the Coastwatchers?"

"Yeah, a handful of navy and marine officers, a couple of Australian commandos, and a half dozen PT crew."

"Does the name Sam Chang ring a bell?"

"No," Kelly said, giving it some thought as he fieldstripped the Lucky. "Can't say it does. Sorry, Billy, I wish I was more help. The war is bad enough even on a good day. I can't understand anyone bumping off some of our own."

"Yeah," I said. "It's worse than murder back home." We were silent for a moment, the words hanging in the heat of the day. "Anyway, when you docked at Guadalcanal, did some of the passengers get off?"

"Yeah, the Aussies and the marines had air transport out of there. The rest stayed on board and got off right here, at Sesapi."

"Everyone departed, along with whoever hitched a ride," I said. Kelly nodded his agreement. "Could you show me where the men were?"

"Sure. Some guys like to sit in the sun, others look for shade. They could have been anywhere," he said, gesturing around.

"Up here?" I asked, walking toward the stern end of the ship, where the fantail was, considerably lower than this working deck.

"Yes, now that you mention it. We had a PT up here under repairs. A few people did wander up to take a look."

Steel cables ran along each side of the deck, forming a chest-high fence. Crates of machine parts and oil drums were stacked near the cranes, giving anyone up here a perch from which to observe the activity on the fantail below. I watched two sailors talking, one lighting a cigarette for another. They didn't look my way, ten feet or so above and behind them. I tried to imagine Daniel Tamana standing at this very spot, suddenly seeing something—no, someone—that surprised him. Then stepping back, completely out of sight.

So what happened next?

"When you docked here at Sesapi," I asked Kelly, "did you keep track of departing passengers?"

"Billy, we're not a cruise ship. We don't bother with all that. We got a manifest with names on it at Rendova, but once we made sure they were all on board, that was the end of it. Tulagi may not be much, but everyone who could leave did, and we didn't stand in their way."

"I get it," I said. "You don't happen to remember anything else about the native Coastwatcher, the one who got on at Guadalcanal?"

"I have a vague recollection of the guy we took from Rendova, but only because his speech was so surprising. I was expecting Pijin and got the King's English."

"Okay, thanks. You've been a big help."

"Wait a minute," Kelly said, snapping his fingers. "There was a GI up here, dressed in fresh fatigues. A little guy. He was pretty dark-skinned, but I thought it was a tan. He wore a big-billed cap, so it was hard to see his face. Not that I tried. But he could have been a native."

"Daniel Tamana. He'd been pulled out with his partner, who was sick with dysentery," I said. "They were flown straight to Henderson Field. His clothes were probably in tatters from living in the jungle. They must have outfitted him on Guadalcanal."

"Makes sense," Kelly said, nodding.

It did, but it didn't answer the important question: *What had*

Daniel seen? I leaned against the rail, wondering if he had done the same thing.

"What's going on with that PT?" I said, looking to the boat below with its tubes and depth charges removed. I was vaguely curious, and uncertain what to do next. Asking questions came naturally, and seemed easier than admitting I was at a loss.

"That's PT-59," Kelly said. "We're turning her into a gunboat. She's getting two forty-millimeter guns and extra machine guns, all in armored turrets. The idea is to use her against Jap barges moving men and supplies down the Slot."

"Not a bad idea," I said, remembering what Jack had said. "A guy told me the torpedoes are often slower than the destroyers they fire at."

"True enough," Kelly said. "And the barges are shallow draft, so the torpedoes run right under them. Ought to be a nasty surprise for our Jap friends. Let me know if there's anything else I can do, Billy. Good luck."

I wished him the same and stood for a minute where Daniel Tamana had stood. I walked along the starboard side of the main deck, keeping an eye on the lower deck where the group from the fantail would have stood as they waited to go ashore. With Daniel watching and listening. Seeing and hearing whatever got him killed.

CHAPTER TWENTY-THREE

"HELLO GENTS," I said to Archer and Gordie as they organized supplies on the dock next to PT-169. Sailors carried crates onboard as the two men checked them off lists flapping in the humid breeze on clipboards marked with grease and rust. Spam, medical supplies, whiskey, ammunition. All the essentials.

"Scuttlebutt is you're coming with us tomorrow," Archer said. "Part of your investigation?"

"I heard Daniel Tamana worked on Rendova," I said. "Thought I'd ask around and see if anyone remembers much about him."

"Ah, the search for clues continues, eh?" Gordie said, grinning as the sweat ran in rivulets down his face. He was the quintessential jolly fat man, always ready with a friendly greeting. Did that smile hide a deadly intent? I had no reason to suspect him of any foul play, other than proximity. But that didn't rule him out.

"My dad always said, if you turn over enough rocks, you're bound to find something slimy."

"Especially true out here," Gordie said, chuckling. "Slimy and dangerous. I'd watch out if I were you. In the bush, the smallest rock can hide the deadliest creature."

"Your dad a copper, too?" Archer asked as Gordie turned back to his checklist.

"Yeah," I said, eyeing Gordie and wondering if he'd been making a joke, giving me a friendly warning, or something more sinister. "Family business back in Boston."

"Funny how these things go," Archer said. "My old man had a station in New South Wales. That's a ranch to you Yanks. I fancied taking over from him, but there was a terrible drought. Some of the local blokes made it through, but we'd recently come out from England and weren't properly prepared. The cattle died and the bank foreclosed when his money ran out. As soon as I could, I headed out here, where there are no banks. Thieving bastards, they are."

"Hard to disagree with that," I said. "I bet a lot of planters came out here to get away from civilization. Silas Porter, for one."

"Our reformed hermit," Gordie said, sticking a pencil behind his ear. "He was famous for his lack of hospitality. We islanders tend to stick together. Not many of us, you know. But not Silas; he was a man who liked his privacy. Still, his plantation wasn't the easiest place to get to, so it wasn't like he was turning people away. But you knew not to expect him at any sort of gathering."

"Man's got a right," Archer said. "That's why a lot of us are here, isn't it? To make our own way."

"Sort of like the Wild West back home," I said, to nods from them both. "Tell me, that's the ship you came in on, isn't it?" I hooked my thumb in the general direction of Kelly's ship.

"Yeah," Archer said. "PT tender. They treated us well, didn't they Gordie?"

"Food and drink, smooth sailing, and no Japanese aircraft dropping bombs. Delightful trip," Gordie said.

"Do you remember what you talked about?" I asked. "You were all on the fantail, right?"

"I'd say we all were," Archer said. "We gabbed a fair bit, but I'm damned if I can remember about what. You, Gordie?"

"Cold beer, women, decent food, cigarettes that hadn't gone moldy—that sort of thing, I expect. Nothing that sticks in my mind."

"You had company, right? Marines, navy officers, Australian commandos," I said, hoping to prompt their memories for anything that might throw some light on Daniel's behavior.

"That's right," Archer said. "Some PT crew as well. But they stayed in the ship's mess most of the time."

"And you didn't notice Daniel Tamana?" I asked. "It's fairly certain he went from Henderson Field and got a ride on the tender to this very place."

"Well, if he did, why wouldn't he make himself known?" Gordie said, his brow wrinkled. "It doesn't make sense."

"Given that neither of us had met him before," Archer said, "we could have walked right by him and not realized who he was."

"But still," Gordie said, "it wouldn't take a genius to figure out what we were all about. How many Australians in filthy khaki and slouch hats were on that boat? And John Kari was there, for goodness' sake."

"What do you mean?" I asked.

"They're both natives and part of the Coastwatchers. They must have known of each other. It'd be natural enough to want to meet a chap like yourself," Gordie said.

"But I thought you only knew each other by call sign," I said.

"Word travels," Archer said. "The natives know much more than they let on, believe me."

"Besides," Gordie said, "didn't they both work on Pavau? They must have met at some point."

"Not according to John Kari," I said.

"Then why did Daniel hide himself?" Gordie asked.

"But only on the boat," I said, thinking it through. "He came right to Hugh Sexton's place, right?"

"That he did," Archer said, nodding. "What does it mean?"

"He felt safe there," I said. "But not on the boat."

"Because Hugh was there, you mean," Archer said, his voice suddenly hard. "Are you accusing us of making him fear for his life?"

"It does make sense, doesn't it?" I answered, watching for Archer's reaction.

"I should knock your teeth in for that, you cow," Archer said, stepping closer, his fists bunched at his side. His face was red and a vein throbbed at his temple. Interesting.

"Hey, just thinking out loud, Archer," I said, holding up my hands, palms out.

"Do it quieter, then," he said, and spun on his heel, stomping off the dock.

"Why'd he call me a cow?" I asked Gordie, who as usual was smiling.

"A Yank'd say bum or bastard. If he were feeling charitable, that is."

"My insinuation didn't seem to bother you," I said, wiping the perspiration from my eyes, glad to have avoided Archer's swing. He looked like he knew how to use those meaty fists.

"About Daniel being afraid of one of us? Hells bells, I've got bigger things to worry about, like the Japanese Army and Navy," he said. "Besides, I know I didn't hurt anyone. Not on our side, at least." He flashed a grin and went back to work, leaving me to wonder at that singular statement of innocence.

I couldn't think of any other rocks to turn over in Sesapi, and I had some time to kill before I picked up Kaz at the PBY base near headquarters. I decided to pay Jack a visit and see how he made out with Cluster, angling for a new boat. If he managed not to irritate me, I might even tell him about the report I filed with Ritchie, absolving him of any involvement in the murder of Daniel Tamana.

I found Jack in his hut, whistling a happy tune while he stuffed clothes into a white canvas sea bag.

"I guess it went well with Cluster," I said, thinking that most guys would be happy about going home, not hanging around the Solomons to give the Japs another chance to burn, drown, or maim them.

"I'm getting a new boat, Billy," Jack said, his grin wide and his eyes on fire. "And I've got you to thank for it. Ritchie told Al Cluster about your report, and that sealed the deal."

"You're welcome," I said. Not that Jack thanked me directly. He was good at alluding to things without coming out and saying them. A real pal tells you thanks straight up. A rich kid says it like he owns you. I was already irritated.

"It's not only a new boat, it's a new experimental craft," Jack said, jamming a pair of tennis shoes on top of his khakis. "A gunboat, armed to the teeth."

"I think I saw her at Sesapi," I said. "PT-59, moored next to the PT tender. They were removing depth charges and torpedo tubes."

"Yeah, that's the plan. They're installing forty-millimeter guns, more machine guns, armor plating, the works. We're going after Jap barges bringing men and supplies down the Slot," Jack said, cinching his sea bag closed. "That's where the war is, Billy, not waiting like a sitting duck for destroyers. If the Japs can't keep their garrisons manned and supplied, we'll send them to hell and gone."

"You discharged from the hospital, Jack?" He was excited, walking on air, but I wasn't so sure about him captaining a gunboat. He was still rail thin, and I could see he was disguising a limp, walking around the bed like a drunk determined to stay upright. The slightest of winces played across his face, hidden by an eager smile. Some guys feigned illness to get sack time in the sick bay. Jack feigned wellness to get out.

"Clean bill of health and a new command," he said. "Never felt better. All I need to do is gather up a crew and oversee the finishing touches on the 59 boat. Al said they might rename her Motor Gunboat Number One. Has a nice ring, doesn't it?"

"Jack, are you sure you're ready?"

"I'll tell you what I'm not ready for, Billy. I'm not ready to be sent home before I pay the Japs back for sinking my boat and killing my men. Don't get in my way, okay?"

"I'm not in your way, Jack," I said, stepping closer and holding my hands behind my back to keep them from grabbing Jack by the collar and shaking some sense into him. "If I were, that report would have come out differently. Not everyone who disagrees with you is trying to get in your way."

"Okay, okay," he said, holding up one hand in half surrender. "I didn't mean anything by it, I just can't wait to get out of here and get on with things. Come on, sit down. Have a sandwich, I'm not hungry." Jack sat at the small table and pushed a plate of Spam sandwiches in my direction, sending newspapers and magazines fluttering to the floor. Jack was never much for housekeeping, but now that he was on his way out the door, he was even more careless.

"Thanks," I said, biting into half a greasy sandwich, knowing that Jack's stomach could never take anything like this and keep it down. I didn't say anything else, letting the brief burst of temper settle back down.

"Anything new on Deanna?" Jack finally asked.

"I thought I might have had something," I said, telling him about John Kari driving through Chinatown and the Cosmoline, which I thought implicated him until I saw the others with it.

"Pretty common stuff," Jack said. "But it does put those four Coastwatchers in the frame, doesn't it?"

"It doesn't clear them, that's for sure," I said. "Did you know that Daniel came over from Guadalcanal on the same PT tender they were all on? He apparently didn't make himself known, which raises even more suspicions."

"No, I didn't. Wouldn't have any reason to. Who do you think is the most likely suspect?"

"I think Kari is hiding something," I said, tossing down the remains of the Spam lunch. My stomach wasn't crazy about it either. "He and Daniel were on Pavau at the same time, but he claims never to have met him. I think he must have, though, since they both would have been present when the Lever boat picked up copra deliveries."

"On some of those outlying islands, the arrival of a boat carrying mail and supplies is a major event," Jack said. "There'd have to be a good reason for them not to have taken notice of each other."

"Especially since Kari worked for Lever, keeping track of copra deliveries and selling supplies to the planters."

"Didn't Silas Porter come from Pavau?" Jack asked.

"He has a plantation there," I said. "But apparently the north end of the island is cut off by a mountain, and there's little contact between the leeward and his place on the windward side. Didn't seem like they ever had the chance to meet. And Porter was something of a recluse back then. The war changed him after the Japs massacred his workers."

"Sounds familiar," Jack said. "Things have to get really bad before a man is forced to change his ways. But when that happens, there's no going back." His eyes drifted, not fixed on anything in the room, or even outside the open windows.

"What's next?" I asked, in an effort to bring him back from the place where things got really bad.

"I could use a lift to Sesapi," he said, the weariness in his voice weighing it down. I didn't bother telling him he should stay here.

"Sure. Come on, I'll even carry your bag." That got a smile, a real one, and I was reminded how damn likable Jack was when he wasn't playing the angles. As we stood up, a muscular, tanned navy ensign entered the hut.

"Jack," he said. "I just heard. Congratulations on the new boat."

"Thanks, Barney," Jack said. "Billy, I want you to meet the lookout on PT-109, Barney Ross."

I didn't know what to say. I watched Jack's face, and then the ensign's. Finally, Jack's stern face dissolved and they both laughed, enjoying my discomfort. It was a classic Jack Kennedy move: cracking a joke that made you chuckle and put you in your place at the same time. It was obvious they'd pulled this routine before, and Barney was as much a part of it as Jack. But I still wondered, if it were repeated often enough, would it create the impression that the loss of PT-109 wasn't entirely Jack's responsibility?

Barney and I shook hands as I tried to dispel my cop's suspicions. I couldn't help it. Being raised in the Boyle household meant a constant state of awareness, observing what people said and did in order to discover the hidden meanings behind even the most innocent of jokes, comments, and silence. As my dad always said, there are no coincidences, and nothing is ever as it seems.

"Barney came along for the ride that night to man the thirty-seven-millimeter cannon we'd scrounged from the army," Jack explained.

"We didn't get off a shot," Barney said, "but the timbers we used to lash down the gun came in handy. The guys who couldn't swim hung onto them. Probably saved a few lives."

"This time we'll have real firepower," Jack said. "No more

jury-rigged single-shot cannons. Two forty-millimeter Bofors guns, how's that sound?" The crazed gleam was back in Jack's eyes, and I left the two of them to talk about gunboats and killing plenty of Japs. Barney had a jeep and said he'd take Jack to his new boat, so I promised Jack I'd visit him onboard the 59 at Sesapi, but I can't say I looked forward to it.

I DROVE TO our quarters and told Kao to have some dinner ready for Kaz and me in an hour or so. Then I headed down to the PBY base, passing Captain Ritchie on the road. He ignored me, which is the best possible relationship to have with a senior officer. I sat in the jeep, waiting for the PBY to come into sight, thinking through everything that had happened since Kaz left. I'd have to tell him about Deanna. Kaz liked new and interesting experiences, not ones that reminded him of the past. I was worried how he'd react to the news. I did my best to keep him distracted, but memories of Daphne were always at the edge of everything, as with all great losses.

Trying to think of less depressing matters, I began to catalog all the events and people in this case of triple murder. What had I learned about all the known suspects? Was there a wild card out there, someone whom I didn't even suspect, or perhaps even know?

I went through all the names and faces I'd encountered, but all that did was leave me with the vague feeling that I'd missed something. Maybe it was vital, or maybe a meaningless loose end. But there it was, that empty space behind my eyes, where sat the niggling feeling of questions begging to be formed and asked, maybe even answered.

I'd given up by the time the PBY came into sight and landed as gracefully as a twenty-thousand-pound twin-engine aircraft can manage in heavy, rolling waves. It moved to its mooring as a launch departed shore and took on three passengers, Kaz included.

"I believe I have had enough of air travel for quite a while," he said as we drove back to our quarters. "I would almost prefer luxury accommodations on a steamship at this point. With smooth waters, of course."

"And no submarines," I said.

"Or Kawanishis," he countered. "Perhaps we could wait out the war on Tulagi, and book cabins on the first decent passenger vessel that comes along. Unless every ship in the Pacific is sunk first."

We went on in the same vein for the rest of the drive, dreaming up exotic means of transportation, none of which involved enemy encounters. It didn't seem right to blurt out news of Deanna's death then, so I waited until we were back at what passed for home, sitting on the verandah, whiskey in hand, watching the last glimmering rays of sun descend over the horizon—which looked far too much like the Japanese Rising Sun banner.

"Deanna Pendleton has been killed," I said, after a healthy drink.

"What? An accident?"

"No," I said. "She was knifed. In Chinatown, by someone who knew what he was doing."

"Tell me every detail," he said, sitting bolt upright in his chair. So I did. I gave him a blow-by-blow description of meeting Jack, finding Deanna, speaking with Jai-li, and the subsequent medical report from Doc Schwartz, along with my discussions with the Coastwatchers and the ubiquitous Cosmoline.

"You are certain Kennedy is not involved?" Kaz asked.

"I can't say for certain," I said. "He can be a bum, but it's hard to see him killing a woman." What I didn't say was that Jack was used to getting his way. Deanna was the kind of woman who didn't give in to the male ego, and Jack's ego was formidable.

"Are you sure?" Kaz said, giving me a hard look. I nodded, keeping my darkest thoughts to myself.

"And someone may have tried to kill me," I said, changing the subject. I told Kaz about the runaway fuel drums.

"Someone may be getting nervous," he said.

"I sure am. Tell me, did you find Dickie Miller?" I asked, now that the bad news was out of the way.

"In hospital, yes," Kaz said. "He is still quite ill and weak, but he should recover. He had nothing but good things to say about Daniel Tamana. 'Smart chap for a native,' that sort of thing. I got the sense he actually respected him, but found him hard to categorize. He said they got along well in the bush, but he wondered how Daniel would get along in the world of Europeans after the war."

"John Kari told me he was thinking of politics," I said. "There's talk of independence for the Solomons after the war. Maybe Daniel would have chosen the same path. The Solomons will need educated leaders."

"Miller said Daniel had talked about that as well. He said it might be the only place for him, as a spokesman for his people. Daniel said he doubted he could ever go back to village life or be accepted as anything other than a native outside of it. I had the feeling Miller felt sorry for him at some level."

"That's pretty thoughtful on Miller's part," I said. "Not that it helps us much. Did you find out anything useful?"

"Only that Miller said nothing seemed amiss with Daniel on their voyage to Henderson Field. He said Daniel was with him every minute, until he was put on the transport plane. All that does is confirm what we thought, that it was something Daniel saw or heard on his way to Tulagi."

"And now we know that our four Coastwatcher friends were all on the same vessel Daniel was," I said, filling Kaz in on my visit to the PT tender, and what I found out about Daniel and John Kari both working on Pavau.

"Miller said Daniel enjoyed his time on Pavau. He wanted a Coastwatchers assignment there, but apparently Hugh Sexton vetoed the idea. Since it is a relatively small island, it would be easy for Japanese patrols to run them down. Daniel claimed he knew every path, hiding place, and secret cove on Pavau, but finally agreed it would place the natives in greater danger."

"How so?"

"The Japanese would have fewer villages to terrorize on a small island. If they suspected Coastwatchers were there, they could simply start killing natives until one of them betrayed their location, or at least the likely location of the radio. Without a radio, there's no use for a Coastwatcher."

"That makes sense," I said. "Not that it's helpful. Did he say if Daniel ever met John Kari?"

"Not that he knew of. Since Kari was the only one you actually saw in Chinatown, he seems to be the most likely killer," Kaz said. "But what would his motive be?"

"No idea," I said. "Money or love, that's what Jack reminded me when we first got here. I'd told him back in Boston those were the two most common motives for murder."

"You are sure Kennedy is not involved in the other two killings?" Kaz asked.

"Yes," I said. "There's nothing to connect him with Daniel Tamana. He did see Sam Chang that night in the hospital, but Chang was alive when he left." I told Kaz about the report I'd given Ritchie and his promise to allow us to stay on to investigate.

"Now that Kennedy is in the clear," Kaz said, "isn't it time you told me what grudge you have against him? Not his family, but him personally?"

"Kao," I yelled. "Bring out the bottle."

Kao fetched the half-empty bottle of whiskey. Then he carried out plates of fish, rice, and taro and placed them on the low table between us. I filled our glasses and figured there was enough to get me through the story, as long as Kaz didn't hog the bottle.

"It was the spring of 1937," I said. "I was still a rookie and pulled duty with the vice squad one night. They were going to raid a brothel on North Street. Queen Lil's, it was called. Fancy place with a doorman and a reputation for clean girls." I stopped to take a few bites of fish and wash it down with the whiskey. "Lil hadn't kept up her protection payments, so it was time to teach her a lesson. We weren't supposed to arrest any of the girls, only the customers."

"Why?"

"Because she needed them working, to keep the cash flowing to the powers that be," I said. "The idea was to show we could embarrass her clientele whenever we wanted. If we kept that up, Queen Lil's would just be another cheap whorehouse in the Black Sea."

"The Black Sea?"

"That's what they call the area around North Street and North Square. It's near the docks, with a lot of brothels and bars catering to sailors. A good deal of gambling, too. Queen Lil's was at the top of the heap in the Black Sea, and her payments were probably a considerable source of income for the higher-ups. So it was a delicate operation. No damage to the premises, and leave the girls alone. Collar a bunch of customers and haul them away."

"Wouldn't that hurt her business even more?" Kaz asked. "I'd think the public exposure would keep the elite clientele away."

"I thought the same thing at first," I said. "It was only later I learned that the men were never booked. They were tossed in the paddy wagon in front of Lil's and taken within a block of police headquarters. They paid a fine on the spot and were cut loose."

"A bribe," Kaz said. "But Queen Lil did not know that either."

"Exactly," I said. "Anyway, we go in like gangbusters, making a lot of noise and grabbing guys with one leg in their trousers. A vice detective has me check the back door and then the top floor. When I get up to the third floor, there's a sitting area at the top of the stairs. Plush red velvet chairs. In one of them, sitting with his legs crossed and smoking a cigar like he didn't have a care in the world, is a young skinny kid. Nice suit."

"He hadn't been taken away?" Kaz said.

"Nope. He looked calm, like he had every right to be there, and to be left alone at that. Two detectives walked right by him, and he gave them a little nod, enough to send a message: you can't touch me."

"Which you did not take well to, if I know you."

"Right. So I asked him who he was and what he was doing there. He smiled and said he was Jack Kennedy, and he was waiting for a friend. I asked where his friend was, and he showed me a room down the hall. A uniformed cop, a sergeant, was standing guard at the door. I was confused and didn't know what to do. But vice had given us our marching orders, and I didn't want to get in trouble with them. Or with my father, since he'd hear about how I did from his pals. So I grabbed Kennedy by the arm and hustled him downstairs."

"Did you know it was Ambassador Kennedy's son?" Kaz asked.

"No. Back then I mostly read the sports section and the funny pages. All I knew was that he was some Harvard rich kid, out catting around. He kept telling me I was making a mistake, which is what a lot of these clowns say."

"But I get a sense you may have been," Kaz said.

I nodded, and dug into the food and drink to fortify myself.

"How was I to know at the time?" I said. "When we got outside, this Kennedy kid asked if we could wait for his friend. The paddy wagon was crammed full, so I said fine. We had plenty of squad cars, and I said we'd give them both a ride to the station. While we're waiting, another kid comes up and starts asking Jack what's up. Turns out it was his older brother, Joe Junior."

"Was he visiting Queen Lil's establishment as well?" Kaz asked.

"Apparently. He began to get testy with me for taking Jack into custody, and with Jack for allowing himself to be caught. Joe worked himself up to the point where I was ready to smack him with my billy club, but Jack laid a hand on my arm and shook his head. It was strange, my own prisoner touching me like that. I should have had him in cuffs, but somehow I never thought to do it. He was so confident, I couldn't picture him doing something as low as running off. I took his advice, and told Joe to hold his horses. It was a bit tense, until Commissioner Timilty showed up."

"That's the police commissioner you mentioned before," Kaz said. "The man who demoted your father because he investigated Joe Senior. Why would the commissioner of police be present at a raid on a brothel? Isn't that unusual?"

"He wasn't there for the raid. Turns out, he was a regular at Queen Lil's. That was the friend Jack had been waiting for. The guy behind the door guarded by the police sergeant."

"Oh no," Kaz said.

"That was almost the end of my career, then and there. Timilty tore into me like I was responsible for the entire raid, and then demanded to know why I was harassing upstanding young men like the Kennedy brothers, and did I know who their father was. It went on like that for quite a while."

"Upstanding young men visiting a house of prostitution," Kaz said.

"Hey, it's Boston, no reason why the two things can't go together. We'd just had a mayor who was also head of the Irish mob in the city. James Curley himself, as crooked as they come. The only way to get him out of town was to elect him to Congress."

"What happened next?"

"Needless to say, I didn't take either of the Kennedy brothers to the station. They drove off in Timilty's automobile, his sergeant at the wheel. Timilty's last words to me were that he'd have my badge by morning."

"I take it he calmed down?"

"No. The vice detective who organized the raid was demoted to the traffic division. It turned out that Jack put in a good word for me and got Timilty to back off from firing me. I was sent to walk the beat in East Boston, around the shipyards. Not the choicest assignment, but it could have been worse."

"If not for Jack's intervention," Kaz said.

"Right. He came to see me at work the next day and apologized. I think he'd gotten the lowdown from someone, maybe his brother, about how Timilty had punished my dad. Maybe he felt bad about giving a second generation of Boyles a kick in the gut. It's the odd kind of thing Jack would do; get you in trouble and then fix things as best he could."

"You became friends, it seems," Kaz said.

"Yeah, we struck up a friendship. Both of us were Irish kids, our families not too long off the boat. He's a big Red Sox fan—I prefer the Boston Braves myself—and he invited me to a game. Best seats I've ever been in, right by the first-base line. I'd been to plenty of games but always in the bleachers."

"I thought you were telling me the story of how you came to dislike Jack Kennedy so much," Kaz said, finishing the food on his plate.

"I'm getting there," I said. "You got anywhere else to go?"

"Yes, actually," Kaz said. He refilled my glass. "But I am tired from the long flight. Continue."

"Oh, right," I said, thinking of Jai-li. I guess I was honored. "Okay, so we're pals. Not the closest of friends, but we get along. Jack invited me down to Hyannisport a couple of times that summer. There were usually a bunch of guests, all of his brothers and sisters inviting friends for sailing and football. I had a crush on his sister, Kathleen. They called her Kick, and it turned out that every guy Joe or Jack brought along fell for her. I liked Rosie a lot, too. She's the oldest sister, a really sweet kid with a great smile. Even better looking than Kick, but the family made it clear that the girls were out of bounds for male visitors. They were pretty strict, old-fashioned Irish Catholics. Attendance at Mass was obligatory."

"You met the ambassador?" Kaz asked.

"Only in passing. He'd finished a term as head of the Securities and Exchange Commission and was waiting to be appointed to some important post by FDR. It was the following year when he went to England. He basically ignored his kid's guests. Not the friendliest guy around."

"How did you get along with Joe Junior?" Kaz asked.

"I couldn't take a liking to him. He had a mean streak. All the Kennedy kids were competitive in everything they did, and sailing was no exception, but Joe was the worst. He brought his little brother Teddy along on a race one day, and Teddy screwed something up, causing Joe to come in way behind the pack. Joe threw him in the water, not close to shore either. I know kid brothers can be a pain, but the little guy nearly drowned. Whatever they did, you couldn't criticize any of them without the rest of them ganging up on you. Joe treated Jack pretty rotten at times, but I think either of them would go down fighting for the other."

"So far, all I know is that Jack befriended you and you went to a baseball game and sat at first base instead of the bleachers, whatever they are. Then you went to what sounds like an ocean resort and went sailing. Did Jack throw you overboard?" Kaz laughed as he polished off his drink.

"It was fun, I admit," I said. "One nice thing about Jack was that he didn't lord his riches over you. He didn't flash cash around. We'd go out at night but never anywhere I couldn't afford."

"A prince among men," Kaz said, leaning back in his chair.

"Jack went to Europe later that summer, with Lem Billings, a good friend of his. He sent me a note when he got back, and we went out to a club once, but he was busy at Harvard and I'd started working the night shift. I didn't hear from him again until November, right after the Yale-Harvard game."

"More baseball?" Kaz asked.

"No. Football, American style," I said, raising the glass to my lips. It was empty, and I set it down. "I got a letter from Jack. He wrote that the night of the game, he accidently backed into a woman's automobile. There was some slight damage, and she wanted to call the police. In his words, she was a 'shit' and he gave her 'a lot of shit' in return. So he backed into her car again, four or five times, then drove off. But not before she wrote down his license plate number, yelling that she'd be reporting it to the Registry of Motor Vehicles in the morning. When the police came calling, Jack told them he'd loaned the vehicle to a friend, who had returned it with the rear bumper crumpled."

"The friend he named was you," Kaz said, his voice low.

"Yeah. The letter said Jack was sure I could work it out and that he didn't want his father to find out about the accident."

"Did you work it out?"

"I almost lost my job. Again. This time Jack didn't come to my defense, since I was his alibi. I got called in front of a disciplinary hearing. I could either tell the truth, and risk bringing down the wrath of the Kennedys, especially if Jack's old man got involved, or admit it was me."

"What did your father say?"

"I tried to keep it a secret, but he found out soon enough. I told him the truth, and he made me promise never to have anything to do with the Kennedys again. I gave him my word, and I meant it. He and Uncle Dan showed up at the hearing wearing their dress blue uniforms. They never said a word. I got a reprimand, which was basically a slap on the wrist."

"You never heard from Jack?"

"Nope. Not until we were summoned here. I was nothing but an alibi, when all was said and done. A convenient sap. Jack's got a lot of personality, I'll give him that. Too much. It blinds you to his shortcomings."

"Do you think he was drunk at the time?" Kaz asked.

"He doesn't touch the hard stuff. Why?"

"As much as he comes across as a scoundrel for his treatment of you, I have to wonder about a man who would lose his temper like that when confronted by a woman. To excuse his behavior by describing her as a shit is terribly self-centered, don't you think? If he could repeatedly ram her automobile over a perceived slight, what else might he be capable of?"

"That's a stretch, Kaz. It happened years ago. It doesn't make him a killer."

I drained the whiskey from my glass. It didn't mean anything, I told myself.

Right?

CHAPTER TWENTY-FOUR

I WOKE UP beneath mosquito netting, clutching an empty bottle. The good news was that I'd made it to bed and even managed to close up the netting. The bad news was that sooner or later I'd have to move my head. I did, along with the rest of my body. I was glad there wasn't a mirror in the room.

"You look like hell, boss," Kao said as I stumbled out of the bedroom. "You don't smell so good either."

"Thanks, good morning to you, too," I said. "Shower. Kopi." I was pretty impressed with myself that I managed to remember the Pijin word for java.

"I can heat up water for the shower if you want."

"No thanks, Kao, but make the kopi strong and sweet." I headed out back to where an outdoor shower was rigged up to a rainwater barrel. Yesterday Kao had added hot water and the shower had been lukewarm, but this morning I needed a cold shock—or as cold as water can get in the Southwest Pacific.

Turns out, that's pretty damn chilly. But it chased away the cobwebs and took my mind off the throbbing in my head. I shaved and got dressed in clean khakis, courtesy of the redoubtable Kao. By the time I was clutching a cup of coffee on the verandah with Kaz, I felt almost human.

"That was quite a story you told last night," Kaz said. "I hope you don't tell another; your liver might fail you."

"Very funny," I said. "But that's it. Now you know the full story of the history between the Kennedy and Boyle clans, such as it is. As soon as we get out of here, I'll be glad to never hear of Jack or his family again."

"Hey boss, you want a Spam and egg sandwich?" Kao asked from the doorway.

"I think I'll skip it, Kao. But thanks. Say, are you from Tulagi? How'd you end up with this job anyway?"

"No, not from Tulagi," Kao said, coming out to the verandah and leaning against the railing. He had a slight physique and a lighter skin tone than most of the natives I'd seen. "My family is from Buka Island, north of Bougainville. They sent me to missionary school on Vella Lavella. The Japs came, and I escaped with my teachers. They found this job for me. Not bad work. Better than on plantation or unloading ships. I'm not strong like my brothers." He looked downcast, maybe at the memory of being teased or missing his folks—big, strong brothers and all.

"Have you heard from your family?" Kaz asked.

"No. Buka full of Japs. Big airfield there. I hear they make all island men work to build it. Many die."

"I am sorry," Kaz said.

Kao shrugged, as if to say condolences were nice but of little value.

"Did you ever hear of Sam Chang from Bougainville?" I asked, as much to change the subject as for any information Kao might have.

"Sure, everyone in those islands knows Sam. He brought supplies to the mission every month. Smart man. I asked if I could work for him someday, told him about my grades in arithmetic. Best in my class."

"What'd he say?" I asked.

"He said maybe he'd have a job on Pavau for me in a few months. Something about an opportunity there, some deal he was working on with Lever. But then the Japs came and everything ended."

"That's all he said?" Kaz asked.

"Yes, boss. He said it was a big secret, and to not tell anyone. But I don't think it matters now."

"Hardly what John Kari told me about Chang's dealings on Pavau," I said, once Kao had gone.

"He didn't want to compete with Lever, I believe you mentioned," Kaz said. "It may not be a contradiction."

"No, but Chang working a secret deal with Lever might have been bad news for Kari. Could have put him out of a job."

"Or perhaps Chang was expanding and would have put both Daniel and John to work, for all we know," Kaz said. It was hard to dispute his logic. We really didn't know much.

"It's a loose thread," I said. "It deserves pulling."

"I may know the perfect man to help," Kaz said. "A fellow by the name of George Luckman was on the flight from Brisbane with me. He works for Lever Brothers and is touring the Solomons to assess how soon the plantations can get up and running."

"How does a soap executive rate transport on military aircraft?" I asked.

"Because glycerin is used in making soap," Kaz said. "They produce nitroglycerin now, given the shortage of raw materials to make soap. And for the good of the war effort, of course."

"Sure," I said, "but now that the Solomons are being slowly liberated, it's time for people to lather up again."

"I would think that is in Lever's interests," Kaz said. "Luckman is traveling under the auspices of the Australian Department of Trade and Customs, so it is logical to assume the government is interested in new tax revenues as well."

"The taxman always wants his cut," I said. "Do you know where Luckman is hanging his hat?"

"With Hugh Sexton, so he can get up-to-date reports from the Coastwatchers."

"Makes sense, since so many of them are planters. Let's grab our gear and pay him a visit."

We packed up and told Kao we were headed for Rendova and weren't sure when we'd return. We tossed our bags into the jeep and paid a visit to Sexton's headquarters. We found him hunched over his map table, a small-scale map of the Solomon Islands spread out from end to end. An older man in nondescript pressed khakis held a pointer, tapping it on the islands to the north.

"Ah, Lieutenant Kazimierz, good to see you again," the gent said, his English accent proper but without the lazy cadence of the upper classes. He stood ramrod straight, his short-cropped hair grey at the temples and thinning on top. He looked old enough to have served in the last war and intelligent enough to have made a lot of money since then. Kaz introduced us and I watched Sexton as he did so. His eyes darted between us, confused at the familiarity until Luckman explained that he and Kaz had been traveling companions.

"What can I do for you?" Sexton said. "We're a bit busy at the moment, if you don't mind."

"Actually, I have a few quick questions for Mr. Luckman, if you don't mind the interruption," I said, idly gazing at the map unfolded across the table. It wasn't a military map. At the corner, in fancy print, the legend read: *Lever Brothers Limited—By appointment—Soapmakers to H.M. The King.*

"Glad to help, although I don't know how I can," Luckman said. "The lieutenant told me a bit of your inquiry. Dreadful business, murder during wartime, especially so close to the front lines. Practically aiding and abetting the enemy."

"There must be quite a pent-up demand for soap," I said, ignoring his pompous little speech. "Are you here to reopen the plantations?"

"Is this part of your investigation?" Sexton said, his irritation clear.

"No, just idle curiosity," I said, tracing my finger along the islands on either side of the Slot. The map showed ports, towns, roads, and plantations. Some were colored red, others blue. "What are the colors for?"

"The red are plantations owned by Lever Brothers and managed for us. The blue are independent properties," Luckman said. Like most people, he didn't mind talking about a subject he knew well and cared about. "Several on Guadalcanal are back in operation already. The fight was mainly contained on the northeast side of the island. The plantations were hardly touched, except for the buildings. If the Japanese patrols didn't burn them out, your chaps bombed them. But it's the trees that are important. It takes ten years for a coconut tree to reach peak production. Compared to that, rebuilding a house is simple."

"Does it matter to you if a plantation is one of yours or owned by the grower?" I asked.

"Individually, no," Luckman said. "There's really no one else to sell to, so it's not a matter of access to resources. But to establish quality and a reliable crop, it pays to run the majority ourselves."

"So on Pavau, for instance," I said, studying the island northeast of Choiseul where one blue section stood alone. "There's one local plantation on the north side, and the rest on the south are all Lever. Any difference in the copra production?"

"None," Luckman said. "Why do you ask?"

"No special reason. Just curious about a fellow who worked for you there. John Kari, a native fellow. Well-spoken."

"Kari?" Luckman said, furrowing his brow. "On a plantation? Can't recall the name. Was he a foreman?"

"He worked in the harbor," I said. "Keeping books on the copra deliveries and managing the sale of supplies your ships brought in, if I remember correctly."

"Kari, yes, now I remember," Luckman said. "We do employ staff at some of the harbors where several plantations bring their crops. Easier to manage that way. Not a very demanding job, except when the ship docks. Once or twice a month it was, at Pavau, I think."

"He's a Coastwatcher now," Sexton said, trying to pull the conversation back to familiar ground.

"Really?" Luckman said, a look of surprise on his face.

"We have several natives working as Coastwatchers," Sexton said, somewhat defensively. "Plus those who serve as scouts and porters. All good men."

"I don't doubt it," Luckman said. "But I wouldn't count John Kari as good. My memory is that he's a thief. We were about to sack him and bring him to Tulagi to be put under arrest. But then the Japanese swept through the islands and the matter was forgotten, until you reminded me of his name."

"Let me guess," I said, "this happened after you cut a deal with

Sam Chang. He was going to pay you to give up the supply business in the islands where he operated. Which would have put John Kari out of work."

"You are well informed, I'll give you that," Luckman said. "It was about the same time, yes. But that doesn't give Kari an excuse for out-and-out theft. He was overbilling the customers and keeping a good portion for himself. Not exactly grand larceny, but still, we couldn't stand for it."

"Did Sam Chang report this to you?" Kaz asked.

"Yes, he was the first to have his suspicions. He had talked with several plantation managers, finding out what they wanted from more frequent deliveries. When he saw what they were being charged for a case of whiskey, he thought Lever was gouging them."

"Surely you didn't mind making a profit from the sale of supplies?" I said.

"A profit, no. As is stands, the ships go out empty, so why not use the space? But we also want our people happy with the arrangement. Our focus is the regular delivery of copra, not being a greengrocer. We were happy to turn it over to Chang. He's a good businessman. I hope we can still come to an agreement when the fighting moves on."

"That'll be tough," I said, noting that he didn't say *when the war is over.* This businessman didn't look far beyond next quarter's profits. "He's dead."

"Don't tell me," Luckman said, looking to Kaz. "He's one of the two victims."

"Three now," Kaz said.

"Bloody hell," Luckman said. "The Japanese are bad enough. I hope you catch him."

"That's going to be tough as well," Sexton said. "By now he and Silas Porter are deep in the bush on Choiseul. They went up to Rendova yesterday and were dropped off early this morning."

"Porter?" Luckman said. "The hermit? I didn't figure him for the Coastwatcher type."

"That's what everyone says," Sexton offered. "But he was keen on it after the Japs massacred his workers."

"The assistant manager as well?" Luckman asked.

"Peter Fraser," Sexton said. "Yes, he and all of Porter's workers were killed in a reprisal. At least as far as we can determine. As you can see, that area of Pavau island is cut off from the rest." He tapped on the spiny mountain range that cut off the north third of the island.

"Yes, I know the lay of the land well enough. Pity about Fraser, we had our eye on him. He worked at our soap factory in Sydney before he came out to the Solomons. Didn't stay long with us, though. There was an accident with a lorry that crippled his father. When the old man died, young Peter decided to light out for the islands. Did a fine job for Porter the short time he was there, from all reports. Manager material, definitely."

"High praise," I said, trying to sound enthusiastic. If Peter Fraser had a tombstone someday, I hoped that wouldn't be his epitaph. "Does the name Daniel Tamana mean anything to you?"

"No," Luckman said, rubbing his chin as if to coax the words out. "Another native chap?"

"Another dead man," I said. "What about Fred Archer? Or Gordie Brockman?"

"Archer?" Luckman said. "Yes, a bit of brute, if you don't mind my saying. The kind of man who leaves one step ahead of the constable and makes for the outback or the islands. His plantation was productive, I'll give him that. Brockman doesn't ring a bell though. Wasn't a Lever manager; I'd know all of them."

"Thanks," I said. "Hugh, please keep us posted on Porter and Kari. We're going up to Rendova but should be back in a few days."

"Do you think John Kari is the killer?" Sexton asked.

"No," I said. "It's not certain. But I'd like to talk with him some more. I can understand him keeping his sticky fingers a secret, but I have to wonder what else he may be hiding. Lying gets to be a habit after a while, and he may have information we need."

"Kari has saved many lives," Sexton said, leaning over the map table. "Consider that before you accuse him of these murders or even suggest he was involved. He may have stolen from Lever, but he's acted bravely since. I can't see any reason why he'd turn on his own people."

"I don't think we'd pursue charges, not at this late date," Luckman said. "Sounds like he's done his bit and more."

"I just want to talk to him," I said, holding up my hands in mock surrender. "I agree that petty pilferage is best forgotten after all he's been through. Thanks for your help."

We shook hands all around, wished each other good luck, and left with distrust hanging thickly in the air.

"They do not like the idea of one of their own as a killer," Kaz said once we were on the road. "Sexton can't imagine a Coastwatcher being a murderer, and Luckman wouldn't want Lever associated with one."

"What do you think?" I said as I accelerated up a winding, hilly road. It began to rain, a light mist that was refreshing, breaking the morning heat.

"You've taught me the three cardinal virtues of a crime," Kaz said as he wiped his glasses with a handkerchief. "Means, motive, and opportunity. John Kari had the means in all three cases. We've seen him kill. He slit the throat of that Japanese sentry on Malaita quite efficiently."

"So he could have easily brained Daniel on the beach," I said. "And overpowered Deanna before he knifed her. But what about Sam Chang? He was strangled. Kari isn't that big of a guy. The doctor said the killer had strong hands."

"First, he was unconscious," Kaz said. "Secondly, the killer knew he had to act quickly. His adrenaline would have kicked in, the fear of being discovered giving him the strength he needed."

"Okay, I can work with that," I said. "What's next?" It was beginning to rain harder, the dirt road turning muddy along the tire tracks.

"Motive," Kaz answered. "Daniel Tamana threatened to tell what he knew about the thefts, so he had to be eliminated. Sam Chang obviously knew, and when he showed up alive, he had to be taken care of. But why Deanna?"

"Because he'd seen Daniel speak to her privately. He had to kill her in case Daniel had confided his suspicions to her," I said, without a lot of conviction.

"But she wasn't killed right away," Kaz said. "Why the delay?"

"Let's move on," I suggested, having no answer to that.

"Opportunity," Kaz said. "He lured Daniel to the beach, saying he could explain things, perhaps appealing to their bonds as natives and fellow Coastwatchers. As for Chang, anyone could have walked into that hospital at night and gained access to the room where the Chinese patients were kept. Perhaps it was a stroke of luck that he saw Deanna alone in Chinatown. An opportunity for him to silence her in case she knew his secret. And we know Kari was driving through around the time of Deanna's murder, a stiletto on his belt."

"It fits," I said. "But the motive is weak. Why murder three people over a theft from more than a year ago? The whole world has changed since the Japs swept through here. Everything's been turned upside down for the Solomon Islanders. It doesn't feel like his thievery would be that important in the long run."

"His life could still change for the better or the worse," Kaz said as we drove along the harbor in Chinatown. I avoided looking at the desolate alley where Deanna had met her end. I slowed for a pair of sailors stumbling out onto the street, bottles of beer clutched in their hands. They looked up, seemingly shocked at the rain soaking their denims. Then the rain stopped suddenly, and they laughed as if it had been a joke staged for their benefit. Leaving them behind, I envied their carefree joyfulness while steam rose from the earth, clouds parted, and shafts of sunlight beat down on us, turning the cool downpour into stifling humidity. "He could be killed. Or return home a hero to his people."

"So why risk murdering three people? What would he have to gain?"

"Not enough," Kaz said. "Unless he were a madman."

"*Gwai lo,*" I said.

"The white ghost," Kaz said. "An elusive being."

We drove on, the misty greyness dissolving the boundaries between the jungle and the road, the treetops and the sky, the water and the islands beyond. Ghosts were all around us, white ghosts floating above the earth, writhing among the palms and tiger grass. Elusive? They were everywhere.

CHAPTER TWENTY-FIVE

SESAPI HARBOR WAS busy, PT boats coming and going, and destroyers steaming out toward the Slot. Native workers unloaded truckloads of supplies, and sailors stripped to the waist carried them from the docks to their waiting craft. The action had a frantic air to it, the rush to complete each task mingled with nervous laughter and foolish grins among the newer men, while the old hands ignored them, stacking ammo like split wood against freshening winter winds. Something was up, another big push up the Solomon chain in the offing, and we were being drawn along in its wake.

We dropped our gear off at Cotter's boat and kept going, down to the end of the pier by the PT tender. I'd told Jack I'd see him on his new command. We had an hour or so before we left, or hauled anchor, or whatever the navy types called shoving off, so Kaz and I decided to check out the new boat.

"Impressive," Kaz said as we took in the big forty-millimeter guns fore and aft. PT-59 bristled with armament and activity. Two turrets amidships sported twin fifty-caliber machine guns, and where the torpedo tubes had formerly been, more machine guns were being installed behind armored shields. An arc welder spit out white-hot sparks as a crewman worked on one of the mounts.

"That's a lot of firepower," I said to Jack, who waved us aboard.

"How do you like her?" Jack was all grin, shirtless in the heat, grease on his hands, and spoiling for a fight.

"A lethal vessel," Kaz said admiringly.

"Exactly, Baron," Jack said. "Now we've got the firepower to take on the Jap barges and shore installations. They won't know what hit them." He was positively gleeful, but I was more interested in how he looked as opposed to his boat. I could count his ribs, and though his skin was tanned nearly bronze, it had an odd tone to it, a shade of dark yellow that didn't look healthy. His knuckles were a dark brown, even deeper than the rest of him. He caught me looking, and grabbed for a faded khaki shirt, pulling it on but not bothering to button it.

"I'm taking her out, Billy, as soon as I fill out the crew." It was a challenge, a dare to even question his fitness.

"I'm sure you'll do fine, Jack," I said. It wasn't my fight. If the navy saw fit to give him this gunboat, then that was the navy's business. I hoped he didn't get his men killed as he sought his revenge for PT-109.

"All set, Skipper," a sailor said from behind us, flipping up his arc welder's helmet. "That's the last mount in place."

"Well done, Chappy," Jack said, stepping by us to inspect the welding job. The steel shields gave the gunners decent protection, at least from small-arms fire. Jack settled in behind one of the fifty-calibers, testing the rotation and angle of fire. "How'd you get the swivel to move like that? It was tight as a tick this morning."

"Oil, elbow grease, and the right tools, Skipper," came the answer as he removed the helmet.

"Hey, aren't you the gunner's mate from Al Cluster's boat?" I asked, remembering the trip from Guadalcanal and the downed Jap flyer.

"Yes sir," he said. "Commander Cluster thought Lieutenant Kennedy might need an experienced hand getting these new guns installed."

"And I'm not giving Chappy back," Jack said. "I still need to fill out my crew, and a gunner's mate is a good start. Consider yourself shanghaied, sailor."

"Fine with me, Skipper. I was hoping you'd say that. This boat is a gunner's dream come true." Chappy left, clutching his tool kit along with an oilcan.

"I'll probably see you two on Rendova," Jack said. "We're headed up there as soon as everything's ready and I have enough men."

"It looks like you've got reinforcements," Kaz said. A group of five sailors approached from the dock, seabags carried on their shoulders.

"Oh my God," Jack said, a look of surprise on his face as he watched the men come on board. "What are you all doing here?"

"What kind of guy are you?" the lead sailor answered. "You got a boat and didn't come get us?" It seemed like an odd exchange between a swabbie and an officer, but smiles had broken out among the group as Jack waded in amongst them, shaking hands.

"Kowal, Mauer, Drewitch," he said, pausing a moment before each man. "Maguire, Drawdy. You guys sure you want to come along? I can't guarantee this is going to be easy."

"Hell, Skip, we wouldn't ship out with anyone else," one of them said, a radioman second class by his two stripes and lightning-bolt insignia. Jack stood among them for a minute, his hands stuffed in his pockets, his head downcast like a shy schoolboy. Then he turned away, heading to the bow of the gunboat, his arm draped around the barrel of the forty-millimeter cannon.

"Who are you guys?" I asked the radioman.

"We're all from the 109," he said. "Maguire, sir. Me and Mauer were on the 109 when she went down. The other guys had been wounded a few weeks ago and just got out of the hospital. We heard the skipper got a new assignment, so here we are. Don't tell me they got the army on this boat, too?"

"No, we're just visiting," I said. "You feel okay about shipping out with Jack after what happened?"

"He got me back alive," Maguire said. "He never gave up. I'd trust him with my life."

That wasn't a sentence I ever heard or expected to hear about Jack Kennedy. I mumbled something appropriate and moved away, the men from the 109 mingling with the rest of the crew as they stowed their gear. I worked my way forward, past the bridge, up to where Jack stood. His thin arm was still holding onto the gun barrel, the other shading his eyes as he gazed out over the water. I stepped closer and saw that he wasn't shading his eyes from the light.

He was hiding them. From my vantage point I could see tears coursing down his cheeks, salty drops hitting the steel deck at his feet, vaporizing in the heat.

Jack Kennedy weeping. Another thing I never expected to see in this life.

I stepped back, unwilling to intrude, marveling that this rich, spoiled playboy had inspired so much loyalty. And that a guy who never seemed to care much about anything stood alone, crying at the thought of the trust these men had placed in his hands.

Kaz was chatting with the new crewmen at the stern. The gunner's mate was working on another machine gun setup, this one on the starboard side. I strolled over, watching him work as I waited for Jack to get a hold of himself. I noticed his name, Ellis, stenciled on his denim shirt.

"Why do they call you Chappy?" I asked, leaning against the bulkhead and enjoying a spot of shade.

"That's 'cause of these tools I use," he said, grabbing a small leather case filled with rachet bits. "My uncle owns a company called Chapman Manufacturing. They make all sorts of hex keys, slotted screwdriver bits, ratchets, that sort of thing. When he heard I was a gunner's mate, he sent me this kit. Whatever the navy throws at me, I can take it apart and put it back together again with these babies. So the guys started calling me Chappy, and it sorta stuck."

"Doesn't the navy have enough tools to go around?"

"Not out here, Lieutenant. We have to scrounge for most everything. But with this tool kit, I'm a walking machine shop. I can even get some Jap hardware working if it's not too banged up."

"Lieutenant Kennedy is lucky to have you aboard, Chappy," I said. "There's plenty of gunnery here to keep you busy."

"It's a whole lotta firepower to throw at the Japs," he said. "I get the feeling the skipper is itching to get back at them for what they did to his old boat."

"Can't blame him," I said. I wished Chappy luck and climbed up to the bridge, where I found Jack, shirtless again, wearing aviator sunglasses and a fatigue cap pushed back up on his bushy hair. The sun was harsh, but I figured he'd donned the glasses mainly to cover his reddened eyes.

"Take care, Jack," I said, offering my hand.

"See you in Rendova," he said, giving me a firm shake. "I hope you find your man."

"I will," I said. "I don't have all the answers yet, but we'll find them. There's always a clue. There's always something."

I clambered down off the boat onto the dock and turned to see Kaz stop to speak with Jack on the bridge. I waited, wishing I had a pair of sunglasses like Jack's as the afternoon sun beat down.

"What was that about?" I asked as we walked back to PT-169.

"I asked Jack about the incident with the automobile," Kaz said.

"Why the hell did you do that?" I asked, stopping to face Kaz, surprised at my own anger. I didn't need Kaz fighting my battles for me, and I sure as hell didn't want Jack thinking I did.

"Because I was curious about the kind of man he is," Kaz said. "I am still suspicious of him."

"Well, what did he say?"

"He has no recollection of the incident. He thought it amusing when I recounted it, but it apparently meant little enough to him at the time."

"So what does that prove?" I asked, irritated at hearing the answer to a question I knew I shouldn't have asked.

"That he is exceedingly self-centered," Kaz said. "I believe such a man could kill more easily than not."

"Yeah, murder is a pretty selfish enterprise," I said, continuing on down the dock. "Nothing earth-shattering about that." Why was I defending Jack? Hadn't I thought the same myself not very long ago?

"True," Kaz said, nodding his head as we walked. "Although the man described by the PT-109 crew is quite a different character. Intrepid, loyal, even inspiring."

"What does that tell us?"

"That Jack Kennedy is a complex man, capable of pettiness as well as sacrifice," Kaz answered. "His actions involving you in the automobile accident demonstrate a disregard for others, and perhaps a fear of disappointing his powerful father. After all, who else would care, or be in a position to chastise him? But his resourcefulness here, in keeping his crew together after the sinking of his boat, demonstrates the complete opposite. From all accounts, he went far beyond what could be expected of any captain."

"That may be why I'm having a hard time understanding him," I said. "He's not the guy I knew. I think maybe that guy went down with the 109. Did he say he was sorry at all? About the car?"

"No, he did not," Kaz said.

"Well, maybe not all of him went down with the ship."

"Boyle!" Cotter yelled from the bridge of PT-169. "Hustle up! We're pulling out. Aircraft headed our way!"

CHAPTER TWENTY-SIX

"THERE'S A LARGE force of enemy aircraft headed our way from airfields on Bougainville," Cotter said as he eased PT-169 out of the harbor and into Ironbottom Sound. "They could be going for Rendova, Henderson Field, or Sesapi. No reason to hang around and find out."

"The trip will be more dangerous in daylight, won't it?" I asked.

"Yes, if we run into patrol aircraft. But this is a big raid. They won't break formation to go after one PT boat." That sounded good, as long as the Japanese remembered to play by the rules.

"What can we do?" I asked.

"Take these," he said, handing Kaz and me binoculars. "Go forward and watch for aircraft."

We'd seen Archer and Gordie positioned aft, scanning the skies as we pulled out. We went toward the bow, behind the twenty-millimeter gun, which was manned by a kid in a big helmet, life jacket, skivvies, and shoes; enough clothing for a hot run in the Solomons.

We each took a side, bracing ourselves between the bridge super-structure and a forward torpedo tube. As Cotter opened up the engines, the ride smoothed out into a steady *thump thump* against the rolling waves, fooling you into thinking you didn't have to hang on. I realized Kaz and I were the only ones without life jackets, and that nobody had taken time to toss a couple our way. On the one hand, if we got hit, we were all going up in a giant fireball anyway, but it wouldn't take much work to get tossed overboard either. I could swim pretty well, but not all the way back to Tulagi.

It wasn't long before a shout went up from the stern, Gordie and Archer having sighted fighters coming from behind. Cotter announced they were ours, flying up from Guadalcanal to intercept the Japs. Even so, every gun swiveled to target them as they flew high overhead.

"Hold your fire," Cotter yelled, knowing how trigger-happy his men could be. Out here, there was nowhere to hide, and dozens of swarming, snarling fighters were downright intimidating. Then I began to worry. Would they mistake *us* for Japs, and open fire?

They passed over without incident, and I let out a heavy sigh, not realizing how nervous I'd been. I watched the fighters, figuring they were being vectored in by radar, or perhaps Coastwatchers. Soon I lost them, and gave the horizon a quick check. Dead ahead I saw an island, too far away to make out anything but a smudge of green.

"Is that Rendova?" I asked the sailor manning the twenty-millimeter.

"Naw, that's Russell Island. We ain't even close yet, Lieutenant."

Cotter kept on course for the island. I strained to see anything at all in the sky, alternating between the binoculars and my eyesight, trying to take in the full arc of the blazingly bright heavens in front of us. It was all azure blue, nothing but foaming water rising into a robin's egg sky; so much to watch, and it all looked exactly the same.

"There!" Kaz shouted, pointing up off the starboard side. Contrails swirled in all directions, evidence of a high-altitude dogfight. I trained my binoculars on the telltale vapor trails, but all I got was the occasional flash of sunlight off a fighter.

"Keep a sharp lookout," Cotter bellowed from the bridge. "If they're making contrails, they're too high to bother us. Watch for fighters breaking away." I waved back, signaling my understanding, and returned to scanning the horizon, sweeping back and forth, dividing the sky into quadrants.

Then I saw it. Black smoke instead of white contrails. Heading for us and losing altitude fast. I picked up the aircraft in my binoculars, but the billowing smoke and dead-on view obscured any markings. It was obvious he was in trouble.

"It's got to be one of ours," I said to the gunner. "Probably headed back to Henderson Field."

"I don't like the way he's heading for us," he said, training his weapon on the incoming fighter.

"Don't fire, wait!" I yelled, focusing on the smoke, glimpsing a brief image of another airplane, then another. "Behind him, two Zeroes!"

"Yes!" Kaz screamed. "He's coming to us for cover!"

The gunner acknowledged a second later, saying he had the two Zeroes targeted. Cotter shouted to hold fire, and then suddenly the first plane was close enough to see, white stars clear against the blue paint job. Smoke poured from under the engine cowling as the Wildcat pilot went into a steep dive, bringing the Zeroes closer to our guns.

The Zeroes were now unmistakable, their bubble canopies and red Rising Sun insignias stark against a light grey background as they closed in on the Wildcat, guns chattering, bursts of tracer rounds bracketing their quarry. The American fighter drew closer, no more than a couple of hundred yards above the water. As he banked to our right, giving the PT boat a clear shot at his pursuers, he lost even more altitude. I could make out oil streaks across his canopy and bullet holes along the fuselage, and I hoped he'd make it back if our fire could manage to distract the Zeroes.

Then all hell broke loose and I wondered if the Zeroes were glad to trade targets.

Great spouts of seawater rose up around us, the machine gun and cannon fire from the Jap planes creating a maelstrom as the two twin fifty-calibers behind me opened up, their rapid fire a counterpoint to the steady, slower hammering of the twenty-millimeter cannon. I ducked, shielding my ears from the clamoring of the weapons, the raging screams of men firing at the enemy, the snarl of engines, and the blood pounding in my head.

Rounds thumped into the wooden deck, sending splinters flying past my face. I hung on as Cotter took evasive action and watched as the Zeroes pulled away, each arcing off in a different direction to divide our fire. One of them spat out a couple of white puffs of smoke as his engine sputtered and he continued on away from us. The crew cheered at the evidence of their marksmanship. The Wildcat was now a good distance to our rear, flying low and steady. If he didn't make it all the way to Guadalcanal, he could probably ditch with a good chance of rescue.

"Look!" Kaz shouted. "Twelve o'clock low!" The other Zero wasn't escorting his pal home. He was coming back for us. This time he was flying close to the wavetops, perhaps hoping we couldn't lower our guns enough, or maybe to maximize his own flame. Whatever the reason, the Zero looked like a demon breathing fire as it bore down on us. Cotter zigged and zagged, which I figured was to throw the Jap's aim off, but it did the same for our gunners. Tracers zipped back and forth, filling the air between the plane and the boat with lines of burning phosphorous, deadly stitches of yellow-white seeking to destroy, to eliminate the enemy threat.

It all happened at once. We were hit again, this time the gunner by my side taking a round in the head. His body dropped like a heavy sack just as the Zero blossomed into flames, parts blowing off as the plane stayed on course, inertia and momentum carrying it forward, straight for the splintered and bloody bow of our ship.

Cotter spun the wheel hard to port, and once again I hung on, grasping the handrail and hoping that if I got tossed over, I'd make it clear of the boat's propellers.

The Zero lost more altitude, one wing dipping drunkenly, the pilot by now likely a dead hand on the stick. The wingtip brushed the surface of the waves, tossing up a delicate plume of water, a glimmering, incongruous spray against the trailing flames. The wingtip of the Zero seemed to balance on the water perfectly, until the aircraft cartwheeled and slammed hard on its back, the sea around it burning with aviation fuel.

Cotter turned, slowed the engines, and circled the wreck, but there was nothing to see but flames, nothing to feel but intense heat rolling off the water, nothing to care about but being alive.

For most of us, anyway.

The gunner's torso lay against the bulwark, his life's blood drenching the deck, the top half of his head nowhere to be seen. His lower jaw hung down, ribbons of muscle and flesh flung back above it, his tongue obscenely huge and pink against a dark, red space of nothingness. Shattered bone and brain were strewn against the steel bulkhead, splashed with blood. A single twenty-millimeter shell can do a hell of a lot of damage, taking only a split second to turn a living, breathing man into a riven carcass.

I had to tear my gaze away, the butchery of war as compelling as it was ugly and brutal. Deep inside, I knew why I had to look—not out of pity for the dead man, or the guilty thrill of carnage avoided, but to consider the possibility that I was no more than blood and gristle myself, that it could as well have been my own body cast asunder, revealing no visible soul, no humanity, no memories, nothing but cooling pink flesh.

I checked the damage to the boat, not interested in having it sink out from under us just as the fight had been won. The bow was pretty chewed up, and bullet holes decorated the bridge as well.

"Anyone else hurt?" Cotter asked, leaning over the bridge, wincing as he took in the scene below. No one spoke. I couldn't get a word out, not even a grunt. I gave him a wave, trying to look like I was just fine. I saw flecks of blood on my hand and felt more running down the side of my face. I looked at Kaz, who had the presence of mind, if not the courage, to step into the gunner's post and man the cannon. His face was spotted in blood as well—a fine, delicate red mist. Cotter increased throttle, and water soon broke over the bow, turning the pooled and darkening blood into a pink foam as it washed back over the side.

I leaned over the rail and vomited.

"I hope that pilot made it back," Kaz said, wiping his face with a handkerchief. "Otherwise his maneuver held little merit."

"And we could still be in trouble, if either of those pilots radioed our position," I said, wiping my face with my sleeve. "Do you know how to work that thing?"

"I watched him," Kaz said, his hands on the grip, his eye peering through the sight. "It seemed straightforward enough, but I hope for a more long-distance duel if we are attacked once again."

Not for the first time, I marveled at Kaz's ability to deal with any situation he found himself in. I guess after losing everyone you loved in the world, there was little surprise left in it. I went back to my binoculars, watching the sky for approaching fighters. Contrails drifted high above, thinning out as the planes dove to lower altitudes to bomb and strafe.

A few minutes later, I heard Archer shout from the rear of the boat. "Formation at two o'clock high! Twelve bandits!"

"On a course for Tulagi," Gordie added.

I found them. Betties, it looked like.

"Fighters behind them," Archer said calmly.

Cotter barked orders for the information to be radioed to Henderson Field, and then turned the boat to starboard.

"We'll make for Russell Island and hide out until nightfall," he told us. "We can't get caught out in the open again. Those Betties might give us a working over on their return trip."

We kept eyes on the aircraft as they passed by, intent on delivering their deadly loads to our home base. Lower and far behind, I made out a ragged formation of Wildcats, probably the squadron that had been scrambled to intercept the first group over Rendova. I hoped they had enough fuel and ammo left in case the Japs were headed for Henderson Field.

Cotter slowed as he approached one of the outlying islands. Crewman came forward to wrap the dead gunner—I never did catch his name—in weighted canvas for interment at sea.

"There's no burying ground at Rendova. The base is on a small island, Lumbari, that's basically a swamp surrounded by ocean," Cotter explained, looking glum at the prospect of having to dump one of his men overboard with little time for ceremony. But he had the living to think of. A few words, bowed heads, a splash, and it was over. But some in this war had even less homage in death.

He took the boat past the small island, under cover of overhanging palms on the shore of Russell proper. The water was gentle here and slapped at the side of the hidden boat, rocking it like grandpa's chair on the porch. Kaz and I rinsed ourselves with saltwater until all traces of blood were gone. Then we sat in the shade, a quiet, peaceful, drowsy rest as we waited for daylight and the war in the air to pass us by.

"You're both lucky to be alive," Gordie observed as we all relaxed amidships. "That was a damn close-run thing, as Wellington said at Waterloo."

"I don't know about Wellington, but if I were really lucky, I wouldn't be wringing a dead man's blood out of my socks," I said, laying the pair of them out to dry and rolling up my trouser legs.

"Can't say I appreciate that pilot bringing the Zeroes down on us," Archer said, his voice an angry snarl. "Nearly got us all killed, the selfish bastard."

"We had the firepower, and he was in trouble," Cotter said, rising to go below. "It was a risk, and he took it. I'm going to check in with Rendova."

"Calculated with the odds in his favor," Archer said to Cotter's back. "I've managed to keep myself alive so far. I don't need a crazy Yank giving the Japs a leg up on doing me in."

"Steady on," Gordie said. "No need to blame the Yanks."

"Steady on yourself," Archer growled. "There's blame enough to go around. First we lose Daniel, and it's that Yank Kennedy who's first on the scene. Then the Chinaman, and lo and behold, friend Jack was there, too. Poor Deanna gets knifed in Chinatown, and what do you know, she was his girlfriend when it suited him. I've had my fill of Yanks for a while. The bush is sounding like a safe place for a change." He stalked off to the stern as the sound of aircraft droned overhead. We all ducked, as if that might make a difference.

"Don't mind him," Gordie said. "Nerves, that's all. The past few weeks have been hectic, and with the killings, it's been hard to relax and prepare mentally for the hard road ahead."

"What's the current situation on Ranongga?" Kaz asked. Gordie and Archer were headed back to their previous station.

"We don't know," he said. "The good news is that the invasion of New Georgia is bringing the war closer, and the island could be taken in the next few months, if I read the tea leaves correctly."

"What's the bad news?" I asked.

"That the Japs understand that as well, and may have established a garrison there. They have a small base at Emu harbor at the northern end of the island. They'd occasionally send patrols out, but by the time they got anywhere near us, the natives would have given us ample warning."

"It is not a very large island," Kaz said. "It must be hard to hide."

"Easy enough if you have time to take the radio down and go off into the bush or up into the mountain. But if the Japs have established other bases since we left and manage to coordinate against us, it'll be a different matter altogether. We've had our share of good luck so far, but since we came out, luck seems to have eluded us. I think that's what got Archer spooked. Me, too, for that matter."

Everyone turned silent as we heard the distant approach of aircraft. Not the steady hum of a formation, but the oncoming sounds of diving whines and turns, throaty open throttles and the sudden chatter of machine guns.

"It's not healthy out there," Cotter said, returning from below. "The PT base at Rendova's been bombed, as well as our positions on New Georgia. The Japs sent fighters on down the Slot to draw our Wildcats away. That's what we're hearing." He jerked his thumb up, toward the leafy palm tree cover, the noise of dogfights ebbing and flowing over the island just out of sight. "Soon as the sun sets, we'll head for Lumbari. The fighters will all be home by then, drinking their saki or scotch."

"Then all we have to worry about are the Kawanishi," Gordie said. "Delightful."

"You knew that when you signed up for the cruise, Gordie," Cotter said, slapping him on the shoulder. "I'm going to get some shut-eye."

"He seems like a decent guy," I said, keeping my voice low.

"You mean not the type to leave his comrades in the lurch?" Gordie said.

"More that I'm surprised he'd lie about it. From what I understand, he still insists he carried out a search."

"Which seems unlikely, given the flames from the burning fuel on PT-109," Kaz put in.

"Tell me, either of you," Gordie said, "how long did you think that Zero was attacking us before it went down?"

"Forever," Kaz said, to which I nodded my agreement.

"I'd say less than four seconds, but it likely felt much longer facing it head-on. Time is different out here," Gordie said, stretching his hand out toward the water. "On the sea, I mean, in one of these flimsy plywood crates filled with fuel and explosives. Daylight or darkness, it makes little difference; it seems as if the entire Japanese air force and navy is determined to blast you to hell. At night, the lines from tracers burn your eyes and the fire from a destroyer's guns is a blindingly bright, vivid white. Shore batteries, too, not to mention the threat of deadly Kawanishi overhead. Maybe he saw the burning fuel and mistook it for enemy fire. He may have searched, and thought he'd done so for thirty minutes or so."

"It could have been much less?"

"Quite possible. I can't say for certain, but perhaps by the time they docked at Lumbari, every man jack among the crew swore they carried out a full-scale search. And believed it themselves."

"It is quite easy to conjecture," Kaz said. "But we were not the ones left adrift and alone. Lieutenant Kennedy and his men certainly see things differently."

"Less forgiving, I'm certain," Gordie said, lighting a cigarette. "Say, I heard you both met up with old Luckman. What did you think of him?"

"How'd you hear that?" I asked.

"Telephone, old boy. I checked in with Hugh before we departed. You are the suspicious type, aren't you?"

"Sorry, occupational hazard. I thought he was hurrying things a bit. Not much that the government can do until the Japs are cleared out."

"I think it may have more to do with the natives and getting them back working at prewar wages," Kaz said.

"How are you going to keep them down on the farm, isn't that how the song goes?" Gordie said with a smile. "Very likely. Luckman's a big cheese with Lever Brothers, don't let that government stuff fool you. They're working hand in glove."

"It sounds like he's working in your best interests as well," I said. "It's going to be hard getting your plantation back on its feet once the fighting is past. Don't you want the natives to return to work without demanding higher wages?"

"Look," Gordie said, "I want to profit from my work as much as the next man. What I paid my workers before the war was fair, by the standards of the day. Things have changed, I understand that. But I'm not a Lever man and wouldn't work for them if I were down to my last shilling. Some of us came out here to make our own way, not to take pay from a corporation."

"Did you ever run into Luckman?" I asked.

"I heard him speak at some gathering in Buka Town, on Bougainville, before the war. Drinks with the islanders, Lever seeking out new talent to run their plantations. I wasn't interested, except for the drinking. He knew his stuff, I'll give him that. Wasn't afraid to get out into the bush and visit the more remote plantations. I made it clear Lever wasn't for me, so he passed me by. He saw plenty of others, though."

"He remembered Peter Fraser, Silas Porter's assistant," I said. "Thought he was manager material."

"Don't mention that around Archer," Gordie said. "He spent time kowtowing to Luckman, only to be told Lever wasn't interested in him. Too rough with the natives, which is true enough. Archer didn't take it well."

"I thought he came out here to get away from civilization after his father's ranch went under," I said. "Working for Lever doesn't quite match up."

"I think he feared another failure if his plantation didn't prosper. He'd had a run of bad luck, and his treatment of his workers didn't help. Too much stick and not enough carrot, if you know what I mean. Lever would at least mean security, and he'd still be an islander, in charge of his fiefdom."

"It sounds as if you do not like the man," Kaz said, glancing back to be sure Archer was out of earshot.

"Not a matter of liking or not," Gordie said. "I trust him. He knows the bush, and he's not afraid of a fight."

"Good with a knife?" I asked, glancing at the stiletto on Gordie's belt.

"There's several dead Japs who can attest to that," he said. "But I doubt he'd turn on his own." Gordie's eyes shot to the shore, where two natives had stepped silently out from the jungle.

"Aftanun ol'ta!" Gordie said loudly, drawing the attention of the rest of the crew. He waved cheerfully, and they smiled back.

"Good afternoon?" Kaz asked.

"Very good, Baron," Gordie said and rose to speak to the natives, who approached the side of the PT boat, one of them carrying a spear. They had a rapid-fire conversation in Pijin I couldn't follow, and one of them handed over a map to Gordie. He gave it a quick once-over, handed it to Cotter, and went below. Crewmen tossed them cigarettes and chewing gum. Gordie returned with two cans of Spam, which were even more eagerly accepted.

"Tanggio tumas," Gordie said. "Thank you very much."

"No wariwari," the one with the spear said, waving to the rest of us. They turned and vanished silently into the thick bush, footprints in the sand the only evidence they'd been here. In a second, waves cleared away even that.

"Spooky buggers," Archer said, returning to our group. "Glad most of 'em are on our side. What'd they say?"

Gordie lit a cigarette before returning to his seat. "A Zero went down about a mile offshore on the other side of the island. Men from their village paddled out when they saw the pilot parachute into the water."

"Did they get him?" Cotter asked, looking up from studying the map.

"Hemi daefinis," Gordie said with a smile. "He's dead, finished. Came down bleeding, evidently. Sharks got to him before the native chaps. There was enough of him left attached to the 'chute for them to find that map."

"Looks like they came from Buka, as reported," Cotter said. "Routes to Lumbari and our lines on New Georgia are marked. Not much value as intelligence, but I'll pass it on to G-2 when we get in tonight."

"Things are pretty quiet right now," I said. "We haven't heard a plane in a while."

"There's still plenty of time for another daylight raid," he said. "We stay here until dark. Get some rest."

There wasn't much else to do. I found a life jacket, not wanting to be without one on this trip again, and used it as a pillow, propping myself up against one of the torpedo tubes. Kaz did the same, along with the crewmen who weren't on watch. Gordie and Archer sat at the stern, aloof now, perhaps steeling themselves for their upcoming mission. My eyes wandered to the dense, green jungle, thinking about the natives and how quickly they had disappeared from view.

Just as John Kari surely had, back on Choiseul with Silas Porter.

I'd been right about Kari lying when he said he hadn't met Daniel on Pavau, but for the wrong reasons. Even if he were an unrepentant thief, that didn't make him a triple murderer in my book. I couldn't blame him for putting the past behind him and trying to start over, all the while hoping the war would cut memories short.

I tried to sleep. Even with my eyes closed, I could picture the natives melting into the bush. One second they were there; the next, they were gone. There and then gone. It felt important, but I had no idea why.

WHEN I OPENED my eyes, the sun was skimming the horizon, and the cook—or I should say the poor slob assigned that duty—was distributing Vienna sausages and pickles for dinner.

"Sorry about the fare," Cotter said. "We got more pickles than anything else for some damn reason."

"I have been to Vienna," Kaz said, eyeing the short, canned hot dogs coated in something that might have been tomato paste. "And I can tell you, the sausages there are nothing like this."

"A delicacy for us, Baron," Gordie said. "Or it will be in memory, after the first month of taro and sweet potatoes every day."

"I never knew how brave Coastwatchers were," Kaz said, forcing himself to chew and swallow.

A few minutes later, the engines started up, a deep rumble signaling our departure. Cotter eased the boat out from shore, negotiated the narrow channel, and headed northwest. The sun was down, the far horizon lit by the fading light, the sky above already sparkling with stars. A clear night. A dangerous night.

We tightened our life jackets as a crewman distributed helmets and weapons to the four of us along for the ride. A Browning Automatic Rifle for me, a Thompson submachine gun for Gordie, and M1 rifles for Archer and Kaz. We were instructed to take up watch aft, on the lookout for Kawanishi or anything else that followed the luminescent trail the propellers would leave.

"Be careful," Cotter warned us when he came down from the bridge. "Don't go off half-cocked. If you fire at anything, everyone else will, too. We'll be lit up like a Christmas tree and visible for miles, so be sure before you shoot. Best to signal a crewman first if you're not certain."

"Remember, the bastards will cut their engines and glide in along our wake," Archer said as Cotter returned to the bridge. "By the time you hear them, it's too late, so stay sharp."

Kaz and I squeezed in next to the rear torpedo tube, port side, while Archer and Gordie took up position starboard, all of us facing aft, along with the twenty-millimeter gunner amidships. I hefted the BAR, aiming it skyward. The thing weighed a ton, but I figured that wouldn't matter if the lead started flying. Kaz did the same with his M1 and nearly lost his balance. It was one big rifle for a little guy.

"Brace yourself if you fire that," I said. "The recoil might send you over the side."

"Very funny, Billy."

"I wasn't joking," I said, and then grinned to show him I was. Sort of.

As we cruised on, the dusky light at the horizon faded into black, and all that was left was the twinkling of more stars than I'd ever seen. This wasn't like being offshore on Massachusetts Bay, where the lights of civilization glowed in the distance. This was pure darkness. No moon, no electric lights, nothing but inky-black velvet heavens draped around us, blending into the dark ocean, the play of starlight on the waves making it impossible to see where air and water joined, the horizon an invisible thread.

The engines rumbled, the vibration felt in the deck beneath our feet, running through my body until the sound became one with the wind whipping my face and the blood pumping in my chest. It was loud and soft at the same time, a monotonous drone that soon became little more than a backdrop to the grandeur surrounding the boat as it sped through the night. If it hadn't been for the wind, I might have thought we were standing still, suspended in blackest night, wrapped in a cocoon spun from the warmth and darkness, alone in the universe.

"It is profound," Kaz gasped, staring up at the dome of stars.

"Look," I said. Our wake was bright greenish-blue, almost neon, spreading out from either side, a giant V-shape that pointed right to us. It stretched out for more than a hundred yards, impossible to miss. "Now I know why Jack was idling his motor that night."

"It does leave little doubt as to our position," Kaz said, gripping his rifle even tighter, leaning against a funnel for balance, and scanning the night sky. "I never considered I might leave this world because of plankton churned up in the South Pacific Ocean."

That had never crossed my mind either. I kept my eyes busy looking for Japs on the surface or in the air, trying to avoid thoughts of death due to miniscule sea creatures, or any other cause, for that matter. I'd seen a lot of death already, more than most guys my age. There were corpses enough in Boston, and since getting into this war, plenty more from Norway, North Africa, and Sicily. I'd fought, killed, been wounded, and lived. I'd been scared plenty of times. But it never seemed I had this much time to think about it, to wait for death to come swooping down or roar over the waves, out of the inky darkness.

I'll admit it: I'd never been so scared. There was something about being out here, trailed by a glowing arrow, alone and awaiting an attack

from any direction, that unnerved me. I felt sweat drop down my
backbone, as a pit of fear opened up in my belly. My hands went
clammy and I wiped them one at a time on my trousers, gripping the
BAR and wishing I'd never met up with any of the Kennedys.

I blinked.

I thought I'd seen something slide across the sky, a disturbance in
the stars, a blackness, there and then gone. If it were a plane, where
was it? I cocked my head, turning an ear toward where I'd seen it. I
didn't hear a thing, didn't see anything out of place. I blinked again,
once, twice, trying to clear my vision.

Suddenly I understood.

The plane had spotted us, banking and momentarily blotting out
the twinkling stars.

I couldn't see it silhouetted against the backdrop of stars since it
was heading straight for the boat, giving us its smallest profile. Narrow
wings, tip of the nose, machine guns. I strained to find it, worried about
being wrong, not wanting to sound the alarm and light up the night
with our gunfire. If there wasn't an enemy plane, there would be soon
enough.

Then I saw it.

I raised the BAR and sighted in on the blank space coming at us,
no doubt in my mind, unable to speak, knowing there wasn't time for
it anyway. I fired a burst, then another. By the time I squeezed the
trigger again, the twenty-millimeter had joined in, followed by every
other gun on board.

Cotter turned the boat hard to starboard and I emptied my clip
at the dark form, which seemed to snarl back at us, its four engines
starting up and the forward machine gun answering our fusillade. We
clearly outgunned the Kawanishi, but Cotter knew the big threat wasn't
from machine-gun rounds. It was the bombload we had to worry about.

Water erupted off to my right, about where we would have been
if Cotter hadn't quickly altered course. The Kawanishi roared overhead,
filling the sky, its wings enormous, blocking out the light of a thousand
stars.

Everyone kept firing. Kaz had himself well braced, taking aimed shots at the plane, pulling the trigger calmly and quickly. Archer was spraying the air with his tommy gun as Gordie loaded a new clip in his rifle. The twenty-millimeter kept pumping out shells as the plane turned away and gained altitude. I shook Kaz by the shoulder, signaling he should stop firing. The Kawanishi was out of range for small-arms fire and becoming invisible again against the heavens.

Until the explosion. A soft *pummpf* echoed across the water, and a belch of flame erupted, probably from an engine. We'd hit her, caused some damage. A cheer went up, and we waited to see what she would do. Head for home, or try for one more attack?

Cotter throttled the engines down to idle. We began to drift, the telltale wake dissipating behind us. The sound of the Kawanishi's three remaining engines slowly faded into the night. Home was their choice; they'd die another day for their emperor. Our engines roared back into life, but not at full throttle. I saw Cotter glance back at our wake, slowing a little until he was satisfied, sacrificing speed for survival, reducing the glowing arrow that signaled to our potential destruction to less obvious dimensions. I wasn't about to ask him to step on it.

Dawn broke as we eased around the western side of Rendova, hugging the coast, ready to dart for the cover of overhanging palms at the first echo of aircraft. We soon entered a protected bay, shielded from the currents by a string of small offshore islands. Within the bay was a larger island. Lumbari, our destination.

It wasn't impressive. It was marked on military maps as a PT boat base, but all I saw was a line of PTs tied up along a crescent-shaped stretch of sandy beach. Tents and Quonset huts were scattered beneath the palms, camouflage netting strung up between them in an attempt to disguise crates of supplies and fuel drums stacked everywhere. Burned trees and the blackened hulks of scattered oil drums marked the hits from yesterday's raid.

The netting may have worked on land, but there was nothing to cover the PT boats on the shore. Bomb craters dotted the landscape near the beach, where one of the PTs sat low in the water, still smoldering from a hit on her stern.

"Welcome to Lumbari," Cotter said from the bridge, slapping a mosquito on his neck as he guided the boat to a spot on the beach. The sun was barely up, but the temperature was already climbing and the bugs were feasting. Sweat soaked my khakis, making them feel thick and heavy against my skin.

"This place is worse than Guadalcanal," Archer said, "which is not something you'll hear too often."

"Why is the PT base located here then?" Kaz asked.

"It's a fair anchorage, protected from the heavy currents," Archer said. "But I think the real reason Commander Garfield selected this spot is the bunker."

"It's a spectacular one," Gordie put in, seeing the questioning looks on our faces. "The Japanese are quite good at constructing bunkers made from coconut tree logs. This one is two stories deep, covered in vegetation, expertly disguised. Has a decent view of the channel and New Georgia in the distance."

"Safe as houses," Archer said, sending a stream of spit into the water. "The way Garfield likes it."

"Word is he never leaves," Gordie said.

"Sure he does," Cotter shot back as he eased up on the throttle, letting the bow bump into the sandy beach. "It doesn't have a latrine." His crewmen laughed, enjoying their skipper taking a shot at a superior officer. Cotter had taken enough shots after PT-109 went down, so I figured he liked dishing it out in another direction.

"What about missions?" I asked.

"Commander Garfield does not go out on missions," Cotter said, his voice lower now. "He directs missions from his bunker. He doesn't ride on PT boats. He's an Annapolis man, in all the worst ways. He probably wishes he were on a battleship instead of running a forward base for PT boats."

"He wouldn't authorize a search for Kennedy and his crew," Gordie said. "Or so I heard."

"That's right," Cotter said. "If Jack wants someone to blame for being left out there, he doesn't have to look any farther than Garfield. He wouldn't let us search, and he sent us on operations in other sectors the two nights following."

I was going to ask why, but the look on Cotter's face told me to drop it. He was caught up in a triangle of guilt, blame, and bad feelings. He'd had enough of Jack and the drama of PT-109, I could tell. It was a familiar feeling.

We took a rickety gangplank ashore, as work crews clambered aboard to rearm, refuel, and repair the 169. She had a fair number of bullet holes, and I didn't envy Cotter and his men the job of getting her shipshape. After the long night's journey, I planned on some shut-eye before moving on to find Josh Coburn and his coffee plantation.

We found the tents allocated for PT-169. Two for the crew and a third, smaller one for Cotter and his XO. The officer's tent was in the high-rent district, given that it was on slightly higher ground than the other two, avoiding the overflow from a languid trickle of foul-smelling water that ran alongside the path. We looked inside one tent, frightening off a snake that had curled up under one of the cots.

"Don't worry about him," Gordie said. "It's a brown tree snake. They hunt at night. He was only looking for a place to rest in the shade, as we are. No wariwari, as our native friends say."

"I would wari if I weren't so tired," Kaz said. He tossed his musette bag on the floor and sat to take off his boots.

"Best to keep your boots on," Archer said. "You might find a surprise inside if you have to put them on in a hurry."

Archer and Gordie laughed, the kind of good-natured laughter you'd get from experienced hands showing a new guy the ropes. All in good fun. But they kept their boots on.

CHAPTER TWENTY-SEVEN

SLEEP DIDN'T COME easy, or stay long.

Heat, humidity, visions of snakes snoozing beneath me, and the sounds of a forward base at work all conspired to get Kaz and me moving before noon, first in search of java and food, and then Commander Garfield. We made it to the mess tent seconds before wind whipped the palm trees into a frenzy and rain came down in hard, hot sheets, heavy drops beating against the canvas and blowing in sideways. It ended in less than a minute, leaving thick, humid air and steam rising from the muddy ground.

We went through the chow line and got a plateful of powdered eggs and biscuits. At least I think the yellow stuff had been eggs at some point in the distant past.

"What's our first move?" Kaz asked, grimacing as he sipped coffee from a chipped enamel mug.

"We report to Garfield, arrange transport to the main island and find out where Coburn's plantation is. That's assuming Kari and Porter are already on Choiseul. If they've been delayed for any reason, we interrogate John Kari."

"You are still thinking he is the killer?" Kaz asked, in a way that said he certainly wasn't.

"He fits the bill better than anyone," I said. "He had the opportunity and a motive. Plus he's no stranger to killing."

"But you have to agree," Kaz said, "all that is a weak motive to support three savage murders."

"A weak motive is better than none," I said, trying to muster a belief in my own theory. "Besides, we know John Kari hid his past from us. Even if he isn't our man, who knows what else he's hiding?"

"Secrets," Kaz said, attacking his eggs with grim determination. "What would we do without secrets to discover?"

I grunted my agreement and did my best with the food at hand. The coffee cleared my head a bit, and as I drained the last dregs from my cup, I thought about the natives vanishing into the jungle last night. Why did that image stay with me? Was it a key to some secret? What did it remind me of? I had no idea, no way even to form a question and ask Kaz about it.

We got directions to Garfield's bunker, stomping through muck and ooze on our way. The thing was impressive, shaded with layers of camouflage netting, two stories of crisscrossed coconut logs covered in dirt. Plants and small trees had sprouted, making it look like a small hillock, except for the antennae bristling along the length of the dugout.

A sentry let us in. As soon as the door shut behind us, I understood one of the attractions of the place. It was cool. Steps led down to the first level, which opened out into a spacious room with a concrete floor, lights strung along the walls, and wooden tables where sailors filed papers, typed orders, and fiddled with radio knobs. We found Garfield at the far end of the room, huddled over a map table with a couple of junior officers.

"Lieutenants Boyle and Kazimierz reporting, sir," I said, as soon as he deigned to look up. He had a sparse head of hair, a thin face, and an expanding waist.

"Are you those army officers investigating some murder on Tulagi? I was told to expect you and provide what assistance I can. Which isn't much."

"Yes, sir." I answered.

"Murders," Kaz said, perhaps surprised at my politeness to a chairbound superior officer. "There have been three."

"I hope you don't suspect any of my men," Garfield said, tossing down a pencil as if it were a knife. "I can't afford to lose any crewmen."

"Or officers, I assume," Kaz said. I enjoyed watching this.

"Well, certainly, if an officer of mine is guilty of any infraction, he should be dealt with," Garfield said. "I'm a busy man, Boyle, so please excuse me."

"We need some transport, Commander," I said, before Kaz could make a remark about murder being a bit more than an infraction. "To the main island, and then a jeep."

"Very well," he said, calling out to a clerk to arrange a launch to take us to Rendova, and to have a jeep waiting at the harbor. I think he was glad to see us off his little island.

"One more thing," I said. "Can you tell us if two Coastwatchers have been brought over to Choiseul yet? Porter and Kari."

"Yes, they went in last night. Landed safely."

"I assume you're in contact with them," I said. "Do you know where they are on the island?"

"You assume incorrectly, Lieutenant," Garfield said. "Coastwatchers are in radio contact with their headquarters on Guadalcanal. We get orders from there if our assistance is needed. Now you must excuse me."

"If you get any orders to send a boat in with supplies or anything like that, please let me know, sir."

"Is one of them a suspect?" Garfield said, showing the first genuine interest in anything I'd said. Everyone loves a mystery.

"We have to ask some questions," I said. "I'd like to get to them before the Japs do."

"Good luck with that. Now get out, I've got operations to plan."

I looked at the chart on the table. Red lines stretched out from Lumbari north into the narrow strait off New Georgia. Blue lines arced in from above Bougainville, the likely route for destroyers of the Tokyo Express. A neat little war game with colored pencils in a safe, cool underground bunker. Garfield noticed I was staring at his handiwork, and it was as if he'd read my mind.

"That launch won't wait all morning, Boyle," he said, waving his hand as if to swat me away.

"Jack Kennedy sends his regards," I said, turning to leave.

"It sounds like he's calmed down then," Garfield said.

"I doubt it. I was kidding, by the way."

The heat slammed us as we left the bunker, but it was better than the chill inside.

"Infraction," Kaz said, spitting out the word.

THE LAUNCH DEPOSITED us at a dock across the bay, on the main island. There were a few older civilian boats, rust-streaked and rotting, tied up next to us. Tin-roofed huts were arranged along the beach, where sailors, stripped to the waist, labored over engines and machine parts. The unglamorous but necessary work of combat-zone repair.

A jeep was provided as promised by Garfield. Our main problem was that no one knew where Coburn's plantation was, so we headed out on the only road available, trusting our luck.

"It's an island," I said to Kaz. "How hard can it be?"

We drove past a field hospital, the giant tents marked with red crosses standing alone in a clearing, a good distance from other military installations. Then along Rendova's east shore, passing a barbed-wire enclosure patrolled by GIs with bayonets fixed to their M1s.

"Japanese POWs," Kaz said. Groups of sullen prisoners squatted in small groups inside the wire. Maybe a hundred or so.

"I didn't think that many would have given up," I said. "They must be from the fighting on New Georgia. That doesn't look like a permanent camp." There were a few huts and Quonset huts outside the wire. Inside, tents with their side flaps rolled up provided shade for the POWs. Most were shoeless, dressed in tattered, rotting uniforms. They were all painfully thin.

"They look much more frightening when they are trying to kill you," Kaz said as we left the barbed wire behind.

"You take weapons and gear away from soldiers who've been fighting for weeks straight, and all you're left with is dirt and ragged, stinking clothes. It's as if belts, helmets, straps, and packs were the only things holding them together."

"In North Africa, German and Italian POWs ranged from sullen to deliriously happy," Kaz said. "Those men looked neither. They appeared lost."

We reached a fork in the road. "Speaking of lost," I said, "which way?"

"Inland," Kaz said. "A coffee plantation would be at a higher elevation, not sea level."

As always, Kaz was right. I'd given up asking him how he knew so much. He'd shrug, as if to say, how is it you *don't* know these things?

The dirt track took us higher, looping around hills until the sea was far below us and the gently sloping ground was cleared of thick jungle and planted with rows and rows of shoulder-high bushes. Workers moved through the rows, wielding hoes and attacking the weeds that threatened to overwhelm the coffee plants. We drove to the top of the hill, where a house with the usual wide verandah stood, flanked by a large shed with a corrugated roof and another long, narrow building on stilts, roofed native-style with palm fronds.

"This is much better than Lumbari," Kaz said, stretching as we got out of the jeep. A mild breeze swept up from the sea, slightly scented with salt, cool and crisp after the stale, thick air of the base.

"Are you gents lost?" The voice held the trace of a Scottish accent, softened by years in the Solomons.

"Not if you're Josh Coburn," I said to the tall figure who'd stepped out of the shed. He had a full white beard, wore a wide-brimmed hat, and walked with one stiff leg. He came closer, eyeing us suspiciously.

"Who might be asking, then?"

I did the introductions. "We don't mean to bother you, but we're investigating a murder. Three of them, actually. We need to ask you a few questions."

"Why? I haven't killed anyone. Which is a claim few can make these days."

"You are Josh Coburn, I take it?" Kaz asked.

"I am guilty of that," Coburn said. "Now, how'd you like to taste some real coffee? If you're going to talk at me, I might as well take a break."

"We'd be fools to turn down a cup of java from a coffee plantation, Mr. Coburn," I said. A few minutes later, we were seated on the verandah, sipping the best coffee I'd ever tasted, marveling at the view. The wind caressed the green jungle beneath the ordered rows of coffee plants, the sparkling sea beyond deceptively peaceful.

"This is extraordinarily delicious," Kaz said. I nodded an eager agreement.

"It's the peaberry that does it," Coburn said. Noting our quizzical looks, he launched into an explanation. "I'm sure you've noticed the shape of coffee beans. The cherry—the fruit of the coffee plant—holds two seeds, which is the bean itself. They grow together, which flattens the sides that face each other. But a very few plants will produce a cherry with single seeds. Then you get a nice oval bean, perfect for roasting. You'll never get it as fresh as this."

"Remarkable," Kaz said.

"Fine stuff, isn't it?" Coburn said. "Commands a good price, too. I roast some beans for myself; the rest get bagged up and sold. Or will be, when the commercial traffic starts back up."

"Your place seems to have weathered the occupation," I said.

"I'm lucky the Japs prefer tea," he said with a laugh. "They had a lookout post up here for a while, but didn't cause too much damage. Shot a half dozen natives for no reason I can figure, then lit out when your army landed. It's mainly a case of beating back the bush after a couple years of neglect. Now that you've had your lesson, go ahead and ask your questions."

"Did you know Daniel Tamana?" I said, feeling the jolt of caffeine kick in.

"Sure I know him," Coburn started, then caught himself. "You put that in the past tense. Has Daniel been killed? Is he one of the three?"

"The first of the three," Kaz said. "Next was Sam Chang."

"Christ," Coburn said. "Sam was a fine man. Forward-thinking. Don't tell me those damn fool sisters of his are mixed up in this?"

"No," I said, glancing at Kaz. "They are mystified as well. The third victim was a woman, Deanna Pendleton."

"Not the lass from the Methodist mission? Dear God, what's going on? When and where did all this happen?" Coburn stood, pacing on the verandah, trying to take in the terrible news.

"On Tulagi, very recently," I said. "We were wondering what you could tell us about Daniel. What kind of man he was, and if he had trouble with anyone."

"Hardly a man back then," Coburn said. "He came here to work when he was a young lad. Smart, spoke good English. I wasn't surprised when he moved on. If I'd had a better job to give him, I would have."

"Did he have trouble with anyone?"

"No, not that I recall. Kept to himself a lot. Always reading, trying to improve himself. Which meant that he didn't make friends well. The other native boys likely thought him stuck-up. Neither fish nor fowl, as they say."

"But no arguments or serious disagreements?"

"No," Coburn said, shaking his head. "A bit of resentment maybe, but nothing more."

"Would you say he was honest?" I asked, wondering if there might be some criminal connection between Daniel and John Kari.

"Yes, I'd peg him as an honest chap. No reason not to," Coburn said as he refilled our cups from an enamel pot. "Brave, too, although you probably know of his service."

"Did you ever run across another native, John Kari?" Kaz asked. "He is a bit like Daniel. Well-educated, suited to European ways."

"Kari, you say?" Coburn said, rubbing his beard. "No, doesn't ring a bell."

"Have you been on Pavau much?" I asked, trying to jog his memory.

"Now and then," Coburn said, raising his eyebrows and giving a slight shrug, inviting me to explain the question.

"That's where Daniel ended up. This John Kari worked there as well, for Lever," I said. It might have been the jolt from the strong coffee, but everything began to converge on the island of Pavau, like the phosphorescent wake of a PT boat. "Sam Chang was looking to expand his operations there as well."

"Right, right," Coburn said, snapping his fingers. "Young fellow, worked down at the harbor, keeping accounts for Lever or something."

"You know a lot of people," I said. "You must get around the islands a fair bit."

"Used to," he said. "Before the war I had my own little cutter, sailed between here, Bougainville, and all points in between. We islanders pay a lot of social calls, helps to ease the monotony. A native can be a good friend, but there's nothing like the sound of your own language spoken by one of your own." He gazed out to the sea, shaking his head slowly, perhaps at the memories of friends lost. He sat again, silent.

"You were almost captured on Bougainville," I said, hoping to shake him out of his reverie.

"Nearly ran out of luck that time," Coburn said, taking a drink and smacking his lips. "I've got another plantation up there, and I wanted to get my people out when it looked like the Japs were about to descend. Some of my workers are from Bougainville, but the rest are all from Malaita, and I'd planned on arranging transport for them."

"Daniel was from Malaita," Kaz said. "Were there any kinsmen of his working here?"

"No," Coburn said. "My workers were mainly from New Georgia and right here on Rendova."

"Why did you bring others all the way from Malaita to Bougainville?" Kaz asked.

"Malaitamen are good workers," Coburn said. "And tough. I was clearing out a new section of bush for planting and I knew I could count on them for hard labor and no complaints. Some say there's still headhunters up in the hills there. I wouldn't be surprised."

"Did you happen to see Sam Chang on Bougainville?" I asked. "He went into hiding when the Japs invaded."

"No, I didn't. I docked my cutter at Arawa and was looking for a vehicle when the Japs began bombing. They blew my sailboat to pieces and strafed the harbor. That's when I knew I'd waited too long."

"You never made it to your plantation?" Kaz asked.

"No. I went south, along the coast road, hitching a ride with some Australian troops who'd been ordered to withdraw to the island of Balalae, where there's a dirt airstrip. We were bombed again and two of them were killed. I decided that the Japs were likely to attack and capture any airstrip within miles, so I left their company. Ended up in a coastal village within sight of Oema Island, beyond which is Choiseul. I gave a native what cash I had and took off in his canoe. This leg's no good anymore, but there's nothing wrong with my arms, I'll tell you that."

"That's a long way," I said, remembering the maps I'd seen. "And close to Pavau, too. Did you stop there?"

"No, by God! It doesn't look far on a map, but I had no time for visits, not on that trip. I rested on Oema and then paddled all night to get to Choiseul. Nearly did me in." Coburn rubbed his eyes, weary at the recollection of his voyage.

"Daniel also escaped to Choiseul," Kaz said. "From Pavau."

"He did. I met him there, along with a boatful of nuns he'd gotten out. I told you he was brave. That was a risky run he made. Two ships left Pavau harbor that day. One was an old island ferry, crammed with refugees. It capsized under the weight and the Japs machine-gunned those who weren't drowned straight off, or so the story went from the few who made it out after that. The currents brought the bodies straight back to Pavau, washed them up for days. Daniel was smart, he only took what his small boat could hold. A half dozen nuns, a wounded flier, and three other Malaitamen."

"Is it possible Daniel turned anyone away, and they held a grudge?" I asked.

"Well, I suppose anything's possible," Coburn granted. "But likely is another story. The nuns on Bougainville were well thought of. I doubt anyone would contest their need to escape the bloody Japs."

"No, I don't suppose so," I said. I watched the workers hacking away at the jungle growth as I finished the coffee in my cup. Even though it had gone cold, it was good enough to keep the wheels turning in my mind. "You said a minute ago that you didn't have time to stop at Pavau during that trip. But you had previously? When?"

"I did, a few days before I went on to Bougainville."

"Did you meet Daniel? Or see John Kari?"

"No, I went around to the north side, to stop in at Silas Porter's place. He's somewhat of a recluse, lives on a remote part of the island. I wanted to let him know what was coming. He didn't have a radio, so I knew he'd be out of touch. Which is the way he wants it, but there are times to intrude on a man's privacy."

"He's a Coastwatcher now as well," I said.

"Porter? I wouldn't have thought it of him," Coburn said, his forehead furrowed. "Not the type."

"You've been away from the Solomons since your escape, I take it," Kaz said.

"Yes, as soon as I got off Choiseul, I went down to New Caledonia. Stayed with a friend from the French export firm that handles my beans. Came back up here as soon as I heard Rendova had been taken. All the natives thought I was dead, after not coming back here from Bougainville. Porter? Really?" He was having a hard time believing it.

"Really," I said. "The Japs massacred his workers and Peter Fraser, his assistant manager. Porter escaped only because he'd gone to get their boat ready."

"Apparently somebody shot a Japanese soldier when they landed," Kaz said. "It was a reprisal."

"Well, I could see how that would get old Silas's blood up," Coburn said. "I'll have to look him up and let him know I'm alive. He probably thought I'd bought it on Bougainville."

We chatted some more but it was evident Coburn didn't know much of any consequence about Daniel Tamana. We shook hands, complimenting him on his coffee, and headed back to the jeep.

"Pavau," I said, stopping to look out over the fields, the plants laid out in neat rows, gracing the curves of the hills. "Why do all roads lead to Pavau, and what does it mean?"

"Perhaps it's simply an island where a number of people have traveled to and from," Kaz said. "Like many in the Solomons."

"There's something I can't quite put my finger on, some thread that we haven't yet unraveled. An inconsistency. But what is it?"

"Something about Pavau, then," Kaz said, leaning against the jeep.

I watched the workers, hauling bushels of pulled weeds out from the cleared rows, dumping them at the edge of the jungle. They walked between plants, crossing rows, holding the baskets high to avoid damaging the plants. I saw the natives on Russell Island again, fading into the bush, disappearing into the dappled shadows.

They moved gracefully, I thought. Those on Russell and these workers in the fields of Rendova. Brought up in the bush, did they learn from childhood how to glide quickly and quietly through the dense greenery? The sense I had on Russell Island was that they had vanished, leaving not a leaf disturbed by their passing.

So what of it?

What was it that bothered me about natives moving through the bush, quietly or otherwise?

What did it have to do with this case?

Pavau. Why did everything come back to Pavau? Daniel Tamana worked there and he was killed, victim number one. Sam Chang went there and spoke to John Kari about expanding his business. Victim number two. Deanna Pendleton hadn't been there, as far as I knew, but she must have known Chang from Bougainville, and she definitely knew Daniel. Victim number three.

"Billy!" Kaz said, in a voice loud enough to tell me it wasn't the first time he'd said it. "Are we going?"

"Where? What's next?"

"You're not giving up, are you?"

"Dammit, Kaz, I'm out of ideas," I snapped. "This image of natives moving through the bush keeps eating away at me. I don't know what it means, and I don't have much more than that to go on. What about you?"

"I think you are correct about Pavau," Kaz said, taking a seat in the jeep. "It is at the center of things, but not in a way that sheds any light on the matter. I wonder how many Japanese are on the island right now."

"You're not serious," I said, hoisting myself into the driver's seat.

"No," Kaz said. "Although if there were Coastwatchers there to guide us, I might consider it. A visit could help pull the pieces of this puzzle together."

"Daniel wanted an assignment there, didn't he?" I said. I felt my mind shifting into gear, images and memories falling into place, and I finally began to see things clearly.

"Yes, that's what Dickie Miller said. Sexton vetoed it because the island was too small to hide in."

"And what else did Dickie tell you about Pavau and Daniel?" I said.

Kaz rubbed his chin, coaxing out the recollection. "That Daniel knew the island very well," he said, still unsure of where I was going.

"Every path and hiding place, that's exactly what you said. You were quoting Dickie Miller, right?"

"Yes, those were his exact words," Kaz said, his face brightening as he sat bolt upright. "And how could he know every path on the island—"

"If he hadn't been to the north coast, where Silas Porter's plantation was. So not only did John Kari lie about knowing Daniel, Porter lied as well."

"But does that follow?" Kaz said. "Perhaps Daniel simply went overland to visit a friend working at Porter's plantation and never talked with the owner himself."

"The way Coburn described Daniel, he was more of a loner," I said. "If John Kari had worked there, I could see Daniel looking him up, since they were so much alike. But no one else."

"But why would he have gone?" Kaz asked.

"To better himself," I said, trying to put myself in Daniel's place. "To see if there was a job available. He would have to have met Porter."

"Why would Silas Porter lie?" Kaz said. "I am still not convinced."

"No," I said, finally understanding the importance of those natives retreating into the bush. "Daniel crossed to the north side. Everyone's been talking about the difficult terrain, but they were looking at it from a European's perspective. Well educated or not, Daniel knew the jungle and its ways. So the question remains, why did Porter lie?"

"We know why John Kari lied," Kaz said. "Because he'd been a thief."

"But who could Silas Porter have stolen from?" I said. "He's the independent type. I don't think he'd worry about other people's opinions."

"Do you see a motive in Porter's actions, whatever the reason?" Kaz asked, not unreasonably. I shook my head, trying to figure that one out.

"If you boys are going to hang about, I might put you to work," Coburn said, coming out of the house and giving us a wave. He walked to the barn with his rolling gait, his bad leg not seeming to hinder him much.

"He's pretty spry for an older gentleman," Kaz said.

"It must be the coffee," I said, and went to start the jeep. Then my hand froze.

"What is it?" Kaz asked.

"Old. He called Porter *old Silas*, didn't he?"

"A figure of speech, old chap," Kaz said. "What of it?"

"Come on," I said, jumping out of the jeep and following Coburn into the barn.

"What now?" Coburn barked as he turned, wrench in hand, about to get to work on a tractor engine.

"Describe Silas Porter for me, will you?" I said. "Then no more questions."

"Silas? Oh, about five foot ten, I'd say, a stocky man. Bald patch on the crown of his head. Black, wiry hair, going grey. Thick beard, last I saw him, almost as long as mine. Why? I thought you knew him."

"I thought so, too," I said. "I'm sorry to say he's dead. And if you see Peter Fraser, be careful. Your life is in danger."

CHAPTER TWENTY-EIGHT

"BUT PETER FRASER is dead, not Silas Porter," Kaz said as I drove the jeep down the steep path to the coast road.

"The man we know as Porter is over six feet tall. Brown hair, no bald spot, with a wiry, not stocky, build. I think he's Peter Fraser."

"Oh dear God," Kaz said. "That explains everything."

"It does. Daniel Tamana met the real Silas Porter, and Peter Fraser for that matter."

"Then the Japanese come, and Peter Fraser finds himself the sole survivor of a massacre," Kaz said, working it out as he went along. "Hardly anyone knows Silas Porter, so he takes on his identity in order to secure possession of the plantation. He counted on the chaos of war to cover his tracks."

"Right. And remember, he had good reason to think the three people he had to worry about were dead."

"Josh Coburn, because he had left for Bougainville and walked right into the Japanese invasion," Kaz said. "Sam Chang, also on Bougainville. As a Chinese national and a man of military age, he was likely to be killed by the Japanese. And finally Daniel Tamana."

"Yes," I said. "The loss of the ferry with all those refugees must have been a well-known fact. Porter—I mean Fraser—may have even seen the bodies when he took the launch and made his escape. It was a calculated risk that Daniel was among them, but a good one."

"But then Daniel saw him on the boat from Guadalcanal. Or he saw Daniel."

"Or John Kari," I said. "Remember, Daniel was on the high deck, and saw the group of them below. He may have heard someone call Fraser by Porter's name. However it went, he bided his time. Once on Tulagi, he went looking for Sam Chang, a man he knew could confirm what he'd seen."

"Why did he not simply go to the authorities?"

"I don't know. Maybe he thought a native wouldn't be believed. That may be why he went looking for Chang. He'd be cautious in challenging a white man and may have wanted someone to back up his story. Or perhaps he did speak to Fraser."

"That's possible," Kaz said, hanging on as I took a sharp turn. "There had been no real crime committed at that point. Perhaps Fraser promised him a job if he kept his mouth shut. Assistant manager, his old post."

"Or maybe Daniel forced the issue. We know he wanted to move up in the world, and his chances were limited."

"You mean he blackmailed Fraser?" Kaz said.

"It's a possibility. But it may be more likely that he simply hinted at the potential for exposure, telling him he knew Sam Chang was alive and could identify him."

"So Fraser concocts an offer, one that Daniel decides to consider," Kaz said. "An offer of a job or a share of the profits from the plantation."

I nodded. "They meet at the beach, where no one can see them, so as not to arouse suspicion."

"Reasonable," Kaz said, constructing the scenario. "They discuss terms, and Daniel agrees to tell Chang it was all a mistake."

"Although we don't know if he ever actually talked to Chang," I said.

"But Fraser doesn't know that. Daniel could have held out the possibility as an inducement, to insure that he was needed."

"Right, and then Fraser asks who else he's talked to," I said, the chain of events falling into place.

"He names Deanna, and once that's done, Fraser has all he needs," Kaz said.

"He kills him, and then Sam Chang," I said.

"But why wait so long to kill Deanna? She hadn't accused him."

"He couldn't take a chance that she would. She was probably harder to get alone. He may have heard from Gordie that he was dropping her off in Chinatown; there were calls back and forth from Sesapi and the communications center. So he sent Kari on an errand, drove there, and knifed her, leaving a smear of Cosmoline to implicate his partner."

"Now all we need is proof," Kaz said.

"Of murder," I said. "We know Fraser took over Porter's identity in order to steal his property. Fraud does qualify as a crime, even out in these islands. But I want him for three murders."

"Yes, I am sure Porter's family would agree, if he has any," Kaz said as I passed the POW enclosure and turned off the main road, making for the nearest Quonset hut. "Why are we stopping here?"

"To check out a long shot," I said. "You don't speak Japanese by any chance, do you?"

"*Konnichiwa,*" he said. "Which means hello. It is the only word I know."

"Well, you just might learn a few more," I said as we approached a sentry in front of the hut. I was about to ask for the commanding officer when shouts rose up from a nearby tent. POWs surged to the edge of the barbed wire, guards raced in from various directions, and two officers burst out of the Quonset hut, shoving us aside as they made for the tent.

"I'll kill that sonuvabitch, get out of my way!" It was a voice filled with rage, the words turning into one long scream. A high-pitched stream of Japanese followed, drowned out by other shouts, furniture being overturned, and bodies thumping to the ground in an embrace of violent struggle.

Two GIs hustled out a frightened Jap POW, each with a firm grip on an arm, practically lifting him into the air. The guy was so scared his legs were pumping, toes barely touching the ground. Guards at the entrance to the wire enclosure motioned with the tips of their bayonets for the POWs inside to back off. They did, and their pal was tossed in quickly, the gate closed and locked behind him.

"Let go of me, goddammit!" came a voice from inside the tent.

"Settle down, Harrison, that's an order!"

We turned back to check on the hubbub. Harrison was a marine sergeant, his face red and his eyes wild. The guy giving the order was an army lieutenant. But that wasn't the only difference between him and Harrison. The officer was Japanese. Japanese-American, I should say.

The tent was a mess. An upended table, chairs knocked over, papers scattered over the wooden plank floor. A couple of GIs held Harrison as he struggled against their grip. Finally he gave up, shaking his head. "I knew those guys, Lieutenant. I knew them."

"Yeah," the officer said, motioning for his men to release their grips. "I don't blame you one bit, Sergeant. Go get some coffee, okay?"

"Sure," he said, shuffling morosely out of the tent. The lieutenant motioned with his head, telling the GIs to go with him, as Harrison continued muttering, "I knew them, I knew them."

"Who the hell are you?" the lieutenant said, startled as he noticed us.

"Lieutenant Billy Boyle. This is Lieutenant Kazimierz. I see we've come at a bad time."

"Lieutenant Joe Sakato," he said, offering us his hand and glancing at Kaz's shoulder patch. "You're a long way from home, Lieutenant Kazimierz. You're the first Polish officer I've run into."

"And you are the first Japanese officer I have seen. In an American uniform, that is," Kaz responded.

"Japanese-American," he corrected Kaz. "I'm a nisei, born in California. My parents emigrated from Japan, but we're a hundred percent American. Not that everyone believes that, but what the hell can I do?"

"Looks like you're doing plenty," I said. "Interrogation?"

"First you tell me what you're looking for," Sakato said. "But not here, let's go inside."

We sat across from Sakato in his small office, which accounted for the rear section of the Quonset hut. The table behind him was covered in Japanese documents, maps, and booklets. His desk was clean except for a pad of paper and a single sheet, covered in Japanese characters. He took out a pack of Luckies, offering them around. We both shook our heads and he lit up, clicking his Zippo shut and tapping it against the wooden desktop. He seemed shook up.

"We're investigating three murders on Tulagi for the navy," I said, figuring we should establish our credentials before asking what Harrison's threats were all about.

"Why are you two doing the navy's dirty work?" he asked, tossing the lighter aside.

"Fair question, but it's a long story," I said. "Quick version: you heard of Ambassador Joe Kennedy?" This got a quick nod. "His kid Jack is in PT boats and got too close to one of the victims."

"So you're sent out with a bucket of whitewash?" Sakato said with a laugh.

"There are those who would not mind the entire affair being swept under the rug," Kaz said. "But we prefer to find the killer."

"I assume it's not the Kennedy kid then," Sakato said. "Otherwise, whoever sent you here would have you on a slow boat to the Aleutians."

"Last I heard, the Aleutian Islands were still occupied by the Japanese," I said.

"Exactly," Sakato said, blowing smoke toward the ceiling.

"Smart guy," I said.

"You have to stay on your toes out here, especially when you look like the fellow everyone else is trying to kill. Okay, I'll bite. How can I help you?"

"First, you want to tell us what that was all about with Sergeant Harrison?"

"Harrison is our liaison with marine intelligence," Sakato said. "We're attached to the Thirty-Seventh Division, as part of the Allied Translator and Interpreter Section. There's one other nisei with our section, but he's on New Georgia right now, trying to talk isolated units into surrendering."

"Much luck with that?" I asked.

"No," Sakato said, dragging deep on his cigarette. "Especially if there are any officers. They order their men to hold grenades under their chins. Or stage suicide charges. Senseless."

"It is the Japanese warrior code, is it not, to avoid capture at all costs?" Kaz asked.

"Bushido, yes," Sakato said. "But Japanese propaganda also tells their soldiers that, if captured, they will face torture at the hands of the American devils. We've found that fear of torture leads many to suicide, even without an officer present."

"Then how did you get all these POWs?" I asked.

"There are always some who wish to live, in any group. And we've had some success in getting our guys to take prisoners more readily. With all the evidence of atrocities, GIs haven't been going out of their way to accept surrender. Especially since some of the Nips fake surrender, and then pull out a grenade or a knife."

"Nips?" Kaz asked.

"Nipponese," Sakato explained. "The Japanese word for Japan is *Nippon*."

"You don't mind those terms?" I asked. He didn't seem ready to talk about Harrison yet, so I let the conversation move on. "Japs, Nips?"

"Not when it's shorthand for the enemy, no. I doubt a German-American minds it much when German troops are called Jerries or Krauts, do you?"

"No," I said, thinking his reply was a bit too quick; it sounded like a stock answer he didn't much believe in. Easier that way, I guess. "So, how do you get these guys to give up?"

"Like I said, our men have been bringing more of them in. We've demonstrated how useful information from POWs can be in saving American lives. That helps a lot. And we've begun dropping leaflets behind the lines." He reached back into the mass of papers on the table and picked out a couple. They were written in English and Japanese, with the phrase *I Cease Resistance* emblazoned across them.

"It does not mention surrender," Kaz noted.

"Correct," Sakato said. "We got that idea from some of the first

POWs we took. Ceasing to fight is more palatable than surrender. And the note guarantees safe conduct. So far it's paid dividends."

"Do you get good information from the prisoners?" I asked.

"Quite good. Once a Japanese solider has given up, he feels that ties to his homeland have been severed. He knows his family would be ashamed and that the military would never acknowledge his capture as anything but traitorous. We are all he has. And once he sees a nisei, he has his eyes opened. Obviously the Americans are not the beasts he was taught to believe in. Give him food and medical care, often much better than he was receiving from his own people, and he's very willing to talk and tell us what he knows."

"We have some questions for your POWs," I said. "But first, if you don't mind my asking, what was going on with Harrison?"

"It's hard to talk about," Sakato said, looking for a moment like he did mind. Then he pulled a tattered, thin notebook from the pile of papers, leafed through it, and gave a great sigh as he ground out his cigarette. He shook another out of the pack, flipped open the Zippo, and thumbed the wheel. A bright flame bloomed and he lit his cigarette, holding the orange flame near the edge of the notebook, close enough to catch fire.

He snapped the Zippo shut.

"I'd been translating this," he said, tossing the notebook onto the desk. "It's the diary of a medical orderly we captured a week ago on the outskirts of the Munda airbase. His unit was stationed near Segi Point, which was one of the landing sites for the Marine Raiders. Harrison belonged to that outfit. He'd been wounded on Guadalcanal and sent for liaison duty with us after he recovered." Sakato took a drag on his cigarette and spent some time watching the glowing embers turn to grey ash.

"So he knew the guys in the Raiders who landed on New Georgia," I said, prompting him.

"Yeah, yeah. He did. The fighting was pretty light at Segi Point, not many casualties. But the Raiders lost two scouts. Missing in action, as they say."

"There is something about them in that diary," Kaz said.

"Yes." Sakato rubbed his eyes with the palms of his hands, as if to erase the words he'd read and translated. "They were captured and brought to the medical section. The orderly, Kenji Doi, describes a very interesting lecture by his major, a doctor. His own words, *very interesting*. The major said that in case he was killed, the orderlies should know the basics of surgery in order to carry on. He had the two scouts lashed to trees and performed human vivisections on them. No anesthesia. They were gagged so the major could make himself heard over their screams. He showed the positions of all the main organs, and removed a lung from one man. It was all *very interesting*, according to Kenji. Ironically, he seems a nice fellow, even gentle. Takes good care of his men with the medical supplies we give him." Sakato was staring out the window, into the nothingness of the green jungle beyond.

"That was Kenji Doi who was carried out of the tent," Kaz said. Sakato nodded.

"And Harrison knew the scouts," I said.

"They were his buddies. He was a scout himself. I didn't want him to see the report, saw no reason for it. It was with some other documents he'd already seen, and the file was ready to go up to division headquarters. But he wanted to check something he'd read and grabbed the file a few minutes ago. I'd asked for Kenji to be brought into the interrogation tent so I could ask him about the major, get a name at least. That's when Harrison saw him and made his move."

"Harrison's lucky he wasn't armed. That would be a court-martial offense," I said.

"No weapons allowed when we interrogate POWs," he said. "Eliminates temptation for all parties. Although in this case, a lot of people would have looked the other way."

"What's going to happen now?" Kaz asked. "To the orderly."

"That's up to Division, thank God," Sakato said. "I'll interrogate Kenji and get the name of the so-called doctor who did this. He'll go on a list. A long list of those wanted for war crimes."

"Harrison?"

"He'll be okay. If there were any place to go around here, I'd give him a few days' leave. But there's nowhere to go, nowhere to get away from anything." He flipped through the notebook, reading the daily jottings of an ordinary Japanese soldier. A man who sat through a display of horrendous torture and pronounced it interesting. Not to others—to put on a brave face, to show he was a Bushido kind of guy—but to himself, in his private diary. *"Kisama!"* Sakato shouted, and threw it across the room.

I didn't bother asking for a translation. We sat, silent, for a long minute. Sakato picked up his Zippo, flipping it between his fingers. It seemed to calm him.

"What did you want?" he asked, irritation showing in his furrowed brow, as if he'd forgotten everything we'd said before he told the story of the scouts. "Wait a second, let's get the hell out of here. I need some fresh air."

He led us outside, walking along a well-worn path paralleling the barbed wire. He stopped at a small rise that gave a view out over the hills and down to the sea. He lit another Lucky, fresh air helping only so much.

"We need to know if any of the POWs here were part of the landing party on Pavau," I said. "Especially if they came in on the northern side. We'll need your help to speak with them."

"It will take some time," Sakato said, turning to look out over the enclosure. "Come back tomorrow morning." Prisoners gathered at the edge of the barbed wire, drawn by curiosity, or more likely, by the smell of tobacco. Sakato looked at the half-smoked cigarette, then at the closest POW, locking eyes with him as he dropped the butt and ground it out with his heel.

WE DROVE IN silence for a while. After what we'd heard, words could only say so much. Finally, Kaz spoke. "Do you think we might learn anything useful from those prisoners?"

"It's a long shot, but they probably didn't keep that many troops on Pavau. It's small, and there's no airstrip or large harbor. They could have been sent down to Guadalcanal, in which case they're probably all dead. Or to New Georgia, where the fighting is now. But we could get lucky."

"What do you think a Japanese soldier will tell us? How he massacred the natives at Porter's plantation?"

"I don't expect a confession," I said, as we descended from the hills and took the road along the coast. I inhaled the fresh salt air, hoping it might wash away the images burned into my mind. *Very interesting.* "But I'd like to know more about how it got started. We heard someone killed a Jap first. If there is a living witness, I think he'd readily tell us about that."

"And then relate his own version of what followed," Kaz said.

"Right. But I don't care about that. I care about who started things."

"Porter—I mean Fraser—are you saying he fired the first shot? Intentionally?"

"Convenient, wasn't it, that everyone on the plantation who could identify him was killed? I think maybe things happened much like he said, except it was the real Porter who stayed behind to gather people together while Fraser hid the boat from the Japs."

"So everyone is in one place, and as the Japanese approach the plantation, Fraser fires on the soldiers," Kaz said, pulling his brim low over his eyes as we drove into the fierce afternoon sun.

"Who react in rage at the nearest natives and Porter. Fraser makes his escape, and becomes Silas Porter. Out here, no one would question him. Porter is well-known as a hermit, and his story of survival is readily accepted, especially since he volunteers with the Coastwatchers." No one questions a hero.

"Which is dangerous, but also an endeavor that keeps him hidden. The entire Coastwatcher operation is shrouded in secrecy."

"Right," I said. "A risky venture, but with a big payoff. After the war, he returns to reclaim his plantation on Pavau."

"He's killed three people to keep his secret," Kaz said. "And believes Josh Coburn to be dead. He must be feeling rather secure by now."

"We'll have to use that against him," I said, with as much confidence as I could muster, having no idea how to actually make that work.

We arrived at the dock in time for the air-raid sirens to wail. We made for a slit trench crowded with sailors and natives who'd been loading supplies. The ground was so wet, we were ankle-deep in mud, but no one minded when the bombs began to fall. The earth shook and geysers rose up from hits in the water, but there was no serious damage. It was over in minutes, a nuisance raid. We stuck our heads above ground and watched the Betties fly over Lumbari, about a mile away. Antiaircraft fire pocketed the sky with dark puffs of explosions and bright white tracers, but the bombers stayed on course, dropping what looked like small specks in wavering, wobbly lines that found their way to the PT base, sending distant, faint *crumps* into the thick afternoon air.

Silence descended like dust. The bombers made for the horizon and the guns stood mute. We clambered out of the trench, smiling. That idiotic grin at the joy of living after a brush with death plastered on our faces, Fuzzy Wuzzies and crew cuts alike. Everyone likes being alive, and even though most won't admit it, more so when others are freshly dead.

We waited while a crew of natives pulled the launch from the water, where it had been swamped by the bombs that had struck off shore. An hour later, we were back on Lumbari, walking through thick smoke from the fires still crackling in the heat. A supply dump had taken a direct hit, thick, oily smoke rising from the shattered fuel drums. A jeep filled with wounded sailors drove past us, heading for the hospital tent. Nearing the beach, we saw a PT shredded by a bomb, luckily not Cotter's PT-169.

We made for the communications center in Garfield's bunker, and waited for things to settle down so I could have two messages sent out. The first was to Captain Ritchie, asking him to contact the Sydney police for a description of Peter Fraser, who'd once worked at the Lever soap factory. The second was to Hugh Sexton, inquiring if the man he knew as Silas Porter had come to the Coastwatchers with a hunting rifle back in 1942. I was betting the answer would be yes.

We ate in the mess tent. Greasy meat stew for Kaz and me, and powdered eggs and reconstituted potatoes for Cotter and the crew of

PT-169. It was getting dark. In theory, they'd slept during the day to rest up for their night patrol, but between the stifling heat and the bombing Betties, they looked beat; listless and hollow-eyed. Still, they shoveled in what passed for breakfast and guzzled coffee, readying themselves for another rendezvous with the Tokyo Express.

"I think I prefer Algiers to these islands," Kaz said, exploring his stew and picking out an unappetizing clot of gristle. "Let's get this killer and go home."

Home. Funny how the North African desert and mountains felt like home, now that we were away from it. For me, Diana Seaton was what made it special. I hoped she was still there, not off on another SOE assignment. I imagined her in the Hotel Saint George, in the very room where I'd left her. It was a pleasant daydream, but it didn't last long.

"Yes," I said. "Tomorrow we'll see if Sakato has any POWs for us to talk to. Then check on those radio messages. If things add up, all we'll need is a ride to Choiseul."

"Simple," Kaz said, pushing away his unfinished stew.

CHAPTER TWENTY-NINE

THE ANSWER FROM Sexton came quickly the next morning. Yes, Porter had brought his own weapon with him. A Mark II Ross, a Canadian rifle. It was still at Sexton's headquarters. He ended the message with a single word. *Why?*

I knew the Ross. It was highly accurate, a sniper's rifle. But it had little tolerance for dirt and dampness. It tended to malfunction if not kept completely clean. Long and heavy, it certainly wasn't suited for jungle warfare. My dad told me he'd met Canadian troops in France during the last war who got rid of them as soon as they could pick up a Lee-Enfield from the British dead. Except for the snipers. They loved the Ross.

"Are you going to answer him?" Kaz asked as we motored across the bay.

"No, not yet," I said. "I don't think Sexton would want Fraser to get away scot-free, but I could see him wanting to keep a valuable Coastwatcher in place for now."

"There is logic to that. We could simply wait until he is withdrawn from Choiseul," Kaz said.

"Well, we're not waiting around for that," I said. "And Fraser is smart. He might decide to pull another disappearing act if he senses anything is up. The last thing he'd expect would be for us to apprehend him behind enemy lines."

"There is some logic to that as well," Kaz said with a sly grin.

"Besides, I don't think either of us wants to hang around the Solomons any longer than we have to," I said, hoisting myself out of the launch and heading for our jeep, still in one piece after yesterday's raid. Heavy grey clouds blew in from the east, winds moving the hot, humid air without providing one bit of relief. Our khakis were soaked with sweat, and it was still early morning. When the rains came, sheets of warm water washed us clean for a moment, and then stopped abruptly, leaving us wet, steamy, and smelling slightly of mold.

At the POW enclosure three trucks were being loaded up with prisoners. We watched the small convoy depart, jeeps with GIs cradling Thompson submachine guns following each of the transports. The prisoners looked worried, perhaps wondering if the propaganda had been right and they were being taken off to be executed.

"Don't worry," Sakato said, approaching us from the Quonset hut. "None of those are of interest to you. I found four men who were on Pavau. You can see them whenever you want."

"Great," I said. "Where are those prisoners headed? They looked pretty glum."

"New Zealand," Sakato said. "Some guys have all the luck. They're frightened of going to a larger camp. More chance of running into hard-core types."

"Hard-core types wouldn't surrender in the first place, would they?" Kaz asked.

"Not willingly, no. Some are found wounded or unconscious and wake up really unhappy to be alive. If they don't find a way to commit suicide, they make life miserable for everyone else. But your four men aren't in that category. How do you want to handle this?"

"Let's talk to them one at a time, okay?"

"No problem," Sakato said as we followed him inside. "I'll have them brought into the interrogation tent. You guys leave your pistols in my office. No weapons, remember?"

"I thought you said these four wouldn't be a problem," Kaz said, unbuckling his web belt.

"No reason to tempt fate," Sakato said. "I speak the language like a native, but there is still much I don't understand about Japanese people. I wouldn't put it past the mildest, most peaceful prisoner to kill himself and take some of us with him. It's been beaten into these men from birth."

"Cheery guy," I whispered to Kaz as we stashed my .45 automatic and his Webley revolver in Sakato's office.

"Another man between two worlds," Kaz said. "I do not envy him."

"I don't envy anyone on this island except Josh Coburn and his coffee," I said, as we made for the interrogation tent. The flaps were rolled up to let in what breeze there was, except for the side that faced the POW pen. No reason to advertise. Guards flanked the entrance, rifles with bayonets fixed at parade rest. Sergeant Harrison guided in the first prisoner, ushering him to the chair opposite Sakato. A small table separated us, with Sakato in the middle and Kaz and me taking a back seat on either side.

"Taku Ishii, Private First Class, 20th Division," Sakato said, looking up from the file in front of him. The soldier nodded, bowing deeply to Sakato, hands straight at his side. Sakato nodded his head slightly in return, and gestured for the man to sit. He did so nervously, bobbing his head and chattering in what seemed like endless thanks. He was nearly bald, what hair he had cropped short. He was thin and bony, with a long face and sad eyes. His light-brown uniform was worn but clean, and I knew his condition was far, far better than what our boys were enduring in Japanese camps.

"Ask him where and when he landed on Pavau," I said. Sakato rattled off the questions in Japanese and listened to the answer, jotting notes as he did so.

"It was in May of 1942," Sakato said. "He doesn't remember the date. He was on a destroyer that docked on the southern tip of the island. He says there was no fighting, no resistance."

"Did he hear of fighting anywhere else on Pavau?" I asked.

"No," Sakato said following their exchange. "He says he was there for less than a week, and pulled out when the navy garrisoned the harbor. He does remember bodies washing up on shore, but says they were civilians drowned in a ferry accident."

"Did he go to the northern end of Pavau?" Kaz asked. No, came the reply. He never left the harbor area.

Next up was Matsudo Kufuku, Leading Seaman with the 3rd Kure Special Naval Landing Force. He performed the same bow before taking his seat. He looked tough, not quite as nervous as the first guy. His faded green uniform hung loosely on his frame.

"He's a marine, right?" I asked.

"Naval infantry, yes," Sakato said. "Our marines don't think much of them, but that's to be expected."

"Can we give him a cigarette?" I asked, noting how Matsudo studied each of us. Wary eyes, but unworried. I had the sense he was a survivor.

"Sure," Sakato said, shaking two Lucky Strikes from his pack, rolling one across the table to Matsudo, taking the other for himself. He lit both from his Zippo, and Matsudo leaned back, drawing the smoke in deep and smiling as he exhaled. Sakato asked the first question.

"Yes, he remembers. May, 1942. His platoon landed on the north side, in an armed barge, covered by destroyers. He says there was a small dock, but no enemy ships opposed them."

"The north side? Are you sure?" Sakato repeated the question.

"*Hai,*" with the self-assurance that told me it meant yes.

"Ask him if they encountered resistance," I said.

"Yes," Sakato said, after listening to what sounded like an angry response. "First an ensign was shot and killed. He was popular with the men, since he didn't treat them harshly."

"Then?"

"They fired into the bush where they thought the shot had come from," Sakato said. "They were all very angry."

"It was a single shot?" I asked. That got another *hai,* followed by a more subdued response.

"He says," Sakato began, releasing a deep sigh, "that the road from the dock led to a plantation. A big house, surrounded by smaller buildings. They fanned out, worried about the sniper. Natives came out and began waving their arms and shouting, but no one understood. He thinks they were being friendly, but others thought they were threatening."

"Did he see a white man?" I asked.

"Yes. An old white man, he says. He came out of the house and stood with his hands held high. He spoke to the lieutenant in charge, but no one understood him. Then another shot was fired."

"By the sniper?"

"Yes, Matsudo is certain of that. It didn't hit anyone, but the natives started to run, the old man was shouting, and suddenly there was a lot of firing."

"They killed them all," I said.

Hai.

The next two POWs were of no help. One soldier who'd also landed on the southern shore and a mechanic who worked at a seaplane base on Pavau weeks after the invasion. But we only needed to hear that story once.

"What are you going to do with him?" Kaz asked Sakato when we were back in his office, buckling our web belts.

"Not much I can do," he said. "He denies taking part in the slaughter. His story is that most of the other men had never been in combat, and that they were nervous and upset after their ensign was killed."

"That has a ring of truth to it," Kaz said. "Once the shooting starts, it can be hard to stop."

"I think he's telling the truth," Sakato said. "He fought in New Guinea before being transferred to the Solomons, so he's had combat experience."

"How was he captured?" I asked.

"It was at Enogai Point on New Georgia. His unit had been pushed back into the ocean. The few who were still alive swam out into the water and blew their heads off with grenades. Matsudo came out of a cave with his hands up. He told me he'd been the only survivor of his platoon in New Guinea, and now again on New Georgia. He thought it was a sign that he was meant to live." Sakato shrugged, as if a bit embarrassed by the story.

"If all that is true, he seems a decent man," Kaz said. "He didn't murder anyone, sees the value in living, and was honest with us. One could ask for worse in an enemy."

"I didn't ask for any enemies," Sakato said. "But I've got plenty. Back home they put my folks in an internment camp, and out here I'm considered a traitor to the emperor, except by the pitiful handful who surrender. Sorry, I mean cease resistance."

"This must be hard, Lieutenant, but you've been a big help," I said, extending my hand. I felt for Sakato, a decent guy stuck out here, forever cut off from the land of his ancestors, alone in the midst of his own people. We shook.

"You've helped us catch a murderer," Kaz said as Sakato fired up another cigarette. I wondered if Kaz felt some sympathy for the nisei, a man cut off from family and homeland by friend and foe alike.

"That's funny," Sakato said. "Bodies are being bulldozed into ditches on Munda Field, right across the strait. And you're looking for someone who killed three people? Small potatoes, boys. See you in the funny papers." He grabbed a stack of captured documents and spread them out across his desk, ash from his smoke scattering across the delicate, dancing script.

"Well, we got what we came for," Kaz said as we made for the jeep. "It was a long shot that paid off."

"Yeah," I said, wishing that it had cheered me up some. I climbed into the driver's seat and looked into the POW pen. Standing by himself at the wire was Matsudo Kufuku, his sun-bleached green uniform unlike all the brown army clothing the other POWs wore. A man alone and apart, straddling two worlds, unready for death, uncertain of life. Like Daniel Tamana, John Kari, and Joe Sakato, each filled with his own brand of loneliness and longing.

Like Peter Fraser, except Fraser chose to break with his old world and start anew. Too bad it meant getting blood on his hands.

Like Kaz, with his family and perhaps his nation forever gone.

Like me? Separated from the only world I ever thought I'd inhabit, Boston and the sacred confines of the Irish brotherhood of the police department.

War makes white ghosts of us all.

■   ■   ■

DARK CLOUDS BLEW overhead as we drove, churning thick and low, about to burst and crackle lightning. The pungent, zesty smell of rain ready to fall filled our nostrils as swirling winds lifted the palm branches high, showing us their light undersides as they rose toward the heavens. We might get soaked, but it would keep Betty and her friends at home, which was well worth a drenching.

We ended up with the best of both worlds. Thunder boomed in the distance and lightning bolts stabbed at the sea, the rains a grey wall moving northeast to the Blanche Channel, separating Rendova from New Georgia.

Back at Lumbari, we checked in with the communications center. There was a response to the question I'd asked Ritchie to pass on to the Sydney police. A description of Peter Fraser: six feet one inch, a hundred and eighty-four pounds, brown hair, brown eyes. No record of arrest. It was signed by Yeoman Howe, who had added *Good luck*. We were going to need it.

"That settles it," Kaz said as we stepped out of the bunker and into the grey afternoon. "We have his description, the rifle, an eyewitness account of a massacre orchestrated by a hidden sniper, the testimony of Josh Coburn—what else do we need?"

"If I were laying this out to the city prosecutor back in Boston, he'd tell me we have a good case of fraud for Fraser taking on Porter's identity. But murder? Circumstantial evidence, some of which was provided by an enemy soldier."

"He had means, motive, and opportunity in all three cases," Kaz said. "If he didn't do it, who did?"

"It's good enough for me," I said. "Our job is to bring him in. We'll let an Australian court-martial decide the rest."

"Now what we need is a way to accomplish that," Kaz said. "Are you sure you don't want to ask Hugh Sexton to recall him?"

"No, that would spook him for sure. We need a reason for a rendezvous, something that won't raise his suspicions."

"Radio? Food?" Kaz suggested as a throng of sailors surged past us, heading for the beach where the PT boats were moored.

"No, they have all they need," I said. "They were bringing in weapons for the natives when they were loading their boat. Maybe more weapons, to prepare for an uprising."

"That sounds plausible," Kaz said. "With New Georgia almost under control, it would make sense for there to be more landings. Choiseul could be next, or it would make a decent diversion. It makes sense militarily."

"Okay," I said, noticing a hubbub down by the beach. "What's going on down there anyway?"

"Everyone is gathered around that PT boat," Kaz said. "Is that Kennedy's new gunboat?"

"That's Jack alright," I said, spotting the bushy hair and the aviator sunglasses. "A guy who owes me a favor, and happens to command a whole lot of firepower."

"He may have orders beyond providing us transportation," Kaz said.

"He's not the only one with friends in high places," I said. "Come on, let's get back on the radio."

At the communications center, we worked on a message to Sexton. It began with the word IMPERATIVE and asked for orders to be sent to Porter and Kari to receive an additional shipment of arms the following night, and to advise the best time and place.

A second message was sent to Ritchie, meaning that the resourceful Yeoman Howe would take care of it. It also began with IMPERATIVE and asked for orders to be sent to Garfield directing that PT-59 take Kaz and myself to Choiseul tomorrow night. I ended it with KENNEDY CONCURS. I figured that would be all Ritchie needed to hear to give Howe the okay. Jack owed me, so one little white lie didn't bother me a bit.

We made our way back to the beach, where most of the crowd had broken up. There were still a few sailors gawking at the forty-millimeter guns, clearly impressed. We clambered up the ladder, Jack greeting us with a wide grin as we saluted the ensign and asked to come aboard.

"I didn't expect to see you fellows so soon," he said. "But they want us on standby for something the marines are cooking up. We're still on shakedown, but things are coming along. Right, Chappy?"

"If you say so, Skipper," Chappy said, from where he sat next to the forward gun, his hands grimy with grease. "I'm having trouble with the swivel getting stuck and the armored plate on the bridge isn't secured properly, and with all due respect, she's a real pig in the water. But other than that, we're in great shape."

"You're doing a fine job, Chappy," Jack said, leaning down to clap him on the shoulder and winking in our direction. "And you're right about the boat. Heavy and slow with all the armor and added guns, not to mention extra crew. She guzzles fuel like crazy, but believe me, the Japs aren't going to know what hit them."

Jack led us down into his wardroom, which was about as big as a broom closet. A crewman brought in coffee, even though below deck it was as hot as Hades. Which wasn't much different from being in the sun above deck, so we drank it.

"We need your help, Jack," I said. I outlined what we'd figured about Peter Fraser, aka Silas Porter.

"He killed three people over a copra plantation?" Jack asked. "That's nuts."

"And he probably didn't mind it that you were a suspect," I said, making it as personal an affront as I could.

"What can I do?" Jack asked.

"Take us to Choiseul," I said. "Tomorrow night."

"You're crazy," Jack said.

"Don't worry about orders," I said. "We're working on that."

"It's not orders I care about," he said. "You two are going to get yourselves killed. Don't you know there's about five thousand Japs on Choiseul?"

"No," Kaz said, giving me the eye. "We did not know there were quite so many."

"They're half-starved remnants from units withdrawn from other islands. But a half-starved Jap can kill you just the same."

"How do you know all this?" I asked. It struck me odd that Jack would have such precise knowledge about any single occupied island, having been sidelined in the hospital recently.

"That's why I've been ordered up here," he said. "Tonight, a battalion of marines is landing on Choiseul. The brass wants some firepower on hand in case they get in trouble."

"Why only a battalion?" Kaz asked. "That's only five or six hundred men."

"It's a diversion," Jack said, grabbing a chart from the rack behind him. "I don't know where the real attack is going to be, but these guys are supposed to keep the Japs focused on Choiseul instead. They're being landed by destroyer transports and establishing a base at Voza, here." It was a coastal village up on the northern part of the island, facing the Slot. "There's a Jap base on the northern tip of the island, here at Choiseul Bay, and south of Voza at Sangigai. South of there, the island is free of Japs."

"It's safe to assume John Kari and Fraser are involved in this," I said.

"Sure. I don't have the details, but they're likely to be organizing native scouts and porters to help the marines."

"They were bringing crates of weapons to arm the natives," Kaz said.

"I doubt that will happen, at least not right now," Jack said. "The whole point of the operation is to draw more Nips to Choiseul. If there's a native uprising and we leave, they'd be slaughtered."

"I would venture to say that Kari and Fraser will not be told it is a diversion," Kaz said.

"There'd be no need for them to know," Jack said.

"Good," I said. "If all goes as planned, Hugh Sexton will order them to meet us tomorrow night for a shipment of arms. We grab Fraser and come back. Simple."

"Leaving the marines with only one Coastwatcher," Jack said.

"That, or take a chance on Fraser getting away," I said. "Besides, John Kari knows what he's doing. Who better than a native to work with the natives?"

"Are you both sure you want to do this?" Jack said, looking first to Kaz and then to me. "You don't have to, you know."

"He killed Deanna, Jack," I said.

"I know. That's why I'll take you tomorrow, orders or no, although orders would be nice. I'd like to avoid a court-martial if possible. But if you end up dead, it's on your shoulders. I've gotten two guys killed already and I don't want any more on my conscience."

"Agreed," I said, extending my hand. Kaz did the same. "It's on our shoulders."

CHAPTER THIRTY

BY MORNING WE'D received responses to our radio messages. Without asking why this time, Hugh Sexton had set up a weapons drop on a deserted stretch of beach south of the village of Nukiki, the area where Kari and Porter were operating in support of the marines. He confirmed that they'd be waiting at 0100 hours, staying for no more than thirty minutes. They'd shine a flashlight out to sea to let us know it was safe to come ashore. Ritchie also gave his okay for Jack and PT-59 to ferry us out and wait for us to bring Porter back from the beach. The only downside was that Ritchie ordered Jack to wait only twenty minutes for our return.

That meant we had to get there right on time, given that the Coastwatchers would not stay exposed on an open beach for long. The same for PT-59; hanging around off the beach was an invitation to get trapped by a Jap destroyer and pushed too damn close to shore batteries and concentrated small-arms fire. We'd be on a tight schedule, but if all went according to plan, it would work.

Kaz and I drew weapons from the base armory; an M1 Carbine for him, an M1 rifle for me.

"Odds are we won't need these," I said, "for either Porter or the Japs. But if we do, don't count on one bullet to take a man out. The carbine is lightweight, but so are the rounds."

"I much prefer this weapon," Kaz said, hefting the short carbine. "I am lightweight myself, but still quite dangerous."

"That's the spirit," I said as we went off to check in with Jack. PT-59 was covered in camouflage netting, as much for the dappled shade it provided as for cover from the air. Crewmen were carrying crates of fifty-caliber ammo aboard, and Chappy was busy greasing the swivel on the forward forty-millimeter gun. He gave us a smile and a lazy salute, seeming to be satisfied with his handiwork.

"I got my orders from Ritchie," Jack said, climbing onto the bridge. "Seems like he thinks it was my idea in the first place."

"I figured he'd take to the idea easier that way," I said, trying to read Jack's face, which was tough with his aviator's sunglasses and brimmed cap pulled down over his bushy hair. "Ritchie's got connections with your father through ONI, and I didn't want him to hesitate about putting you in harm's way. And I don't want to be your fall guy again."

"After the baron reminded me of how I treated you back in Boston, I probably deserved that," he said, and laughed, his eyes lighting up as he removed the sunglasses. "But harm's way is exactly where I plan to go. Let's head below and I'll show you the route in."

We followed, as I lifted my eyebrows at Kaz, astonished at what amounted to an apology from Jack. I had to admit, he wasn't quite the same guy I knew back in Boston. Harder, and a touch more humble. Just a touch though, since he had to qualify his statement with "probably."

"Here we go," Jack continued, rolling out a chart in the tiny wardroom. "The marines landed here, at Voza, along the north central coast." He tapped his finger about three-quarters of the way up the coast of Choiseul. "There's lots of Japs south of there, down to Sangigai, here. We're going in at Nukiki, which is north of Voza but not close enough to Choiseul Bay to worry about the Japs up there."

"Why not simply go in at Voza, where the marines are?" I asked.

"They've already gone inland, established a base in the mountains, to raid north and south," Jack explained. "The whole idea behind this diversion is to have the Japs think a full division has landed. The brass is even announcing the invasion on the radio. According to them, twenty thousand marines are now on Choiseul."

"But the reality is six hundred or so," Kaz said. "Not very good odds for them if the enemy rushes reinforcements to the island."

"That's what we want," Jack said. "Then we hit their transports by sea and air, and get the marines out of there."

"Sounds good on paper," I said. "But then so does our scheme. What are the waters like off Nukiki?"

"Here," Jack said, laying out several photographs on the table. "I got these reconnaissance photos from Garfield. This shows the beach right next to the village. There's an opening in the reef that runs offshore; see where the water is calm? We can bring you in close and put you on a rubber raft."

"How about rigging up a dummy crate of weapons?" Kaz said. "We could ask Porter to come back with us to get more. Once aboard, it would be simple to secure him."

"If he buys it," I said. "If not, we'll need a length of rope to tie him up."

"We'll have both in the raft," Jack said. "I'll have the boys put K rations in a crate; that ought to work fine in the dark. We have enough canned pickles for a regiment."

"We shall have to take him quickly," Kaz said. "John Kari might intervene, if only out of confusion and shock."

"They're both in the thick of a fight right now," Jack said. "They're going to be keyed up, ready for anything. Watch yourselves out there. The Japs aren't the only ones to worry about."

"Jack," I said, "if we're not back pretty damn quick, don't wait more than those twenty minutes. If it takes longer than that, we're done for."

"Don't worry, Billy. I like you two fellas, but I'm not going to endanger this boat. Now get some shut-eye if you can. Be onboard by eighteen hundred hours. We'll be in the Slot by dark, and then it's a hundred-mile run. Don't be late. If you're not here, I'll have to go after the bastard myself." Jack flashed one of his patented grins, all white teeth and lively eyes. It was hard to resist his eagerness and his charm, and as we faced this hazardous mission together, I really didn't want to.

■   ■   ■

SLEEP HAD BEEN elusive in the heat and thick, humid air, with sunlight blazing and baking our canvas tent. But that didn't matter now; we were slicing through the waters of the Blanche Channel, Lumbari at our backs and a cool wind on our faces. Explosions reflected off the low clouds, the sounds and sudden flashes of light like fireworks on a summer's night. Deadly up close, but at a distance, in the full South Pacific night, it was otherworldly, even glorious.

"They're pounding the last Jap stronghold on New Georgia," Jack said, his voice raised to be heard over the motors. "We might spot some barges bringing troops out."

"Be hard to see," I said. It was a cloudy night, not even reflected starlight to see by.

"We finally have radar," he said. "If they're out there, we'll find them."

Kaz and I exchanged glances. That wasn't what we were out here for. I gave him a little shrug that told him not to worry. Jack wanted Porter taken as much as we did. He also wanted revenge, but I was hoping he'd hold off on hunting Japs until the return trip.

"This is Blackett Strait," Jack said, his voice grim. He slowed the engines and turned to one of the crewmen who'd come from PT-109. "Mauer, get the boys up here."

The four other veterans of PT-109 stood with Jack on the bridge as he raised his arm to the port side, out into the inky-black night. "Right about there."

They stood quietly for a minute, hands on shoulders, crowded together on the tiny bridge, holding each other close, as they must have done that night in the water while flames licked the waves and every other PT boat left them alone and adrift—nothing between them and the Japanese but sharks, sharp coral reefs, and guts.

Then they broke up wordlessly, hustling back to their duty stations, scanning the sky and the horizon. We turned north, picking up speed as we moved along the perimeter of Kolombangara, the almost perfectly round island off New Georgia.

"Radar contact," said the radio operator. "Bearing one-four-nine."

"Changing course to one-four-nine," Jack said. "Distance?"

"Two miles out, heading west by northwest."

"Jack?" I said. He didn't respond. Kaz and I stepped back, grabbing hold of the radio mast as the boat accelerated and Jack went for the targets ahead. So much for caution.

Less than a minute later, I made out two dark hulks churning through the water ahead. Japanese Daihatsu barges, each about sixty feet long, crammed with soldiers, and armed with machine guns mounted at fore and aft.

They were no match for Jack's gunboat. He kept straight on course for the second barge, the forward forty-millimeter firing away, joined by the twin fifties in the turrets on either side of the bridge. A burst of bright orange leapt from the barge, an explosive burst of fuel catapulting men into the water and scorching those who remained on board, their uniforms catching fire as they scrambled through the flames and over the side where machine-gun rounds stitched the ocean into geysers of blood and fire.

Jack slowed and turned, coming at the first barge with a full broadside. It didn't catch fire, but splintered and broke apart under the heavy machine-gun and cannon fire, bodies broken and shattered, dancing under the staccato light of tracers as the impact of multiple rounds sent them careening against each other. Ending in death's calm embrace only when Jack signaled cease fire.

He did a circuit of the barges. Screams—whether in agony or anger, it was impossible to tell—echoed out over the water. Jack ordered full speed ahead, leaving the carnage behind, a satisfied grin on his face, delight showing in his eyes as they met mine.

"I had a crewman when I first came out here. He was wounded on patrol, and transferred to another PT boat after he recovered," Jack began, in answer to the question I hadn't asked. "A few weeks later, they sank a barge, like that one, and pulled four survivors out of the drink. He had them covered with a tommy gun. One of them begged for water, and being a nice kid, he leaned forward to give him his canteen. The Jap grabbed the Thompson and killed him with it. That's what comes of doing the decent thing out here."

"Decency and war seldom go together," Kaz said as Jack turned

away, fiery eyes forward. "But here, they seem not even to have a nodding acquaintance." That was something coming from Kaz, who'd lost
his family as well as his nation to the Nazis.

"Jack," I said, stepping up on the bridge. "If we're making good
time, I wouldn't mind going ashore before oh-one-hundred."

"So you can get a drop on him?" Jack asked. I nodded yes. "But
we're still only waiting twenty minutes, there's no way around that.
We'll put you in the rubber raft about quarter of. The twenty-minute
clock starts ticking once you hit the beach. Clobber him over the head
and paddle back as fast as you can."

We crossed the open waters of the Slot at full throttle, more than
making up time for the brief, one-sided engagement. As the island of
Choiseul showed up on the radar screen, Jack slowed the boat, lessen-
ing the phosphorescent wake and the chances of being spotted by a
Jap lookout. We moved slowly, the sound of breaking waves increasing
in volume. I could make out the whitecaps where the tide drove water
against the coral reef, a rolling, crashing tumult that threatened to rip
open the hull of any small craft that went against it. Or the feet of any
man swimming over it, as Jack had done trying to signal a friendly
vessel in Blackett Strait.

As I was considering the chances a rubber raft had of riding those
waves, I saw the opening. A river of calm water between the breakers.
I looked at my watch, the luminous dial reading quarter of one.

"Ready?" I said to Kaz. He nodded, and we both slung our rifles
and went aft, where Chappy and Mauer were putting the raft over the
side. The crate filled with food and two coils of rope were in place.
Next was us.

"Good luck," Jack said. "As soon as you get onshore, the countdown
starts. Don't dawdle, fellas."

"Not planning on it," I said, trying for a nonchalance I didn't even
remotely feel.

"Speed is the essence of war," Kaz said as he lowered himself into
the raft. Jack gave a knowing nod and helped shove us off.

"Is that a quotation?" I asked, a bit irked that Kaz could always
come up with a pithy saying.

"Sun Tzu, from *The Art of War*," he said. "Jack seemed to know it."

"Of course," I said, digging in with my paddle. "He's a Harvard boy. Now row, before we're swamped." It took both of us at maximum effort to keep the small raft from drifting, the current pulling us away from the smooth, glassy water ahead. We finally made it past the breakers, and with a few easy strokes were up on the sand, dragging the raft into the bushes.

We squatted beneath the overhanging palms. I checked my watch. Ten of one. If we weren't back in the raft and close to the boat by ten after, we were out of luck. Stuck on Choiseul with a killer and several thousand Japs on high alert. What the hell had I been thinking?

Blood was pounding in my head, masking all other noises. Or was that the surf? Kaz stuck his head out and glanced up and down the beach, shaking his head when he saw nothing. As we waited, I began to sense the sounds around me with increasing clarity. The wind through the trees, the breakers out on the reef, and the softer sounds of water lapping at the white-sand beach.

Nothing else.

Five more minutes passed. It was one o'clock on the dot.

Nothing.

We stuck our heads out from the undergrowth and scanned the beach in both directions. I didn't see any movement, but suddenly a figure was standing on the beach, a few feet out from the arched palms. A pinpoint of light flicked on and off.

I tapped Kaz on the arm. He nodded and took up the coils of rope. There was nothing to do but walk over, with no sudden moves. We had to be quiet enough not to alert the Japs and deliberate enough not to panic Porter and have him shoot first and ask questions later.

Then the flashlight shined in our direction. The pinpoint of light hit me full in the eyes, and I shielded them with one hand, keeping the rifle at my side with the other. We stood and walked to the light.

"Kari?" I said. "Porter? Turn that thing off."

"Sure boss," the figure said, his cadence and accent pure Pijin. He was a native, bare-chested, wearing a tan *lap-lap*, a big machete on a cartridge belt around his waist, and a Lee-Enfield rifle slung over his shoulder. "Nem blo' mi Ariel."

"Wea nao ples blong John Kari? Silas Porter?" Kaz asked, after he'd made introductions. I was pretty sure he asked where Porter and Kari were.

"Warrior River," Ariel said. "They scout for marines. Many marines lost. Too many Japan man."

"How far?" I asked, resisting the urge to make walking motions with my fingers.

"One day, no Japan man. Two days, lotta Japan man. You bringim gans?"

"No guns," I said. "Guns tomorrow, food today." I figured we might as well pass out the food and get back to the boat kwiktaem.

"You bringim Silas and John here tomura?" Kaz asked.

"No, too much fight, too many Japan man. We takim food, takim you to marines. Both with marines." Ariel waved a hand and four more native scouts appeared around us. Two of them hoisted the rations and the others drew their machetes and quickly sliced the rubber raft into pieces.

"Japan man no find, is gut, namba wan, yes Billy?"

"Yeah, great, number one idea," I said, my mouth gaping. I watched them use the paddles to scrape a depression in the sand and cover the remains of the raft. I looked out to sea, wondering how long Jack would wait. Five more minutes by my watch.

"Well, we came to do a job," Kaz said. I had to agree. Ariel and his pals were ready to take us to Porter, so why not? Well, I thought of a lot of reasons why not, but with no raft and Jack heading back to Rendova in a couple of minutes, it really didn't matter.

"Usim marine wailis," Ariel said. "Send for more gans. We killim plenty Japan man."

"Wailis?" I said, falling in behind Kaz as the group filed into the bush, each man nearly invisible in the darkness and thick undergrowth.

"Wireless," Kaz said. "We can use the marine's radio. As soon as we get there, we can contact Jack."

"If the Japs don't mind," I said.

"Kwait, no ken mekim nois," Ariel whispered harshly.

"Wait a minute," I said in a low voice. "One question. How did you know where we were? You shined the flashlight right at us."

"You smellim like waitman. Bad smell, but not bad as Japan man. Hariap."

Ariel took off, taking fast, sure steps, as if we were walking through an open field in daylight. We haried ap for the rest of the night, not stopping until the faint light of early dawn.

CHAPTER THIRTY-ONE

"I CAN'T BELIEVE you endangered these men, Lieutenant, and in the middle of an important operation, goddammit!"

Colonel Victor Krulak paced in front of us, one hand wiping sweat off his crew cut, the other resting on his holstered .45 automatic. I hoped his arm was just tired. His lungs sure weren't. This was about ten minutes into a full-dress tirade, and he wasn't done yet.

"These scouts and the Coastwatchers have been invaluable," Krulak said. Ariel seemed to enjoy the spectacle, even if he might not understand most of it. I tried not to think about the nickname his men had given Krulak. Brute. "Now you want to arrest Porter in the middle of a battle, after Ariel walked through Jap lines to get you here? What the hell are they thinking back on Tulagi?"

"Probably that three murders shouldn't go unpunished, sir," I said in my most respectful voice.

"The man you know as Silas Porter may be unstable, Colonel," Kaz said. "He is not to be trusted."

"We've been trusting him and the other Coastwatcher, Kari, with our lives," Krulak said. "Not to mention Ariel and the other scouts. But I don't want to harbor a murderer, even if he's good in a fight." He sighed, and grabbed his helmet from where he'd thrown it to the ground during the start of his lecture. "Johnston, get over here," he yelled to a group of marines watching the proceedings.

"Yes sir," Johnston said, eyeing us as he approached, tommy gun slung over his shoulder.

"Lieutenant Johnston is taking a platoon to the area in which Porter and Kari are operating," Krulak said to Kaz and me. "Go with him. Don't get in the way and don't get anyone killed."

"Sam Johnston," the officer said as we introduced ourselves. He was tall, lean, and filthy, sweat and mud caked on every part of his uniform. After only one night in the jungle, Kaz and I were cultivating much the same look. "I didn't expect the army to tag along, especially the Polish Army."

"First to fight, as they say," replied Kaz.

"That's what Krakowski was always saying. He wanted the marines to invade France and take on Hitler. He'd enjoy talking with you, but he's dead."

"The first to fight often are," Kaz said. "Now, what is the situation?"

"I'll explain as we walk," Johnston said. "Damn, I wish Krakowski could've met you."

In short, the situation could have been better. The marines had been busy raiding up and down the island. They had four Higgins boats hidden on a small island off Voza, where the battalion had been put ashore. The boats carried detachments up and down the coast, hitting Jap installations, then disappearing, keeping the Japs guessing about the size of the force.

Early yesterday, two of the landing craft had dropped off a company north of the Warrior River, under the command of Major Bigger. The Higgins boats were to return to the mouth of the river this morning and extract the marines, after they'd raided an enemy base near Choiseul Bay. The marines didn't make the rendezvous at oh-six-hundred. Worse yet, there'd been no radio contact, and Major Bigger should have checked in by now.

"Your man Porter is with them," Johnston said. "Along with the other guy, Kari. Our job was to make contact. They were supposed to have left a radio team and a security detachment at the river mouth, but there was no sign of them either."

"That doesn't sound good," I said. "What is one platoon supposed to do about it?"

"One marine platoon, you mean. With the Polish Army contingent, of course. Not to mention the US Army's contribution, Lieutenant Boyle. You know how to use that thing?" He thumbed in the direction of my M1.

"I had some practice in North Africa," I said. "Although I prefer a Thompson like yours. They were out at the armory, or the navy didn't want to let one go."

"They're good for jungle work," Johnston said, holding up a hand for the column to halt. Ariel came in from the front at a trot, his head low. I took a hint and went down on one knee. Kaz did the same as Johnston waved his men off the track and they moved several yards into the bush, poised to face any potential threat.

I heard Johnston curse under his breath as he listened to Ariel, who spoke slowly, using as much English as he could muster. He ended by shaking his head slowly. "Mi sori."

"We're getting close to the river," he whispered to us and a sergeant who gathered around, along with the radioman. "There's a dead white man tied to a tree about a hundred yards up."

"A marine?" asked the sergeant.

"Ariel can't tell. He's naked. In bad shape. Real bad."

"Are you going to march the entire platoon right by him?" I asked. I knew these guys were no strangers to corpses, but this sounded worse than the standard-issue battle carnage.

"Damn right I'm going to," Johnston said, the bitterness so sharp in his voice I wasn't surprised when he spat. "Sergeant Trent, get his dog tags if he's one of ours. Either way, cut him down. After the men have a chance to see what kind of enemy we have here."

"It's Gallaher," the radioman said as soon as we came to the body. I don't know how he recognized him.

"Corporal Gallaher was in charge of the company radio," Johnston said. "Now we know why we haven't heard anything." He stood next to the bloody tree, staring at the body as his men marched by. Most looked. None for too long.

Gallaher was stripped naked and bound with rough rope, his hands pulled back around the tree. There was a rope cinched tight in his mouth, and around his legs, immobilizing him against the wide coconut trunk. He must have had a hundred wounds. Bayonets had struck him everywhere. Arms, legs, shoulders; some of those wounds wouldn't have killed him at first, but the blood loss would have done it sooner or later. His abdomen was peppered with bayonet slashes, his intestines protruding, blackening in the broiling heat.

His genitals were gone.

"It wasn't quick," I said.

"No," was all Johnston said, his eyes fixed on the flies feasting on what had been Gallaher's eyes. I joined the column, still wanting Porter, but letting thoughts of revenge elbow their way forward and take their rightful place.

We came to the river. Johnston signaled his men to take cover, and they faded into the bush, working their way along the riverbank on either side of us. "That must be where the landing craft went in," Johnston said. The opposite side of the wide river mouth was a gravelly stretch of even ground leading gently up into a stand of coconut trees. Some were fallen, or snapped off at the top—from age or artillery, it was hard to say. They were planted in even rows, part of an old plantation, most likely. On our side, the banks were steep, loose stones and gnarled roots sticking out where the curving flow of water cut away at the ground.

"What now?" I whispered as we edged back into the bush.

"I'd bet the Japs have that area covered," Johnston said as he scanned the opposite bank through his binoculars. "It's the only place the LCs can get to. Too risky to cross here."

"Not to mention how deep the river looks," Kaz said, displaying his standard unease with any water deeper than a bathtub.

"Yeah," Johnston said. "We'll find a crossing farther upriver."

We crept back from the river's edge and began the slow process of hoofing it through the dense bush. There was a narrow, overgrown footpath along the river, but that was an invitation to an ambush. Or maybe booby traps set up to warn the enemy of our approach. Machetes would have helped, but slashing at the choking greenery is damn noisy, especially when there are thirty or so guys having at it.

So we pushed past fronds as big as elephant's ears, stumbled over giant roots snaking out from tree trunks covered in vines; orchids in pale yellows and greens dazzled the eye while black ooze threatened to pull the boots from our feet with each step.

Ahead of us, Ariel raised a hand, signaling halt. The other he cupped around his ear.

Voices. The sound of footsteps on hard-packed ground.

People were on the path and they weren't speaking English. A small group, chatting. Probably no officers or noncoms around to enforce silence. They were complacent. Happens when you think no one's around except the guy you just butchered and left tied to a tree.

Johnston handed me his Thompson and put a finger to his lips for silence. He drew his Ka-Bar combat knife and tapped several men on the shoulder, Sergeant Trent among them, as he passed silently through the hidden platoon. Along with Ariel armed with his machete, they moved in crouched steps toward the path. In seconds they were gone, swallowed by the dense growth.

The sounds from the path drew closer. I figured five or six men, from the tromp of feet, the creak of leather, the faint sounds of packs, canteens, and other gear bouncing against bodies in motion. I guessed their rifles were slung. Maybe their intelligence was faulty, maybe they were cocky, or simply thought they could deal with outnumbered Americans.

The rhythmic sounds of movement stopped, replaced by a sudden rustle of leaves, grunts, thrashing, one high-pitched cry cut off before it could carry above the jungle canopy, and finally, the gurgling sound of a man choking on his own blood.

Trent pushed through the bush, signaling with one bloody hand, and we came forward, each end of the column spreading out on the trail, watching for other Japs.

There had been six. All were dead, except for one man who would
be in seconds. He clutched his throat, blood bubbling out between his
fingers, rivulets of red flowing between clenched teeth. The others
were strewn about the trail, most with their big Arisaka rifles across
their shoulders. Slit throats had sent streams of blood pumping out,
spraying the green leaves chrysanthemum red.

Ariel and Johnston were busy cleaning their Ka-Bars. A sergeant
stood over the dying Jap, watching as he cleaned his knife on the man's
service cap.

"Is that a stiletto?" I asked, as the Jap tried to speak, forming nothing but bubbles of blood that popped pink, as if he were chewing
bubble gum.

"Yeah," the sergeant said, offering it to me by the hilt, his eyes
riveted on the man at his feet. "Traded with an Aussie commando for
it. Think this is one of the guys who did that to Gallaher?"

"Hard to say for sure," I said. "But I'd guess so. There were only
bayonet wounds on his body. No sword slashes. Which suggests no
officers present, same as with these poor bastards."

"I heard you were a detective," he said. "Pretty smart for an army
man." He rolled the Jap facedown with his boot, then kicked his arm
away from where he held the wound. An arterial gush of blood damp-
ened the jungle floor, and then silence.

"This isn't the same as those marine stilettos," I said, motioning
for Kaz to join us. "It has a hard wood pommel, bigger than the metal
one on the marine version."

"That is the same size as the wound in Daniel's skull," Kaz said as
he studied the weapon. "Porter said he had owned an Australian commando knife, but lost it."

"I bet I know exactly when and where he lost it," I said, handing
the weapon back to the sergeant. "In that small inlet off the beach
where he killed Daniel. If we have the bottom searched as far out as
a man could throw one of these, we'll have the murder weapon."

The bodies were dragged off the path, their weapons tossed into
the river. We continued on, sweat soaking our clothes, the air so thick
and hot it felt like walking through a steam bath filled with snakes,

lizards, and spiders. I took a swig from my canteen, the water hot and tasteless.

A distant *pop pop pop* sounded, echoing from the hills above. More gunfire, and soon the rapid hammering of a machine gun joined in. We strained to determine the direction, sure only that it wasn't behind us. It seemed to be everywhere else.

"Choiseul Bay is that way, due west," Johnston said, studying his compass as he conferred with Ariel, who nodded his agreement without bothering to look at the device. "That's where Major Bigger and his men were to attack a Jap base in the harbor."

"Could that be the attack?" Kaz asked.

"No," Johnston said, checking to see if Ariel agreed. He did, giving the slightest nod. "The harbor is too far away. But they could be fighting their way back to the river. We need to cross here and find them."

"Agri," Ariel said. "Yumi faetem, kill Japan man gut." With that, he beckoned us forward, to the river. I had to think about what he'd said, and then I agreed, too. You and me, we fight 'em.

Within minutes Ariel had led us to the riverbank. Johnston sent two men over first, wading in waist-deep water to the other side. They gave the all-clear sign and we forded the river, which was much calmer than it had been downstream. Kaz didn't even look concerned, until a water snake rippled its way along the line of men. That got everyone moving fast.

We spread out, moving up a ridge, scrambling over moss-covered rock that dripped water from between rocky seams, making the going as slippery as it was tough. When we reached the top, I was about done in. A grueling march, too little sleep, and heat that wrung out every ounce of strength had left me limp on the ground, gasping for air. Only the volleys of gunfire got me to roll over and scan the ground below. The sounds were closer now, more distinct, with each weapon sending its signature rhythm echoing out into the valley below. The dull crump of mortars mingling with the rapid *blam blam blam* of M1s and the slower but steady cracks of the bolt-action Arisakas.

"Up there," Johnston said as he swept the hills with his binoculars, one arm extended to the next ridgeline. I could see the explosions, small bursts in the thick green cover. Those were the mortars, but it was impossible to tell whose or where the opposing forces were. Directly below us, stretching off to our left, was the plantation we'd glimpsed earlier: rows of coconut trees extending to the river's edge, undulating with the landscape, cresting over a small hill below us. At the edges, the jungle had already begun encroaching on the cleared land, tall shoots of tiger grass overcoming the palm trees and erasing the precision of the planted rows.

"Look!" Kaz said. "There, a man running between the palms."

I saw him. Darting from tree to tree for cover and looking over his shoulder each time. The Sten gun dangling from his shoulder. The dirty khakis, the slouch hat.

"That's Porter," Johnston said, finding him with his binoculars. I didn't correct him. He ordered two men to hustle ahead and intercept him before he got to the river. The rest of us followed slowly, fanning out in the brush, alert for any signs of the enemy.

"Do you think he is running away?" Kaz asked as we pushed aside tiger grass, its sharp edges slicing at our fingers.

"I don't know," I said. "Where would he run to? And why wait this long? Seems like he's coming from a helluva fight." Choiseul seemed a million miles away from Tulagi. Here, the Japanese were the terrible and immediate threat. I had to remind myself of Daniel Tamana and how his young life was cut short; Sam Chang, and how he survived months hiding in the jungle only to be killed in his hospital bed; and Deanna Pendleton, knifed in a filthy alleyway. The man who called himself Silas Porter was a killer far more dangerous than the enemy. He killed his own kind, and for nothing but lucre.

We finally broke through the tiger grass, the entire platoon spreading out to advance into the grove of trees. Ahead, I saw that the two runners had caught up with Porter, who was seated on a fallen palm tree, drinking from his canteen. I held Kaz by the arm and we stood back as Johnston, Ariel, and the radioman approached Porter.

"Where's the G Company radio team?" I heard Porter ask Johnston. "They're supposed to be across the river."

"Gallaher?" Johnston asked. Porter nodded, a frown forming on his face as he worked it out. "Dead. The Japs got him alive."

"Bastards," Porter spat. "Does your radio work? We had another set with us, but it crapped out."

"Sure," Johnston said. "What's the situation up there?"

The radioman took the heavy pack off and he and another marine began fiddling with it. As they knelt, Porter caught sight of Kaz and me.

"Boyle! What the hell are you two doing here?" His face revealed nothing but surprise. Either he had a good poker face, or was too exhausted to realize why we were with the marines.

"Never mind us," I said with a smile I didn't feel. "Lieutenant Johnston needs a briefing."

"Yes, of course," Porter said. "Kari and I, along with two scouts, guided Major Bigger and his men to Choiseul Bay. It took us a damn sight longer than we expected. Tough going if you keep off the trails. We attacked a Jap base and surprised them, did a lot of damage. Then we pulled back into the jungle and began to encounter patrols coming in from the eastern shore. That's when John was wounded along with one of the scouts. The other was killed."

"Are there many casualties?" Johnston asked.

"Three dead, about a dozen wounded," Porter said. "The biggest problem is the radio. When the Japs hit us a few hours ago, Bigger sent me to try and make contact with our radio team across the river."

"To call in the landing craft, I assume," Johnston said.

"Yes. We're being pressed hard right now. The major figured if the Japs occupied the river mouth, the LCs would never be able to get in and pick us up. Did you have any trouble?"

"No," Johnston said. "We crossed further upstream after we found Gallaher. No sign of the other men, or the radio, for that matter."

"Can you radio for a pickup now? I'll head back and let the major know," Porter said, looking anxious to leave our company. Johnston nodded and ordered the radioman to make contact with the landing craft. Then he called for a corpsman.

"Lieutenant, there's some urgency here," Porter said, his eyes darting nervously between Johnston and me. "Major Bigger's held off the Japs so far, but they're bringing in more troops and nearly have him surrounded. He didn't want to make a break for the river until he knew the landing craft would be there. Otherwise they'd be cut to pieces with their backs to the water."

"Don't worry, we'll take care of everything," Johnston said. "Give our Coastwatcher friend some Atrabine and salt tablets, Corpsman. Can't take chances with malaria and dehydration out here. How's G Company fixed for medical supplies?"

"Running short on these things," Porter said, accepting the pills and the proffered canteen. I figured Johnston was deliberately giving me an opening, so I stepped in while he had the canteen raised to his lips and relieved him of the Sten gun hanging loosely off his shoulder.

"What the bloody hell!" Porter roared. "Give that back. Are you mad?"

"Not me," I said, holding the Sten on Porter. Kaz darted in and took the .38 revolver out of Porter's holster. Even though I knew his real name now, Porter stuck with me.

"Lieutenant Johnston, are you going to let this idiot get away with this?" Porter's face turned red and his eyes widened, rage building up inside him. "There's a company of marines that needs help up in those hills."

"The knife," I said. "Drop it on the ground."

"I will not, not until you explain yourself, damn you." Veins bulged on his neck, his hands balled into trembling fists.

"Josh Coburn is alive and well," I said, stepping closer, the short barrel of the Sten gun aimed at his belly. "It's all over."

The fight went out of him. His face collapsed, the rage dissipating in the heat of the sun and the burning truth. There was still a witness alive. His deception and his crimes were out in the open. He fumbled weakly for the knife, not even realizing that Ariel had stepped in silently and slipped it out of its sheath.

CHAPTER THIRTY-TWO

"DIG IN!" JOHNSTON commanded. "Set up the thirty-caliber over here." The machine-gun team hurried forward with their gear and began digging out a firing pit with their entrenching tools. We were on the crest of the hillock we'd spotted from the ridgeline. It had a good field of fire covering the coconut grove, with a commanding view of the route to the river. The slope was a tangle of fallen trees, and Kaz and I helped to drag several of the trunks to the crest to help shield the machine-gun nest.

"What's the plan, Lieutenant?" I asked Johnston as I took a gulp from my canteen, careful not to spill a drop. The late-day sun was still withering on the exposed hilltop.

"Anything more from Porter?" Johnston said, sitting on the edge of the foxhole he'd excavated.

"Nope," I said. "Just the general direction of G Company, and that he ought to be the one to contact them." Porter was slumped glumly against a log, his legs stretched out in front of him, oblivious to the work going on around him.

"He is playing his last card," Kaz said, wiping the sweat that dripped into his eyes. "There is a chance he is sincere about getting back to Major Bigger, but if so, I wouldn't trust him one second after he does so."

"Agreed," Johnston said. "Making contact with Bigger is too

important to leave to the likes of him. I'll take Ariel and another man and go myself."

"You won't make it," Porter said, his voice dull and low, his eyes on Johnston. "Send me."

"Not happening," Johnston said.

"When are the landing craft coming?" I asked.

"Oh-seven-hundred," he said. "It's too late to bring them in today; we'd never get G Company here in time. So the plan is I make contact now, then we come back through here at first light, and head for the landing area. My platoon will provide covering fire and be the rear guard if we're pursued. Then everyone goes home."

"You'll be pursued," Porter said. "We should bring them back tonight, quietly, in small groups."

"Negative," Johnston said, without looking at Porter. He handed his binoculars to Sergeant Trent. "Trent is in charge while I'm gone. I'll see you fellas bright and early."

We wished him luck, and waved to Ariel as he jogged off with Johnston and the sergeant who'd wielded the Aussie commando knife. Kaz and I finished scraping out a trench behind one of the coconut logs, and pulled Porter in with us.

"They'll kill him in no time," Porter said. "Why don't you send me? I'm a dead man anyway."

"Shut up," I said.

Kaz rummaged in his musette bag and came up with three cans of chopped ham and eggs, and a supply of crackers. Porter looked surprised when Kaz handed him his share, but took it eagerly.

"I'm not an evil man, you know," he said, running his finger around the edges of the can to get the last of the egg mix. "Just a bloke from Sydney who started down a road without thinking about where it might end."

"You murdered three people on Tulagi," I said. "Not to mention the deaths you caused on Pavau."

"That wasn't my fault," he said. "At least not directly."

"What really happened?" Kaz asked, using a few drops of precious water to rinse his fingers. Ever fastidious.

"What I told you before was true enough," he said, licking his fingers. "Except it was me who went to hide the boat and Silas Porter who gathered the workers together. They were scared, having heard stories about the Japs on Bougainville. No one wanted to stay."

"You took Porter's Ross rifle," I said.

"Right. He gave it to me to take away so the Japs wouldn't find any weapons in his house. On my way back, I saw Japs coming up the road from the dock. They had two natives in tow, and it looked to me like they were being forced to carry supplies. They were stooped over with heavy packs on their backs. One of them tripped, and this Jap officer took out his sword and chopped his head off. For tripping."

"So you shot him," Kaz said.

"I did. Without thinking. I was ahead of them, in the bush along the roadside. Good concealment, only a hundred yards or so. Put the bastard down with one shot. But then I realized what I'd done, and tried to get back to warn the others."

"Doesn't seem like you did," I said.

"No, I couldn't get there, even though I tried my best. If I'd taken the road, they would have spotted me. I hoped the shot would have alerted the others, but even so, I tried to make it through the bush. About a quarter mile out, I checked the road and saw the Japs coming at a trot. I figured I'd riled them up plenty, and they were looking for anyone to take it out on. I fired one shot wild, to slow them down, but that only got them screaming and running faster."

"So you ran off," Kaz said.

"Yes! I ran, and no man can say he'd have done different, unless he was there. I didn't mean for it to happen like that, but it did. I ran into the nearest grove and climbed a coconut tree. I watched Silas stand in front of his workers, trying to protect them. The Japs killed them all, shooting and bayoneting everyone. They set fire to the main house after that. Their blood was up, and it was likely my fault."

"Likely?" I said.

"Well it was, I guess, but you never know with the Japs. I heard in some places they were almost polite to the plantation owners. In other places, they burned them out. So the same thing might have happened even if I'd never pulled the trigger."

"Either way, you decided to take advantage of the situation," I said.

"Yeah, I did. Silas didn't have any family I knew of, and no friends, really. The only visitors had been Josh Coburn and Sam Chang. Josh had set off for Bougainville the day before the Japs invaded, so I figured him for a goner. I'm kind of glad to hear he's alive, even if it did bugger me. He's a good old bloke. As for Chang, I heard the Japs were murdering Chinese everywhere they found them. So why not take a chance? Folks aren't big on paperwork in the Solomons, so I decided I'd take over as Silas Porter and work the plantation after the war. A fresh start, after I'd done my bit."

"So far, you have only committed the crime of fraud," Kaz said. "What made you decide to become a murderer?"

"Take a look at that sky," he said, arching his head back and sighing. The sun was edging low, tinging the thin clouds with streaks of orange, the sea sparkling in the distance. "I wanted a peaceful life, with money and the beauty of these islands around me. I couldn't face going back to Sydney after the war. I didn't want to die a broken man, like my father, his health ruined after a lifetime of factory labor, his legs crippled."

"Luckman told us your father had been in an accident," I said.

"Yeah, a lorry backed into him, crushed his legs. It was a contractor's vehicle leaving after a delivery, and Luckman claimed my dad had been negligent in stepping behind it, so it wasn't the company's responsibility. Best he would do was to give me dad's job, so I could earn enough to provide some care for him. I took it, of course, hating every minute of working in that damned, sweltering factory."

"And you left after your father died," I said, trying to feel some pity for him.

"Yes, I wanted to start over. When the Japs came along, it was like everything fell into my lap. I knew that after the war I could rebuild and work hard, hard enough to turn a profit and sell the plantation."

"But any buyer would want a deed, some proof that they owned the property," Kaz said.

"I knew that," he said. "Before I left I'd helped Silas bury his strongbox. It held cash, the deed to the property, a few gold coins, some other papers. All I had to do was come back after the war and dig it up. I thought I had everything worked out. When Daniel Tamana came along and threatened to ruin everything, I snapped. I surprised myself, really." He shrugged, as if admitting to a minor character flaw.

"He recognized you," Kaz said.

"Yes, but he wasn't about to go running to the authorities. He wanted my old job when the war ended. Said he knew what it took for a man to succeed out here, and he wanted his share."

"You went along with it," I said. "Lured him to the beach."

"Yeah, and I might have made that deal with him. There's enough work to go around, and he seemed eager enough. We went to the beach separately, so no one would suspect we had any connection. But then he told me about Sam Chang, and how if I double-crossed him, he'd get Sam to confirm his story and take it to the authorities. Well, that was that. I couldn't trust him if he was going to blackmail me. Who knows what he would have demanded next?"

"So you hit him on the head with your Australian commando knife and then threw it into the water," I said.

"Damn, Boyle, you *are* a detective. That's right. I didn't plan it, really. It was like my anger took over, and suddenly the knife was in my hand, Daniel gazing out to sea, and then he was dead on the ground. It sickened me, to tell the truth. But after that, I couldn't leave Chang as a loose end. I had to eliminate that threat as well. Very distasteful, but it left me safe and secure."

"Why did you kill Deanna?" I asked, my voice soft and soothing, wanting the details to keep coming.

"Oh God, that was awful. I called the signals section from Sesapi, the day you showed up there. I got Gordie on the telephone. He mentioned that Deanna was on the prowl, looking for some Chinese woman. I knew exactly what that meant; she was looking for the Chang sisters. She and Daniel had been friendly, and I figured he'd blabbed the story to her. So when Gordie told me he was dropping her off in Chinatown, I took my chance."

"You met her there, and killed her in that alley," I said.

"Yes," he said, shaking his head sadly. "I'd sent Kari off on an errand, and I knew if I acted quickly, I could be back at the dock before he returned." His face clouded over, the pain and guilt overcoming his desire to tell us how clever he was. I'd seen this before, the criminal's need of an audience to appreciate his audacity and skill, to share his belief in his own superior intelligence.

"You had it figured pretty close," I said. "I saw John Kari in Chinatown, but I missed you."

"Jesus, if I knew things would end up like this, I never would have started. I'd be glad to be plain, penniless Peter Fraser again. But I was in so deep, I didn't see any other way out. I mean, after two killings, it's almost a sacrilege to let the fear of a third stop you. Otherwise, the first two would have died in vain," he said, in the remorseless logic of a murderer. "Don't you see, Deanna's death would have finished things? I'd be Silas Porter for the rest of my life. A plantation owner, a man of property, and a war hero to boot."

"Except for Josh Coburn being alive," Kaz said. "Do *you* not see? You never would have gotten away with it."

"I'm sorry," he said, shaking his head, tears streaming down his cheeks. "It was like a curse came over me, and I had to protect this terrible secret. The first killing was almost an accident, then the second was so easy; it was as if it were fated. I never imagined it could be so easy. The rage I felt towards Daniel was nothing like I ever felt."

"It was fate that made you stick a knife into Deanna's heart," I said evenly. "Not greed or fear?"

"I didn't mean it like that, Boyle. Yes, I was afraid of being found out, terribly afraid. I think it was fear more than money. The fear of public shame and ridicule. I desperately didn't want to be found out, to be unmasked as a common murderer. Now that it's over, I'm almost glad you found me out. No, I *am* glad. I never really felt like Silas Porter. Sometimes I felt it was him doing those things, not me."

"The insanity defense isn't going to work, Porter," I said. "So can it."

"Believe what you will. I've finally told you the truth, such as it is. All I want is to ask you to do me one small favor."

"What?" I said, disdain for this pitiful killer foul in my mouth.

"Could you call me by my real name? I'm tired of being Silas Porter. I am Peter Fraser, after all."

Kaz and I were both silent, stunned at the fawning self-justifications of this man. Whose name I could not speak.

CHAPTER THIRTY-THREE

THE LATE-AFTERNOON SUN cast shadows through the coconut grove, long slivers of darkness lengthening between the rows. We were on lookout, searching the ground in every direction, watching for an enemy expert at infiltration. Everyone except Porter, who sat slumped against a log, passive amidst the activity around him.

"There!" Trent focused his binoculars. "Hold your fire! It's Ariel."

He was alone, and he didn't look good. His weapon was gone. Blood flowed from his shoulder, and he grimaced as he ran, his one good arm waving back and forth. Trent sent two men to help him up the hill and into the perimeter.

"What happened?" Trent said as a corpsman handed Ariel a canteen and began cleaning his wound. It looked like a through and through in his upper shoulder. Not bad, if you were near an aid station. Out here, it wasn't good news.

"Hem dae," Ariel gasped, then took another drink.

"Who? Johnston?" Trent demanded.

"No, other marine. Jap takim Johnston. We cross stream, see no denja. Japs jump us, shoot marine, shoot me, grabim Johnston. Hitim, drag away. I come kwiktaem." His eyelids fluttered, and he collapsed.

"He's lost a lot of blood," the corpsman said. "But he's alive." He and another marine carried Ariel to rest under the shade of a shelter half rigged up to a coconut tree.

"Now what?" Trent said, looking to the two officers present, even though we weren't marines. "G Company still has no idea we're here or the boats are coming."

"Send your most expendable man," Porter said. "We all know who that is."

Trent looked to me. "He's got a point. And he knows the way."

"What if he skedaddles?" I said.

"Boyle, where the bloody hell am I going to go?" Porter demanded. "You know who I am; there's nowhere I can hide. If I fail, well then justice has been served. If not, then those men have a fighting chance and we're back to where we started."

"Why?" I asked. "Why volunteer?"

"Two reasons," he said. "First, think about my reputation as a Coastwatcher. Has anyone ever said anything about a lack of dedication?"

"No," I said. "Sexton seems to hold you in high regard."

"Right. This is part of my job. It's what we do."

"And the second reason?" Kaz asked.

"To start balancing the books. There's a lot of lives need saving up there, John Kari included. Just because I'm a right bastard doesn't mean I want them on my conscience, too."

"Okay, but I go with you," I said. "And you go unarmed."

"Wait, Billy," Kaz said. "You don't know your way around the jungle."

"But he does, and I'm not letting him out of my sight," I said. "Sergeant Trent, you okay with this?"

"Yeah, I think it's our best chance," he said, giving Porter a hard stare. "You mean all that?"

"I do, mate."

"Okay, here's what we do."

Trent gave me a flare gun with two red flares. Once we reached G Company, we were to send them both up, Porter assuring us they could be seen from our position. That would tell him to expect Bigger and his men by morning, as planned. A fire team of four marines would accompany us to the edge of the plantation, ready to move in if we ran into trouble. But only for the first thirty minutes. After that, we were on our own. Kaz, of course, was coming along with the fire team, promising four tough marines he'd pull his weight. They chuckled, not knowing how deadly he really was.

It was dusk as we walked through the coconut grove, nearing darkness as we came to the end of the cultivated rows. Porter explained to the corporal in charge where we'd be entering the bush and the route we'd be taking. Passwords were given: the call "little" and the response "Lulu" because of the difficulty the Japanese had pronouncing the letter L.

"Good luck, Billy," Kaz said. "Keep an eye on him."

"He'll be in front of me the whole time," I said. I was about to tell Kaz I'd see him in the morning, but it seemed like bad luck to repeat what Johnston had said not too long ago. So we shook hands, and I turned to follow Porter into the black jungle.

Once we were under the canopy, my eyes adjusted and I began to make things out. There was a partial moon and the reflected light filtered through the dense overgrowth, casting shades of black and grey everywhere, as if I were watching a motion picture.

"Stay with me," whispered Porter.

"Right behind you," I said. When I'd asked Porter why he didn't balk at not having a weapon, he'd said it wouldn't matter. If we stumbled onto the Japs, they'd have us in no time. Our only weapon was stealth, he said. Still, the feel of the M1 in my grip was damned reassuring.

We made our way through the bush, the sound of a stream off to our left, the distance never varying by much. I figured that was how Porter was navigating, but I wasn't going to ask any questions. We walked carefully, Porter sometimes halting to point out a root or slippery stone. We were both wearing the new rubber-soled canvas boots, and it made for quieter going. My eyes had become accustomed to the dark, and as long as I kept focused on Porter's back, I could make out where we were headed.

Stepping over a rotting log, Porter snapped a twig as he came down. We froze, the noise deafening even with the usual jungle sounds around us. There were no shouts, no sudden rustling of branches that signaled a Japanese patrol heading our way.

Porter looked at me and exhaled. I smiled, nodding, relieved that the misstep hadn't drawn the enemy to us. Then I remembered: this man was the enemy. Out here, alone in the darkness, it was easy to see him as an ally. I needed to guard against thinking of him that way. A temporary ally, perhaps, but not one to count on.

We neared the stream, Porter looking up and down the waterway, listening for signs of movement.

"Is this where Johnston crossed?" I whispered. He nodded yes, his finger to his lips, his eyes fixed on rocks jutting out from the stream. I tried to focus, but I didn't get it.

"Boots," he whispered. Then I saw what I had thought were rocks. We moved silently, going stone to stone to avoid the splashing sound of water. Porter leaned down and lifted the torso up to remove his dog tag. "Not Johnston," he said as he dropped the disc into my palm. It was the marine who'd had the Australian stiletto.

I followed him up the opposite bank, senses on alert, fear tingling in my gut.

The landscape opened up as we walked over limestone rocks, climbing higher every minute. The bush was less dense, the trees farther apart, the grasses thicker underfoot. A few feet ahead of me, Porter stopped. He hadn't stumbled or held up his hand to signal a halt; he stood there, staring into the darkness. I walked closer, moving toward whatever he was looking at.

Some sort of large plant? A tree trunk? My eyes couldn't put together a shape that made any sense. Then I saw.

It was Johnston. His hands tied with vines stretched between trees. His legs bound with more vines. He was still. Thank God.

Long slashes had left his skin in ribbons, from his chest to his thighs. His face was half cut away, his jawbone obscenely on display in the moonlight.

"Swords," Porter said. "This was done by officers. Their sport for the evening."

"My God," was all I could say. I wanted to remove his dog tag, but as my hand neared the bloody mess that was his neck, it shook like a leaf.

"Sorry, Boyle," I heard Porter say, and I thought how odd it was that he was giving me condolences over the tortured death of Lieutenant Johnston.

Until the lights went out.

I awoke on my back, hidden in the tall grass. The M1 was by my side, and a bloody dog tag was pressed into my palm. The flare gun was gone, and so was Porter.

Pain raced through my skull as I got up. Porter knew a thing or two about lethal force, and he had held back on me, but my head still hurt like the blazes. I stuffed Johnston's dog tag into my pocket along with the other and drew my knife, about to cut him down. I stopped, realizing that if the Japs came by this way again, they'd notice someone had moved their handiwork.

"Sorry, Lieutenant," I whispered. "You've got one more job to do."

I headed back, having no idea which way G Company was, barely certain of the way to the coconut plantation.

At the stream, I gathered water in my cap and doused my head, washing away the drying, sticky blood, wondering what Porter was up to. He could have slit my throat and taken my weapons, but he hadn't. Maybe Bigger and his men had a chance after all.

After an hour and a couple of wrong turns, I heard the password. "Little."

"Lulu," I answered, as loudly as I dared.

"Billy, what happened?" Kaz asked, rushing forward to help me, marines at his side.

I told him and repeated the whole thing for Trent back on the hill.

"They butchered Johnston," I said, draining what little there was in the canteen I'd been handed. I winced as the corpsman put iodine on my wound, telling me it was a little scratch.

"Look, Sarge!" a marine said, his face raised to the darkness.

There, in the distance, two tiny red dots rose into the night sky. Porter had made it.

CHAPTER THIRTY-FOUR

I WAS EXHAUSTED, but sleep would not come. My eyes felt like they were coated in grit, my head hurt, my muscles ached, and my throat was parched. I took a careful, small sip of water, shaking my canteen to take a measure of what was left. One good gulp. A couple of guys volunteered to take canteens to the river and fill them, but Trent vetoed the idea.

"No one else is getting taken by the Japs," he said. Case closed.

"How's Ariel?" I asked Kaz as he joined me in the trench.

"Stoic," Kaz said. "He refused water, saying if he couldn't fight he wouldn't drink. How are you?"

"Fine," I said. "Just can't sleep." Mainly because I kept seeing Johnston's mutilated body whenever I closed my eyes. But I was fine. Really.

"Do you think he'll come back with Bigger?" Kaz asked.

"If he's Porter the Coastwatcher, then yes," I said. "He has to guide them here. And I think he means what he says about doing his job. But if he's more Fraser the murderer, then all bets are off."

"A strange man," Kaz said. "He has talked himself into thinking he's acted rationally. It makes sense to him, each act leading to the next in a logical sequence, even if the end result is one he now regrets."

"Mainly because he was caught," I said. "Regret usually comes after an arrest." I was feeling bitter, but I had to admit Porter might be feeling genuine regret. Hard to tell. Perhaps he was his own white ghost, haunted by what he'd done and how close he'd come to getting away with it.

"We have radio confirmation the landing craft are on their way," Trent said as he knelt by our trench. "It'll be daylight soon. If G Company makes it, you'll have to secure your man and get him to the landing site pronto. We're not waiting around a second longer than we need to, Lieutenant."

"Got it," I said. "You're staying up here until they're clear?"

"Yeah. Once Bigger's men get to the river, I'll send squads down one by one. The machine-gun team last, in case we need covering fire." As soon as he said the words, gunfire erupted beyond the coconut grove, the sounds echoing along the hills.

"Over there," Trent said, looking to our right. Small sparkles of light dotted a distant hillside like a swarm of angry fireflies.

"Can't tell how far away," I said. "No way to know if that's all of them or one small group."

"Porter said coming out in small groups would be best," Trent said. "I hope that's a rearguard action, and they're not having to fight their way through the Japs."

"Should we go to their assistance?" Kaz asked.

"Negative," Trent said. "If we split our forces and get lost out there, we might not be able to stop the Japs from getting to the river. We need to stay put. And it looks like we might need suppressive fire at the landing site." He called for the radioman to request PT boat assistance at the Warrior River.

After that, we waited, watching a running firefight draw closer and closer, the drumbeat of shots growing louder as faint lines of rosy light appeared in the eastern sky. Finally, figures appeared on the fringes of the coconut grove, moving between the neatly spaced rows. Every man in the platoon aimed his weapon, jittery after the night of waiting and watching.

"Hold your fire," Trent said calmly, his binoculars to his eyes. "They're ours." A wary marine led the way, waving to Trent who had stood up, his helmet held high. More riflemen followed, guarding a group of wounded marines, their filthy bandages stained with dried blood. These were the walking wounded, followed by two stretcher cases. I could only wonder at how difficult the trek had been for them and their bearers. Gunfire sounded behind them, moving closer as the rear guard gave ground.

"Sarge," hollered a marine who jogged up the rear slope. "LCs have been sighted, still a ways out."

"PTs?" Trent asked. He shook his head no. "Okay, head down and lead the wounded to the river. They go first. Lieutenant, you two can look for Porter if you want. But don't stray far."

"No wariwari," Kaz said, and we both clambered over the logs and descended into the grove.

"Have you seen Porter?" I asked the first G Company man I saw. "The Aussie?"

"He went back to help the rear guard," he said, "soon as we got to the edge of the plantation."

We hustled to the edge of the jungle, passing more marines walking numbly out of the bush, sunken eyes ringed with fatigue, blinking in the dawning light. John Kari stumbled by, supported by a native scout, a bloody bandage wrapped around his head and covering one eye.

"Keep going boys, almost there," I said, as dozens more filed by.

"Are you Boyle?" The voice belonged to an officer sporting a major's oak leaf insignia.

"Yes. Major Bigger?"

He nodded. "Porter told me to look for you, said you'd likely be waiting. What's the situation?"

"Landing craft are within sight. We've asked for PT boats to provide cover, but they haven't been sighted yet." More gunfire sounded, followed by the *boom* of grenades. Close enough that I flinched. "Where's Porter?"

"With the rear guard. I've got to get the rest of the men to the river. Porter and the squad he's with are going to hold them up for ten more minutes, then hightail to that hill. Johnston's platoon still there?"

"Yes sir. Sergeant Trent is going to send men down to the river by squads, as soon as you're all clear."

"It's going to be close," he said. "There's beaucoup Japs on our tail." With that he was off, shepherding his company through the grove, leaving Kaz and me alone, waiting for the last of our men, not to mention the enemy. The firing reached a crescendo a few minutes later amidst another round of grenade explosions. The first man to appear nearly fell out of the jungle path, clutching his leg, blood oozing from his thigh. Two more marines followed, scooping him up as they passed us.

"Porter?" I yelled.

"Back there," was all one said, not wanting to hang around and chew the fat. The firing was close enough now to make out each weapon. Two M1s and a Thompson, against a whole lot of Arisakas.

Finally, two marines burst from the bush, a tommy gun firing away behind them.

"Is that Porter?" I asked.

"Yeah," said a corporal. "He's laying down covering fire. Get ready to run, mac."

"I am quite ready," Kaz said as they darted into the trees. "Do we really want to wait for this man?"

"Hell yeah," I said, trying to sound like John Wayne in *Flying Tigers*.

Porter came into view, backing into the open field, firing his Thompson until it was empty and tossing it to the ground. He pulled a pin on a grenade and flung it into the bush, turning and pushing off into a sprint. He spotted us, barely hesitating.

"Run!" We didn't need prompting. Hard on his heels, we were breaking speed records when the grenade went off. We had a few second's grace but the Japs soon opened fire, bullets zinging overhead, slamming into tree trunks, and kicking up dust ahead of us.

Porter's arms were pumping, Kaz close behind him. My M1 felt like it weighed a ton, my legs were weak and wobbly, but a whole lot of Japanese guys trying to kill me was a great motivator. I followed the two of them as they zigged and zagged between trees, once turning around and thinking of squeezing off a few rounds to slow our pursuers down.

I didn't have enough bullets.

They were pouring out of the jungle, forty or fifty of them, I guessed. With the rear guard gone and an open field ahead of them, all the pent-up energy of the slow night's fighting had been unleashed. They were screaming, a couple of samurai swords held high, Arisakas with fixed bayonets an undulating sea of steel in the morning light.

Good.

The hill came into view. I waved and signaled the Japs were behind us as we raced around it, but Trent and his men needed no prompting. They waited a few seconds for the full mass of men to come into view. The attacking Japs slowed, someone obviously on his toes, noticing the fortified position ahead.

The machine gun opened up. Lead ripped into the front line, dropping half a dozen of them. Then everyone else fired, M1 rounds dispatching even more. The machine gun chattered away as the Japs faltered and began to retreat, using the trees as cover, much as we had.

Trent signaled the machine gunner to cease fire.

"Think there's more?" Trent asked Porter, who was lying on his back, gasping for air.

"Plenty more," Porter said. "They tried to encircle us. There's at least a company moving through the bush on each flank. And I'd bet some heavy weapons aren't far behind on the trail. They hit us with mortars a few times."

"LCs?" I asked Trent.

"Should be approaching the river now. But it's going to take some time to get everyone on board, especially the wounded. We've got two PT boats on the way as well."

"Listen," Porter said, sitting up and accepting a canteen from Trent. "You should all head to the river. Leave me here with the machine gun."

"No," I said.

"What's the matter with you, Boyle?" Porter said. "I'm sorry to cheat the hangman, but I'll do more good dying here than in some bloody prison in a few months. Who will that help?"

"It'll take more than one man to hold them off," Trent said. I didn't like that he hadn't put the kibosh on Porter's suggestion entirely.

"Position your men below, so they can hit the Japs as well. Then pull out fast after the next attack and get to the river. What have you got to lose?" Porter looked to each of us. I could see the idea had some appeal.

"Can we trust you?" I asked.

"Christ," he said, "you must be crackers. I saved your life last night, giving you that whack on the head. You were making so much noise, a deaf Jap would have heard us in Tokyo. Sorry about that, but I didn't think you'd agree with my suggestion. You must admit, it all worked out."

"He's got a point," Kaz said.

"You too?" I knew when I was beat. "Okay. But I'm staying up here, until the last minute. Sarge, when you pull out, I'll come down the rear slope and join you quick as I can."

"As will I," Kaz said.

No one had a chance to comment. Another wave of Japs had come out of the jungle, but this time they'd moved stealthily, and were well into the trees before we spotted them. We poured fire into them, but they returned it as well. We'd been lucky the first time, catching them unawares. That wasn't going to happen twice. Bullets hit the coconut logs and split the air above us. Then a marine went down, hit by fire coming from our right flank.

"That's the other company!" Porter yelled. They were working their way through the tiger grass, creating waves of movement targeting their position. The machine gunner swiveled and fired bursts into the grass, forcing the survivors back.

"There's not much time," Porter said, stating the obvious. "Once they get machine guns and mortars close enough, they'll hit us from two sides and they won't stop."

"Okay," Trent said, ordering his men to fall back and block the path to the river. "Porter, whatever it is you've done, I appreciate what you're doing for us." He stuck out his hand and they shook.

"You two," Trent said, "watch our position. When we pull out you better be damn close behind us. You'll need these." He handed me the binoculars and followed his men down the back slope and into the grove, taking up positions behind the tall trees. I could see him sending a runner down to the river, probably to check on the landing craft.

"You know how to operate that thing?" I asked Porter, as he took over at the machine gun.

"Yes," he said. "They trained us on Jap and Yank weapons. I guess I'll be an expert in short order." He pulled an ammo box closer, checking the belt, readying himself behind the gun, and settling in with a smile. He was a strange one, all right.

"You seem to be in a cheerful mood," Kaz said.

"Why not? I'm outside, with the breeze on my face and the sea at my back, doing heroic things under an open sky. A lot better than being imprisoned in a dark hole for months before they hang me. You blokes are doing me a favor."

"Delighted," Kaz said. "Look there." The Japs to our front were making another push, moving man by man, taking cover behind the trees, in the three rows to our left. Then I spotted movement in the tiger grass and fired my M1, getting rifle fire in return.

Porter squeezed off bursts at the figures behind the trees, but they had good cover. Trent and his men had a better angle and peppered them with shots, pushing them back. I fired another clip into the tiger grass, and heard a scream. It was the ones who didn't scream that worried me.

Kaz crawled over to check on Trent. "They're pulling out," he said. "Time to go."

I checked my ammo. Three more clips. I unloaded into the tiger grass again, just to be sure.

"All set, Porter?" I said, eyes still on the tiger grass.

"Boyle?" Porter said.

"Yeah?"

"Call me Peter, will you?" He smiled, the grime and sweat on his face glistening in the sun. He actually looked like he was enjoying himself, and I almost gave in. Then I thought of Deanna.

"No. Count yourself lucky I don't drag you back to a dark cell." With that, I followed Kaz over the logs and down the slope. He might be the hero of the day here on Choiseul, but I knew him from Tulagi.

We ran low, taking cover where Trent and his men had been. It was about two hundred yards to the river bank, and I could hear the landing-craft engines. I raised my M1, looking for Japs among the trees. I spotted one, his hands and feet visible as he shinnied up a tree. A sniper, looking for a good angle on the machine-gun nest. Worse still, he'd see there was only one man left on the hill. I aimed at his hand—a tough shot, not because of the distance, but because it was a small target. I fired. Once, twice, and then he fell, his scream signaling a hit.

"Billy, how long are we going to stay here?" Kaz asked. The landing-craft engines were louder now, as if they were straining under a heavy load. Porter opened fire, short bursts into the trees.

"Okay, let's go," I said. "Nothing else we can do here."

We edged back, and I felt a gnawing sense of worry as we left our fate in the hands of a murderer.

At the river, it was chaos. One overloaded landing craft was hung up on the coral reef offshore. That was the revving engine we'd heard. A second LC was also crowded but pulling away, while the third was taking on the last of the men. The only good news was the two PT boats fast approaching. One of them was PT-59. Jack to the rescue.

"What's happening up there?" Trent asked.

"They're moving in again," I said. "He can't last long."

A shrill whistling sound came from overhead.

"Take cover!" Trent shouted. An explosion shook the trees on the riverbank. Then two more mortar rounds hit the water, sending up harmless geysers. Harmless until they found their range. The machine gun was firing steadily now, and I wondered if Porter was making his last stand.

More rounds hit closer to us, and a couple of men went down, wounded by shrapnel.

"Lieutenant, can you go back up there and see what's happening?" Trent asked. "I need to know if they're closing in. I'll send men up if we need to fight."

"Sure," I said, scrambling up the bank, Kaz next to me. We ran to a stack of coconut trees that had been cut down years ago, about a dozen of them rotting into the earth. It made for a good hiding place and gave us some elevation. The machine gun was still chattering, a constant stream of lead flying through the coconut grove.

The machine gun stopped abruptly, the silence strange and disconcerting.

"Did they get him?" Kaz asked.

"I'm not sure," I said. I couldn't see the top of the hill from here, but I didn't hear any rifle fire from the Japs, only the mortar rounds heading to the river. Maybe the gun was jammed. Or maybe the Japs had rushed him from the side. I scanned the ground ahead with the binoculars, looking for an immediate threat. I leaned forward to get a better view of the rear of the hill.

Nothing.

Then I saw him. Shirtless.

"Son of a bitch," I said. "Porter."

"What?" Kaz said. "Where?"

"Hightailing it upriver, near the tiger grass," I said. "I bet he used his shirt to tie down the trigger. Shot off all the ammo to cover his escape. Goddammit!" I raised my rifle in his direction, but he was too far gone into cover to get a bead on him. "Kaz, go tell Trent there's nothing between the Japs and the river but yours truly. If you hear me fire, send help. I'll stay five minutes and then head your way."

"No more," Kaz said.

"No wariwari."

I kept watch through the binoculars, looking up every few seconds to avoid tunnel vision. Then I spotted a couple of Jap soldiers running toward the hill. I didn't fire, figuring that would draw them to the landing area once they realized it was just one guy. Pretty soon they were standing in the open, certain that they'd won the ground. Which they had. An officer appeared, his boots gleaming and his sword reflecting sunlight. He was barking orders, loud enough for me to hear, gesturing with his sword. I swung the binoculars in that direction.

Porter was being brought forward at bayonet point, his hands held above his head.

He hadn't escaped after all.

A crowd gathered, and I could see the officer laughing as one of his men smashed his rifle butt into Porter's ribs. They tied him to a tree, ropes around the wide trunk holding him secure. They screamed at him, the kind of curses you probably give to any machine gunner who's just mowed down a bunch of your pals. Good thing for us they were taking their time with him. Bad for Porter.

More mortar rounds sailed through the air and exploded behind me. Kaz ran back, crouched low. "The last LC is stuck on the riverbed. The tide is going out, and it was overloaded. One of the PT boats is rigging a line to pull it off. We need to go now."

I handed him the binoculars. I didn't need them to make out what was about to happen. They were about two hundred yards away, maximum. I could see the officer waving his sword in front of Porter, taunting him with what he was about to do.

I heard Kaz gasp.

I stood, cupping my hands around my mouth, and shouted.

"PETER FRASER!"

I dropped, and could make out faces turning in my direction. I had a few seconds, no more.

I filled the sight with Peter Fraser's torso. I let my breathing steady, put a slight pressure on the trigger, and exhaled.

I pulled the trigger. A good hit. A second shot, to be sure. His body slumped, held by the ropes.

We sprinted to the river, leapt off the bank, and ran onto the ramp of the last landing craft, Trent signaling us to hurry. The PT boat surged ahead, the steel cable connecting it to the LC going taut as we scraped bottom, engines revved high. Kaz leaned close, whispering.

"It was a clean shot, Billy."

We came off the bottom with a jolt, and men grinned and laughed as we made our way out of the river mouth. I joined in, not wanting to think about what I had done. Being judge, jury, and executioner didn't sit well with me. The cable was cast off, and the PT boat moved away, on watch for any enemy movement on shore. The second boat was Jack's PT-59, and he edged closer to us, putting his boat between us and the riverbed. He spotted me and waved, and I did my best to respond. I should have been happy; everyone around me was delirious with joy. But I was empty, gutted.

Gunfire rippled from the shore. Jack's boat answered, machine guns and cannon fire chopping up the ground and jungle, taking down small trees and sending the few Japs who weren't hit scurrying away. A ragged cheer went up from the marines. Then a more immediate concern demanded our attention.

We were sinking. Water was rising in the LC, probably from damage on the rocky river bottom.

I waved to Jack, not fifty yards away. He waved back, smiling, as did his crew. For a minute, they thought we were congratulating them. But it didn't take long for the list to become noticeable, and Jack drew PT-59 alongside the landing craft.

The navy crewman on the LC kept her steady while the men packed in the landing craft clambered up the side and were pulled on board the PT. The crewman came last, and Jack throttled forward, heading slowly out to sea.

"Chappy, put a few rounds in at the waterline and sink her," Jack commanded. Chappy, in the gunner's seat on the forward forty-millimeter, complied. Four shells blew her side in, and the LC was gone in seconds.

"We'll get you all back," Jack said to the marines crowding his deck. "But we've got to take it slow. We're low on fuel."

"Sir, we have one badly wounded man," Trent said. "Do you have a bunk we could get him in?"

"Put him below in my cabin," Jack said. "Mauer, show them where, and break out whatever medical supplies they need. Kowal, get those cans of peaches and pass them around."

The peaches were a hit. Trent opened a can with his Ka-Bar and offered it to me. I wasn't hungry. Kaz took it and tried to get me to eat, but I told him later. I slung my rifle and went below deck to look for Jack. I found him standing outside his captain's quarters, which contained one bunk and a tiny desk. Luxurious for a PT boat. In it, a corpsman was removing the wounded man's field bandage, dirty and caked with blood. It looked like shrapnel wounds to the chest, probably in that last barrage. He was a kid. Not even twenty years old, by my best guess. They all looked younger stripped of their helmet, web belt, and gear. A kid with freckles and a dirty face.

His breathing was ragged, a small pink bubble forming on his lips with each breath. His eyes opened, and he tried to speak. His mouth would form a word, but nothing came out. Then a sudden gasp, a gurgle, and he was gone, his lips holding that last word hostage forever.

Jack smacked the bulkhead with his palm and went up on deck, cursing under his breath. He checked in with his executive officer on the bridge and walked among the marines lying everywhere, accepting their thanks, asking how they were doing. He clapped Kaz on the shoulder, gracing him with that grand smile. Even though that kid's death got to him, it wasn't something he could show the world. It wasn't so much that his smile was a lie. It was a mask.

I wandered along, not wanting to talk. Finally, we both ended up on the bow, wind snapping at our faces. Jack was silent. I knew the death of the boy in his bunk would haunt him much as the death of his crewmen had. There was nothing more he could have done, but it seemed to add to the burden of responsibility he felt so keenly.

"I thought you were done for when you didn't come back to the boat," he finally said. "Glad to see you're both okay."

"Yeah," I said.

"What happened? With Porter, I mean."

What happened? How to explain it? That he'd been a hero, a fraud, a cold-blooded killer, a liar, a con man, and that I shot him?

"The Japs got him," I finally said. True enough.

"Killed him, or got ahold of him? I heard some of the marines talking about men being tortured. Trent said you found his lieutenant."

"Yeah," I managed. "The Japs got hold of him, Jack. But the end was quick, that's all I can say. All I want to say."

"Christ," Jack said, stuffing his hands in his pockets. "It's a hell of a goddamn war we have out here. I never imagined it would be anything like this."

"Me neither," I said, our eyes meeting. Whatever beef I'd had with Jack and his family, this war had put it all in perspective, burned away the pettiness, eliminating any need for forgiveness or recriminations. Nothing mattered but what we'd shared out here; nothing in our past could compare with what the Solomon Islands had done to us. Death, terror, beauty, joy, and sorrow were daily offerings from the gods of the South Pacific. It was a new beginning, or the perfect ending. Either way was fine with me.

I looked away, not trusting my emotions. I stood at the rail, feet braced against the heavy roll of the PT crashing through the waves. The rifle hanging from my shoulder grew heavy as the strap dug into my flesh. I took it off, holding it with both hands, feeling the weight of the thing, its heft and perfect balance, the beauty and solidity of this lethal tool, wood and steel smelling of oil and gunpowder. I swung my arms, threw it overboard, and watched it disappear into the seething and sullen sea.

AUTHOR'S NOTE

THE HISTORY OF the Australian Coastwatchers operation is truly fascinating, full of colorful characters, amazing courage, lonely death, and final triumph. In all my research, I came across no such villain as the Coastwatcher character in this book. He sprang purely from my imagination, a creation at odds with those who served in those hidden outposts.

Writing about a hero from my youth—I was thirteen when President John F. Kennedy was assassinated—was quite a challenge after researching his early life and upbringing within the close-knit Kennedy clan. While young Jack was often charming and generous with his friends, he did have a darker, self-centered side. The story behind his and Billy's estrangement—the incident with the car, as described in Chapter 23—actually happened, but to Lem Billings, a close friend of Jack's. That he found it convenient, or necessary, to lay the blame for his accident and subsequent actions on someone else demonstrates a sense of entitlement and selfishness I found disturbing and disappointing.

Jack Kennedy was recovering in the navy hospital on Tulagi in August of 1943 after the sinking of PT-109. At the same time, Richard Nixon was working as an Air Transport officer across Ironbottom Sound at Henderson Field on Guadlcanal. If I had any basis to think that their paths would have crossed, I would have taken literary advantage of that opportunity. But I did not. Future presidents Gerald Ford and George H. W. Bush also served in the South Pacific, well after events in this novel.

As mentioned in the narrative, Jack Kennedy should never have been in the navy. If he had undergone a routine medical examination, he would not have been accepted, much less instantly commissioned as an officer. His special treatment was due not only to his father's political connections, but also to his own competitive nature. His older brother Joe Junior was a bomber pilot, and even though it was Joe who was being groomed for future political office, Jack had no desire to sit out the war without a combat record. By all reports, Joe was not pleased by Jack's status as a hero in 1943, and felt himself eclipsed by his younger, sickly brother.

Some of the historical events in this book have been altered slightly to fit the requirements of the narrative. Kennedy did take command of PT-59, the first converted PT gunboat, but it was in October 1943, not August. On November 2, he did participate in the rescue of marines from the 2nd Parachute Battalion, who had been trapped on the island of Choiseul after a lengthy raid, which I also moved to August for purposes of the plot. The capture and torture of Corporal Gallaher and Lieutenant Johnston did happen during that raid in circumstances very close to those described in this book. The story of the two marine scouts and the diary of the Japanese medical orderly also is true. That incident occurred during the earlier Guadalcanal campaign.

Jacob Vouza was a real-life character, a retired sergeant major in the Solomon Islands Protectorate Armed Constabulary at the time of the Japanese invasion of Guadalcanal. He was captured and tortured and then escaped as described in these pages, in time to warn the marines of a major Japanese attack. The Battle of the Tenaru River was a major victory for the marines, and might have turned out quite differently but for the courage of Jacob Vouza. He was awarded the Silver Star for bravery and was made an honorary sergeant major of the Marine Corps. He also received significant honors from the British government.

Over the years, many readers have asked about the possibility of

Billy being sent to the Pacific for one of his investigations. I hope fans do not mind this step backward in time for Billy and his good friend Kaz. When I saw the gap in his timeline between the second and third books, I thought it would be interesting to pair him up with Jack Kennedy, who was ultimately sent back to the States in January 1944, suffering from a variety of medical conditions, including his back injury. By the end of that year, he was medically discharged from the service.

Two characters in this book were named as part of a fundraiser for the Waterford Country School in Connecticut, a facility designed to meet the special needs of children and families at risk.

Gunner's Mate "Chappy" Ellis was named for Chapman Manufacturing, which manufactures American-made precision hand tools in Durham, Connecticut. Chappy used Chapman tools, as many members of the US military still do today. Chapman Manufacturing is a keen supporter of the Waterford Country School.

The character of Deanna Pendleton was so named as the result of an auction held at the Waterford Country School fundraiser. Her father won the bid for a character naming and passed the privilege on to his daughter. This character also has a basis in reality. Merle Farland, a New Zealander, was a Methodist nurse on Vella Lavella. She was evacuated to Guadalcanal in December 1942, where a rumor spread that she was Amelia Earhart. Farland had shown courage in staying behind on Vella Lavella after the initial Japanese invasion, working with Coastwatchers and providing medical assistance to downed American aircrew, at great personal risk, until her evacuation was deemed necessary. Merle Farland continued to serve as a nurse and survived the war.

I AM INDEBTED to Ted Cummings, of Manchester, Connecticut, for the time he graciously spent describing his experiences as a Browning Automatic Rifle (BAR) man with the 1st Marine Division on Tulagi and Guadalcanal. The story of the piano on Tulagi came from Ted, who witnessed a marine playing "I'll String Along With You" as

they marched into battle. The details Ted shared about the terrible
conditions on those islands helped to inform the narrative and provide
a more accurate picture of what our soldiers, sailors, airmen, and
marines endured in the Solomon Islands Campaign.

ACKNOWLEDGMENTS

I OWE A great debt to my wife, Deborah Mandel, for her constancy in all things. Her support, understanding, companionship, studied reading, and first draft editing all go a long way in making these novels what they are.

Early reader Michael Gordon, family member, memoirist, and writer, continues to provide lucid and vital comments to my first drafts, improving each story in important ways.

Soho Press, a fine independent publisher under the inspired leadership of Bronwen Hruska, is due a debt of thanks from me and many, many readers for giving Billy Boyle such a supportive and friendly home. Mark Doten (a superb author himself) is my third editor since this series began over ten years ago, and he is continuing in the great tradition of Laura Hruska and Juliet Grames. His red pencil is gentle, thoughtful, and unerring.

And to Dan Cosgrove, illustrator; thanks for the terrific covers. Your artistry has helped shape the brand for the Billy Boyle novels.